The Mynah's Call

The Mynah's Call

by Paula Favage

Electra Press, LLC
Salt Lake City

Library of Congress Cataloging-in-Publication Data is available on file.
ISBN 978-0-9991573-3-6

ACKNOWLEDGEMENTS

I wish to thank all the brave men and women of the mujahedin along with the Afghan people for the valiant fight they put up against oppressing enemy forces. May their battle for an independent Islamic Republic of Afghanistan not have been in vain, and may peace reign once and for all throughout South and Central Asia.

Contents

ONE

The name engraved on the bracelet read only "Marta." She had come to Milwaukee from Hungary as a transfer student, but her studies had little to do with education. Mostly, they had to do with men.

She stood five-foot-six, her blonde hair streaked with white, the overall illusion of which provided her the appearance of a peroxide-bottle baby. But it was full and thick hair, naturally wavy, the way no hair from a bottle could ever be. And she put it to good use.

On March 23, the woman attired herself in designer jeans, a low-cut T over a pushup bra to show off her extraordinary architecture, and five-inch black pumps. Usually on such occasions she stuffed an extra pair of panties in her bag ... just in case. But not this time. This time, she wouldn't need them. She could count on that.

When she finally arrived at the bar inside the Giorgio Hotel, she found the man of her dreams gently caressing his third Old Fashioned. With two dead soldiers already at his flank, he appeared to be waiting for someone. Marta approached slowly and paused before sliding onto the stool next to him. She set her bag on the bar and grabbed hold of his arm just above the elbow, that most sensually suggestive spot on any man's anatomy. The bartender, smiling, asked what she was drinking that night. She smiled back and said softly, "Negroni."

On most any other night, two hours later would have seen Marta showing her date to her home. It would have been midnight, tops. She would have walked through the door into her apartment with three hundred-dollar bills stuffed inside her purse. And an hour later, she would have crawled beneath the covers, naked and alone, and turned out the light.

But this night was to be different. This night, she would hold his hand against her arm as the two walked through the door of her apartment together. Her purse would be empty. The two would cuddle and caress one another with each step. And then they would disappear into one another's arms for days.

Steven, she had decided only recently, wasn't like any of the other men she'd met. She felt it the moment she first saw him. Yes, he was a mark. Yes, he had once paid for her services. Yes, she had looked forward to the money. But before long, she began turning the money away ... and opening herself up to his charms.

That alone made him different. *Definitely* different. Warm, caring, outgoing, quick to smile. She would never have wasted two hours of her valuable time over dinner with him if he'd been anything else. She would never have spent that much time. But he wasn't anything else. He was the one man in her life she believed she could love. The one who she honestly felt was unique. The one who had her thinking seriously about giving up the lifestyle for good. In fact, beyond thinking.

Planning.

Marta took a quick look around the bar--force of habit--and turned her gaze back to him. She ran her perfectly manicured fingers up his arm, stopping only when they reached past his neck to rest against the back of his head which she pulled slowly closer to her confident, moist lips. The wildly passionate fragrance of his *Aramis* caught her attention as it mingled with the delicate scent of the jasmine she was wearing. It was an exquisite combination, just the way she hoped the two of them would be together--exquisite.

Except for one thing.

She wasn't wearing jasmine.

* * *

Marta forced the key into the slot in the lock and opened the door slowly. She hesitated before stepping inside. Placing her bag on the cocktail table several feet in front of the console TV, she flipped off first her right pump and then her left before walking through the darkened house toward the master bedroom. Reaching in, she flicked on the lights and crossed the room toward the bed. She pulled off her shirt and wriggled out of her jeans before smoothing the wrinkled bedspread and continuing on to the dresser. There, the woman looked around for several seconds, finally picking up a watch that had been carefully set out on a velveteen pad and slipping it over her wrist. Snapping the diamond-studded clasp in place, she looked at its face and smiled before unclasping it, slipping it off her wrist, and setting it back onto its saddle.

Ambling slowly across the room past the dressing area to the recessed tub, she reached around and undid the snaps on her bra, allowing it to fall to the floor as she bent forward to turn on the water. She stood up again, bra in hand, and carried it back to the dressing area, where she placed it on the corner of the table. She studied herself in the mirror, analytically, taking in every curve, every swell, every contour and bump, every spot, every hair, every pore, every nuance of who and what she was until finally she reached around to the back of her neck and, grasping her hair with both hands, lifted it up over her head.

Noticing for the first time how tired her eyes looked, how sad and spent they appeared, she shifted the hair into her left hand and reached down to an open drawer, pulling out a solitary ornate silver barrette from inside. She snapped it closed just above the nape of her neck and repeated the exercise with a second barrette placed higher up so that it held her mane firmly in place.

Slowly slipping out of her panties, she stepped free, bent down to pick them up, and folded them neatly before setting them next to her bra. And then, giving herself one long, final, disapproving look in the mirror, she reached once again into the drawer.

TWO

Islamabad, Pakistan, 1971

We were barely an hour outside of Islamabad, and I was already miserable. The suffocating heat of the midday sun had infiltrated the fumes from the gaudy war-surplus Willys that somehow managed to masquerade as a bus. Bob and I had squeezed into the next-to-last seat where we received the brunt of the summer day's assault. The scent of human bodies broiling in our portable oven washed over us like the rising and falling waves of the ocean, rolling gently, gaining in intensity, roaring past us, pulling us under, engulfing us until we popped back up gasping for air.

"How far have we gone?" I asked.

Bob looked at his watch. "About thirty miles, I guess."

"Thirty miles? That's it? We've been traveling two hours!"

"Sure--at fifteen miles an hour. At this rate, we ought to be in Kabul by ..." he checked his watch, "--noon tomorrow."

I rubbed my palm across my face and lifted some of the sweat clinging to my forehead. "Why can't he go any faster?"

My words were swallowed by a sudden swell of noise from the engine, the angry gnashing of gears followed by a loud *froomp* and a large bellow of smoke belching from the exhaust. Several rows ahead of us, a small baby released its grip on its mother's breast and began to cry. The mother shifted the baby to her left, popped out her other teat, and muffled the infant's sobs in the thick, tawny flesh.

Suddenly a strong, pungent odor hit me--the smell of dead fish steaming under the hot summer sun. I looked around and peered down at the old man seated behind us. "Oh, my God," I said, whirling back around.

"What?"

"The man behind us … is *peeing* on the floor."

Bob smiled. "That's not unusual for this part of the world. There aren't a whole lot of public toilets in rural Pakistan."

I shook my head and sighed. "I wish we were in Afghanistan."

Bob broke into a grin.

"What's so funny?"

"There are even *fewer* there."

I looked back at the man, stuffing his limp organ inside his baggy cotton pants. He smiled above a stubbled white chin before settling back against the corner of the bus and closing his eyes.

"Oh, Jesus."

"What now?"

"Don't you smell it? I think I'm going to puke." The odor of fish had vanished, replaced by the choking-thick smell of ammonia. "I'm not kidding, Bob. I think I'm going to lose it."

"Oh, great. That's just what this bus needs--one *more* sensuous scent. Look," he said, squirming around in his seat as though suddenly attacked by a swarm of ants, "let's trade places."

I shook my head. "I don't think I should move."

"Come on. Up with you!" He struggled to his feet in the cramped space between seats. "Sit by the window for a while. It'll help."

Bob raised himself up and over my legs as I slid across the worn vinyl. I lowered the window as far as it would go and stuck my head into the dust and fumes swelling up from the road.

"This isn't going to work," I said, craning my head

back inside. I sat back as he reached over and slammed the window shut.

"There. Better?"

I glared at him before realizing the smell had actually dissipated some.

"Thanks," I said, irritated with his smugness.

He paused for several moments. "Don't mention it."

The coach rumbled on across the country as I kept my eyes trained on the dry, desolate landscape. For miles, I saw no one but an occasional solitary figure on horseback or a herdsman walking alongside his sheep or goats. From the moment we'd landed at Islamabad National and jumped aboard the bus to cross the Pakistani frontier toward the Afghan capital, the land had grown more ominous. I wondered how anyone could live in such a country, how anyone could *survive*. There was no sign of water and only an occasional glimpse of green. We were driving straight into hell, and I couldn't help wonder if what lay ahead could possibly be any worse than what we'd left behind.

Our language tutor with the Peace Corps had warned us that Central Asia was a wild, untamed part of the world. I'd expected sand, dust, and dirt; I had *not* expected this.

After another hour of riding blindly through paradise, I turned to Bob. "Level with me. Does it get better or worse?" I looked over at him, his head bobbing up and down against his chest. I thought about nudging him, but if he was sound asleep, I didn't want to wake him. I listened to the small, motor-like sounds coming from his chest, like the purring of a contented cat. It was a peculiar little noise he made whenever he slept, a reminder of a childhood battle he nearly lost to rheumatic fever. It made me feel comfortable, lying in bed at home and listening, assured that someone was near; but now it made me feel awkward, ill at ease. It brought back memories I'd just as soon have forgotten, painful memories of events that had led us to join the Peace Corp, led us here--events that had nearly ended our relationship.

It was a muggy April afternoon in Milwaukee when I learned of Marta's death. The elderly lady in the apartment below her had heard a loud crackling noise followed by the sound of the body hitting the floor. She called the super, and they rushed to her aid, but it was too late. Marta was gone.

Marta and Steve had met in a lit course at the University of Wisconsin. That's what she'd told me at any rate. They were good-looking, intelligent, and popular-- well, she, mostly. After a whirlwind courtship, she had planned on getting married to him and living the rest of their lives together. But six weeks had gone by, and still no sign of a ring. And then one day, when he returned from a business trip for the Midwestern branch of a major oil company for which he worked, she met him at their favorite bar at the Giorgio Hotel. And that was the last time she ever saw anyone again.

When the news reached us over lunch on the Union terrace, I could only sit, wrist limp, my fork dangling over my plate. After a few minutes, I became aware of Bob, still eating as if nothing had happened. I stared at him in disbelief.

"What's the matter?" he asked, pushing a forkful of potatoes into his mouth. He dropped the tool on the table and downed a couple gulps of beer. "Don't you like it?"

"You eat like a pig, you know that?"

He picked up his fork, unfazed. "What the hell'd I do?" He took in another forkful, the forever gluttonous hamster. His long brown-and-gold hair, frizzed from the wind and sprouting in all directions, added to the image.

"You mean you don't *know*?"

He dug his elbows into the table and slowly leaned forward, his small, round eyes widening to nearly twice their normal size. "Well, I didn't fuckin' *insult* you, at least I know *that*." He leaned back in his chair and shoved a fork at a piece of chocolate cake.

"You even *talk* like a pig." I flung a plastic spoon at

him.

"Jesus Christ, Paula!" He glanced around. "What's the matter with you? What's gotten into you, anyway?"

"*Me*?"

He raised his brows. "*You.*"

"Well, for one thing, I'm hurting, okay? I'm hurting … *bad.*"

"About what?"

I hesitated, but I'd come too far to stop. "About your ultra-sophisticated, man-about-town approach to Marta's death. I mean, really, Bob, we saw her just a few days ago, and she was alive. Today she's dead. *Dead!*" I felt the veins in my neck straining, my fists involuntarily clenching. "Doesn't that *mean* anything to you? Doesn't that count in your super-educated, ultra-liberal approach to life? She's dead. A good friend of ours is *dead.*"

"Yeah, I get it. People die all the time. You never went to pieces over anyone else."

I stared in disbelief. "So it doesn't make sense to you that I'm hurting?"

He paused, glanced up at me, and then he continued eating. "Not really."

"And why not? Can't you fit my feelings into your personal philosophy? Can't you share my pain? Show some empathy? Or *won't it float*, Bob? That's this week's catchphrase, isn't it? This won't float, and that won't float!"

I paused, waiting for some reaction, the tears welling in my eyes. "Well, Marta's death won't float with me, Bob. I just can't accept it. I don't understand it. I ..." I struggled to draw in a breath. I paused. I relaxed my grip on the table. "Why did she do it? She had everything to live for, *everything!* Don't you think it's odd that someone who has everything to live for would kill herself? Don't you think it's really strange?"

He shrugged and took a sip of beer.

"I'm serious, Bob. I want to know. Tell me. Tell me something, here. Tell me *anything*. Please. Tell me *your* point of view."

He sat there digesting the words as calmly as if I'd just handed him the extended weather forecast. *Cloudy and humid with a chance of showers Wednesday. Warmer and mostly clear through the weekend.*

"You don't want to know."

"Oh, yes. Yes, I do. I want to know more than anything else in the world."

"Okay, you asked for it." He set his fork down, lifted his closed fist up to cover his mouth, and gazed off toward the horizon for several seconds. This was getting serious. "First of all, I'm not surprised. Oh, maybe a little by the *way* she did it. I mean, she could have taken a couple dozen sleeping pills or something sensible like that. But plugging a fingernail file into a wall socket while standing in the middle of a bathtub. *Jesus!*"

"That's not too smart, huh, Bob?"

"Well, Marta never struck me as a particularly well-balanced person emotionally. Not necessarily dumb--just not too stable."

"So you *were* surprised." I paused. "Or weren't you? Please. Help me out. I'm ... I'm not quite sure, here."

"More like amused, I'd say." He picked up his fork again and gulped down the last bite of chocolate cake. Wadding up his paper napkin and stuffing it into an empty cup, he wiped his face on his sleeve. "See, Marta never seemed to have any particular goals in life--I mean, beyond the obvious. And she did *that* pretty well. But once she met Steve and started planning for the future, once he got that good job with the oil company, I think it kinda bugged her. I mean, she never even finished sophomore year. She never seemed to know just what the hell she wanted out of life. All she had was a great body and a knack for doing what comes naturally. But without a goal ..." He shrugged. "Why bother?"

"Her goal was to become a good wife to that cheating jackass boyfriend of hers."

"I never noticed that in her."

"How could you? You never got around to looking past her *tits*. What is it really, Bob? Upset that she never came on to *you?*"

"That's crass, Paula,"

"That's *true*, Bob. Don't think I haven't noticed."

"See, that's the difference between you and me. You think I'm only interested in chasing every piece of ass that comes along."

"No. Not *every* piece."

Bob's eyes grew suddenly cold. "What's *that* supposed to mean?"

"What do you *think* it means? You're so Goddamn busy checking out every other good-looking woman who crosses your path, you forget you're married to *me.*"

"I'll ignore that."

"Oh, please don't Bob. Pick it up and run with it. Analyze and expand upon it. Do anything you want with it, but don't *ignore* it."

"I think you've been working too hard."

"You're Goddamn right I've been working too hard!" I looked around the patio and quickly dropped my voice. "Of course I've been working too hard. But if I stopped, we wouldn't have a place to sleep or food to eat or clothes to wear!"

"Oh, Christ, here it comes again."

I took a deep breath, exhaled slowly, and continued. "We wouldn't have our stereo or our secondhand bedroom set or our Salvation Army sofa or that piece of rusted-out junk we call a car. We wouldn't even have a damned pot to pee in. That's what would happen if I ever stopped working so hard. We'd lose everything we own, everything we ever bought with my earnings."

"What do you mean, *your* earnings? I thought they were *our* earnings. I thought we were married--a couple, a unit, a *team.*" He leaned forward, thrusting his chin to within inches of mine. "I thought we were *partners.*"

"*Partners!* You don't know the meaning of the word!"

"That's *right--partners.*"

"All right, then, *partner,* what have you contributed to the household lately?"

"Don't be smart. You know I'm going to school. I

can't study and hold a job, too, not with the load I'm taking,"

"Which, by the way, you wouldn't *be* taking if I weren't working so hard."

"Don't worry; you'll get it back," he snapped, "every last cent and then some."

"When, Bob? When you graduate and get a job?"

"That's right. When I graduate and get a *good-paying* job."

"And when will that be? You were a junior when we got married three years ago, and you're *still* working on your B.A. I know I agreed to help put you through school, but I never thought it was going to take a lifetime! You change majors more often than I change socks. Let's see, what's it been so far? Economics, history, sociology, language ..." I counted them off on my fingers.

"You forgot philosophy."

"Oh, no. How *could* I forget philosophy! Philosophy for the philosopher. Philosophy for the energetic young man who continues to burn up the academic world in his attempt to make the *Guinness Book of Records* as the world's oldest living professional student. Philosophy for the man who's able to rationalize the suicide of one of his wife's best friends, the man whose personal creed over the years has developed into, 'It's better to have a wife who's putting me through school than to have no wife at all.' How *could* I have forgotten philosophy?"

"Is that what's bugging you--the fact that I don't have a full-time job?"

"Full time? When have you ever held a *part-time* job for more than a week?"

"I *do* occasionally tutor incoming freshman. Remember?"

"If you've made two hundred dollars in the past year, I'd be shocked. And whatever money you *have* made you've spent on CDs and pipes and stash--all the stuff *you* want. I'm talking about work, Bob, *real* work--not goofing around."

"Well, if that's what's making you so Goddamn bitchy,

just come right out and say so. Because if that's it, I'll go out and *get* a job. I'll flip burgers at McDonald's or stuff size-nine feet into size-eight shoes or shovel cat shit in a pet shop or *something*. Hell, any one of those top-notch executive positions ought to net me thirty, maybe even forty bucks a week.

"Of course," he continued, the sarcasm dripping from his voice like wax from a spent candle, "if I'm working days, I'll have to go to school at night, which means it'll take me longer to get my degree. I'll have to cut my load from full time to four or five hours tops. After all, I won't have as much time to study. And my grade-point average will probably slip."

"You're only a C student now. If it slips any further, you won't have to *worry* about studying."

"But," he went on, ignoring the remark, "if I continue going to school *full* time, I'll probably be able to get my degree in Eastern languages within a year. I've already started looking into job opportunities as a translator for the government. With the years I spent in Iran in the Peace Corps, I'd probably be able to start at, oh, thirty or thirty-five grand a year. But, of course, that's *if* I continue school full time. If I take that thirty-buck-a-week job instead, I could probably get my degree in, oh, three more years. If that's what you think I ought to do." He was playing coyly with his empty plate and cup. "Hell, it doesn't matter to me. In fact, it'd probably be easier to work full time and go to school nights than to continue taking the academic load I've got right now." He paused, still looking down. "Brutal."

"You think you're so damned smart, don't you."

"Why, Paula," he said, his lips curling into a wry smile the way they did whenever he was running a con on me, "whatever do you mean?"

"You think all you have to do is dangle a carrot in front of the old girl and she'll be yours for life. Play on my emotions, and you can get whatever you want."

"Sweetheart," he said, pursing his lips lightly, "that's the name of the game."

"Is that what life is to you--a game?"

He shrugged. "What's wrong with that?"

"Oh, nothing, nothing at all, except that while you're playing, the rest of the world is out there busting ass."

"That's *their* problem."

"No it's not, Bob; it's *yours*. It's *ours*."

"*Uh-uh*. I don't have any problems."

"Well, I'm sorry to be the one to burst your little bubble, but who's going to pay the rent this month?"

His face turned cold. I could tell I'd hit a nerve. I'd shaken his little make-believe world. I didn't want to, I loved him. I *did*. But he was living in Fantasyland, sleepwalking through reality, and I *had* to do something to wake him up.

"You know that *you* always take care of that!"

"Yes, well, I'm not going to be able to take care of it this month. This month I'm short because I had to make a double payment on the stereo because we missed last month's payment so we could make a double payment on the car to cover what we missed the month before that. My check from the hospital only goes so far, Bob. I'm a nurse, not a neurosurgeon. I'm making $10.50 an hour, remember?"

"This is a hell of a time to tell me you don't have this month's rent."

"I told you last month!"

He stared out at the lake, at the billowy white sails skipping across the surface.

"You don't remember that, do you, Bob? You probably just figured, 'Oh, what the hell, she'll come up with the money, she always does,' and then forgot all about it."

"That's peculiar." His voice sounded suddenly far away.

"What?"

"Over there. Did you ever notice how the lake seems to open up into a channel?" He pointed off to the left. "Now, I'll just bet that if we rented a sailboat and headed for that channel, it would take us all the way out to the ocean, and then to Calcutta. Or maybe Kuala Lumpur." He sat back and smiled.

I stared blankly at him. "What are you talking about?"

He leaned forward. "Don't you see it?" He stared off into the distance. "Over there, just to the right of that big group of trees."

"Oh, Bob, what's going to happen to *us*?"

He turned back to me, a deep crease marking his forehead. "What?"

"I'm worried about *us*, Bob, about where we are, about where we're going. I think of Marta and Steve and all they had going together, and look what happened to them." I hesitated, fighting back the sudden urge to cry. I took a deep breath and let it out slowly. "I don't want that to happen to us. I don't want us to lose our way like that."

"That's ridiculous. Nothing's going to happen to us."

"Haven't you been listening? Haven't you been listening to *us*?" I took hold of his arm. "Bob, all we do lately is argue. That's not how it used to be. Don't you remember? We had some wonderful times together. The trips we used to take, bicycling, backpacking through the Rockies. Whatever we wanted, we did. We were a team. Whatever we wanted, we went out and worked for and got it. We had a fantastic time together. Don't you remember?"

"Of course I remember," he said, pulling his arm away and twisting around in his chair so that he could look out over the water again. "I don't see why it has to change. I don't see why it can't be like that again. All we've gotta do is hop a plane and …"

"We don't have any money, I'm telling you! We can't even pay the rent!"

"We can sublet. What do we need with an apartment if we're living in Calcutta?"

"I'm not kidding, Bob. Who's going to pay this month's rent?"

"Or maybe we can borrow from the government. After all, they pay farmers not to farm. Maybe they'll pay us not to …"

"Damn it, I'm serious!" I grabbed his shoulder and

spun him around. "Can you think of a way to come up with four-hundred dollars for this month's rent?"

He looked at me sheepishly, the same little-boy look I had seen in his eyes the night he asked me to marry him. He was hurt, bewildered, cut off from the fantasy of his dreams by the harsh reality of life around him.

He paused, thinking. "Do you remember that time we were taking a sailing lesson and that huge storm came up? And that one boat full of students capsized, and our instructor had to dive in and go to their rescue?"

I stared at him in disbelief.

"He told me to take the helm, and the waves were whipping up ten feet high--maybe more--and I moored that baby on our first attempt. Remember the dockmaster? He thought I was the instructor. Told me what a great job I'd done getting my students in safely."

"That's what I'm talking about, Bob. We used to do things together. We used to work together. We used to play together. We were a team. Why can't we be like that again? Instead of always fighting about money, always quarreling."

My voice had pierced his thoughts, dragged him back to the present. I looked at him sitting across the table, looked into those little-boy eyes, the same eyes I had married so long ago. They hadn't changed a bit. "I'm not kidding."

He sat up suddenly, a new glow settling across his face, his eyes flashing wildly. "Hey. Why *don't* we?"

"Why don't we what?"

"Let's get the hell out of Milwaukee. Maybe not to Calcutta, but *somewhere*. We don't have anything to tie us down here. We don't even have anything to tie us down to the States. We don't have a reason in the world to stay." His eyes were aglow, skin radiant. "There's nothing to hold us here. Let's go somewhere where life is simpler, not so fucking hectic. Or expensive."

"What about my job? It's our only source of income, our one hope for survival."

"But it's *not*. I could get a student loan, drop out of the university, and with that money, we could get away."

"Look, Bob ..." I leaned down to pick up my purse. "Look. I've got to get back to the hospital. When you figure out how we're going to come up with another seventy-five dollars for the rent, let me know. And you can forget about another student loan and leaving Milwaukee. We're not running. We're staying right here and working things out."

"The least you could do is listen."

"Bob, hear me out. I'm through listening, and I'm through being your nursemaid, your free ride through life. There comes a time when everyone has to grow up and accept a little responsibility if a relationship is going to survive. Now is that time." I picked up my plate and dropped it in the trash. "I mean it." I glared at him before turning down the steps toward Milwaukee General.

All the while I was walking, my stomach churned. My fists clenched closed. My teeth were grinding. I was all knotted up, tense, a pitted feeling overtaking me deep down inside. I'd known that feeling before, nearly twenty years ago. I had been in the backyard of our home, throwing a ball to my new puppy, when the ball rolled out into the gangway. The dog bounded after it through the open gate and disappeared. I stood horrified at the screech of the tires and the sickening *thud* that followed. And then the silence. And then the tears.

The one difference between that feeling and this was back then, I hadn't lost only a pet; I'd lost my best friend. Now, I was losing my husband.

Bob opened the door to the cabin and ushered me in with a sweep of his arm.

"This is it?" I looked around in disbelief. "This is really where we're staying?"

"Yeah. This is it. What do you think?"

I walked around the room, my wooden clogs echoing from the hardwood floor, reverberating off the cathedral ceiling. The furniture was sparse, leather, tasteful. A large, overstuffed sofa and two easy chairs formed a conversation pit before a sprawling two-story fireplace. Above the wooden mantel hung the head of a pronghorn sheep. My eyes followed the brickwork down to the floor.

"What the hell is *this?*" I laughed, pointing.

"What does it look like?"

"It looks like a bearskin rug." I bent down and ran my fingers through the brush-like fur. "I've never seen one before. Not a real one."

"Well," Bob asked again, "what do you think? Will this do for the weekend?" He grabbed my shoulders and began kneading them with his hands.

"Will it do? It's fantastic!"

"I thought you'd like it."

"I *love* it. I'd just like to know how much we're paying for it and where we're getting the money."

"Don't worry about it."

"I *have* to worry about it. We don't have enough set aside for the landlord yet, and here we are ..."

"Forget about the landlord. It's all taken care of."

"What is? What do you mean? You've got the money?"

He nodded and kissed me lightly on the lips, the scene of sandalwood teasing my nose. "And this place won't cost us a cent. That's the surprise I was telling you about."

"What do you mean? Why not?"

He fell into one of the chairs and swung his legs over the arm. "It belongs to a friend of mine from school. He works up at Whitecap as a ski instructor in the winter. Bought this place from his folks. Pretty nice, huh?"

"Yeah," I said, confused. "Fantastic. But what does that have to do with us?"

Bob shrugged. "I told you. He's a friend."

"Nice friend." I smiled. "Keep up the good work."

He pulled a large bag from his jeans pocket, opened it, and sniffed the contents.

"I didn't know you had any stash with you. Where did you get it?"

He smiled. "He's a very *good* friend."

I watched as Bob pulled out a pack of papers and

fumbled with the bag while trying to roll a joint. *Something's not right,* a little voice inside me kept saying. *It's too good, too sudden.* "He *must* be, to be giving that stuff away. Or did you buy it?"

Bob ignored the question, sealed up the bag, and tossed it over to me. "Help yourself. It's good quality. Good and strong."

I picked up the bag and sniffed. "*Whew*! Why bother smoking it?"

He set a match to the end of the joint, and it burst aflame before dying back to a glowing ember. He took a long, deep drag. Eyes closed, he held the smoke inside his lungs for several seconds before exhaling. "Here," he said, offering me the joint, "try some. You'll like it."

I motioned him away. "I'm not in the mood. I'd rather know where you got the money to buy this stuff ... *and* to pay the rent."

"Nosy little bugger, aren't you."

"This friend of yours--is he a dealer?"

Bob took another drag. "That's *such* an ugly word." He looked into my face. He knew in a second I wasn't kidding. "I guess you could call him that, but strictly small time, you know? More like a ... *supplier.*"

"And he's got you pushing for him now, is that it?"

"Not pushing, honey." He laughed. "You push the California shit. This is pure Colombian gold. You just hold it up, and everyone comes running with twenty-dollar bills in their hands. You don't have to do a goddamn thing but dish it out and smile."

My palms were beginning to itch. "How much are you ... selling for him?"

"Enough," he said, reaching around to his back pocket. He fished out his wallet and flipped several bills toward me. "Here. This should cover the rent."

"Three hundred dollars! I don't believe it. You made three hundred dollars selling stash since Wednesday?"

"That's better than standing over a hot grill any day, now, isn't it?"

"And your friend offered us his cabin as sort of an

incentive bonus? Is that it?"

He inhaled again, deeper than before, and the ash raced toward the middle of the joint like the flame from a flickering sparkler on the Fourth of July. "Not a bad deal, huh?" He exhaled a long plume of thick white smoke. "Not only do we get ahead in the cash department, but we get to spend a weekend alone together in the north woods. And, best of all, there's plenty more where this came from."

I examined the bills, half expecting to see the word "Monopoly" stamped across the face. "I don't know, Bob. I don't like it."

"What do you mean? What's not to like?"

"It all sounds too easy."

"Sure it's easy. That's what's so great about it. I can do it in my spare time. I make a few contacts, pick up some good bread, and still have time for studying and classes. Everybody comes out ahead."

I looked around the cabin before wandering over to the bookcase. It was stuffed with hard-cover volumes, including several sets with gold-stamped titles, their spines showing the look of age, the look of money: Mark Twain; D. H. Lawrence; Edgar Allen Poe. Whoever Bob's friend was, he appeared to be well read ... not to mention more than a little well off.

I walked across the room, past a small kitchenette with a bar and four padded stools before an island. On the far wall, a smaller bookcase held a number of more current volumes, nonfiction mostly--some history, some self-help--even *The Joy of Sex* and *More Joy*. Next to the bookcase hung several framed photographs, including one of a very attractive dark-haired girl wearing a wide, seductive smile and nothing else. Next to it were several oil paintings and a few antiques, including several old rifles and a shotgun.

"That's the kitchenette," Bob said, pointing. "And through that door on the left is the bedroom, and that second door is the bath. Gene gave me the layout before we came up here," he added, reading my mind.

"Quite a place." I wandered back to the sofa. "This Gene must be pretty well fixed for dough."

Bob shrugged. "I'd say."

"Is that how he makes his money--selling stash?"

"What do *you* think?"

"I mean, is that all he ... he doesn't sell anything else, does he?"

Bob laughed. "No, baby, he's not into the hard stuff. I told you, during winter he's a ski instructor. He's gotta stay clean. This stuff is just a way for him to make a few extra bucks during the off-season, that's all."

"Are you sure?" I leaned against the sofa.

"Sure I'm sure. Don't worry so much. Sit down. Enjoy the place."

"Bob, I know money is money, and I know we need it pretty bad for the rent and all. But ... well, I just don't want anything to happen. I don't want you to get involved in something we'll both regret later. Okay?"

"Hey, this is strictly a low-key operation. Gene buys a little grass, distributes it to a couple of his friends, and then collects some bread, that's all. In turn for passing it around, we're well taken care of. And even you gotta admit," he added, motioning with his head as he drew on the joint, *"this* is being well taken care of."

I slipped down into the sofa. "It just makes me a little nervous, this whole thing."

"What's there to be nervous about?"

"Well, for one thing, it's not exactly legal ..."

"*Ahh.*" He waved me off with his hand. "What can it hurt?"

"Who is this guy again? This friend of yours? Where did you say you met him? I mean, did he come up to you on the street one day and say, 'Hey, you look like a cool dude. Wanna push some dope?'"

Bob shook his head, drawing one last time on the roach. He flipped the butt into the fireplace and blew a long, narrow stream of pungent smoke toward the ceiling. "I met him at the U. We had a coupla beers and started talking."

"And he offered you some stash?"

"Yeah."

"Out of the clear blue sky?"

"Yeah." He stopped. "*No*. Not out of the clear blue sky. We were shooting the shit, you know, and the talk just got around to stash. So I asked him where he got his stuff, and one thing just led to another."

"And he offered you a job selling for him?"

"Yeah, sort of. I don't remember word-for-word, for Chrissake. What's with the interrogation? What are you, a Narc or something? Jesus!"

"*I'm* not, but *he* might be."

"What? What the hell are you talking about?"

"What if this guy's a cop? Did you ever stop to think about that? You don't know him from Adam. He could be setting you up. He could be running a campus sting. It's happened before."

"Look, Paula, the guy already paid me for moving some stuff for him. He invited us to his cabin for the weekend. Why would a dick do something like that? Why the hell would someone go to all that trouble just to nail a guy for selling a few joints? For Chrissake, *possession* in Milwaukee is only a five-dollar fine. That's less than the cost of a parking ticket."

"Possession? You idiot! If you get caught, it's for *selling*, not possession. Selling is a *felony,* and you're sitting here with a sock full of that stuff. That means more than a $5 fine and a slap on the wrist if this guy's not on the level, Bozo. That's more like five-to-ten and a few thousand dollars--*if* you're lucky."

"Get outta here. Besides, don't you think I can tell a cop when I see one? Give me credit for having a few brains, will you?"

"I'm not saying he's a cop. All I'm saying is, you meet a guy over a beer, and before you know anything about him, you're pushing shit for him. What if something goes wrong? Alright, maybe he's not a cop. But what if *he* gets nailed? Don't you think he's going to bargain for his skin? Don't you think he's going to give up the names of the guys dealing for him if it will help keep *him* out of jail?”

Bob waved me off. “You don’t know what you’re talking about. For one thing, I didn’t just meet him over a beer. I’ve seen him around campus a million times. Everybody knows him. He’s an okay guy, so quit worrying, will you? He could turn out to be the best thing that ever happened to us. It could be just the break we’ve been waiting for, a chance to get a few bucks ahead until I graduate and get a job, that’s all. *You* were the one who was bitching about money. *You* were the one saying there’s something wrong with our relationship. We never spend enough time together anymore. We never go camping, we never do this, we never do that. Well, now we've got some extra money, and we’re spending the weekend together at a beautiful place in the north woods, *free of charge*. What the hell is wrong with that?”

“I just wish you had told me about it first. So we could have discussed it.”

“And what would you have said?”

“I would have told you to forget it.”

“I rest my case. So quit worrying about Gene already. *I’m* the one who knows him, not you, so why get in a big snit over it? Once you meet him, you’ll see. He’s a great guy. You’re going to like him.”

“I’m not going to meet him.”

“Hey.” He winked at me and patted the arm of his chair. “What do you say we stop all this arguing and you come on over here, *huh*?”

“For what?”

“For my personal pleasure and gratification.” He grinned.

“I’ve got a better idea.”

“Yeah? What’s that?”

“You come over here ... for *mine*.”

“Shit. You know what your problem is? You’re too goddamned independent.”

I slid into the corner of the sofa and crossed my legs, my white shorts riding up, emphasizing the early tan I’d been working on under the lamp. “You know that’s what attracted you to me in the first place."

Bob settled down at my side. "What attracted me to you in the first place," he said in the worst Bogie imitation I'd ever heard, "were your gams, baby!" He began stroking my legs. "Long, slim, silky ..."

"Don't forget *hairless*." I laughed.

"And hairless."

He ran his palm up my calf to my thigh where it paused, kneading the flesh for several moments, before sliding slowly back down. I watched the expression on his face. He seemed preoccupied, almost as though the rest of me wasn't there. In the fading light of day, he looked deceptively small, much smaller than his six-foot frame. Sometimes I forgot that he was a man, nearly twenty-seven years old. I forgot, too, just what kind of power he had in those hands--until, at times like this, he reminded me.

"*Ummm*," I said. "That feels *good*."

"It sure does." He moved one hand up to my waist, tunneling beneath my short-sleeved shell, and continued up to just below my breast, where it stroked my skin slowly.

"*Oooh* ... I'm beginning to wonder what you've got in mind."

"What do you *think* I've got in mind, sweetheart?"

"I think," I said, wiggling into a reclining position and tugging on my top until my breasts popped free, "that I'm about to be compromised."

"And you know what I think?" His hands pushed up under one breast, cupping it firmly, his fingers moving continuously.

"What?"

"I think you're right."

"Oh, Bob," I moaned as his lips drew near. They parted slowly, blowing a warm, moist breath of air against my erect nipple, sending a sudden surge of energy racing up to my brain and charging down again all the way to my toes. He ran his tongue across his lips, the way a little boy might do standing before an ice cream cart on a sultry summer's day, and then he planted a soft kiss just beneath my nipple, followed by another that barely brushed the tip. Suddenly he fell upon me with his strong wet lips opened wide, push-pulling rhythmically at the flesh.

"Oh, God!" I cried. "Oh, God, Bob, yes."

"Yes?"

"Oh, don't stop ... please, don't stop! It's been so long. Oh, God, it feels so *good*." I pulled his head closer to me, pressing his face against my breast, squeezing so hard that it hurt. I didn't want to let him pull away. Not now. Not *ever*.

Suddenly all the arguing, all the bickering, everything seemed so far away. This was the man I had met and fallen in love with. *This* was the man who loved me in return. *This* was the man I had missed.

* * *

"Bob," I said, jarring him out of a sound sleep. "Bob, wake up. There's someone in the other room." I struggled to see the time on the dresser. "*Bob!*"

"*Huh*? What is it?"

"I hear someone in the living room. I think someone's out there!"

"That's nice," he muttered, burying his face in the sheet. "I'd hate to think you heard someone who's *not* out there."

"Bob, I'm not kidding. I think someone broke into the cabin."

"Oh, go back to sleep, will you? It's probably just Gene."

I rolled over and propped myself up against the headboard. "Gene? Your friend?" I pushed the hair back out of my eyes and strained to see my watch. "What would *he* be doing here?"

"It's his cabin. He's got a right to be here. It's the law."

"I *know* it's his cabin, Bozo." I aimed a sharp jab between his ribs. "But *we're* supposed to be using it this weekend."

"We *are* using it," Bob grumbled. "Now, go back to sleep, will you?"

"I'm not going back to sleep until you answer my question. Stop playing games and tell me what he's doing here."

He raised himself up on his elbows. "I thought I told you."

I flicked on the light. "Told me what?"

He waved his hand as if he were dusting flies from his face. "About Gene. He asked if we'd mind if he joined us for the weekend."

"What!" I stared holes through him. "And what did you *tell* him?"

"Well, what do you think I told him? It's hard to say no to a guy when he owns the place."

"Damn it, Bob! I wish you had let me in on it. I thought we were going to be alone this weekend. I don't want to share this place with some guy I've never met!"

"Good point, he said, rolling over on his side. "I'll introduce you in the morning. Now, turn off the light and let's get to sleep."

"Cute, Bob, real cute." I turned over and fumbled angrily with the light. Within minutes, Bob was making those funny purring noises while I lay on my side awake, listening to what was going on in the other room for what seemed like hours. I checked my watch when the stereo went on--3:30--and then I grumbled and tossed around, trying to bury my head in the pillow. Finally, I nudged Bob again.

He rolled over. "For Chrissake, Paula, what now? Aren't you ever gonna let me get some sleep?"

I stroked his cheek with my hand. "Why, sure I am, baby," I cooed. "I'm gonna let you get all the sleep your little heart desires." I grabbed the covers and yanked them back. "*As soon as* I *can!*"

"Go take a pill."

"It's not insomnia; it's *Abba!*"

"What?"

"It's the Goddamn stereo. What's he playing it at this time of night for?"

"How should I know? Why don't you go ask him?"

"Are you sure he knows we're here?"

"Our car is parked right outside the front door. It's too big to mistake for a lawn ornament."

I reached over and flicked on the light. "Well, then, go talk to him. Ask him if he'll turn it down a little."

"Jesus Christ, Paula," he moaned, *"you're* the one who can't sleep. Why don't *you* go ask him to turn it down?"

"Hey, Bozo, he's *your* friend, remember? I don't even know the guy."

Bob muttered something under his breath, sat up, and fumbled with his jeans, finally managing to slip into them and pull them up over his hips. "What the hell's he going to think," he mumbled on his way to the door, "when I ask him to turn down his own Goddam stereo in his own Goddam house!"

As the first few bars of Waylon Jennings filtered in from the other room, I heard muffled voices followed by laughter--loud, nervous, childlike, Bob's laughter. *Good,* I thought to myself when the voices finally died down, and the silence reached me through the half-open door. But soon the silence was broken by voices again and more laughter--a deep, throaty laugh not at all like Bob's.

I jumped up and swung my legs over the side of the bed. I heard the muffled pop of a bottle and the flat sound of a cork falling on the tile floor and rolling across the floor. I reached for my gown and threw it over my baby dolls before plodding over to the door and peeking out.

A roaring blaze in the fireplace shed long, thin shadows across the stucco ceiling, Peer Gyntian shapes stretched halfway down the wall on one side and halfway up the other, like a scene from the cavernous Mountain Hall. All that was missing was a coven of witches and warlocks cavorting in the corner. Smoke rose in bulbous clouds from above the sofa, dancing in the light from the fire, but it didn't come from the fireplace. It carried with it the thick, sweet smell of dreams, the promises of a fulfilled tomorrow. I stepped out.

"Paula!" Bob spotted me from the sofa. "I thought you were asleep."

I walked up to him and forced a smile. "For some reason, I'm just not very tired anymore."

"Well, great, come on in, join the party. Over here," he said, dropping an ash on the bearskin rug and struggling to sit up. "Here, I want you to meet a *verrrry* good friend of mine. Gene ... Gene ..." He turned to the figure at the far end of the sofa. "Say, whata hell is your las' name, anyway?"

"Just Gene," the figure said.

"Right--Jus' Gene. Paula, I'd like you to meet Jus' Gene. Jus' Gene, Paula, my *wife*." He said the word with a great deal of finality, as though he was proud of the fact ... or perhaps they had just been talking about me.

The figure rose and stretched out a thick palm. "Paula, pleased to meet you."

"Thanks," I said, taking his hand. His large, solid frame and sharply squared chin surprised me. I had expected someone smaller. In his green smoking jacket and dark-brown slippers, he looked out of place. He should have had on thick denims and a flannel woodsman's shirt.

"I hope I didn't wake you. Or at least I hope you won't hold it against me if I did."

I shrugged.

"Naw, you didn' wake us," Bob said, taking another hit.

"If it's any consolation," Gene continued, "you're even more attractive than your husband said you were."

"Oh, I'll bet." I didn't know how to take his words. Mocking? Serious? It wasn't exactly as if I was trying to impress him!

Gene settled back onto the sofa and motioned for me to join them. "So how do you like my little north woods retreat?"

"We love it, don' we, Paula? You shoulda seen her ravin' about the place earlier, didn' you, Hon?"

"How much of that stuff have you had?"

He just smiled and, lifting his glass in an imaginary toast, touched it to his lips and drank, a thin stream of golden-colored liquid running down his chin and onto his pajama tops. He held out the glass to me, and I finished what was left.

I handed the empty to Gene. "It's really nice. Elegant. Must have cost a fortune."

"What doesn't these days?" He grinned, setting the glass on the table and pulling a neatly rolled blunt from a gold-lined cigarette case. He held the joint out to me.

"Thanks." I held up my hand. "Maybe later."

"Oh, go ahead. Take one. I'm not a Narc." He held up one leg and pointed to the sole of his foot. "See?"

I felt flush. "Thanks," I said, taking the joint and leaning forward for a light. I'd been right. They *had* been talking about me. I didn't really want a joint, but I didn't want to insult him, either. I sat back and drew in the smoke, glancing up at him in time to see his eyes flit to my chest. I leaned back against the cushions and exhaled slowly.

"So," he said, "Bob tells me you're a nurse."

With his thick, muscular legs and broad shoulders, he could have been a football player or a wrestler or even a stevedore. He didn't fit at all the image I had of someone hustling dope on a street corner.

"That's right. At Milwaukee General." I took another hit and exhaled the smoke toward the ceiling. Thin, wispy shadows danced along the stucco, and I wondered what would happen when shadows and smoke finally collided.

Gene pulled a small footrest over to him and propped his legs up on it. My eyes instinctively followed the line of his thighs as the smoking jacket parted halfway up. I looked into his eyes, smiling at me, confident.

"I've always admired nurses." He said the words as if they held some special meaning that only we two shared, some secret code we'd developed years ago and guarded zealously ever since.

I looked over at Bob. He was slumped down, his chin resting on his chest, and peering glassy-eyed into the fire. It wouldn't be long before he'd be gone again, gone to where he felt most comfortable--away from reality, away to where he could escape everything and everyone, perhaps even himself.

"Why do you say that?"

"About nurses? Oh, I don't know. They just seem so ... dedicated. I mean, *they're* the ones who hold the hospitals together. *They* do all the work. I've always thought that it's *they* who should be making all the big money. Or, *them.*"

"*They,*" I said.

He smiled. "*They.*" He paused to take another drag before blowing out the smoke. "Instead, some doctor comes in, spends five goddam minutes asking a bunch of fool questions, and then he tells the nurses to keep up the good work. He goes out to play golf the rest of the day and pulls down a couple hundred grand a year. It just doesn't seem right."

"Hallelujah. You know, I like the way you think." I laughed.

"Say, I'm sorry," he said, getting up. "I didn't ask if you wanted anything to drink. Champagne, Sherry, Chablis?"

"I don't know ... when I drink and smoke, I get kinda stupid."

"I'll count on that."

He opened a small cabinet to the right of the fireplace and took out a decanter and two glasses. Pouring carefully, he filled each one three-quarters to the top and returned to the sofa. "Sherry. Amontillado. An elegant wine for an elegant lady."

I took one of the glasses, lifted it up to the fire, and swirled it, watching the amber liquid race around the sides and finally settle into a shimmering pool in the center of the glass. I took a sip--dry and crisp. It went down easily. Without thinking, I drained it as though it were iced tea on a muggy August Milwaukee day.

"My goodness. You really *were* thirsty." He went to rise. "Here, let me get you another."

"No, really," I said, shaking my head, but he'd already taken my glass. By the time he returned, I was feeling warm, feverish. "Wow. This stuff is *potent*."

"Those Spaniards are hot-blooded people. They're not the type to fool around with a *Sauterne* or a *Pouilly-Fuisse*."

"You know a little about wine."

He smiled. "It comes with the cabin. Actually, my father was a wine steward for Maxim's in New York for nearly thirty years. We grew up around wine. *Good* wine. Before dinner, during dinner, after dinner. Did you know," he confided, leaning close to me, "that Louis Pasteur once called wine the most hygienic of all beverages?"

I shook my head and laughed. "No. Louis Pasteur? Why Louis Pasteur?"

"It's true! Served before dinner, it heightens the appetite and sharpens the palate. During dinner, it makes even the dullest meals bearable. And after dinner ..." He paused to take a long sip from his glass. "After dinner, it aids the digestion and stimulates the heart ... as well as various *other* parts of the human anatomy." He smiled, his gaze roaming up and down my frame, settling finally upon my eyes, as though he were looking right through them into my mind, examining my thoughts, savoring my own sensations.

"My goodness." I fanned myself with my free hand. "It's really getting warm in here. It must be the fire." I loosened the ties on my gown. "Would you mind opening up a window?"

Gene set his glass on the table next to the sofa and slid close to me. "I'd rather open up *you*."

He placed his hand on my arm and drew to within inches of me. The orange glow from the fire lighted the right side of his face, emphasizing his large, square jaw and chiseled features. He was good-looking in a rugged sort of way. Rather like what I imagined an early pioneer looked like after facing a hard winter on the trail west. The deep lines around his eyes resembled dried-up riverbeds wending their way along the rims of dual canyons. His face was clean-shaven, yet the smallest trace of tomorrow's growth of beard was struggling to the surface--young saplings breaking the virgin prairie soil. I felt flushed, giddy. I began to giggle.

"What's so funny?" he asked. "I know some of my lines are corny, but--"

"I'm sorry. I was just looking at your skin and imagining ... oh, no. Forget it."

"No, go on. What?"

"This is silly, but I imagined a tiny covered wagon pulling out of your left nostril and wending its way across your chin. Your *chiseled* chin."

Gene laughed, settling back in the sofa and reaching for his glass. "You're right. It's silly. But you ..." He paused for what seemed an eternity.

"What?"

"You are one of the most exquisite creatures I've ever seen."

Creatures? I felt an obligation to be embarrassed. Instead, I found myself flattered. Here sat a young, virile, handsome man of good taste and breeding paying me compliments--*me*, right in front of my own husband. I smiled. "Would you mind saying that again, a little louder?"

"Why?"

"I want Bob to hear it."

"And why would you want that?" he asked, drawing close to me again. His presence alone sent chills up my back. My face felt hot; my head, light. I took another sip from my glass and stared into his eyes as if he had issued me a challenge and I had to prove I dared to meet it.

"Because sometimes ... he forgets."

"I'm afraid," he said, untying my gown and pulling it back, so that only a filmy wisp of nylon separated us, "that Bob isn't in much of a condition to hear anything anymore." He leaned forward and began nuzzling my neck with his lips.

"*No!*" I snapped, pushing him back. "Don't do that."

"Why not?"

"Because it's not right."

"How do you know?"

"Because … it feels … not right."

He smiled. "It's supposed to feel *good*."

"*Uh-uh.*"

He reached for me again, and I jumped up and stumbled back several steps. I watched as well as possible as he picked up a bottle, poured another drink, and plunked something in it. I thought. I suddenly felt as if I had to get away. I climbed up onto the large stone hearth, pulling my gown up around me so that I wouldn't trip.

"Here," he said, holding out the glass. "One more for the road."

"What road?" I asked. "Are we going somewhere?"

I suddenly realized how light I felt, how buoyant and free. And when Gene reached out for my hand, I quickly pulled it back. "*Uh-uh,*" I said. "You can look, but you can't touch."

He smiled, wide. "Okay, no touch. But you'd better drink up. You don't want that to go to waste."

"*Huh?*" I looked at my glass, at the liquid resonating across the surface like a miniature sea calling out to me. I lifted the glass to my lips and took a deep swallow. "This feels good," I said as I moved my body in tight little circles. The rough stone hearth beneath my feet reminded me of the times I used to run barefoot as a little girl, feeling the sensations of cold concrete scraping my soles. I closed my eyes and recalled the sensation.

"You're an amazing woman."

I stopped, opened my eyes, and looked down at him. "I know." I took another sip of wine. "Why?"

He laughed. "Because you're so free. You remind me of a young child--pure, sweet, innocent."

"A child," I mused aloud. I threw what was left of the wine into the fire and listened to it hiss, and then I slowly, deliberately turned back to Gene, tracing my hips with my palms. "What happened to the beautiful woman?"

Gene finished his drink and set the glass on the floor. "All right, then. A beautiful woman-child." He raised one leg up to the sofa and set it down close to his body. The smoking jacket separated to his waist.

"My goodness." I couldn't help staring. "Did I do that?" I tried to feign embarrassment.

"There's nobody else here."

"I'm flattered." I smiled, my head beginning to spin. "But I'm also married. I'm a married woman, Jus' Gene."

"Your husband is the luckiest man on earth."

I felt suddenly overwhelmed--the words I had always hoped to hear from Bob. Coming from a total stranger while Bob slept, slumped over against the sofa. I shouldn't have, I know, but for some reason, I felt happy, confident, at peace with life, sure of myself as a woman. I felt *free*. Totally, inexplicably free. Free from financial worries, free from the stresses of nursing, free from all the marital squabbles, free from everything. It had been a long time since I'd known such a feeling. The wine and grass had helped, I was sure. Still, I was amazed at just how open I suddenly felt to the universe. And everything in it. And it didn't matter why. All that mattered was *what*. I was on a roller coaster of delight, and it had already passed the summit. Nothing could stop it now. *Nothing*.

"The only question remaining, is," Gene whispered, "what are you going to do about it?"

I stepped slowly down off the hearth and walked up to him as he untied his jacket and let it slip to the floor. I knelt in front of him and placed my hands around him, running them around his tight muscular waist, squeezing, stopping, squeezing. I lowered my head, inch by inch, until my lips touched him, and I opened my mouth and took him deep inside.

"Oh, my God, baby," he whimpered. "Oh, yes, do me. Do me, honey. Oh, God ... *fantastic!*"

I was completely free. Free of Bob. Free with Bob. Free because of Bob. I was a wanton young woman aching for a strong man to hold me, to praise me, to make love to me. I bore down harder, taking him deeper into my mouth, deeper and deeper, until I thought surely I would swallow him. I felt him shift forward, felt his warm belly against my head, one hand on the back of my neck, holding me as though he expected me to try to pull away. His free hand reached around my arms and grabbed one of my breasts, fondled it firmly, then harder still until it hurt- -a wonderful, satisfying, throbbing kind of hurt. I felt his fingertips close around my erect nipple. I continued to suck harder and faster as soft, moaning sounds slipped from his lips. It seemed as though we were locked together like that forever when from somewhere far, far away I thought I heard a voice spurring me on--Bob's voice.

But the words were just as quickly lost as Gene slid down onto the sofa, pulling me up on top of him, our lips meeting, our tongues entwined. And then I felt the warmth of him sliding into me. I kept worrying about my baby dolls, wondering how we would ever be able to make love with them on. I wondered whether I'd hallucinated about the voice. Then, suddenly, I stopped wondering. I felt my entire body begin to quiver. It was as though someone had set the fuse, lighted it, and then run for cover as the explosion went off. Deep down inside somewhere, I knew I'd been set up. It was all too obvious. And I knew I'd been set up by my own husband. He wanted me to have sex with his friend. Why, I didn't know. Had he found someone else? Someone better able to support his drug habit? Better suited to put up with him?

All of a sudden, none of that mattered. I was in no position to argue. Not with one explosion after another tearing through my body, ripping through my very reason for being. Until, finally, the explosions stopped, and I settled back, exhausted, spent, unable to move, and I drifted off into a delirious state of peace and warmth.

THREE

I gazed out the window at the Pakistani sun settling down against the landscape. It seemed as though we'd been rolling through the countryside forever. One of my legs was numb; my brain, foggy from the heat. Most of the passengers had dozed off, taking advantage of the cooler evening temperatures dropping to just below the century mark.

I looked over at Bob, still sound asleep, and then back out the window. I blinked as the bus swung farther west toward Afghanistan. Amazingly, some green shrubbery popped in and out of view. For a moment, I thought I was dreaming. Far in the distance, a long line of magnificent snow-capped mountains rose up, foam-crested waves leaping out of an angry sea of brown. They looked as out of place against the stark stillness of the desert as seagulls over Nebraska.

As we drove on, a clump of trees sprouted from the banks of a small pond. The setting rays of the sun cast orange and purple light on its surface, as still and smooth as glass. Within minutes a large herd of sheep, accompanied by half a dozen robed Pakistani horsemen, rolled into view. The men wore the look of dogged determination, swathed in flowing robes and turbans, a picture from the pages of history. I imagined their ancestors riding the plains as free as the wind, fierce warriors, owners of all they surveyed, yet claiming nothing but the sun in the morning and the moon at night.

The Pakistanis were a proud people, even during those

ancient periods of British subjugation. At one time, Britain had laid claim to India, which included the lands known as East and West Pakistan. More than half a century ago, India won its autonomy from British rule, and the community of nations welcomed it and Pakistan into the world.

Not long after, East Pakistan broke out into a civil war that ended in a declaration of freedom from Pakistani rule, and Bangladesh was born. Ever since, relations between Pakistan and India have remained strained, since the Pakistanis had long accused the Indian government of playing more than a passive role in encouraging their neighbors to the north to revolt and form a new nation, a buffer state, between two old and jealous rivals.

We passed several more Pakistani tribesmen and a row of huts molded out of mud. Children laughed and ran along the dusty roads that served as arteries connecting one family's home to another. The coach began to slow, the squealing of the brakes exaggerated by the stillness of the night, a mournful howl like some ominous wild beast calling out to the vanishing sun. We lurched forward as the pads grabbed hold and the bus bucked to a stop.

"What is it?" Bob rolled onto his right side to peer out the window.

"I don't know."

"Peshawar!" the driver shouted. He got up and flung open the doors as the passengers buzzed to life.

"Peshawar."

"Are we in Afghanistan yet?"

He shook his head. "When we reach the border, you'll know."

The old man behind us got up and, smiling at me, said a few words in Persian before following the line of passengers down the aisle.

"Oh, Jesus. That reminds me," I said. "I have to pee."

"We might as well get out. My legs feel like they've been locked inside a kennel for a week."

"You still have legs?"

Outside, the soft beauty of the Pakistani sky washed

over us. The sun was all but gone now, the darkness settling over the land like a quilt thrown across a makeshift bed. Several Pakistanis showed up at the station to meet friends and relatives, with everyone grabbing and kissing everyone else. Soon the passengers paired off and slowly disappeared into the landscape like grains of sand on the wind.

I turned to Bob. "Where do we go?"

He squinted into the night, turning first one way and then another. "I guess there." He pointed toward the desert.

"Where?"

He nodded. "Over there."

"You mean right out in the open?"

"There's a ditch over there. That's as good a place as any."

"Terrific. And I suppose there's hot and cold running sand."

"Just hot." Bob led me by the hand. Suddenly an old man wearing religious beads and a flowing white tunic began flailing his arms and shouting. He pointed as if fingering for the police the ruffian who'd just robbed his aging grandmother of every last cent she owned. Bob and I stopped and looked around as the man drew closer.

"Gunaah khilaaf khuda! Gunaah khilaaf khuda!"

"What's the matter with him?" I felt my heart begin to pound. "Who's he shouting at?"

"I'm not sure, but he seems to be pointing at you."

The man drew closer, his hand flailing in the still night air, until he was right on top of us, so close I could smell his breath, feel the searing heat of his eyes. *"Gunaah khilaaf khuda!"*

"Bob! What does he want?" I tried to shrink away, but the old man slithered after me, not touching me, but not relenting.

Bob began to laugh. "I'm not sure. He's speaking some sort of ancient *Urdu*."

"It's not funny! Get him away from me."

"I think he's letting you know you're a loose woman

because your face isn't veiled in the company of men. It's a Pakistani tradition."

"Well, make him stop!"

"You'd better cover up."

"With what?"

Bob reached into his pocket and pulled out a white handkerchief that the old man grabbed, spat ont, and threw into the night, cursing unintelligibly. *"Gunaah khilaaf khuda!"* He continued his chants. Soon several others had gathered around, and the men all took up the call.

"What am I supposed to do?" I looked around for a place to retreat. "What does he want?"

"I think you'd better get back on the bus." Bob made a few pacifying gestures to the man and spoke a couple words of *Urdu* before leading me away by the arm.

"But I can't. My bladder is going to burst!"

"Gunaah khilaaf khuda! Gunaah khilaaf khuda!"

"Farangi," Bob shouted back, pointing to me and repeating, *"Farangi!"*

"Tell them I'm not Pakistani!"

"I tried. It doesn't seem to matter."

"What should I do? I've got to pee!"

"When in Rome …" he said, making for the ditch.

"Goddamn it, Bob!" I shouted, and I turned and ran back to the bus, half a dozen angry Pakistanis hot on my heels. The driver, standing by the door with an amused look on his face, muttered a few words in Persian to the men, which only seemed to heighten their angst. After several moments, two of them turned and slowly walked off, followed by several others. Finally, the solitary figure that had begun the ruckus waved his fist at me, spat menacingly into the wind, and traced his footprints back into the night.

My hands shaking, I pulled a scarf from my bag and tied it over my face just as Bob and several others climbed aboard, and the driver, slamming the door behind them, slid into his seat. The engine growled to life: The bus lurched forward.

"What's he doing?" I asked. "We can't go yet. I've still got to pee!"

"Sorry, but this ain't exactly Greyhound." He pointed to the scarf. "That's kinda cute, you know?"

"Don't touch me!" I pulled the scarf off my face and swatted his hand away.

"What are you mad at *me* for? *You're* the one who offended them."

"Offended them? You mean ticked them off, don't you? A bunch of old religious goats!"

"You should have worn a veil."

"Just to go relieve myself?"

He slid down in the seat next to me. "When in Rome ..."

"Stop saying that!" I kicked the empty seat in front of us as hard as I could. The pain shot up my leg to my neck. "*Oww!* Goddamn it! This is a nightmare. And I *still* have to pee."

"Well," Bob said, looking over his shoulder, "it appears that the commode is unoccupied at the moment."

I turned around and looked at the empty seat in the back. "You're not serious."

Bob shrugged. "It's either that or hold it 'til we get to the border."

I thought long and hard about it for several minutes. Finally, Bob struggled to his feet.

"Where are you going?" I asked.

"If you're going to pee, I'm moving up front."

We'd been rolling along for an hour, Bob and I and six other passengers. They were Afghans from the Tajik tribe. All people living in Afghanistan are referred to as Afghans, although the country is actually made up of dozens of smaller groups called tribes, each one with its own traditions, heritage, way of dress, and language. The Tajiks speak mostly Persian, while the Pashtuns, the largest ethnic tribe of Afghans, speak a peculiar Persian derivation called *Pashto*, something of a rough Persian that when spoken slowly--a rarity among Afghans--is pretty easily understood by all Persian-speaking people everywhere.

If there is one thread of unity running through the people, it's their religion. Nearly all are Muslim, and Islam is the official state religion. It's been said that more people have died in Afghanistan in the name of--or on *account* of--Islam than for all other reasons combined. I believed it.

As the road deteriorated, the bus bounced from side to side like a channel buoy on a windy day. After some while, the driver downshifted into second and slammed on the brakes as we ground to a noisy stop. He threw open the door and said a few words to someone standing outside. From the window, I heard voices and saw several lights dancing in the dark.

"What's going on?" I asked Bob.

"Pakistani border patrol. We're crossing into Afghanistan. Just keep quiet."

From their voices, there appeared to be two of them. Both seemed interminably slow, as one asked the driver a question in *Urdu*, which the driver answered in Persian. There was a pause of thirty seconds to a minute, and then the other guard asked something else.

"What are they talking about?"

"*Shhh*." Bob motioned with his hand. "They're trying to decide whether or not to search the bus."

As he spoke, one of the guards climbed halfway up the stairs and peered down the aisle. He raised his flashlight and sent a long shaft of light bobbing and weaving from head to head. When it finally settled upon Bob and me, the guard called to his companion.

"What's going on now?"

"I think," Bob said, squirming in his seat, "they've decided."

The second guard boarded the bus with a gas lantern swinging from his free hand. He set it on the top step and pumped it up, sending a radiant yellow glow throughout the vehicle. Bob and I sat motionless as the guard approached an elderly couple and asked them a question.

They exchanged puzzled looks and shrugged. After several seconds, the guard turned to his companion and said something in *Urdu*. Returning to the couple, he repeated himself more slowly, deliberately, as if by enunciating more carefully, he could make the Afghans understand.

"Excuse me," Bob called out to the guard. "Excuse me," he repeated, this time in *Urdu*.

The guard whirled around, shock scarring his face.

"Stay here," Bob said to me. "I think I can get us outa this."

He got up and walked to the front of the bus. As he approached the first guard, the one by the door suddenly shifted his leg up to the top step, flinging his hip into plain view, and on it, a monstrous pistol that looked as though it had received plenty of use. Bob smiled and greeted them in their native tongue. They were surprised that an American would know *Urdu*. Before long, the three of them were bantering back and forth and grabbing one another's arms as if they were long-lost members of the same tribe reunited at the wedding of a loved one.

Finally, Bob turned to the elderly couple and, in Persian, said, "The guards are interested in knowing what you bring with you from Pakistan into Afghanistan. Have you any pistols, knives, or ammunition?"

The old man sneered in *Pashto*. "Do they think I look like a revolutionary?"

Bob smiled and told the guards *no*.

There was more talk in *Urdu*, and again Bob turned to the old Afghani passengers. "They would like to know why you are traveling to Afghanistan and if you plan on returning soon to Pakistan."

The old man replied, "I am traveling to my home near Kandahar, where I shall remain until I die. Tell the guards they are both welcome there and will be treated with dignity and respect, something they surely have not seen much of in their native land, which treats even its own loyal subjects as mindless jackals."

Bob turned to the guards, who were waiting intently

for the translation. He glanced back at the old Afghans and then spoke to the guards in *Urdu*. Though I learned a fair amount of Persian before coming over from the states, I knew little *Urdu*; but my intuition told me that Bob's response must have been abbreviated, as both guards laughed, slapped each other on the arm, and spoke at once.

Bob addressed the couple again. "The guards would like to know at last--of *everyone,* " he added, loud enough for all to hear. "If there is any contraband of any sort in your possession, or if anyone is attempting to take from Pakistan any rupees or any objects of art or any gold or silver artifacts, any paintings, or any livestock."

All at once, the people on the bus chattered loudly as if at a fair, laughing, holding up their traveling bags for inspection, and generally making disparaging remarks in Persian about the parental lineage of the two border guards as well as the inhabitants of Pakistan on the whole.

Smiling broadly, Bob answered to the guards' satisfaction, after which they responded with a few loud words in *Urdu*, made a weak attempt to thank the people in Persian, and stepped down from the bus. As Bob made his way back down the aisle, each Afghan he passed grabbed his hand and thanked him, and he stopped to chat with each one in turn, as is the Afghan custom when traveling. Everyone was amazed that this young *farangi,* as the Afghans call foreigners, had mastered not only Persian, which is difficult enough to understand and nearly impossible for a *farangi* to speak intelligibly, but also *Urdu*, which most Afghans consider little more than rapid belching from the very pit of the stomach.

"Well," Bob said, finally arriving back at his seat after several minutes of center-aisle accolades, "how'd I do?"

"My hero!" I threw my arms around his neck and kissed him on the cheek.

The Afghans in front of us began to hoot and howl as if watching the love scene from a grade-B Western, but their revelry was cut suddenly short by shouting from outside the bus. The driver climbed back up the stairs, and judging from the tone of his voice, he was becoming increasingly annoyed. From the words I could make out, the guards had asked for a stipend, some "earnest money," in order to allow the bus to pass the checkpoint without further delay. And, like all good Afghans everywhere, the driver took great exception to being asked to pay a bribe for something he felt should be inherently *free.*

"Jesus, the driver is really pissed. The guards are threatening to strip down the bus to search for hashish if he doesn't hand over a hundred rupees."

"And what's the driver saying?"

Bob hesitated. "I can't quite make it out. He's speaking Persian, but he's talking so fast. I think it's got something to do with the guards being born to the loins of a stray dog."

"Do me a favor?"

He looked at me.

"Don't offer to translate."

The voices continued to grow in pitch, getting louder as the seconds passed until it seemed the three would come to blows. At last the driver slammed the doors shut and spat against the window. He shoved the transmission into gear and stomped on the accelerator. The coach leaped forward, and the passengers began to cheer. As we passed the guards, two beams of light shone through the windows, like the eyes of some great nocturnal beast, before dimming and finally fading to black.

"What happened?"

"The driver told them they were a disgrace to their country and to their parents, whom he alleged to have known personally."

"Then what?"

"Then he called them a few things even *I've* never heard of before and told them he'd be damned in the eyes of Allah if he turned over even a single rupee to them."

"And they let him go?"

"Not much else they could do. It's a matter of honor. The driver is older than they."

"But I thought the guards didn't speak Persian."

"They speak it well enough. I worked in a few words of Persian when I was translating for them earlier, and they knew exactly what I was saying."

"That's strange."

"That's *fantastic*," he responded softly as if talking to himself. He lifted his feet over the seat in front of him and slumped down as the bus slowly built up speed. "An Afghan will apparently fight for what he feels is right-- anytime, anywhere, even in a foreign land. How many other people would do that? How many Americans would? I wonder."

*   *   *

"Hey, sleepy head."

Gene's voice gently massaged me awake. I opened my eyes slowly and looked up to see him standing before the fireplace. I smiled. And then reality set in. "Gene. Oh, God. Where's Bob?"

"Still out of it." He nodded toward the bedroom.

"How'd he get in there?"

Gene shrugged. "Must have gotten up during the night."

I rolled over on the sofa and looked outside. It was already light. "Oh, my God. What time is it?"

"Seven-thirty," he replied. "Time for all beautiful, sexy, hot young women to think about getting up and starting their day."

"Seven-thirty? In the *morning*?"

"In the morning." He laughed. He finished tying a knot in his blue-and-white-striped tie and tucked the tails of his shirt into his khakis.

"Oh, Jesus. My head." I felt a sharp pain slice deep into my skull. "What happened last night?"

"You don't remember?"

I thought, fighting back the pain. "*Ohh.* Well, I remember *some* of it."

"Baby, I'm gonna remember *all* of it for a long, long time." He bent down and kissed me gently on the lips. I felt suddenly guilty, awkward. I wondered what Bob had seen, what he'd thought, why he hadn't awakened me.

And if he'd known all along what was happening--and why.

Slowly I pulled my body toward the arm of the sofa, like an inchworm crawling along a narrow twig, until I was sitting half upright. "Oh, I can't believe it."

"What?"

"I can't believe we did what we did ... what *I* did. And right in front of Bob."

Gene sat down in the chair and slipped into his black-and-brown, wing-tip Oxfords. "Why do you say that?"

"I've just never ... never done *anything* like that before. Never, you know, cheated on him with anyone."

He peered up at me with a puzzled look on his face, and he returned to tying his shoes. "Don't worry. You were great."

He got up, dusted his pants with his hands, and picked up a midnight-blue blazer from the back of the chair.

"Where are you going?"

"Back to Milwaukee. Business meeting at noon."

"Today?"

"*Um-hmm.*"

I felt suddenly disappointed, confused. I thought we should talk. I thought all three of us should talk. He had other ideas.

"Hey," he said, reaching down and stroking my cheek, "what's the matter?"

"I don't know. I guess ... I guess I've got some things to think through. Some things that are bothering me. I was kind of hoping that, well, we could talk a little before Bob gets up. I really need to get some things straight in my head if ..."

"I would if I could--honest I would--but I've gotta run. Really." He leaned over the sofa and kissed me full and long on the lips. "That's what I like about you." He smiled down at me. "You really give a guy his money's worth. You could teach some of the others a thing or two."

"Some of the others?"

He looked at me curiously for a few seconds, and he

reached back into his pants pocket and pulled out his wallet. "I know we had an agreement." He pulled out a bill. "But, here, take this. Maybe it will help with your *problem* you need to straighten out in your head." He laid a hundred-dollar bill next to me.

"What's this for?"

"For being so good. And I left something on the table for Bob, too. Top quality, from Istanbul. Tell him thanks, that I really enjoyed it and we'll have to do it again sometime soon. But next time, without the coke, okay?"

My eyes popped open. "What?"

"I said, next time, no coke. It just threw him for a loop. Made him a little squirrely."

I squinted up at him.

"What? You didn't know? He dropped a couple hits in his wine."

I sighed. "And then he handed me his glass, and I finished it."

He shrugged. "Yeah, but for you, it worked just fine. You know how to handle it."

"Wait a minute. Hold on a second. I'm having a bit of a delay here. What are you talking about, it worked just fine? You're not making any sense."

"The stuff for Bob, you mean? Coca-Cola, baby; the Silver Witch." He laughed. "What do you think your little hubby was doing last night--Mary Jane? Not even the best stash in the world will knock you off your ass the way coke will. You've snorted. Right? You know."

I shook my head--one of the less intelligent things I'd done that morning.

"Well, anyway, like I said, we'll have to get together sometime and have another little party. Just as soon as I can swing it."

"I thought ... I thought you sold pot."

He paused, squinting through a contorted smile. "I do."

"I mean, nothing else but pot."

"Where'd you get an idea like that?"

"From Bob. He told me that's all you had for him to sell because that's all you handle."

Gene shook his head. "I don't get you, baby. What do you mean, *had for him*?"

"Isn't Bob pushing stash for you?"

He stared at me.

I added, "On campus?"

"Hey, honey, nobody pushes *anything* for me. I deal a little pot, sure. I deal a little coke, some bennies. I deal a little of whatever's in demand, you know? I'd have to be crazy to take in a partner, especially someone like Bob. No offense, but he'd have us both cooling our heels in Waupon within a week."

"But ... but you gave him three hundred dollars."

"Right, and I already told you, you were worth every penny of it. That's why I gave you the extra hundred, to show my appreciation, *comprende, Senorita*?" He picked up the bill and waved it in front of me, and then he shoved it into my hand. "Now, you tell Bob I'll see him around, okay?" He leaned over and kissed me quickly on the cheek. "I'll be in touch, hear?" He stopped as he headed for the door and called back over his shoulder. "Oh, and you two feel free to stay as long as you like. Just be sure to lock up before you take off." And he was gone.

I sat back, my brain a stale egg sizzling in a sputtering pan. As his car's engine roared to life and the wheels bit into the gravel road leading to the highway, I looked down at the bill in my hand. I blinked once, twice, hoping that everything would grow clear, that I'd wake up soon and find it had all been a bad dream--a product of the wine and the drugs. But nothing happened. Nothing disappeared. I glanced down at the bearskin rug, at my nightgown lying on the floor. Slowly I rose and walked, placing one foot methodically before the other, toward the bedroom. Bob was still in bed, sound asleep--or, rather, stoned.

Finally, it all sank in. I'd been used. Used just one more time in a long history of abuse. Bob had lied to me, pimped me out to a perfect stranger. He was in on it from the start. He knew what was going to happen from Day One. Well, this time, damn it, he wouldn't get away with it. This time he'd gone too far. I grabbed some of my things and stuffed them quickly into my bag, and I ran out of the room. In my left hand, I still clutched the hundred-dollar bill.

"Son-of-a-bitch!" I cried, flinging the bill toward the bedroom door, tears flowing down my cheeks. "You god-damn lying son-of-a-bitch! Keep your money! Keep your drugs! Just get the hell out of my *life*!"

I drove home in a blind fury, and the first thing I did when I got there was to collect every item of Bob's I could find and throw it all onto a pile on the back porch. Then I called a local locksmith to come out and install new locks, and I refused to open the door for Bob when he finally showed up late that evening. I refused to let him in the next morning, too, or to talk with him on the phone. When he failed to call for several days in a row, I started thinking about contacting a lawyer. It was over. Definitely. I couldn't go on anymore. Our relationship had turned into hell on earth. I'd done all I could possibly do, and it just wasn't enough. I once thought that nothing on earth could ever make me surrender my dignity, no matter how bad things might get. I was wrong.

The following Saturday Bob called again, and for some reason, I listened to his pleas for forgiveness. He said he didn't know what had got into him. He said he had been scared I would leave him if he didn't come up with the money for the rent. It was the first time I'd ever heard him cry. I told him we couldn't go on the way we were. I couldn't face the thought of running into Gene around town, or into someone who knew him and knew what had happened up at the cabin. I couldn't even face myself in the mirror.

Bob begged for compassion. He thought we could start over. He *knew* we could. We could get away from Milwaukee, from all our problems. We could store our furniture and join the Peace Corps for a couple of years, work together side by side to strengthen our relationship as we traveled the world. The Corps was always looking for dedicated teachers and nurses to work in underdeveloped countries.

It was a long shot, I knew, but somehow it seemed better than facing the agony of divorce; so I told him to come home. I said we would talk about it.

FOUR

Kabul, Afghanistan

The bus lumbered into the capital of Afghanistan where we were to meet a representative from the American Embassy before receiving our permanent Corps assignment. It was a little before noon on the first Thursday in June. As we stepped down from the coach, I squinted up into the bright light. I had expected to find a land as dusty and barren and sparsely populated as that we'd just passed through. Instead, I found hundreds, *thousands* of people milling around a cluttered open-air marketplace that smacked of life in the ancient bazaar.

Women in their traditional *chaderi* balanced stout wicker baskets of food on their heads as they slipped through the narrowest openings in the crowd like the wind through the willows at the edge of a pond. Men, dressed in lightweight cotton pants, colorful shirts, and vest-like overcoats, pushed and jostled their way from one stall to the next. They stopped from time to time to chat with a merchant or to sample some of his wares. Some of the men wore oversized, floppy turbans made from long folds of cloth wrapped round in a crude circle, one end tucked in, the other snaking its way down two or three feet to the middle of the back. Others wore only the traditional skullcap, black with the finest gold thread woven in intricate patterns. The children--dressed in plain cotton blouses and pants the color of sand--went without anything at all on their heads, the sun turning their black hair a murky brownish-grey.

From a distance came the barely audible sound of music. "Hear it?"

I listened. "What is it?"

"The dance," he said. "God, how Afghans love to dance. They consider it one of the highest forms of art."

"Let's go see!" I was excited at the prospect of watching an ancient ritual performed as it was centuries ago, even as Genghis Khan stormed across the Asian plains in his effort to bring the world under his dominion.

"Murghi? Murghi kay-liay farangi?" We looked down at a short, balding man with spectacles and a basketful of chickens tottering atop his head. He pointed excitedly at Bob. *"Murghi? Aap chaahna?"* His voice was high-pitched and crackly so that it was hard telling it from the cackling of the birds.

"Nahein, naheen aaj," Bob replied in studied *Urdu. No chickens today, thank you.*

"Murghi?" The man hoisted the basket down so that we could look inside. *"Dekhna? Murghi. Bohot sahat mand. Bohot mota!"*

I nudged Bob. "Very fat and ... what did he say?"

"Healthy."

I looked down at the birds, squabbling to get out. I wondered if they had any inkling of the fate awaiting them.

Bob shook his head and motioned the man off.

"That's incredible," I said as the peddler pushed past us, struggling up the steps of the bus to offer his *murghi* to the other passengers. "He's going to hit up the other passengers now, just going from one to the other. Talk about cold-calling!"

Bob shrugged. "I guess persistence pays off no matter where in the world you live."

I looked up. "Oh, there," I said, pointing. "The dancers. Let's go see!"

"Soon enough." Bob stepped away from the bus and grabbed my hand. He breathed in the hot, dry air and exhaled deeply, and the sudden smell of exotic spices-- curry, turmeric, allspice, and only God knew what else--

washed over us. He nodded toward the horizon beyond the two-story huts lining the street. "What do you think?"

"Oh, my God." I gasped. "What a magnificent sight! The Kush?"

"Yes. The Hindu Kush," he whispered in reverence, "and there, to the southwest, the Koh-i-baba."

"I've never seen mountains like those before in my life. So tall. My God, they seem to rise forever."

"To the very gates of heaven."

Beneath the golden-grey skies of Afghanistan spread the stark, deep-blue peaks, their tips dabbed in white like an artist's canvas. They must have been a hundred miles away, but their enormous size made them look as though they'd sprouted right across the street.

Kabul had been built on a plateau nearly six thousand feet above sea level, in a bowl surrounded by the mighty Hindu Kush and the lesser Koh-i-baba mountain ranges. Running along the eastern edge, the Kabul River wends its way along the steep banks carved out from clay and rock over the centuries and emptying, finally, into the Indus Sea.

The location--set between the Hindu Kush in the north and the lower passes out of Ghazni and Gardeyz to the south--was chosen less for its beauty than for its practicality. The river was a reliable source of fresh water, and the mountains presented a nearly impenetrable barrier to the wandering tribes and Mongol hordes that periodically swept down across Asia from as early as 1500 B.C. The only practical route from Kabul to the rich trade centers of Pakistan and India to the east was through the Kush along the Khyber Pass, and that was possible only in the summer. During winter, the pass became a treacherous journey to negotiate, even for the surefooted wild sheep and goats--impossible for great armies of men traveling on foot.

"Allah be with you," a voice cried in Persian. "May your journeys through our homeland be always blessed, Sahib Bob." I looked up at the elderly Afghan from the bus.

"Thank you, Ahmad," Bob said.

The old man hugged Bob and kissed him, first on the right cheek, and then on the left, before finally taking Bob's hand and pumping it vigorously. All the while they embraced, his wife stood back several feet, as was the custom, her face cloaked in mystery behind the *chaderi*. As they prepared to depart, the old man reached into a shoulder bag and withdrew a large, flat piece of bread, which he offered to Bob.

"May this food nourish you and sustain you through all your days, as Allah stands judge before us all."

"May the peace of Allah be with you and your family, Ahmad." Bob took hold of the loaf as we watched the two heavily cloaked figures disappear among the throngs of people.

"Well?" Bob held out the bread. "Shall we eat now or save it for later?"

"Eat it! I'm starving."

He tore off a corner and handed it to me before popping a piece into his mouth.

"*Ummm* ... delicious," I said, biting it into tiny bits. It had a fresh, nutty taste, unleavened and somewhat chewy, in the tradition of all Asian breads.

"Not bad. Not bad at all."

"Say," I said, looking around. I took another bite. "Are we early or what?" I swallowed the last of my share craned my head.

"What do you mean?"

"I thought someone from the embassy was supposed to meet us."

"Yeah, at noon Thursday." He frowned and checked his watch. "Well, it's noon, and it's Thursday."

"So where's the Welcome Wagon?"

"I don't know. I don't see ..." His eyes scanned the crowded street--the children playing in the dirt, the merchants hawking their wares, their hauntingly lilting cries combining in a chorus of cacophonous sounds. I stooped down to pick up my bag.

"What are you doing?" Bob asked.

"Well, we can't wait around here all day. We might as well check things out. Maybe we'll run into our contact."

Bob continued scanning the streets for some sign of a friendly face as the driver stepped down from the bus. "You are looking for someone, Sahib?" He spoke in thick Persian.

"Yes," Bob replied. "We were supposed to meet someone from the American Embassy. We're here with the Peace Corps."

"Oh, yes." The man nodded, looking us over as though seeing us for the first time. "With the Peace Corps. Are these your bags?"

"Yes."

"You are wealthy Americans?"

Bob laughed. "If we were wealthy Americans, we wouldn't be here with the Peace Corps."

The driver smiled and nodded. "Of course. But in Afghanistan, it seems as though all Americans are wealthy."

"Then, there are other Americans in Kabul?" I asked in Persian, excited at the prospect of meeting someone from home.

He nodded. "There are always Americans in Kabul. Americans and Germans and British and Canadians--all kinds of *farangis*. The Afghan government hires them to advise our technicians and engineers on a great number of projects. Several years ago, there was a large crew of American workers hired by our government to build a road from Kabul through Ghazni to Kandahar. They did an excellent job." He beamed, as though paying himself a compliment.

"That's a long way to come, from America to Afghanistan, just to build a road," I said.

The driver agreed. "It is a long way, yes, but it is not *too* long if the camel knows only one true path. In northern Afghanistan, not more than five years ago, the government hired a group of Soviet engineers to put in a road at considerably less expense than the Americans charged. It was even longer than the American-built road to Kandahar, and wider, too."

"Why didn't the government use the Soviets to build the Kandahar road, then?"

The man shook his head. "The Soviets built a *terrible* toad. Before the first winter had passed, the concrete had buckled up in so many places because the workers had cheated on the materials, it was fit only for goats and sheep. I myself have driven the road twice on my way north to Khanabad." His eyes rolled toward Allah as he shook his head woefully. "There is an old saying in my country. If you wish to buy a good carbine, see the Russians. If you wish to buy a good road, see the Americans."

I smiled.

"Tell me, do you know the name of the person you are to meet in Kabul? I know several people at the American Embassy. Perhaps I could ..."

"No, I'm afraid not," Bob said. "All we know is that the embassy promised to have someone here to meet us at noon."

The man checked his watch. "It is after noon already, I am afraid. I myself would gladly help you locate your contact, but I must quickly eat lunch and begin the long drive back to Islamabad. I must make three round trips each week if I wish to keep my job. But I think if you go to the American Embassy, maybe you will find your friend there."

"Where is the embassy?" I asked.

He pointed down the center of the street. "It is maybe 200 meters toward the west. Turn north at the sign of Omar the merchant. But I warn you, buy nothing from him, for he is a thief and a scoundrel." He spit contemptuously into the street before continuing. "The embassy is the large building with the American and Afghan flags flying outside the door."

"That's not far," I told Bob. "We can walk."

"Be grateful you are not British," the driver said. "The British Embassy is on the far northern end of town. It would take you all afternoon to travel that distance on foot." He leaned close to us as if about to reveal some great government secret. "The British were determined to build the largest foreign settlement in all of Kabul. Larger, even, than the American, French, and German compounds combined. We Afghans have beaten them off Asian soil twice in the past. Since they could not conquer us from without"--he winked--"they thought they could do so from within."

The man reared back on his heels and laughed a deep, throaty, raspy laugh that shook him down to his toes.

"And so they did," Bob said.

The driver shook his head and drew near again. "When the Afghan government finally agreed to cede to them nearly three square miles of building space, that naturally made the Brits very happy."

"Naturally."

"You should have seen the look on their proper British faces when the colonel of the guard arrived with a large crew of designers and engineers to begin work on the compound, only to find that the land was not even in the city but on its far fringes, where only wolves and jackals prowl at night."

We all laughed. "So they eventually built there, anyway?" Bob asked.

"Yes," he replied, adding with some annoyance, "and I will be a son of a camel if it isn't one of the most beautiful compounds in all the land."

We thanked the driver for his help, grabbed our bags, and started off in the direction he had indicated, each step deeper into the city carrying us further into the strange eroticism that exploded around us. Handsome faces and rugged ones, mysterious eyes of great exotic beauty peeking above richly woven cloth--all held the allure of excitement and joy, of mystery and unfulfilled promises.

We stopped only once to wave at the driver as the bus growled to life behind us before roaring down the center of the road, horn honking, chickens flying from its path. When it was no longer in sight, I felt a strangely eerie veil of darkness descend upon me, like a *chaderi* that covered my body except for the slit over my eyes.

We continued on our way west, seeking out the sign of Omar the merchant.

"Bob," I said, stopping short. "Look at that." I pointed to a circle of young boys playing in the dirt at the side of the road. They were taking turns tossing colored stones inside a small ring that had been etched into the ground with a stick. "What are they doing?"

"They're playing an ancient Persian game, like our marbles. The last boy to remain in the game wins."

One of the boys, squatting on bare feet, looked up at me and wiped a thick shock of black hair from his forehead. His eyes were large and brown, his head a perfect oval. He was dressed in thin cotton pants that seemed to be more dust than cloth and an attractive Indian-style shirt of faded blue. I smiled at him, but he just stared back-- the first blonde-haired, fair-skinned woman in jeans he'd ever seen, I guessed.

Suddenly the others began calling to him. He picked up a stone and hurled it at a group of rocks scattered across the circle from his, missing its mark by several inches. The boys in the group hooted and howled, taunting him, and one shoved him playfully as the next boy took his turn.

"Come on, Paula, we'd better get going. Unless you want to join them."

"Good-by," I said in Persian, waiving at them. The little boy in the blue shirt looked startled.

"God, he's cute. Do you think ..." But Bob had already forged far ahead of me, and I had to hurry to catch up. Suddenly he seemed inspired to reach our destination.

"Hey, slow down. What's the big hurry?"

"No hurry." He grabbed my arm and pulled me through the crowd.

"Well, then, slow down, will you?"

"Let's just get to the embassy and get settled in as soon as possible, okay? Then we can dawdle around town if you like."

We snaked our way through the crowds in the street,

wall-to-wall people so thick that rarely could you see past them to the sidewalks where the blacksmiths and the furriers, the bakers and the leatherworkers had set up stands to hawk their wares. By the time we reached the corner of Omar's shop, the sweat poured off my face. My top was drenched, and I was beginning to feel queasy. Suddenly I remembered we hadn't eaten a real meal since late last night when we shared food with our fellow passengers. My stomach, right on cue, began to rumble.

"Come on, will you?" Bob pulled harder on my hand.

"Hey, take it easy. We're going to be here two years, remember?"

"Yeah, well, I just want to get settled in. I don't like the fact that no one showed up to meet us. What if they forgot we were coming today? What if the Corps in Chicago never wired them? What if everyone at the embassy has gone home? You know how government employees are. Do you want to sleep out in the streets tonight with the jackals and the thieves?"

"What jackals?" I pulled back against him. "And what thieves? *Oww!* You're hurting me."

"Keep up, then, will you?"

"I'm hungry." I stopped for a moment to sniff the air. The pungent smell of roasting lamb suddenly licked at my nostrils. I strained to see past the crowd to where a large cloud of smoke rose up, hanging in the air as if suspended by wires. "Bob, look." I peered past the smoke. "There's food over there. Maybe we could get something to eat. Bob?"

I turned around, and my heart leaped suddenly. I fell back against the crowd as a giant of a man scowled down at me. Someone pushed me back toward him, his long, flowing robe and sandaled feet in marked contrast to the bandoliers crossing his chest. A wicked-looking knife hung from a wide sash of red silk. A large carbine, black and deadly, lay casually slung across one shoulder. His lips curled into a tight ball. But it was his eyes--those steely coal-black eyes--that pierced me.

"Oh!" I shouted as the giant took one step forward.

"Excuse me ... excuse me ... my wife ... have you seen my wife?" I heard Bob's voice in Persian somewhere off in the crowd.

"Bob! Bob! Over *here*!"

"Excuse me." Bob broke through the crowd and froze before the giant. "*Uh*, excuse me," he said softly. "My wife. *Mera biwi.*" He smiled at the giant, took me by the hand, and pulled me away. I looked over my shoulder and saw him still peering after us. "Come *on!*"

We pushed our way through the crowd until finally we were lost to the giant's piercing gaze. Bob stopped and turned to me.

"What in the name of hell is the matter with you, yelling out that way? Do you want to get yourself killed?"

"What *was* that ... that ... that ... *thing*? That man with the knife and the gun and ..." My heart still pounded wildly.

"I told you to keep up with me! Kabul is the melting pot of Afghanistan. God knows what kinds of people are here."

"What *was* he?" I asked again.

"Probably a Pashtun rebel down from the north to buy supplies."

"But he looked so *mean*, like a wild man. I've never seen a man with eyes like that before."

"There are some parts of Afghanistan where a man survives by being wild. Some of the mountain people learn how to kill before they learn to walk. It's a way of life. And death."

I looked back over my shoulder, fighting the tears that were welling up in my eyes. "I was hungry. I just stopped for a minute to ..."

"Well, don't stop again without telling me!"

He took me by the hand and pulled me through the crowd until we reached a large building of sun-bleached clay and stone. Outside, two flags--one American, the other Afghan--lay perfectly still against their masts in the breezeless day, as though yielding in supplication to the scorching, relentless Afghan sun.

We hurried up the stairs and into the building, the cool shade inside a sudden dip in a shallow mountain stream. We walked up to a landing, and we paused.

"I'm sorry," I told him.

"For what?"

"For acting like a child." The words were stilted and faint, choppy. I choked back the tears that tried to follow them.

"Forget it."

"It's just that I wasn't expecting it. I mean, I just turned away for an instant, and when I looked back ..."

"*Forget* it. It's a lesson well learned." He tossed my hair and squeezed my arm lightly. "Come on. Let's see what's going on here."

We walked through a doorway into a small reception area. A young American marine who had been seated in one of the high-backed chairs lining the corridor snapped suddenly to attention. He wore his best dress uniform and had a service revolver strapped to his side.

"Yes, sir!" he said, sounding as official as he could.

"Hi," Bob greeted him. "Say, we're here from America with the Peace Corps, and we'd like to see the ambassador."

"Yes, *sir!*" the marine snapped. "Follow me, *sir!*"

He turned on his heels and walked briskly across the room. Bob raised his eyes and peered back at me before throwing me a salute. Bob mouthed the words, *Follow me, sir.*

We passed through an open doorway into a second room, slightly larger than the first, where the marine held the door as we entered, closing it softly behind us. At the far end of the room, a young woman in her mid-twenties pounded away at an old Underwood typewriter perched atop a small wooden desk.

"Damn it," she said under her breath, picking up an eraser and scratching at some marks on the paper.

"Excuse me," Bob said.

"Oh!" The woman started. "I didn't know anyone was here."

"The guy in the soldier suit let us in," Bob replied. I poked him in the back.

"May I help you?"

"Yes. My name is Bob Favage, and this is my lovely wife, Paula."

I smiled and held out my hand. The woman looked at us quizzically. For a moment, I thought she hadn't understood, although she seemed to have been speaking English. She looked American enough, too: long black hair pulled back and tied behind her head; a neatly pressed lightweight suit over a cotton blouse that revealed too much cleavage when she bent forward.

"Bob and Paula Favage?" he repeated. "We're with the Peace Corps. We just arrived in Afghanistan and were told we would be met by someone from the embassy at the bus depot, but no one showed up."

"Well, how did you get here then?" she asked.

He looked at her incredulously, glanced quickly at me, and turned back to her. "We walked. The taxis don't seem to be running today." Sarcasm dripped from his voice.

"Well, what did you want?"

Bob was still perspiring. Beads of sweat formed on his upper lip and forehead. "We would like to see the ambassador."

"Pertaining to what, please?"

"Pertaining to what? Pertaining to our arrival. Pertaining to just exactly what the hell it is we're *supposed to be doing* now that we're here in Kabul."

"I'm sorry, sir," she said. "I'm afraid I don't understand."

"Look," Bob said, setting his bag on the floor and leaning over the edge of the desk. "Didn't anyone tell you we were coming? We're here to work in Afghanistan with the Peace Corps. You've heard of the Peace Corps, haven't you?"

"Oh, yes, of course. Everyone has ..."

"Good. Now, we were told when we left the states that we would be expected here in Kabul today, that there would be someone at the bus depot to meet us, and that we would be taken to the American Embassy for further instructions. You know, little things like where we'll be staying, when we start work, what we'll be doing. Those kinds of things."

"Oh," she said, the light finally seeping through. "And you say you're with the Peace Corps?"

I felt sorry for her. She was genuinely struggling with the situation. Either she didn't have a lot going for her upstairs, or she was so new at her job that she hadn't experienced anyone from the states yet. Bob wasn't helping.

"Yes, that ... is ... right," he replied, exaggerating each syllable as he spoke. "With ... the ... Peace ... Corps. *And* ... we'd like to see the ambassador. *If* you don't mind."

"Oh, I don't mind." The woman began shuffling through some papers in a basket on the corner of her desk. "I'm really sorry," she said before adding under her breath, "but nobody ever tells me anything. You'd think they could ..." She pulled a sheet from the stack and scanned the first few lines. "Here it is!" she announced triumphantly. "Favage, Robert L. and Paula D. Is that right?"

"Yes, that's right."

I gave Bob a nudge and turned to the woman. "Excuse me, but is there someone here we could talk to? We just this minute arrived on the bus from Islamabad, and we're a little tired and hungry. If we could just speak to the ambassador, he would know ..."

"Oh, yes, of course," she said excitedly. "My, you people have had a long journey, haven't you?"

Bob's head craned slowly around to me, then worked its way agonizingly back to her again. "Yes. Yes, we have. So you'll call the ambassador now?"

Her mouth popped open and her eyes glassed up as if focusing on some object far in the distance. "Oh, my, no. I'm sorry, but I'm afraid that's impossible."

"Why ... is that impossible?" I asked.

"I'm afraid the ambassador is in a meeting at the moment and left explicit instructions that he cannot be disturbed."

Bob sighed. "Well, then, is there someone *else* we can talk to?"

"Oh ... I suppose there must be ... *someone*," she said, picking up the telephone and dialing once. "I'll see if the ambassador's assistant is free."

"Thank you." I turned to Bob and whispered, "See? You catch more flies with honey than with vinegar."

He shook his head. "You'd catch more flies in here," he replied flatly, "with a great big pile of cow ..."

"All right," the woman said, setting the receiver down. "Now, if you'll just go through that door to the third door on the left, you can talk with Mr. Ingersoll, the ambassador's assistant. He knows more about Peace Corps people and the like, anyway. Just straight through there." She pointed. "Through there. Through that door over there."

"Come on, Bob." I tugged at his arm.

"Oh," the woman added, "and you'd better take this paper with you. It might help if Mr. Ingersoll knew what you were all about."

Bob grabbed the paper from her hand, and she turned back to her typing.

"Can you believe that?" he asked as we passed through the dimly lighted corridor. "Can you believe something like that can end up working in a career diplomatic post at the American Embassy? Jesus Christ, with her on our side, it's a wonder America hasn't surrendered to Jalalabad by now."

"You're in a jolly mood."

"And why shouldn't I be? It's a hundred and ten in the shade. We just traveled halfway around the world, the last twenty-four hours by overland stage. We got off in a strange land and were met by a group of kids playing marbles, a bus driver with bad breath, and a Pashtun rebel who wanted to slice us to ribbons and feed us to the jackals."

"I didn't notice that."

"You didn't notice *what*?" he asked curtly.

"That the driver had bad breath."

We walked through the third doorway on the left and found ourselves in a ten-by-twelve-foot cubicle sparsely furnished with two wooden chairs facing an even smaller wooden desk than the one in the reception room if that was possible. Behind the desk sat a fat, balding, greasy-headed man working hard at pushing a pencil across a sheet of paper. His nose, what there was of it, supported a pair of wire-rimmed bifocals. He appeared to be fifty, perhaps fifty-five, and was wearing a rumpled tan suit that had needed a trip to the cleaners six months ago. His white shirt was frayed at the collar, which was open, and a wide blue-and-white polka-dot tie formed a fat knot three inches below his chin. The man didn't look up. I instinctively disliked him.

Bob cleared his throat and dropped the bag at his feet.

"*Yessss*?" the man hissed. "What is it?"

Fists clenched, Bob took one menacing step forward.

"*Uhhh*," I said, pulling him back, "Mr. Ingersoll, is it? We're here with the Peace Corps, and we were told by the receptionist that you may be able to help us get settled in."

At the sound of a woman's voice, Ingersoll dropped his pencil and peered up over his spectacles. "Well, well, well," he said, rising from his chair and tugging at his tie. "Well, do come in."

"Thank you," I said.

"So you're the new Peace Corps people, eh?" He glanced at Bob and returned his smile to me. "George Ingersoll here, assistant American consul general, at your service." He quickly removed his glasses and extended his hand.

"Paula Favage," I said as we shook hands. "And this is ..."

"Well, well, *Miss* Favage, is it? I certainly never expected to see anyone so ... so ... *young*. Or so, *uhh* ..." His beady eyes ran up and down my tight-fitting jeans, across my torso, resting finally on my gaze. "--well, *attractive*, if I may say so. Those Peace Corps people back in the states--I must admit, they're doing a much better job in recruiting than they used to. Top notch. First rate. I can see that we're going to get along splendidly, just splendidly."

"Hi," Bob said, pushing his hand into Ingersoll's free palm and pumping it vigorously. "Bob Favage, here, husband to Paula Favage, whose hand you've been shaking now for the past thirty seconds."

"Why, yes," Ingersoll said, the smile on his lips fading. "How nice to have you here, too, Mr. Favage. I do hope you didn't think I was ignoring you. It's just that, well, you'll learn when you've been here in Afghanistan for a while that it's customary to greet guests cordially. Cordiality, as the old saying goes, is the staff of life. It's considered poor taste, don't you know, an insult and all that sort of thing, to shake and run, as it were." He chuckled. "Very poor taste indeed. So I apologize if you mistook my greeting for anything that may have seemed, well, *inappropriate* from a typical American point of view. I assure you, sir, that nothing could be ..."

"I was stationed in Iran and Iraq during the Sixties, Mr. Ingersoll. I served nearly four years in the Peace Corps and traveled extensively throughout the Middle East and Central Asia, including Afghanistan, Pakistan, Kashmir, and India. I'm well aware of what the local customs are. As well as what they are *not.*"

He hesitated before clearing his throat. "Yes, of course. I'm sure I understand your position. Precisely." Ingersoll looked as though he'd just gotten word that his mother had passed away from gout moments before his father had died of a stroke.

"Now, Mr. Ingersoll, we've been traveling for *soooo* long, and we're so *very, very, very* tired. So, do you think it's possible that we can be shown to our accommodations for tonight?"

"Tonight?"

"Yes," Bob repeated, "tonight. I assume we won't be traveling on to wherever we'll be stationed until the morning, and that we won't need to sleep in the street."

"*Ahh,*" Ingersoll said, his eyes suddenly aglow again,

"to where you'll be stationed. Yes, of course. I see what you're getting at. You wish to stay in Kabul the night before leaving in the morning. May I?"

He held out his hand, and Bob gave him the assignment sheets on us.

"*Aha*! He strained his eyes to make out the symbols on the paper. After some time, he finally slipped the bifocals back over his nose. "Just for reading," he added, cackling. "Normally, I don't wear them at all." He scanned the sheet several times, emitting several grunts and groans as he read, before finally turning to me. "So you're a nurse?"

"Yes."

"A registered nurse from, *uhh*, Milwaukee, Wisconsin, I see."

"Yes."

"The Dairy State."

"That's what they say."

"Yes. Any specialty you have? In nursing, I mean."

"Yes. I worked in cardiology--ER pulmonary resuscitation."

"*Ahh*, yes. Quite. Pulmonary resus- ... pulmonary resus- ... has to do with the kidneys, doesn't it?"

"The heart."

"*Ahh*, yes, of course. Very good. Excellent! The heart. Of course." He scanned farther. "And, Mr. Favage, you have applied as a teacher, I see. A teacher of what, sir?"

"I was told I would teach English as a secondary language at the intermediate level."

"English? Oh, yes. Very big here in Afghanistan. The locals *must* learn English. Oh, my, yes, yes, yes, of course." He lowered his head and craned his neck to one side. "They're very dependent upon us, don't you know. The locals." He said it as if not wishing anyone else to hear. "*Very* dependent. Especially in the sciences, you know--math, engineering, things like that. You ... you don't speak Persian, by any chance?"

"Persian, *Pashto*, *Urdu*, and some Turkish," Bob replied, "although my Turkish is a bit rusty."

Ingersoll's chin dropped. "Rusty, yes. I see. Well, I

must say, it's a rarity to have someone from America who can speak the locals' language ... or languages, I should say. As for myself, I never did do well with Persian." He laughed. "Too damned complicated, with all those hidden meanings behind each syllable. I might set out to ask a local for a glass of water and end up insulting his daughter's virtue!" He laughed again, glanced at me, and stopped suddenly to clear his throat. "Not that I can't speak it well enough to get by, you understand. I'm a career diplomat, myself, six years in Afghanistan. One must learn *something* of the local language in six years, now, mustn't one?"

Bob sighed.

"Yes." Ingersoll quickly folded our orders and stuffed them into his suit coat pocket. "*Uhh*, well, then. I see you are both eminently qualified to perform here. I am sure the country will be the better for your presence. I believe, then, Mr. and Mrs. Favage, that we can put your, *uhh*, talents to good use right here in Kabul: you, Mr. Favage, at the university, where I happen to know the locals are always in need of qualified instructors of English; and you, Miss. Favage ..."

"*Mrs*. Favage."

"Oh, yes, of course. *Mrs*. Favage. At the clinic. I'm sure that with your medical training and past experience in resus- ... resus- ... in that kidney thing, you will find yourself to be quite useful."

"You mean we'll be stationed right here in Kabul?"

"Yes. Yes, you and your lovely, *uhh*, Mrs. Favage, here."

"That's good news, isn't it, Bob? We'll have a chance to settle in and get acquainted with the town."

"Oh, I'm sure you'll find the city charming by day, charming. A trifle hot, perhaps," he added, noticing our damp clothes. He pulled out a handkerchief and dabbed at his forehead. "*Ahh*, but one gets used to the heat after a while." He looked up at Bob. "You already know that, though, don't you? Well, then, there's no need for a long indoctrination program, is there? I mean, if there's anything I dislike about this job, it's going through a long indoctrination program, don't you know. Do this, don't do that; go here, don't go there."

"I think we'll make out okay," Bob said.

"Of course you will, of course, most assuredly. And should you need any assistance, anything whatsoever, my door is always open--to *both* of you." He draped his short, stubby arms around our shoulders and turned us toward the hall.

"I'm sure," I said. "Bob's being here before will be a big help."

"Of course, of course it will. And, if he neglects your education one teeny bit, you feel free to come to me, my ... *uhh*, Mrs. Favage. I would be only most pleased to try to satisfy your specific needs as best I can." He peered at me over the tops of his glasses, and I thought I saw him wink.

Out in the hall, we shook hands goodbye. "Nice to have met you. Good having you aboard." He turned to Bob as an afterthought. "You, too, Mr. Favage. *Both* of you. I ..."

"Is there someone to show us where we'll be staying?" Bob asked.

"Oh, of course. How silly of me. Yes, yes indeed. I'll have one of the locals, Naim, show you to your quarters. You'll be in quite capable hands, I assure you. And tomorrow being the end of the week, well, it seems cruel to ask you to begin life anew at the end of the week, now, doesn't it?" He laughed to himself. "And if there's anything you'll soon learn about old George Ingersoll, it's that he's anything but cruel. So, why don't we expect you to begin teaching, and"--he nodded to me--"*nursing* on Monday. I'll make contact with the respective authorities and send a local for you in the Jeep, so you'll not have any trouble finding your way the first day if that is satisfactory."

"That'll be fine."

"Very well, then, it's all set." Ingersoll stopped, peered up and down the hall, and sucked in his gut. His lips parted and paused before suddenly exploding.

"*Naim!*"

The sound echoed through the narrow corridor for what seemed like hours. When there was no response, he sucked in a second time, and I braced for the blast. Suddenly the door at the end of the corridor opened, and a teenaged boy with dark, straight hair and tawny good looks poked his head out.

"Did you call, Sahib?" the boy asked.

Ingersoll let a rush of air escape from his mouth and sighed deeply as though, he, too, was relieved. "Naim, these two fine young people here are with the Peace Corps. From the States. Take them out to the hut, will you, and help them get settled in. Meanwhile, I will secure their work positions for them and get their papers of introduction in order. On Monday you can pick them up in the Jeep and take them about, show them their jobs and all. Is that clear?"

"Yes, Sahib." Naim closed the door behind him and followed Ingersoll down the corridor. "Perfectly."

Ingersoll squeezed my arm tightly, saying his final goodbyes before slipping, snail-like, back into his office.

"I am sorry," the Afghan said in English as he came toward us, "but I did not learn your names."

"I'm Bob Favage, and this is my wife, Paula." Bob took the boy's hand.

Naim wore sandals, lightweight cotton pants, and a Western-style sports jacket like the ones we'd seen in the street, except that it was several sizes too large for his slight frame.

"Welcome to my country." He smiled warmly. "I hope that you find it has all the pleasantries of your own home."

"So far, I find it hot."

"Oh, yes? It is very hot for you. It is hotter than in the United States of America, I am sure. That is where you are from?"

"Yes," I said, "from Wisconsin."

"Wisconsin." He toyed with the word for several

seconds, as though trying to fit the piece into a giant puzzle and, failing, finally shrugged.

"It's north of Chicago," Bob told him.

"Oh, Chicago." Naim beamed. "The Windy City!"

I laughed. Naim blushed. "I am sorry. I do not speak your language so well, I am afraid."

"No, no." I smiled. "You speak English better than some of our friends back home."

At this Naim seemed pleased. "I am glad. I have studied hard of your country's language and wish to speak it always imperceptibly."

"I'm sure you do." I fought back the urge to smile.

"I will take you to your hut, although I am afraid we will have to make the trip on foot. The consulate's Jeep is being in for the repairs."

"Oh, great," Bob said.

"But it is not so far--no more than three or four kilo-meters."

"Jesus," Bob groaned.

"Well," I said, shifting my bag from one hand to the other, "we'd might as well get going."

"Oh, no," Naim protested, wresting the bag from me. "Let me carry your luggage." He reached down and hiked Bob's case up over his head, slipping mine beneath his arm as though it were a loaf of bread. With that, he coaxed the door to the reception area open with his foot and stood to one side.

"Naim!" Ingersoll's voice boomed from deep inside his office.

"Yes, Sahib!"

"Naim, be sure to tell them about the trouble with those damned Pashtuns. I don't want them going near any of those damned Pashtuns!"

"Yes, Sahib. I will tell them."

We descended the embassy steps into the steamy Afghan day and began the long walk to our quarters.

"What was it that Ingersoll said about the Pashtuns?" Bob asked.

Naim frowned. "It is trouble, for certain. But no more

than usual."

"What kind of trouble?"

"It is a long story that goes back many years. Nearly thirty."

Bob checked his watch. "Well, we've got the time."

"The Pashtuns are a people of the Pathan tribe of old Afghanistan, living in the area of our country that once bordered on northern Pakistan and eastern India."

"In the Northwest Frontier."

Naim looked surprised. "You know of the Frontier? You know of my country's history, then. That is well."

"I've studied it some," Bob said.

"Then you know that in 1950, the Pakistani government annexed the Northwest Frontier as part of their land, with the aid of the Indian nation."

"Yes. And that led to border skirmishes and the closing of the Khyber Pass in"--he paused--"1961, I believe."

Naim nodded. "Very good. Yes. My country has long supported the Pashtuns' claim for independence. It is important that the Pashtuns have the right to choose whatever type of government they will live under--an imposed monarchy under the rule of Pakistan, with strong ties to India, or as a free nation, which the Pashtuns have been since before the days of Genghis Khan."

"With strong political ties to Afghanistan."

"Yes. That is also correct."

"But as I recall, the Pashtuns' land today is still part of Pakistan."

"That is where the difficulty lies. You see, the Pashtun rebels have been revolting against the Pakistani intruders, causing much bloodshed and violence on the Frontier. Naturally, Pakistan believes that my country supports the violence."

"And Pakistan is worried, too, about Russia getting nervous and stepping in on the side of Afghanistan?"

"Well," Naim smiled coyly, "Russia and Afghanistan have been, how do you say it, bed persons since the early 1970s. That is when the Pashtun tribesmen began gathering arms and fortifying large encampments at the foot of the Hindu Kush."

"From which the Pashtuns have been launching raids into northern Pakistan."

"Yes, into northern Pakistan, and even into India and northeastern Afghanistan, in pursuit of Pakistani government forces. There the borders have been in dispute for centuries. The Afghans are reluctant to cede the disputed land to the Pakistanis for fear they will continue their expansion westward into other disputed areas. Then they might attempt to annex those lands in the name of their government and force the Afghans living there to leave."

"And that's the area that Ingersoll wants us to avoid?"

"It is safe, Sahib Bob, to journey no farther north than Chitral. One never knows when or where border skirmishes may break out."

"I understand. With all the tension between Afghanistan and Pakistan, it's a wonder the Khyber Pass is open today."

"There has been talk that if the situation in the Northwest Frontier does not improve soon, this may change."

"Sounds to me as if the Pashtuns are fighting a full-fledged revolutionary war."

Naim sighed. "No less so than your own nation's war with the British in 1776, or in Afghanistan's struggle for freedom with the Imperial Lion. And I am afraid that, until the Pashtuns win their right to a free and independent state, there will be no peace in Afghanistan. They have had their own Boston Tea Party. The conflict that resulted has been very bad."

I stopped short and threw my hands against my hips.

"What?" Bob asked. "What's wrong?"

I shook my head. "You two are amazing. This has been an Asian history lesson for me. I read all the material the Corps sent us, but this is as if you've actually lived it."

Naim smiled. Bob extended his hand.

Naim explained that he was a student at Kabul University during the winter months. He was presently on break and was working for his second season at the American Embassy. While at the University, he studied English, math, religion, and the sciences. He hoped one day to go to America to study engineering, but he was only in his second year at the university and would not be eligible for travel abroad until he had successfully completed his third.

"Is it a religious university?" I asked.

"I do not understand. What is a religious university?"

"Is it run by priests, by Muslim clerics?"

"It is run by the government, like everything in Afghanistan. But the *mullahs*--the holy men--exert great pressure on the government to retain the traditional social and religious values of the past. At one time, the only education available in Afghanistan was through the *mullahs* at the mosques. They taught all that Allah decreed man must know. Mostly, the dictates of Islam."

"And then the government took over the schools?"

"Yes. At some time before I was born. But even though the government today runs many schools, like the university, the *mullahs* demand that compulsory religious education be included in all curriculums, in all schools."

"And the government goes along with them?"

"You must understand the *mullahs*. Naim chose his words carefully. "They have their strengths deeply rooted in tradition. To the people of our country--especially the people outside the great cities of Kabul and Kandahar and Ghazni--the *mullahs* are still the real leaders of the nation, for, in the eyes of most, Allah comes first, and what is left belongs to the government."

"You sound almost as if you'd rather the *mullahs* didn't have so much power."

"Oh, no. I find the study of religion ... rewarding. To come to know Allah, one comes to know life. It is just that ..." he hesitated, "that sometimes there seems to be too *much* of religion. The *mullahs* are fearful there will be a great modernization of thought in Afghanistan, as there has been in Iran. They worry that there will be no one left to take over the task of running the mosques and praying to Mecca. Already many students I know have dropped out of the university because of too much religion. They say they go there to become doctors and teachers and military officers, not *mullahs*. They do not know why they must receive so much religion."

"And you?" I asked. "Have you thought about dropping out?"

Naim broke into a wide-toothed smile. *"Everyone* has thought about dropping out. It is very hard to study there and to maintain good grades. If you do not, you will be asked to leave. But I do not wish to leave. If I did, I would have only to go back to my village and work with my father and brothers in the fields. They own nothing but the sweat on their backs. My father took me aside when I was only six years of age and said to me, 'Naim, I will save up my money, and, when you are ready, I will send you to the great university in Kabul. There you will learn all you need to know to become a great scholar and a gentleman. You will study hard and wear great clothes and not have to toil away behind the ox and the mule, as I. You will be a landowner and have much pride in your accomplishments.' And that is what I wish for, too."

As Naim spoke, he looked straight ahead. Occasionally he glanced at Bob, as though on a dare or out of curiosity, but he would not turn his eyes to me, not even when I spoke to him. It wasn't as though he were snubbing me, as though he felt me beneath his dignity, for I saw a look of great sensitivity and compassion in his face. He was perhaps unrefined by Western standards, but be carried a good deal of pride within him, and that shone in his eyes whenever he spoke. He was sincere, honest, the type of person I had hoped to meet in Afghanistan, the kind I hoped could become a friend.

We approached a tall brick-and-mud wall beyond which I could see the green tips of several trees. There were other similar walls dotting the landscape, and I wondered out loud what lay behind them.

"These are the great estates of my land, the gardens for which Afghanistan is so well known."

"They seem to be all over."

"In and around the cities, yes--in Kabul, Islamabad, Kandahar. Some of the gardens are among the most beautiful of any in the world. One such is the garden at the British Embassy right here in Kabul. It is magnificent, with its pomegranate and apricot trees and quince and mulberries you can pick up and eat right from the ground."

"Really? Is it far?"

"It is not so far when the consulate's Jeep is not in repairs; otherwise, it is a very long walk, yes." He led us up a cobblestone path to the gate of a high fence.

"Where are we going?" I asked.

Naim lifted the iron latch, and the gate swung open. "This is where you and Sahib Bob will stay."

"Here?" I asked, straining to see inside. "Are you sure?"

"This is hut number one."

We walked through the gate and up the cobblestones set into the hard clay. Straight ahead lay a one-story hut with tan walls and a flat mud roof. Along either side stood tall palms, which I guessed to be dates, while an orchard of citrus trees spread far off to the left. Along the walk and on each side of the hut, flowers of every imaginable color and size sprayed their beauty.

"My God," I said, "I've never seen such a garden!"

Naim beamed. "I often help with the grounds work."

"It's like a ... a magnificent splash of paint in the center of a huge white canvas."

"Like an opal in a lump of coal," Bob added.

Naim hurried ahead of us and opened the door. The house had a closed-up, musky smell. Even in the dim light, I could see there was very little in the way of furnishings: a small sofa, two or three tiny tables, and a lamp. I was disappointed. The grounds outside far outshone the interior, what was to be our home away from home for the next two years.

Bob pointed to the lamp. "Is that for decoration, or is there really electricity?"

Naim set our bags inside the door, strode up to the lamp, and flicked the switch. He stepped back and grinned.

"Well, glory be. That *is* an unexpected delight."

"Electricity? We have enjoyed it for several years, I think maybe four. The Soviets helped our people to construct a dam."

"It's certainly an improvement over the good old days."

Naim asked, "You have been to Kabul before, Sahib?"

"A long time ago. On a trip from Tehran to Calcutta."

"You have seen Calcutta?" Naim's eyes glowed suddenly brighter. "They say that Calcutta is a terrifying city, with wild beasts of men who roam the streets of the bay by night, savage men who would rather slit your throat with a stiletto than to look at you, men who kill for the very sport of doing so."

"If I'm not mistaken," Bob grinned, "they say the exact same thing in Calcutta about the men of Kabul."

Naim smiled. "I think ... you are fooling with me as if to tell a joke."

Bob laughed. "Yes, I think I am."

"My instructor at the university says, 'Naim, sometimes you chatter like an old woman.' Perhaps I have talked too much. I should leave you alone now to unpack."

I stepped forward. "Well, I for one, think you've been the perfect host. We really appreciate all you've shared with us. You've been very warm and helpful."

Naim blushed. "I will like to help you all that I can." He turned toward Bob. "I will be most happy to help you." He paused. "You will need food from the marketplace, no, Sahib Bob?"

"Yes, I ... *we* will. We've got some crackers and cheese and a couple candy bars here that will hold us for tonight, but we'll have to stock up tomorrow."

"Then, I can pick you up in the morning, and we will go to the market together to buy food. I will show you which merchants are fair and which will rob a *farangi* blind."

"That's very kind, Naim."

"I am pleased to do so." He backed toward the door. "I will pick up the Jeep from repairs tomorrow early and drive straight here for you and Mrs. Paula then."

We followed him out and stood for a few moments admiring the view. "Do all Afghan homes have such beautiful gardens?" I asked.

Naim shook his head. "Most Afghans are not landowners. Most live in tiny huts here and there around the countryside, or they wander the plains in search of work and a place to sleep or to graze their herds. Our country is not very large. Not everyone can own property such as this."

"Those who don't must resent the fortunes of the rest."

"Resent? Why should they resent? The Afghan people know what belongs to them and what does not. Those who are privileged to own land bring joy to the lives of others by offering employment, food, and great beauty. How could one resent something of great beauty? It is like the shepherd who follows the sun for his entire life, walking over the endless sands because he owns no more than the sandals on his feet. Suddenly there appears on the horizon another herdsman, with a larger flock and riding on the back of a camel. Should the first resent the second, or should he admire him for what he has accomplished through his hard work?

"It is a matter of principle," he added, his eyes staring intently into space. "It is enough for an Afghan to be free, to carry no shackles to his bed each night. Whatever else he finds in life is a bonus, a gift from Allah."

I held out my hand to him. Hesitantly, almost painfully, his eyes brushed mine before darting quickly away as he shook it, and then Bob's, and departed.

"You'll come for us tomorrow, then?"

"I will come," Naim called. "And I will bring the Jeep."

The following morning arrived too hot, too soon. A

loud cawing from the garden woke us at six. I threw open the shutters, expecting to see a crow, and instead a large black-and-gold mynah peered up at me from the ground, where it had been pecking at a ripe orange with its oversized beak. Upon seeing me, the bird cocked its head as if to say, "What on earth are *you* doing here?" Then it picked up the fruit in its beak and, with a loud fluttering of wings, lifted itself up and over the treetops, where it disappeared into the morning sun.

"Hey, Paula," Bob shouted from the bath. "Come here! I can't believe this!"

I hurried into the small cubicle off the living room. Bob was toying with a spigot on the end of a single pipe rising up through the mud-and-brick floor, some ancient periscope poking its head above the sea at its skipper's command. He turned the handle to the left, and the goose-necked head spit up a steady trickle of water that splashed against a small drain hole carved into the floor.

"Running water!" I cried. "Talk about luxury!"

"It's absolutely ingenious. Look. Look here." He pointed to the floor. "When the wastewater runs down into that drain hole, there, it runs through a pipe to the outside wall of the house, where it dribbles into a tile-lined ditch. Gravity carries it out to the orchard, where it's used to irrigate the trees. Take a look."

I peered out the bathroom window and, sure enough, saw the steady trickle of water from the shower worming its way along an open tile ditch toward the garden. Not an ounce of the precious treasure was lost in a nation whose average annual rainfall reaches a scant six inches a year.

"Do you ever get the feeling that the preparation we got back home was just a bit short of the mark?"

We crowded up to a small mirror that had been hung from a nail attached to one wall.

"Shit," he spat, scrubbing his teeth with his finger and spitting into the drain. "If it were a matter of knowing the number of men in the Afghan armed forces or the strength of the troops stationed along the Soviet border, they'd have the latest figures down to a *T*. Ask them a simple thing like is there running water or electricity, and they're still back in the fucking Dark Ages. You'd think the American Embassy here had never heard of a telephone. You'd think we were the first Americans ever to come to this country."

Bob grabbed a damp rag and quickly sponged his naked body, splashing some water onto his hair. "Where's the comb?" he asked. He slipped into his crisp, white shorts and bent over to strap on his sandals.

"What's your hurry?" I rubbed my hands over his damp back. "Naim won't be here for a couple of hours."

"Jesus, Paula," he said, a sharp edge to his voice. "Not now, okay? It's too hot."

"It's only going to get hotter." I slid my arms around his neck and kissed the back of his head. "I can help." It felt like years since I'd been held, squeezed, in Bob's arms. Something about being in this primitive, mysterious, foreboding land turned a fire on inside of me. I wanted Bob to hold me, to squeeze me, to make love to me. "We'd might as well make good use of the time."

"Not *now!*" he snapped, bucking me off his shoulders. "Jesus Christ, can't you take no for an answer?"

I backed away from him, startled. "I'm ... I'm sorry. I didn't mean to ... I mean, I just thought ..."

"No, no, you didn't, Paula. That's the trouble. You *didn't* think. If you had, you'd know I'm not in the mood. When I say no, it means *no*. It doesn't mean maybe. It doesn't mean 'Watch me change his mind.' It means *no!*"

"I *said* I'm sorry. It won't happen again!" I spun around and stormed out of the room. Ripping open my purse, I scattered the contents across the floor. "Here!" I yelled, picking up the comb and flinging it into the bathroom. "Your precious comb!"

"Watch out, will you!"

I kicked the compact and lipstick and tissue pack clear across the floor and ran into the bedroom, tears stinging my eyes.

"*Damn* him," I sobbed. "*Damn* him to hell if he thinks he's going to treat me here like he treated me at home!"

"What are you mumbling about?" Bob called from the bath.

I grabbed a small hand mirror from the chest next to the bedroom window and looked into it. Two full, pouting lips and a pair of runny blue eyes stared back. I wiped the tears from my face. The last thing in the world I wanted was for Bob to know I'd been crying.

"For Chrissake, Paula," he called, "what's this shit doing all over the living room floor?"

"If you don't like it, pick it up!"

"What the hell's Naim going to think when he walks in? This place looks like a pigsty. We're supposed to be the *sophisticated* culture, remember? We're supposed to have the better lifestyle. What the hell's he going to think when he sees this?"

"If you're so damned worried about what he's going to think, pick it up," I said again. I slipped off my baby dolls and stepped into a pair of bikini panties. I could hear Bob stuffing things into my purse. I grabbed a denim wraparound skirt and buttoned it up the front. "If you spent as much time worrying about us as you do worrying about what others *think* about us, we'd be a lot better off."

Bob walked in and flipped my purse onto the bed. "Now, what the hell's that supposed to mean?"

"Why do you always have to ask me what something is supposed to mean? You understand English, don't you? So why don't you just respond?"

"Respond to what? If you made any sense when you opened your mouth, I'd be *happy* to respond. What kind of comment is that--if I spent as much time worrying about us? What the hell's there to worry about? How am I *supposed* to respond?"

I pulled a short-sleeved cotton top from my case and shook out the wrinkles. I slipped it over my head and down around my waist. "There are lots of things to worry about. There's us. There's the way our relationship has been going lately. Don't you ever think about that? Don't you ever think about *us?*"

"What the hell kind of a question is that?"

"It's a *direct* one, Bob. Can't you give me a direct answer?"

"Sure," he said. "Okay. You want an answer? Yeah, I think about us. Okay? Satisfied? Case closed?"

"What *about* us, Bob? *What* do you think about us? Can you tell me?"

"How the hell can I tell you when I don't even know what the fuck you're talking about, for Chrissake!" He turned on his heels and stomped out of the room.

"That's it, Bob. Just walk away from our problems. That's always been your favorite way of dealing with things."

"The only thing wrong with our relationship is in your head!"

"And what's *that* supposed to mean?" I trailed him into the living room. "That it's all my fault? That *I'm* to blame for all our problems?"

Bob threw open the shutters in the front, and the early-morning sun streamed through, illuminating the tiny particles of dust fluttering past the window like fish swimming in an aquarium. "Forget it. You wouldn't understand."

"I don't want to forget it." I grabbed his arm and pulled him around to face me. "Bob, this is serious. There's something *wrong*, here. I'm not kidding. There's something wrong with us. It's not like it used to be. Every other day we're fighting, quarreling. Back home it was the pressure--school, your future, money, rent, all those things. But we're not back home anymore; we're here." I looked around the room. "What do we blame it on now? Those pressures we had back home are gone. You don't have to worry about finals, or about getting a good-paying job, or about how we're going to come up with money for the rent. The Corps is taking care of all that now. So *why are we still fighting?"*

"You tell me," he said flatly. "You're the one who blew up in there."

"Bob," I said, drawing him close to me, "I'm sorry. I didn't mean to. And I'm not looking to place the blame on anyone. I just want to be loved. I want to feel needed. Can't you understand that? Can't you just ... let me feel that you still love me ... sometimes?"

He stood silently--cold, unmoving, a pillar.

"Look," he said softly after several moments, "you'd better get ready. When an Afghan says he'll be here in the morning, he means early."

I looked up into Bob's expressionless face, and I slowly backed away and dabbed at my eyes. "Bob ..."

"Go on, now," he said, as if he were talking to a young puppy he'd just scolded for piddling on the floor. "Go. Into the bathroom with you. And wipe your eyes."

It was useless to protest. It wouldn't do any good. None at all. I knew Bob well enough to know that. He'd made up his mind to sidestep our problems, to avoid confronting them. There would be no changing his mind today. Not tomorrow, either. But maybe, just maybe, sometime down the road, in the future ... with enough work ... enough time. Someday, he would be ready.

Monday morning swept down across the plains more quickly than I'd expected. We had spent the weekend with Naim ferrying us around Kabul. He took us to the British Embassy, with all its gardens, where several of his friends worked six days a week at keeping everything looking perfect. He had driven us to the foothills of the mighty Hindu Kush, where I gazed, stunned, at the spiraling pinnacles. There wasn't a doubt in my mind why man with all of his technological marvels hadn't yet conquered the Kush with his roads and rails, his hands and his brawny back. The Kush would survive another thousand years or more intact, scar-free, virginal. The only concession the mighty mountain made to man was to withdraw its blanket of white each spring so that the nomadic herdsmen could wander across the lower throws of its slopes with their flocks. But no one--not even the sure-footed pronghorn sheep or the surly karakul goat-- dared attempt to traverse the Kush in winter, with its snows so thick, a man could dig with a pickax for six months and barely scratch the surface.

But Nature? She is a marvel. Each spring, the warm breezes wending their way north from southern Asia, from the Tropic of Cancer and the Arabian Sea, trigger a change in the iron will of the Kush. Slowly, grudgingly, the mountains surrender the snow, pulling it back like a mother turns down a blanket from her sleeping child's bed, until, by early summer, all that remains is a pillow of white at the peak. In return, the Kush sends a torrent of life-sustaining water racing down its valley slopes to come to rest, finally, in the Kabul River, where it begins its journey, roaring like a raging madman along the steeply carved banks that lead ultimately to the Indus.

"It is hard to believe, I know," Naim said as we stood on the soft, thin banks of the river, watching this trickle of water wend its way slowly south, fighting the long, hot days of August along the way. "This tiny stream, which a man could easily traverse on foot, swells into the tyrant that storms the countryside in spring." He picked up a small stone and threw it into the river where it landed with a splash. "But you will believe. By next spring, you will believe."

After dropping Bob off at the university downtown, Naim veered the Jeep north along the winding banks of the river, heading west toward the clinic where I was to work. As we rolled over streets built thousands of years ago to accommodate traders on horseback and camel, roads along which Mongol conqueror Ghengis Khan urged his troops, Naim stopped frequently to allow people and livestock to move out of the way until we could pass safely.

"A driver has to be patient in Kabul!" I said, smiling.

"Most are, yes. Some, though, not so much."

"Who are the worst? The Americans, I'll bet."

"Oh, no. American drivers are like lambs in the company of wolves. Compared to a German, they are innocent young children behind the handlebars of a bicycle."

"You're kidding!"

"In Afghanistan, we have a saying: The first thing each morning, the French consulate sends his aide out to check the wine cellar. The British consulate sends his aide out to start the tea kettle. The American consulate has his aide plug in the coffee pot. But the German consulate, he sends his aide out to polish the headlights and wipe the fingerprints from the chrome. And," he added, "to test the horns on their automobiles."

I laughed. "It sounds as if a German driver would feel right at home in New York."

"New York--that is your country's largest city with people, is it not?"

"Yes," I replied. "You know your U.S. geography. Did you study about America at the university?"

He shook his head. "I have a friend who only recently returned from there. He went to the great University called Cornell. While he stayed there, he worked very hard learning engineering, knowing well that he would soon be forced to return to his native land. He told me of many amazing things about your New York: the Statue of Liberty, the Grand Central Station, the Box Zoo."

"The what?"

"The Box Zoo," he repeated. "It is a great place of wild animals on the south side of New York City."

"You mean the *Bronx* Zoo."

He stared straight ahead, puzzled.

"Bronx. B-r-o-n-x. The Bronx Zoo. Named after one of New York's five Burroughs."

"*Ahh*," he smiled, satisfied that he had just learned a great secret that others in his country might not yet share. "The *Bronx* Zoo. *Quite* amazing."

"And your friend? Where is he now?"

"He returned home and is helping his family work the fields."

"What? With an engineering degree from Cornell? Why isn't he working for Afghan government? Or for some big international conglomerate?"

Naim shrugged. "He does what he must. When the season is right for planting winter wheat, you do not go out into the fields with a sack full of oats."

He pulled hard on the wheel, and the Jeep lurched sharply to the right. I was hanging over the side as we lurched to a stop before a small, weathered building with the word "Clinic" inscribed in Persian above the door.

"We are here!"

"Thank God. It was farther from our hut than I'd thought. Ten miles or so, no? About fifteen kilometers?"

"Sixteen. But it is not normally so long. I took us the long way past the university. If we had come up this road"--he pointed to the south--"we would have come maybe three kilometers. No farther. It is not a long distance at all from your hut."

"Not long for an Afghan. I'm afraid we Americans aren't used to walking."

"Yes, we walk nearly everywhere we can."

I grabbed my bag from the back seat. "It will do me good to walk three miles to work each day. Maybe I will make walking an American custom again."

"But surely it is not necessary for you to walk in your own country with so many automobiles and all your fine roads ..."

Despite the fact that he was speaking directly to me, he looked out across the Afghan plains south toward Kabul.

"Naim ... I ..."

"What?"

"Well, I was going to ask you ... I mean, I know you have many customs in your land that I don't understand. But I was wondering ... I mean, it's the custom in America when two people are talking to one another, especially when they are friends, that they *look* at each other. If possible, I'd like us to share that custom here in Afghanistan, as well."

Naim quickly glanced up, and then just as quickly looked away, as if to test my sincerity. Painstakingly, his eyes returned to mine and remained there, nervously, as though held by a tiny thread while a great spring behind each pupil struggled to yank his gaze away again. "Your ... your husband, Sahib Bob, he would not mind my looking upon you?"

"Bob mind?" I laughed. "Of course not. Why should he?"

"Well, in my country it is the custom for men to look at men when they speak together, even when in the presence of women, but never to speak to or look at a woman as though she were a man."

"But, why not?"

He shrugged. "An Afghan woman is the property of her husband. He alone holds the right to look upon her as he holds the right to possess his sheep or goats or, if he is a wealthy member of the royal clan, a great steed. If another man should cast an eye upon the first man's livestock, it is considered an insult. It is as if the stranger means to steal what rightfully belongs to the other."

"But a woman isn't a goat! She's not something to be owned. That would be *slavery*."

Naim looked puzzled. "A man's wife cannot also be his slave. It would be against the Holy Book. A slave does not bear a man's children or cook for him or weave or tend to the marketing. That is the duty of a wife."

"You could have fooled me."

"I am sorry," he replied, "but I don't understand. I have fooled you?"

I laughed. "No, no. Let me put it another way. You have shown me that you are an intelligent young man. You're a student at the university here in Kabul. You hope someday to travel to America to study there, even to live there for a time, as your friend did. You understand and speak excellent English. You meet many *farangis* each year right here in Kabul."

Naim nodded. "All of this is true."

"So when you're ready to marry, I can't believe that *you* would take a woman into your life and treat her as you would a goat or a chair or a loaf of bread. You're the young Afghanistan, the *new* Afghanistan. You're the future of your country. You can't honestly sit there and tell me you would want to *own* the woman you marry. Why would you even *want* to marry a woman who wasn't your equal?"

Naim thought for several seconds. "Perhaps you are right," he said finally.

I beamed.

And then, with a smile, he added, "Perhaps I would marry *several.*"

"You wouldn't!"

"That, too," he said, this time his dancing eyes looking right into my own, "is an old Afghan custom."

He turned the key in the ignition, and the engine growled to life. "I will return to pick you up this afternoon."

"Oh, no. You don't have to. I can find my way home."

"I think it would be best for a time that I drive you until my people get to know you better."

"Well, if you're sure you don't mind."

He nodded.

"When this afternoon, then? What time?"

"When you are finished with your work. I will be here."

He jammed the shift into first gear, and, like a great beast that is weary of travel and balks at the desert heat ahead, the machine growled, bucked, and grudgingly ground its way back toward town.

FIVE

As the dog days of August burned on, Bob and I slowly adjusted to our new environment. For him, life was as comfortable as it was back home. He was familiar with Afghanistan's history and customs. He knew its languages. Everywhere we went, he shocked the locals who found a *farangi* who could speak their own tongue as well as they to be remarkable.

And, as pleased as they were with Bob and his unusual grasp of their country's language and customs, he was enamored of the typical Afghan mind. "These people," he told me one night over dinner, "never cease to amaze me. They're cunning and shrewd, brave, resourceful. An Afghan man is master of his own fate, and he knows it. He'll give a friend the shirt off his back if he chooses, but he'd just as quickly pull a *pesh-kabz* from his sash and slice him to shreds for violating some unspoken principle of tradition or religion."

"And the women? Do they impress you, too?"

He hesitated. "Yes," he said, adding flatly, "They know their place."

I was beginning to enjoy our new life, too--more so than I had anticipated. The task of visiting the market after a full day of work was culture shock, but it was a way to touch base with our neighbors. It was also the only way to live. The embassy had furnished our hut with only a small refrigerator that held freshly butchered meat for a couple days without spoiling, but the Kabul marketplace rarely boasted such meat. Most of the mutton or goat was butchered during the night for sale the next day, and by the time I went to purchase it, it was already eight or ten hours old and beginning to decompose in the hot, thick air that pressed in on us one day after the next.

Fruit and vegetables lasted a little longer, three or four days, depending upon their ripeness when purchased. Afghans do things the way people everywhere used to: They pick their produce when it's ripe. Then it becomes a race to see if they can beat the clock and the heat in getting the produce to market before it spoils.

I frequently ran into Naim at the market. We enjoyed the camaraderie of shopping together after work. Sometimes he brought along the young Afghan student with whom he shared a small apartment. The two of them taught me the secrets of selecting a good cut of meat over one that had lain in the sun too long. They taught me how to get a fair price when buying grain and other dry goods. Afghans are an honest, considerate, and warm people, but balancing the scale so that it yields slightly less than the amount of food being purchased is not below their dignity. In fact, it seems to be part of their heritage. *Let the* farangi *beware!*

At the clinic, I found yet another way of Afghan life. Despite my years of training and ER experience, I wound up teaching small groups of women from different parts of the country in the age-old tradition of midwifery. Hospitals and clinics are rare in Afghanistan, so nearly all pregnant women bear their children at home. The government trains midwives to send into rural areas to aid expectant mothers in the safe, acceptable medical procedures of childbirth. Their goal is to reduce the nation's infant-mortality rate, which is more than ten times that of the modern world.

But helping to ensure safe childbirth wasn't simply a humanitarian gesture. In an agrarian nation, every new farmhand means increased family income and a stronger national economy. A high infant mortality rate is not only morally unacceptable but also economically disastrous.

Dinara, the young Afghan nurse who was charged with

running the clinic, had warned me that my job would not be as simple as it sounded.

"Why not?"

"The *mullahs,* the holy men. They have little accommodation for modern technology and even less for foreign intervention in traditional Islamic ways. Many priests look upon the government's sudden interest in the area of childbirth as yet one more example of secular meddling in affairs that should be left to Allah alone."

Mullahs or not, my workday lasted eight hours--from 8 A.M. to 4 P.M with half an hour off for lunch. At noon, I often ventured out of the clinic and down to the streets of Kabul for sight-seeing or a bowl of *pilau* and fresh unleavened bread steaming hot from the ovens. Afterwards, I took my Nikon camera and wandered around Kabul, looking for exotic scenes to send to friends and family back home. I enjoyed capturing the unique customs and cultural idiosyncrasies of our host country.

And then, one Thursday in early September, after finishing with my class earlier than normal, Dinara surprised me with a visit.

Attractive, like most Afghan women, she sported medium-dark skin, black hair, and deep brown eyes that extended down to her very soul. She differed from others, though, in that her dress ranged from traditional to modern. The government had long ago decreed that Afghan women no longer had to veil their faces in public, although some, especially those living in the smaller rural areas far removed from Kabul, still wore the *chaderi* to conceal their faces out of religious deference. In that, Dinara was a feminist; she alternated between sari and jeans, sandals and wooden platforms. She was an example of the modern Afghan woman, and she knew it.

She was different from most of her countrywomen, too, in that she had studied in France and America and had even lived overseas for a while. I gathered she had come from a wealthy family. Her father had been a prominent military man and landowner outside Pul-i-Khumri just north of Kabul. Her uncle was still called

Khan--an expression of political power and one, I gathered, of traditional respect. He had led a successful Afghan insurrection against the Pakistanis years before.

Dinara was in her early thirties and still unmarried, despite the fact that most Afghan women are wed to a man of the family's choice by the time they reach puberty.

"How did it go?" she asked, pulling up a chair and settling into it gracefully. She moved like a cheetah, smooth and stealthy, her every gesture soft and gentle, cat-like, comforting to watch. With her perfect posture and porcelain Indo-Eurasian features, she resembled a child's doll, something you simply had to pick up and cuddle.

I shook my head. "Sometimes I wonder if they'll ever be ready."

She smiled. "They will be ready. They all seem anxious to learn. Why I don't know. It is such a foreign thing to them, learning. But they have an excellent teacher."

"Thanks." I smiled. "I needed that."

"I know it is trying, taking young girls like these and stripping them of the superstitions and religious customs they have come to cling to over the years. But, once you have succeeded, these girls will spend the rest of their lives helping people all over this land. My government will owe you much gratitude."

I shrugged. "I'm getting paid."

"Hardly enough!" She laughed. "Not for the amount of work you have put in."

"It's more fun than what I was doing back in the states."

"That reminds me. You mentioned that you were going to have your embassy friend over for dinner this week."

"Naim, yes. I had planned to ask him, but I just don't think the scheduling will work out. Unless maybe over the weekend, and that's when Bob likes to have time alone. Once I get home from the clinic and the market, there's just not enough time to cook anything decent. So...well, we'll see."

"Your husband cooks some of your meals?"

"Bob's a great cook. If anything ever happened to me, he'd never starve."

"That is the way it should be. Afghan men, too, are proud of their ability to cook."

"I didn't know that. I would have thought just the opposite."

"Oh, no. It is true. Often, when I was a little girl growing up in Pul-i-Khumri, my mother would have to chase my father from the kitchen so that she could prepare the evening meal as she wanted. Sometimes I think my father would send her to the market just before dinner so that he would have a chance to work up the meal himself."

"He must have really enjoyed it."

"Yes. Most men in my country learn to cook out of necessity when they are very young. It is hard to predict when they will be away from home for long periods of time, either tending the flocks in the mountain valleys"-- her eyes suddenly clouded over, and a look of sadness spread across her face--"or fighting *farangi* invaders."

"Your father--he was killed in battle, wasn't he?"

She looked surprised. "Why, yes. How did you know?"

"One of the other nurses told me. I'm sorry." The words sounded hollow, insufficient.

"He was killed on the fields below the foothills of the Kush, where the mountains sprout from the rich fields of rye and wheat. A group of infidels riding down from the northland on a raiding party struck at several rural villages in the area, and my father happened to be at one of them when they came. They say he was very brave, that he killed many before he, himself, was shot in the leg and, unable to make his escape, was captured."

"What happened to him then?"

She paused. "They cut off his head and stuck it onto the end of a spear, which they paraded around the village for more than an hour before finally disappearing back into the wilds of the hill country."

"Oh, my God ..."

"Say. She perked up suddenly. "I have an idea. Why

don't you take the rest of the day off and invite your young friend for dinner tonight?"

"Tonight. Really?"

"Absolutely."

"Well, I don't know. I still have my afternoon rounds."

"The clinic is nearly empty. One of the orderlies can cover for you. If anyone needs tending, I'll be here."

"And my charting."

"Consider it done."

"Are you sure? I mean, that would be great. I'd really like to repay Naim for all he's done for us. You're sure you don't mind?"

"Not at all. Besides, you have earned some time for yourself. And what is more important than two friends from faraway lands getting better acquainted over a meal to cement international relations?"

"Well, okay," I laughed. "If you insist."

"You can call the embassy from the clinic and set things up. And if he can't make it tonight for some reason, just let me know, and we'll work out another night for you."

"I'm sure he can. He spends most evenings home, reading or studying or talking with his roommate."

She rose from the chair and hugged me. The thick-sweet smell of incense and patchouli filled my nose. "Good. Then go quickly. The marketplace will be crowded soon. Do your shopping on the way home, while you can still find fresh produce."

I thanked her again, changed out of my uniform, and set off for town. Along the way, I stopped at my favorite vendor to buy some fresh lamb, rice, and cracked wheat. Afterwards, I hurried to the hut to prepare a feast of curried *pilau* Afghan-style. A traditional Afghan meal, it's a favorite of ours--a meal Bob learned to prepare when he was in Iran with the Corps during the Sixties.

It was nearly 4 P.M. by the time I'd finished preparing the dough for the bread. I had just popped it into the oven when I heard the unmistakable roar of the embassy Jeep outside. I cracked open the front door and continued with dinner, expecting Naim to come waltzing in. Instead, there was a knock.

"Come on in, Naim!"

"I do hope the invitation extends to me as well." I whirled around at the sound--a louder, deeper voice than that of our Afghan aide.

"Mr. Ingersoll. Oh. I'm sorry. I was expecting someone else. Please. Come in. I was just getting ready to start ..."

"You were expecting ... Naim, did I hear you say? The *Afghan* boy?"

I bristled at the way he said *Afghan*. There was distaste in his tone, even contempt.

"Yes--Naim. I've invited him to dinner tonight." I put aside some dishes and silverware and wiped my hands on a small towel. "He's been very helpful to us in getting settled here in Kabul. I thought he might enjoy knowing just how much we appreciate him."

"*Ahh*, yes." Ingersoll closed the door behind him. "You are a very thoughtful hostess in a primitive land." He took my hand and raised it to his lips. "How good it is to see you again, my dear." I pulled my hand back so suddenly that he very nearly kissed his own fingers. He looked momentarily flushed.

"Oh, my, my, my," he squealed, affecting a sudden air of delight as he looked around the hut. "What you *have* done to this place, Mrs. Favage. It's true what they say about a woman's touch. The last two people to occupy this hut were men, archaeologists from the University of Chicago, I believe. They had the place in a shambles in no time. Horrible little men. Filthy beasts. But you! You certainly have a flair for making the most of a, *uhh*, *Spartan* situation."

"Thanks, but all I've done so far, really, is unpack."

Ingersoll looked mortally wounded. "Not so! Surely you have dusted and rearranged and, *uhh*, and ..."

"Oh, yes," I said as if suddenly remembering a great event. "Yes, you're right. I did move that ottoman, there, from its original spot over there."

"*Ahh*, well. You see? Nothing slips past old Ingersoll. It is the perfect placement." He laughed nervously and checked his watch.

"Is there something in particular I can do for you, Mr. Ingersoll?"

"Please. That's much too formal. After all, we are both Americans, are we not? Why don't you just call me George? And I ..."

I looked at him for several moments. "Yes?"

"I shall call you ... *Paula*." The word slipped out from between his lips as though it were magic.

"That's my name," I replied, going back to the kitchen table and slicing some green onions to add to the *pilau*. "But you still haven't told me what you want."

"Oh, my dear Paula, must there be a specific reason for one American to come calling upon another? Isn't our common bond here in Afghanistan enough? I merely thought I would drop by after a hard day at the embassy and see that you and your delightful young man are getting along well. It's been too long, I'm afraid. I've been so busy. And you, too, I imagine. Time has a way of slipping by, you know. May I?" he asked, pointing to a chair.

I nodded.

"By the way, I had expected to find your husband at home by now."

"What time is it?"

"It's already going on, oh, a quarter of five." He squinted again at his watch.

"He's usually home by five. He may stop off at the market for some *halva* or something."

"Some *halva*, you say? My, my, but the two of you seem to be getting into the genuine swing of things here, I dare say. *Halva*. Can you imagine that? And I suppose you have drunk the Afghan green tea? And eaten cracked wheat? It's excellent of you, really excellent, to rely so on the local foods. It makes the natives, well, *comfortable* around you. It makes them feel as if you fit right in, don't you see." He got up and peered anxiously out the window.

"I, for one, simply can't get used to all that local stuff--that old, smelly goat cheese and those green acorn things the natives crack with their teeth. *Yecch!*" He shuddered involuntarily.

"It's all mind over matter."

"Yes, well, I assure you, my mind would rather be on such matters as fried chicken, ham and eggs, sirloin steak ... *Ahh*," he said, peering out the window, "here comes your young gentleman now." He hurried over to where I was working and whispered in a low, conspiratorial tone, "If you ever have a taste for sirloin steak, come see me at the embassy. I have some purloined away in the freezer there." He winked. "For just such an emergency."

Before I had time to inquire what sort of emergency might demand the presence of purloined beef, he had slipped back to his spot next to the door and begun pumping Bob's hand upon his entry.

"Well, Mr. Ingersoll." Bob beamed. "This is a nice surprise. I'm sorry I'm late. Paula, you didn't tell me we were having such distinguished company tonight."

"It was a totally unexpected pleasure."

"Yes," Ingersoll added, laughing to himself. "It was sort of a lark, if I may say. I was sitting in the office, just contemplating diving into a stack of very dull official papers, don't you know--passports and military requests and the like--when I said to myself, 'George, why don't you go see that lovely young American couple, Robert Favage and his charming young wife, Paula.' So I said, 'To hell with the paperwork. What's more important than a pair of fellow Americans in this strange and hostile land?' And here I am!"

"Hear that, Paula? It's nice to have such good friends."

I cocked my head toward Bob. "Peachy."

"Sit down, sit down," Bob gushed. I kept looking for the stinging sarcasm in his voice, but there was none. I couldn't understand why he was making such a big deal over Ingersoll's visit. "I'd offer you a drink, but liquor is a little hard to come by in Kabul."

"Those damned *mullahs*," Ingersoll cursed. "I always

say, if it's any good at all, the *mullahs* will condemn it, ban it, or throw it into the river."

The two laughed.

"Hear that, Paula? The *mullahs* will throw it into the river."

"Hilarious."

"That's funny, because Paula's friend, Naim, was telling us just the other day about how he found a camera that the *mullahs* had taken from some poor schmuck and thrown it into the Kabul. Isn't that right, Paula?"

"Yes, it is."

"Well," Bob continued. "I do wish I had something to offer you besides green tea ..."

"*Ahh*, but have no fear. I have a little surprise for the two of you out in the Jeep. It won't take but a second to fetch."

"The embassy Jeep?" I peered out the window. "I thought Naim had ..."

Ingersoll disappeared through the doorway as Bob stretched out his arms, sauntered casually over to where I was slicing vegetables, and stopped. "Say, that Ingersoll's not such a bad guy after all, is he?"

"*Uh-huh.*"

"What are you fixing there? *Pilau?*"

"Yes, *pilau.*"

Bob snickered nervously.

"What's the joke?"

"Huh? Oh, I was just thinking about how wrong a person can be about someone."

"Someone in particular, or just any someone in general?" Bob was irritating the hell out of me, and I couldn't figure out why.

"Well, take old George Ingersoll, for example. When we met him at the embassy our first day in town, I thought, 'Jesus, this guy's a loser.'"

"But now you don't."

"Hell, no. He's turned out to be a nice guy, a *damned* nice guy."

"Did you know he was coming over here tonight?"

Bob's eyes widened suddenly. "Who, him?" He motioned out the door. "Me? No, of course not. Know he was coming here? *Tonight?* How would I know that?"

"You didn't seem very surprised when you walked in and found him here."

"Well, I wasn't. After all, we're all Americans, aren't we? Like he said. I guess I just figured that sooner or later he'd stop by."

"Is that so?"

"You know, Ingersoll is the kind of guy who'd be good to get to know better."

"And what kind of a guy is that?" A little bell had gone off in my head. I wasn't quite sure why, but I had a feeling Bob was ringing it.

"You know what I mean. He's in a very influential position. He could turn out to be a very valuable friend if we should ever need something. He could cut through red tape, make life a little easier for us while we're here, things like that."

"What could we possibly want from a man like him?"

Bob shrugged. "Who knows. Maybe one day ..."

I looked deeply into his eyes. "Have you been smoking?"

"What do you mean?" He paused. He sighed. "Okay, I had a coupla cigarettes. Raoul and I ..."

"I'm not talking about cigarettes." I stared at him blankly.

"Oh, Paula, for Chrissake."

"Oh, Paula, nothing. When we decided to come to Afghanistan, we agreed no more dope."

"I told you, a coupla cigarettes, that's all."

"You know what can happen to us if we're caught doing drugs. This isn't Milwaukee; it's Afghanistan. They could throw us in prison for even *looking* at a joint."

"For Chrissake, Paula, I haven't been within fifty miles of any shit. Now, quit worrying, will you?"

I stared at him, searched his eyes for something I could trust, as Ingersoll walked through the door. I whispered to him, "I don't believe you."

"Well, well," Ingersoll announced, struggling with a large brown bag that he set on the table. Reaching into it like a magician preparing to pluck a rabbit from a hat, he pulled out a bottle of Jim Beam. "*Ta-daaa!* Welcome to Afghanistan!"

"Well, will you look at that. *Bourbon.*" Bob grinned, picking the bottle up and examining it as though he'd never seen whiskey before.

"And that's not all." Ingersoll extracted a bottle of vodka, followed by a third bottle and a fourth. "And," he added with great finality, "what welcome to Afghanistan would be complete without *this?*" He handed Bob a bottle of gin--Boodles, one of our favorites. "You'd better guard this with your life," he added softly.

"Why?" Bob asked. "The *mullahs?*"

"*Mullahs,* hell. It's those damned sops over at the British Embassy. If they ever get word that this is around, you'll have the bloody beggars knocking down the door for a nip!"

"Mr. Ingersoll, this is awfully nice of you, it really is. But I'm afraid we can't accept."

Ingersoll looked at Bob. Bob stared at me. I turned back to my preparations.

"Paula, where are your manners? Of *course,* we can accept. I'm sure Mr. Ingersoll went to a lot of trouble to get this for us. It wouldn't be very hospitable to turn it down, now, would it?"

"It wouldn't be very hospitable to our Afghan hosts if we accepted it. You know how they feel about alcohol. It's against their religion."

"Damn the Afghans! We're *Americans!* We've got a right to drink whatever we want whenever we want. It's not against the law. The government couldn't care less if we've got alcohol in our own home."

"It's against their *religious* laws. It's against what most Afghans believe in."

"Yes," Ingersoll said, somewhat shaken. "Well, perhaps I'd best be going. I can see you ..."

"No!" Bob grabbed his arm and pulled him back inside

the doorway. "I mean, the least you can do is join us for a drink. After all, it would be ungracious of us not to share our gift with our host, wouldn't it, Paula?"

"Well," Ingersoll said, "if you're sure it's no problem."

"Nonsense." Bob stooped down before the cupboard and pulled out three glasses.

"None for me." I threw the hair back from my face. "I'm fixing dinner."

Bob scowled and took the glasses to the table. He twisted the cap off the gin and filled all three glasses to the top. He handed one to Ingersoll and took one himself. "Paula?"

I was burning inside. For some reason, Bob was playing up to Ingersoll, and I couldn't figure out why. He was making a complete ass of himself. "I told you. I'm busy, now."

I saw Bob glance at Ingersoll and shrug. "Well ... down the hatch." He clinked Ingersoll's glass.

"Cheers!"

The two gulped down the liquor as if it were lemonade.

"Perhaps," Ingersoll said, placing the drained glass on the table, "if Paula isn't up to it, I should just wander on. Some other time, maybe."

I saw Bob nod some kind of signal to Ingersoll as I bent down over the oven.

"Or," Ingersoll continued, "perhaps she would prefer indulging at a little, *uhh*, party tonight."

"Oh?" Bob raised his voice. "And what party would that be?"

"It's nothing, really. Just a small embassy party of sorts. You know, the usual amenities--cocktails, hors-d'oeuvres, music, dancing, good food. I could send the car around at, oh, shall we say...seven?"

"That sounds terrific, doesn't it? Paula?"

"Terrific. But we can't go. I'm fixing dinner here."

"Well, *pilau* can be refrigerated," Bob said, dragging out each syllable for emphasis. "It's not as if it's anything special. And it's not every day that Mr. Ingersoll comes by with an invitation like that."

"*Pilau* can be refrigerated, but Naim can't. I've invited him over tonight. So I'm afraid we'll have to pass."

"Naim? Tonight? You didn't tell me anything about that!"

"I invited him this afternoon. Dinara gave me half a day off so I could fix dinner."

"Damn it, Paula, Naim can come to dinner some other night. He'll understand."

"I'm nearly through," I said firmly. "The bread will be done in just a few minutes. Besides, Naim is probably on his way here right now."

"Perhaps she's right," Ingersoll told Bob. "Perhaps some other night *would* be better."

"No!" Bob shouted. "I mean, no, tonight would be best. Paula's always complaining about there being nothing to do here in Kabul. This would be *perfect* for her."

"I've *got* something to do this evening." I glared at him. "I'm fixing dinner for our company."

"Look." Bob came up to me and spoke softly, threateningly. "I've got some work to prepare tonight for tomorrow's classes. I can't sit around with Naim all night. Now, there's no reason you should be stuck here by yourself when you could be having a good time at the party. So why don't you just go get ready, and I'll explain to Naim when he arrives. I'm sure he'll understand. After all, Mr. Ingersoll *is* his boss."

I was beginning to see the scheme. For some reason, Bob wanted me out of the house. He'd obviously arranged this whole thing with Ingersoll earlier. He must have thought I'd be dying to go. What better way to get me out of the house so he could be alone than to dangle an embassy party in front of my nose? I *hated* him when he played his underhanded little games. If only he could have been *honest*. Just *once*.

"If you want to be alone, why don't you just say so?"

"No," he protested, "it's not that at all. I told you. I'm just thinking of you. I've got all this work to do tonight, and I don't want you locked in the bedroom all by yourself while I'm out here preparing this stuff. You'll be climbing the walls. You *know* you will. I'm just thinking of you."

I glared at him. "I'll bet."

"Well, I ... I really should be going." Ingersoll turned toward the door. "Perhaps, then, some other night."

"Paula, Mr. Ingersoll wants to know if you'll accept his generous invitation to go to the embassy party with him. Now, it's not very polite to keep him waiting."

"Bob, Mr. Ingersoll already has his answer."

Bob's eyes rolled around in his head, and his face turned crimson. "Goddamit, Paula," he said, straining to keep his voice down, "that is the most ungracious thing you've ever done!" He banged his glass on the table and headed for the door.

"Where are you going?" I asked.

"*Out!*"

Ingersoll looked at him before turning and throwing me a sheepish grin. He shrugged and followed him out the door.

"What about dinner?" I called.

"Eat it yourself!"

It was well after seven when Naim finally showed up. He was dressed in a style that might have screamed, *Prep!* except for the black Oxfords looking a size or two too large for his feet.

"I am sorry if I have been late. We do normally eat at seven or eight o'clock. Your note did not specify at which time you would have preferred me."

"It doesn't matter, as long as you're here."

From behind his back, Naim pulled a bouquet of roses. "For a very beautiful person, very beautiful flowers."

"Oh, Naim ... they're absolutely gorgeous!"

"You do like them?"

"I *love* them." I held them up to my nose and breathed in deeply. They were reddish-pink tinged with violet. I had never seen anything like them. I arranged them in a tall glass of water and set them on the table. "But where on earth did you get them? Roses, of all things."

"One of my friends at the British Embassy picked them for me. He was sure they would not be missed. He selected some of the prettiest."

"That's very thoughtful. Please tell your friend thank you."

"You are most welcome, I am sure."

"Now ..." I motioned for Naim to be seated at the table and brought out the *pilau*, which had cooled to the right serving temperature. In the hot climate of central Asia, few meals are served steaming.

"Ahh," Naim said as I set the dish before him and uncovered it with a flourish, "it smells delicious. I had no idea you were such an accomplished cook in our cuisine. *Pilau* with lamb, cracked wheat, tomatoes, green onions ... It is my very favorite meal."

"Well, even if I didn't believe you, I'm glad that you said so. I learned to make it from Bob. He accumulated quite a few recipes from Asia when he was in the Peace Corps years ago." I brought the bread to the table and set it down across from my guest.

"But where is Sahib Bob? Is he not yet home from the university?"

"Oh, yes, he's home--or was--but he had ... some class preparations to do for tomorrow. I doubt he'll be back before late."

"Preparations? At the university? Did he go there with another instructor?"

"No," I lied. "By himself. Why do you ask?" I wanted in a way to tell him about Ingersoll and what had happened, but at the same time, I didn't want to tarnish the image he might have of his boss.

"It is just that to be alone in Kabul, walking the streets at night ..." Naim looked worried.

I laughed. "Oh. I'm sure he'll be all right. Bob knows his way around."

"Still ..."

"Why? What's the matter?" I could see a lingering look of concern on his face.

"Well, the police in Kabul do not take well to *farangis* walking the streets of the city after dark."

"Well, Bob left hours ago, and it's only a short walk to the university."

"Yes," Naim agreed. "And surely when he is ready to return home, one of his fellow instructors will accompany him."

"Yes. Surely." I filled Naim's plate and helped myself to a smaller serving.

"*Umm*, this is wonderful!" he said, dipping a large piece of bread into the *pilau* and shoveling it into his mouth. "And freshly baked, is it not? What baker made this bread for you at this hour? Most ovens grew cold long ago."

I pointed to myself. "Paula Favage, baker *extraordinaire,* at your service."

"*You* did this? I cannot believe it."

I smiled. "Why not?"

Naim shrugged. "I have never known an American to cook Afghan meals and bake Afghan bread with such great acumen."

"*Acumen!*" I laughed out loud.

Naim blushed. "It is a word I learned only today at the embassy. It means *perception* or *understanding*."

"If you don't quit learning so many fancy English words, you're going to put me to shame."

"Oh, no. My English has quite a long way to go before I am good enough to speak it as you."

"Who used that word at the embassy?"

"Some *farangi* visitor--from Canada, I believe--a political person of some great power, from what I could judge. He came to discuss some problems in the northern provinces. Apparently, there is a Pashtun rebellion taking place there against the Pakistanis. It is not the first time the Pashtuns have fought against the Pakistanis for the right to form their own country."

"Is that who the embassy party is for--the Canadian visitor?"

"Party? What party?" He pulled a large chunk of bread

loose from the loaf and buried it in a mound of *pilau.*

"The party at the embassy."

Naim looked at me blankly.

"The American Embassy," I continued. "George Ingersoll stopped by earlier this evening and wanted to know if I ... if Bob and I wanted to go."

Naim shook his head. "I am afraid I know of no party at the American Embassy."

I shrugged. "Well. I guess it couldn't be important."

"No. I guess not. It is surprising, though." He stopped long enough to pour some tea for me and some for himself. "Usually when the American Embassy hosts a party, they ask the Afghan boys to tend bar and wait tables."

"And nobody said anything to you?"

He shook his head.

"Nor to any of your friends?"

He paused. "I do not think so. Perhaps you misunderstood Sahib Ingersoll. Perhaps the party was for another day. I believe there will be one in two weeks. We have already been asked to serve at that."

"No." I paused, thinking back. "I'm sure he said it was tonight."

"Well, maybe Sahib Ingersoll had meant to invite you and your husband to his home. He frequently enjoys to entertain *farangis* there. It is very large and beautiful, with many fine gardens and much nice furniture both inside and out."

"Maybe, although I'm sure he called it an embassy party. Does Mr. Ingersoll often ask you or your friends to serve at his home?"

Naim shook his head. "Only at the embassy. When he entertains at home, he seldom wants others around."

"Oh? Why is that?"

Naim smiled lamely. "Well, he enjoys the company of his fellow Americans."

"Especially *female* Americans?"

Naim shrugged. "I think maybe so." He shoved more *pilau* into his mouth.

"That explains why Ingersoll looked so disappointed when I said I had other plans for tonight."

"But surely he would have had the most honorable of intentions, as he knows you and Sahib Bob are married."

"Yes," I said flatly, "he knows."

As Naim emptied his plate, I served him more *pilau* and bread. He quickly finished that and accepted a third helping. I had heard that an Afghan can eat enough *pilau* to bury a small goat, yet few of them come even close to being overweight, a tribute to their hard, active lifestyle. And, perhaps, a paucity of Mickey Dees.

As we finished our dinner and I brought out the *halva*, a customary dessert following special meals such as this, I paused. "Naim? May I ask you something that requires a frank answer?"

"What is this word, frank?"

"I mean, I don't want you to be embarrassed, and I don't want to force you to answer if you don't want to, but I need to ask you and hope you will feel free to answer honestly."

"I will tell you whatever I am able."

"If Bob *weren't* at the university tonight ... I mean, if he went out somewhere else, alone, would he be in any danger?"

Naim grew suddenly silent. Finally, he replied, "That would depend upon where else he went. But," he added, brightening, "as long as he is at the university, I am sure ..."

"That's just it. I wasn't totally honest with you. I'm not sure where he is. When Ingersoll asked us to the party earlier, Bob said he couldn't go because he had to stay here to prepare for tomorrow's classes. He told me to go on ahead without him. I told him I didn't want to go, and we had sort of a ... *fight*."

"Oh." He smiled. "In my country, married people do fight frequently, also."

"As in every country. It seems as if it's part of the tradition. But what I'm wondering is, if Bob *didn't* go to the university, where might he have gone?"

Naim thought for several seconds. "Did he and Sahib Ingersoll leave together?"

"Yes."

"Then, perhaps he went with him to his home."

"Does Ingersoll often invite men to his home?"

Naim shook his head. "Usually only women."

"Oh, I'm just being an old worrywart!" I filled Naim's cup with tea. "Bob's a grown man. I'm sure he can take care of himself. He speaks the language as well as ..."

"Perhaps, Paula Favage, I should go in search of Sahib Bob. Yes?" His eyes held a look of genuine concern. "There has been ... some talk around the embassy of ..." He stopped suddenly, as though realizing he should say no more.

"Talk of what?"

Naim looked at me sheepishly.

"What, Naim? Please tell me."

"I do not wish to upset you, for I am sure it does not concern Sahib Bob. But, there has been talk of a married woman--an Afghan woman--on the arm of a young American man."

"An Afghan woman!"

"The embassy is quite alarmed, as it should well be, for if the *mullahs* should find such a couple walking the streets of Kabul, they would not take kindly to them."

"What would they do?"

Naim shrugged. "It is hard to predict what the holy men would do. They might scream and curse them and publicly rebuke them for carrying on in the eyes of Allah. They might threaten to tell the woman's husband. They might even ..."

"What? Might even *what*?"

"I do not wish for you to worry. It is not nice to talk about. It is like a great sin from my people's past, something few educated Afghans are proud of. But the *mullahs* have been known to ... to *stone* such a couple ... to death."

"Stone them!"

"It is a holy matter in their eyes. Allah prohibits a

Muslim woman from consorting with an infidel who has not yet come to know Him. And, of course, to commit infidelity. The *mullahs* see it as their religious duty to separate such couples whenever they can, *however* they can."

"You don't think ..."

Naim shook his head. "I am sure it is someone else. There are many Americans in Kabul these days: diplomats, teachers, military personnel, advisers, young men who have been separated from wives and sweethearts for too long. One of them could easily have turned to the willing arms of another. It is said that *farangis* find Afghan women to be very beautiful. Perhaps some young diplomatic aide knows not of our customs. It is for him that the embassy is concerned."

"If you're sure it's someone else, why did you say you think you should go look for Bob?"

"The *mullahs*. If they should see an American out and about the streets of Kabul, they may assume he is returning from a clandestine meeting with the woman I spoke of unless he can convince them otherwise or show that he was in the company of an Afghan male."

"But surely the police would prevent the *mullahs* ..."

"The majority of my people still consider the *mullahs* as the rightful lawmakers and enforcers in Afghanistan. The police are a symbol of a weak attempt at Westernization by the government. It is seldom that you will find the Kabul police risking a confrontation with the *mullahs*. Their very lives--and the reputations of their families--would be at stake."

Naim looked into my face, saw the worry I felt deep within, and quickly dabbed at his mouth with a napkin before excusing himself. He said he would return to the embassy to pick up the Jeep and then drive around Kabul to try to locate Bob. He told me not to worry, that Bob was likely with a friend he'd met at the university. But if he *was* out walking alone ...

I watched as Naim hurried down the path through the courtyard gate. The stars above already glowed brightly, hanging low over the Afghan countryside. The moon was hidden, so it was difficult to distinguish the figures that passed in the darkness. Perhaps that would be to Bob's advantage. *Wherever* he was.

SIX

I rolled over in bed and turned on the light as the front latch jiggled. The door squeaked open and quickly slammed shut again. It was after midnight. I turned off the light and slid back down into bed, wiping my swollen eyes on my nightgown. Before long, the bedroom door swung free, and I heard Bob muttering to himself as he stumbled across the room. He was struggling out of his clothes, taking far longer than usual even in the dark. I stretched out and flicked on the light. He looked stunned, shielding his eyes from the bright glow that spilled over him.

"Are you okay?" I asked.

"Kill that light, will you? It's too bright."

"Where have you been all night? I was worried sick."

"I said kill that fucking light!" He lashed out with his arm and sent the lamp sprawling across the room. The bulb shattered against the wall. "Goddamn it, when I say it's too fucking bright, I mean it's too fucking bright!"

He struggled around to his side of the bed, groaned, and flopped down. He smelled of gin.

"I've been waiting for you for nearly six hours. Where have you been?"

He rolled over sluggishly. "What the hell do you care where I've been? What's it to you? You had your little party, didn't you? Just you and Naim. That's all you wanted, wasn't it--your little party with your little Afghan friend, Naim?"

"Yes, you're right. I *am* interested in my friend. I'm

also interested in my husband and what he's been doing for the past six hours while I was sitting home alone, not knowing whether he was dead or alive."

"Alone? *Oooh*, whatsa matter? You and Naim have an argument? Huh? Is that what happened? You two have a little ... lovers' spat?"

"That's not funny."

"*Oooh*," he said again. "Touchy, aren't we?"

"Not that it will matter in your state, but Naim left around eight to go look for you."

"Look for me? What the hell'd he wanna go and do that for? He's *your* friend!"

I reached over, grabbed a tea candle, and lit it before sitting back against the headboard. "He was worried that you might have been wandering around town alone and gotten into trouble."

"He said that? He told you I was gonna get in trouble? Why that lyin' li'l sneak. He's got his nerve, you know that? First, he forces me outa my own home, and then he fills my wife's head with all kinds of lies about how I'm gonna get into trouble. What kinda trouble, huh? Did he say what kinda trouble? Did he say I was running around with a bunch of dopers? Huh? Is that it? Is that what he tol' you? Did he tell you I found some guys who had all the stash a fella could ever want, and they were gonna share it with me? Or did he tell you I was secretly meeting a beautiful blonde secretary who works at the British Embassy? Is that what he tol' you? Yeah, that's it. That's what he prob'ly tol' you. Or maybe that I'm smuggling guns for the revolutionaries. *That's* it, isn't it? I'm a gum rummer ... a gum *runner*." Bob laughed out loud. "Wanted dead or alive, the American gum-rumming revolutionary traitor, Traitor Bob. Payment for his skin, 20 million *afghanis*, no questions asked."

"That's not funny."

"Oh? It's not? Well, I think you los' your sense of humor, then, you know that? Because I think i's *damn* funny!"

"And I think you're drunk."

"Me? Drunk?" He laughed again. "You're damn right I'm drunk, baby. And you know somethin'? You wanna know somethin' about it? It feels good. It feels *damn* good. In fact, it feels so damn good, you oughta try it sometime. You really oughta see what it's like, you know that? Little Paula oughta see what i's like to get smashed, boppo, blitzo--Little Miss Perfect who never does anything wrong, never gets into any trouble, never ever lets her goddamn hair down."

"If you weren't so stone-cold drunk," I said, slipping out of bed and into my slippers, "I'd leave you tonight." I bent down and reached under the bed for my sleeping bag.

"Like hell you would! Where you goin'?"

"What do you care?"

"I care plenty. That's what I care. I care plenty where my wife's goin' in the middle of the night. And I'll tell you something else, baby. You wanna know what I'd do to you if you ever left me? Huh? You wanna know what I'd do? I'd *slap* you, that's what I'd do. I'd slap you so hard, your teeth would ... I'd ..."

I unrolled the bag in the living room, flung it against the wall, and climbed on top of it, using a pillow to screen out Bob's drunken chatter. I was tired, my body aching for sleep. My head throbbed. I felt a sudden sorrow welling up inside me. At first, I thought it was sorrow for Bob, for the condition he was in. And then I thought it was for us, what our relationship had become. But as the evening unfolded, I realized that it was sorrow for having cried over Bob in the first place. Sorrow for having wasted the tears.

I listened to him chatter on for nearly fifteen minutes, and then there was silence. It seemed as if I had just fallen asleep when I awakened to the smell of eggs frying in the kitchen. I lifted the pillow off my face and looked up into the light streaming through the shutters. Bob was standing before the stove.

"Hey, sleepyhead, time to get up. I've got breakfast just about ready." He slipped the eggs out of the pan and onto a plate and began squeezing orange juice from some fruit he'd gathered in the garden. "You want one piece of toast or two?"

I looked around to make sure I wasn't dreaming. We were in Afghanistan, I was on my sleeping bag, but Bob certainly wasn't the same person he'd been the night before.

"I don't know." I yawned. "Two, I guess."

"Two it is, coming up. And you want some *pilau* on the side? It looks good."

I leaned forward and slowly shook the grogginess from my head. "It *is* good." I climbed to my feet and walked over to the kitchen table. I plopped down on one of the chairs. My back ached, deep down inside my body, just between my shoulder blades--a gnawing, dull sort of pain that I got sometimes back home when I was nervous or upset or hadn't had enough sleep. "At least it was good last night."

"Hey, I'm sorry about last night, about missing dinner. I really am. I don't know what got into me. I was just frustrated, I guess. I had a rough day at school. I mean, it was murder. You ought to try teaching a dozen eighteen-year-olds English when they can barely speak their *own* fucking language." He placed our plates and two glasses of fresh juice on the table and sat down.

"Yeah." I tried not to sound too jaded. "It sounds tough."

"Look, I don't blame you for being sore. I shouldn't have walked out on you last night; I know that. But sometimes what you do and what you *should* do just aren't the same thing, you know?"

"What *did* you do?"

"Didn't I tell you?"

I shook my head

"Not much, really. After I left here with Ingersoll, he dropped me off at Raoul's. You remember, that fellow teacher I told you about, the one who went to Berkeley?"

"And you were there until after midnight?"

"Was it that late? Yeah. I guess so. He asked me to stop by sometime for a drink, but I was always too busy, you know?"

"But Afghans don't drink. It's against their religion."

"Well, one thing I learned about Raoul. He's sort of ... *different*. He picked up some 'Perfectly abominable habits while in the Americas,' as he puts it." Bob laughed. "He also picked up some fantastic Irish whiskey. *Whew*! It'll knock your socks off before you know what hit you!"

"So I noticed."

"I was pretty bad, huh?"

"Bad would have been three steps *up*."

"Well, I shouldn't have done it, I know. I should have told you where I was going."

"And you spent all that time drinking with your ... with this ... Raoul?"

"So help me," he said, stuffing a forkful of *pilau* into his mouth before hoisting the fork up like a Boy Scout about to take an oath. "It was after midnight when I finally left. Raoul had one of his servants drive me home to make sure I got back safely."

"If you wanted to go to your friend's house last night, why didn't you just tell me instead of lying?"

"What do you mean, lying?"

"That story about having to prepare for your classes today. And trying to palm me off on Ingersoll to get me out of your hair."

"Hey, that was no lie. I'd intended to stay home last night to prepare, just like I said. Really. But when we had that fight about the party and all, well, I just figured what the hell, I might as well go out."

"That wasn't very considerate. You could have gone to see Raoul some other time. You know how much that dinner meant to me. It was the first time we'd had a guest over, and you weren't ..." I paused, fighting back the tears. I felt so weak, so foolish. So hurt. I didn't want to rag on him, I really didn't. But I couldn't hold back my anger, my frustration, and my disappointment.

"Hey, I said I was sorry." He washed down the toast with a mouthful of juice. "But when a wealthy Afghan asks you over, you don't just say, 'Gee, I'd love to, but I can't make it. My wife has other plans for me tonight.' Afghans don't accept stuff like that. They don't understand it. The men make the social plans for the family. When they want to do something special, they do it. It's part of their tradition. The women don't have a damned thing to say about it."

"Wait a minute. You just said you made plans to meet with Raoul last night. Before that, you said you were planning on staying *home*. Which is it?"

"Yeah, yeah," he said, waving his fork at me, "that's what I meant. I didn't think you'd mind me spending the evening working on that stuff for class if you had something else to do. That stuff about Raoul, I just ended up there, that's all, when you said you were staying home."

"Speaking of which, Naim told me there *was* no embassy party last night."

"What do you mean? How would he know?"

"Ingersoll has the Afghan boys work all the embassy parties. Naim said nobody knew anything about a party last night."

"That's ridiculous. Why would Ingersoll lie?"

"That's what *I* was wondering. Naim thinks maybe Ingersoll was planning a smaller party--a *much* smaller party--at his own home. He apparently has a bit of a reputation for entertaining young, eligible women ... alone."

Bob laughed nervously. "But Ingersoll knows you're married. Why would he try pulling a stunt like that? Besides, he's too nice a guy. You saw the liquor he brought us as a welcoming gift."

"A welcoming gift ... or a bribe? We've been in Afghanistan over a month, now. It's a little late to welcome us to the country, isn't it?"

"You heard him. He's been busy. I don't see ..."

"Bob, are you leveling with me? About Ingersoll and the party? About going to your friend's house last night?"

"How can you even ask a question like that? Why would I lie? If you want, you can ask Raoul, yourself.

He's coming by to pick me up for work. Just ask him."

"Forget it."

"Hey, look, if something's bothering you ..."

I shook my head. "Let's just forget about everything, okay? Only don't try palming me off on Ingersoll again, because I don't like it. He gives me the creeps."

Bob shrugged. "I was only thinking of you."

We finished breakfast in silence. I could feel the distance growing between us. It had started long before we'd arrived in the Middle East, and it had only gotten worse. It was as though we were strangers out on a first date and had run out of things to say. Any more words would have sounded strained.

After clearing the table, I went into the bedroom to dress while Bob cleaned up the kitchen. Before long, I heard a car grind to a halt, and Bob's voice was calling something from the living room. There was laughter, some muted talk; and then Bob called me out.

There before us stood a tall, handsome Afghan in a perfectly pressed three-piece suit and patent-leather shoes. From his breast pocket peeked a neatly folded handkerchief. With his manicured good looks, he could have been a Brooks Brothers model.

"Hello," I said, extending my hand.

"Paula, I'd like you to meet Raoul, the friend I was telling you about. Raoul, my wife, Paula."

Raoul took my hand and shook it lightly. "I am very pleased at last to meet you," he said in perfect English. "Bob has told me much about you, but he failed to tell me of your great beauty."

I smiled. "Are all Afghan men so debonair when they meet a woman?"

He shook his head. "No. But then, most of the women we meet are not as stunning as you."

"I told you, honey..." Bob winked. "You'd better watch out for this guy. Mr. *Smooooth*. Hey," he added, turning to Raoul, "you want some tea before we go?"

"It would be very welcomed, but I'm afraid we're running late. Besides, I have something I want you to see outside--a little surprise I brought for you."

"A surprise?" Bob turned to me. "Now what could that be?"

We followed Raoul out into the courtyard, where he motioned off to one side. There, leaning up against the fence, sat an old, balloon-tired Schwinn. It had been perfectly reconditioned so that it looked brand new. I glanced at Bob, who was taking the sight in like a kid with his first car.

"From one friend to another." Raoul grinned.

"Wow," Bob said, running his hands over the bars. "I don't know what to say."

"You can tell me that now you won't have any excuse for being late for class in the mornings!" He laughed.

I turned to Bob. "You've been late?"

"*Ahh*, he's just kidding." Bob looked back at Raoul. "It's been years since I even *saw* a bike like this."

"Not just a bike, but an *American* bike. I thought you might particularly enjoy using it to explore the countryside around Kabul. There are so many beautiful sites that are far easier to reach on a bicycle than on foot."

"It's a gift?" I asked.

"Please, you must accept. It will make your stay in Kabul more enjoyable. And it will make me happy."

"But American-made bikes must be awfully hard to come by," I said.

He smiled and replied with obvious pleasure, "It is easier to find a Jeep or a great horse. It is said that one bike is worth many camels and even more Jeeps, and I am sure that it is true. After all, camels need food and drink. Jeeps need petrol. A bicycle asks for little in return for years of good service."

"That's really very nice."

"Yeah. But maybe we could give you something in return. We have some good gin ..."

"You must accept it as a *gift*. It is the custom in our land to offer a gift from the heart and to take only great pleasure in finding its acceptance. Besides, it is one of three that I own."

"Three? You have three Schwinns?"

"Raoul is rather … *uhh*, well off. You should see his home. It's fantastic. It makes Disneyland look like a trailer park."

"I have been very fortunate, it's true. My family is only one of few to have once ruled vast areas of this country. My great uncle was Muhammad Sayed Khan. My father and his father before him ruled nearly half of Afghanistan during the days of the Great Dynasty. We live very comfortably still, even though the Dynasty was long ago replaced by an elected provisional government." He spoke with some sadness, as though he regretted not being himself the lord and master of all he purveyed. And perhaps, with his good looks and superior education, he was being bred to assume the role of ruler, should the era of the Afghan feudal lords return one day.

"But what do you need with three bikes?" I asked. I found Bob's friend intriguing, a polished diamond in a cave filled with stalactites.

"They are actually my wives' bicycles. The two youngest still ride theirs around the estate."

"You have three wives?"

Bob smiled. "One for each bike. How perfect."

"It is a tradition, I know, that Americans find difficult to understand, but one I am not eager to change."

"Raoul's youngest wife was once Miss France."

"Miss Alsace-Lorraine. Yes. She is my child bride. The other, my middle wife, is of the Tajik tribe, an Afghan."

"And the third?" I asked.

"She was the owner of this." He pointed to the bike. "A Pashtun."

"Oh, God, we can't take it. She'll miss it, won't she?"

"My third wife," he said blankly, "is a pig. Fat and greasy and lazy. She no longer deserves a roof over her head, let alone such amenities as this. Still, she has borne me five children. As long as she remains faithful to me, I am bound by the laws of Islam that she shall remain under my roof. It is all that she lives for. She has no other purpose in life, so I must provide for her. It is the custom."

"Well, look," Bob said, glancing quickly around, "we really appreciate this."

"I am sure you will find the roads of Kabul rougher pedaling than those of your own home in Wisconsin. Still, I believe it will be easier to travel from one end of town to another on a bicycle than on foot."

"Say," Bob said, looking at his watch, "we'd better get going, or we'll be late for class."

"You are right. Time flies. Are you ready?"

"In a minute." Bob ran inside and grabbed his briefcase. Raoul again expressed his appreciation for my beauty and charm as Bob emerged and pecked me on the cheek before flying out of the courtyard to the car, a red Citroen, and the unlikely duo sped off toward town.

I was running late, too, and had a long walk ahead of me in the already hot Afghan sun. I hurried back into the house, grabbed my bag, and locked the door on my way out when it suddenly hit me. I didn't have to walk to work. I could enjoy the luxury of a real road machine--a two-wheeled one, to be sure, but certainly better than walking!

I threw my bag in the basket and wheeled the bike past the large iron gate out to the street. It was bigger and bulkier than the ten-speed I rode back home, but it worked. I started my slow, steady trek to the clinic.

At the crossroads just a few blocks from our home, I turned east into Kabul, from where another road--recently paved and still relatively smooth--ran north to the clinic. That route was a little longer than if I had traveled northeast directly from our hut, but the newer road was less traveled and would be easier pedaling, better suited to the bicycle. Besides, I was anxious to show off my new acquisition. I could just picture the locals turning their heads at the blonde-haired *farangi* pedaling through town on an old Blue Zephyr.

As I rolled down the street, I passed a group of young children playing on the corner. The first boy who saw me held a mixed expression of awe and shock on his face.

Then the others caught sight of me, and all six of them began running behind.

"Nice, isn't it?" I called in *Pashto*.

"Aap hona alu!" they shouted. *"Aap hona alu!"*

"Who's a potato?" I called back over my shoulder, laughing at one boy who had caught up with me and was poking at the spokes of the bike with a small stick, sending a terrible grinding noise echoing through the alleyways.

"Don't! Don't do that! Please. *Stop that!"*

The boys continued calling out to me. One grabbed the rear fender of the bike and shook it as I pedaled. I pumped faster as the youngsters bore down until finally I left them standing in my dust. I was upset. I wondered what the problem was. Afghan boys were usually so shy and polite with their elders, particularly so with foreigners--but I wrote the experience off as little children having fun with a strange object, and I pedaled on, past a sudden turn in the road that took me by a Shiite mosque. Suddenly I heard a roar, the sound of an angry boar on the attack. Looking back, I was startled to see a grown man not a hundred feet behind me and bearing down fast, all the while shouting ominously in thick, rapid Pashtun. Startled, I pulled to the side of the road to see what had upset him.

Soon enough, I realized he was shouting at *me*. And he was drawing closer! In a second, three more men, all dressed in black flowing robes and sporting long grey beards and turbans, emerged from the mosque and joined their friend in pursuit.

"Mullahs!"

I lunged forward, jumping up and forcing all hundred twenty pounds of me against the pedals, and the chain began to grind. I could tell by the frenzied voices that the men were gaining on me. I didn't know what they wanted, but I knew enough about the *mullahs* so that I was in no hurry to find out.

In seconds the first *mullah* drew so close, I could see the look of rage in his eyes as I peered back over my shoulder. He slowed down just enough to scoop up a handful of stones from the side of the road and hurl them toward my head in one sweeping motion. They missed their mark by inches.

"Hey," I shouted, "what are you doing! Are you *crazy?*" Soon the others joined in, and a hailstorm of stones cut the still morning air, some just missing me, others stinging my back and legs. All the while the men yelled and cursed as though I'd just brought their temple crashing down around them. I was beginning to regret having gotten out of bed.

As the first *mullah* pressed hard on my heels, his fingertips brushing the bike's saddle, I jumped up on the pedals and pumped with all my might to the top of a hill. As I crested it, I began picking up speed. Finally, I left the *mullahs* far behind, still cursing and hurling stones in my wake. After several minutes, I noticed that one of the stones had sheared a spoke, the dangling thread of metal making a horrible gnashing sound with each revolution of the wheel. I pedaled on, not about to stop to inspect the damage. Spokes could be replaced; my body was one of a kind.

It seemed like an hour had passed before I finally bucked to a stop at the clinic. Several amused onlookers watched as I hopped off the bike, throwing it down against the hard Afghan soil. My heart beat wildly, the tendons in my hand strained and twitching. I burst through the doors before I realized that I'd left my purse in the basket and had to go back for it.

Inside, Tashad, one of the Afghan nurses who sat in on my classes and acted as a translator when I got into trouble, pulled me to one side and asked what was wrong.

"My God," I said, panting, "I was almost killed on the way to work this morning."

"By bandits?" A look of terror creased her face.

I shook my head. "Not by bandits. By *mullahs*. Down by the mosque."

"*Mullahs*! What did they want with you?"

"I don't know. As I passed by the mosque, one of them

came out and started chasing me, shouting at me in *Pashto*. Then three others came out and took up the chase. They began throwing stones at me." I pointed to some red marks on my arms. "Some of them hit me." I fought back the sudden urge to cry.

"They chased you but did not catch you?"

"I think they would have killed me. When I reached the top of the bill, I picked up speed and managed to get away."

"I do not understand. You were in a car when they attacked you?"

I shook my head.

"Then how did you outrun four *mullahs* on foot?"

"On the bicycle. I was on a bicycle. One of Bob's friends gave it to us just this morning, and I decided to ride it to work. If I'd been on foot, they would have caught me for sure." I shuddered at the thought, tales of incensed *mullahs* avenging their religious fervor on their hapless victims dancing through my head.

"You ... you rode a bicycle ... past the mosque?"

"Yes, why?"

"And the *mullahs* stoned you and chased you?"

"Yes," I replied, puzzled at the light smile that had formed on her lips. I was having trouble finding any humor in the situation. "And before that, some young boys in Kabul ran after me and called me 'Potato.' One of them even poked at the spokes with a stick. He broke one of them."

"You're fortunate that's all that was broken."

"Why? What do you mean?"

"It's not your fault. You could not be expected to know."

"Know what--that the *mullahs* are killing Americans this week?"

She laughed. "No--that in Afghanistan, a woman alone does not ride a bicycle. It is considered an affront to the dignity of those Afghan men who must walk through the countryside. That is why the young boys chased after you and called you 'Potato.' It means ..." She thought for several seconds. "It means one who makes fun of society, an outcast."

"Oh, great. Terrific. But what about the *mullahs*? They could see I meant no disrespect. Surely they knew I was a *farangi* unfamiliar with their ways."

She shrugged. "Who can explain the actions of the *mullahs*? At times they avoid *farangis* like the plague, not seeing them, not hearing them, not bothering with them. At other times ... well, perhaps they felt you were being disrespectful by riding by a place of public worship in such a manner."

"But I didn't mean ..."

"I know you didn't ... and it's not your fault. The *mullahs* have been upset with all *farangis* since the government removed the ban on women showing their faces in public."

"But that was years ago."

"Yes, more than a decade. But the *mullahs* ... they do not forget quickly. And they do not forgive. They have felt all this time that it is the influence of the Western *farangis* in Afghanistan--the British, the Americans, the Canadians--that is slowly leading to the disappearance of the *chaderi* in our land--and with it, the gradual weakening of the influence of the *mullahs* and respect for *Allah*. If they could, they would overturn the laws tomorrow. They still feel that it is a great sin for a woman to expose her face in public."

"You'd think they'd be a little more understanding after ten years!"

"The *mullahs*?"

Suddenly it struck me. "How am I going to get the bike home? I'm sure as hell not *riding* it!"

"I would think that to be a wise decision. But perhaps we can find a ride for the bicycle, as well as for yourself. Or I will have one of the orderlies to ride your bicycle home for you if that is all right."

"Would you?"

"Yes, of course, if you're sure you do not want the pleasure of riding it yourself." She grinned.

"That's one pleasure I can do without!"

As the days of September slowly wound down, I left the incident with the *mullahs* far behind me--a bad dream that had taken only seconds out of a lifetime. The clinic was growing steadily, both in size and in the number of patients we treated--a lot of cases of malnutrition, especially in young children. The country was going through its third year of drought--dry even by Afghanistan's standards. Crop production was poor. That was devastating to the small landowners and farmers who depended upon the Afghan plains to yield enough crops to sustain themselves and their livestock. The children, whose growing bodies were least able to cope with the lack of nutrients, were the hardest hit. It broke my heart to see them in the condition they were in before their parents finally surrendered their pride and showed up at the clinic door. But at least we were able to help a good number of them ... for how long, no one could say.

One morning, Dinara burst into my class. She was upset about something, nearly frantic.

"Paula, can you come out to the ward?"

"What's the matter?"

She motioned for me out to follow her and disappeared into the hall.

I asked Tashad to take over my class and followed after her.

"What? What is it?"

"It's Farij," she said over her shoulder. "She's found three young children with an unusual-looking disease, large red welts, some open sores all over their bodies. I thought if you could take a look ..."

We entered the ward and approached three youngsters sitting at one end of a folding cot nearest the door. "Here. These are the children. You see? These red sores?"

Three pairs of eyes peered up at me. There were two boys, about seven and five years of age, and a three-year-old girl, looking far more feverish than frightened. All had dark red splotches covering their skin, just as Dinara had said, but the worst was on the face of the girl. Her splotches were so large, they'd burst open into weeping boils and were beginning to drain. Scratching had spread the pustules and made the infections worse.

"Have you taken their temperatures?"

"Yes. The boys are each one-hundred-two, and the girl is slightly over one-hundred-four."

"*One-O-four*? Wow. Did you ask Dr. Rashad to look at them?"

"That is the problem. Dr. Rashad left last evening for a week-long tour of the northern provinces. We cannot reach him until he checks into the clinic from Khanabad on Friday."

I removed the children's clothing, speaking softly to them in Persian to comfort them. I learned they were from the same family, from a small tribe not far from town. The oldest boy said his sister had been the first to break out nearly four days earlier, and the two boys only recently began showing similar signs.

As I examined them, a nurse brought two more young children into the ward--a brother and sister suffering from the same symptoms.

"What *is* it?" Dinara asked.

I shook my head. "I wasn't trained to diagnose, but I'm pretty sure we have an outbreak of measles on our hands."

"That is what I feared. But I wanted your opinion before acting."

"What is wrong with the children?" Farij asked.

I examined one of the children more closely. "It's measles."

She looked at me blankly.

"Measles," I repeated louder. I turned to Dinara. "How do you say 'measles' in Persian?"

She shrugged. "I ... I do not know. I don't think there is such a word in our language."

"But you must ..."

"Measles are unknown in our country. They are a Western disease. Few Afghans have ever heard of such a thing, let alone contracted the disease. I learned of them in

France, where I was studying at the University in Paris. But I only saw the pictures, never the actual disease."

"Wonderful. So no one else here has the faintest idea of how to treat them."

She shook her head. Suddenly the young girl on the cot began to moan. Instinctively, her long, thin fingernails reached for the blisters on her face.

"Hold her," I told Farij. "Hold her hands like this. Don't let her scratch. Scratching will only spread the disease." I turned to Dinara. "We have to get these children cleaned up and isolated from the rest of the ward. Have the orderlies bathe them in cool water and diluted alcohol, and then put them to bed in one of the smaller rooms. Their fingernails should be clipped so they can't re-infect themselves by scratching, and they must be watched closely--their temperatures--understand?"

"Yes, of course. It will be done."

"Do we have any calamine lotion on hand?"

Dinara shrugged. "I'm not sure. If not, I will have the pharmacy make some up."

"Good. Make sure we have plenty. It should be applied every couple of hours to help dry the blisters and ease the itching. Also, let's see how quickly we can get some vaccine here. Maybe, if we work fast, we can keep this thing from getting too far out of control."

"It will be done."

I followed her out into the corridor. "I'd better cancel my class. If this turns out to be as bad as it looks, we're going to be plenty busy the next few days."

"How serious are these measles?"

"Usually, they're not bad if caught early enough. In America, we have programs for inoculating the children in school. Before the inoculation programs, it was not uncommon to lose thousands of patients a year to the disease."

"You mean ... death?" She thought for several seconds. "And in a land where measles is unknown, and inoculations do not exist, how bad could it get?"

I shrugged. "I don't even want to think about it."

I looked down the hall as a worried father led two young children into Admitting. Their eyes were puffy, their skin red with rash.

"What I don't understand is where this outbreak is coming from. If measles are unknown in Afghanistan ..."

"It is easy enough to understand. We have a growing number of *farangi* visitors in Kabul. Sometimes these people bring with them diseases that can infect ..." Dinara stopped short. She blushed.

"That's okay," I told her. "I understand. I would feel the same way if the circumstances were reversed."

"I didn't mean that you ..."

I grabbed her hand and squeezed it. "I think you'd better check on that lotion. And it might not be a bad idea to inform the staff that they may be called to work overtime. They should be informed that the disease is very contagious and encouraged to avoid contact with others, especially young children. They may well be carriers. In fact, I think it would be best if we quarantined the clinic and kept everyone who has come in contact with the disease here under observation. Just to be safe."

"It will be done," she said. "And ... Paula?"

I looked up at her. "Yes?"

"I will appreciate your taking charge of the clinic until Dr. Rashad returns."

"Me? I can't ... I mean, I'm not ..."

"You have had experience with the disease. That is something no one else has had. Including me. We would be as the blind leading the blind."

Dinara called an orderly to her side and asked him to phone the American Embassy to relay word to the families of the staff that they would be quarantined for several days. "Have the young boys working at the embassy notify everyone on the outside as soon as possible to stay clear of the clinic unless there is an absolute emergency." She turned back to me. "Would you like any special message sent to your husband?"

"That won't be necessary. I've already had ..."

"Yes, you have already had the disease, I know. But

we will need you here around the clock to stand watch. I am sorry, but I must ask you to stay."

"Yes. Of course. Just tell him…tell him I'm … quarantined. And that I may not be home for several days." I looked down the hall at a family of five entering the clinic. "If then!"

* * *

Working at the clinic night-and-day for a week straight was like spending a month living out of a suitcase. Six nurses, four orderlies, and half a dozen clinic support personnel shared five spare rooms and worked around the clock to keep watch over the patients. We had three spare beds to begin the week and ended up shifting those into the wards. We crafted several makeshift cots for our patients. We scrounged up enough calamine lotion to treat an army, and we exposed more than enough frayed nerves to go around.

But none of that helped one of our greatest problems-- the Afghans, themselves--especially the younger nurses-- had no previous experience with quarantines and proved less than up to the self-imposed rigors of confinement. They continually tried sneaking out to share a meal with their families before sneaking back when they thought we weren't looking. Our cook, an Afghan man of 70 with a long, scraggly beard and bulging blue eyes, steadfastly refused to be locked "in jail," as he put it. So each night after dinner, he walked haughtily past the personnel on night duty, disappeared through the front door, and returned the next morning at six.

Those people we knew were breaking the quarantine we tried to keep away from the patients as much as possible, although the cook's youngest child, an eight-year-old boy named Sayyid, did break out and had to be admitted for treatment on Friday. By then, the first patients to check in had rotated out, the vaccine had arrived, and spirits were slowly growing among the staff.

Somehow, our quick action prevented a regional outbreak of the disease. Friday morning, Dinara finally reached Dr. Rashad in Khanabad, and by that evening he had returned to Kabul.

Dr. Rashad was a young Afghan, about thirty, who had received his medical training from Johns Hopkins in the states. After quickly checking out the patients in the isolation ward, he expressed amazement at how efficiently we'd handled the quarantine and how few new cases of measles had been reported during the previous twenty-four hours. That evening, he called me into his office.

"You have been invaluable to the clinic during this week of my absence," he told me in a thick accent. "For this, Paula Favage, I will be always in your debt."

"I'm just glad I was here when the outbreak occurred. And," I added, laughing, "I'm glad I had measles when I was a kid, or else I might not have been able to diagnose them so quickly!"

"You've done more than you were expected. You have worn yourself to the bone. I am prescribing a good night's rest for you ... at home."

"Home? Really? *Tonight*?"

He didn't have to tell me twice. I looked at my watch. *Nearly eleven. Too late to phone. Bob will be asleep.* A young lab technician volunteered to drive me home, since night was no time for a *farangi* woman to walk the streets alone.

I thanked my driver when we arrived at the house and slowly dragged myself up the walk to the door. The demands of the past hundred hours were only beginning to catch up with me. I was ready to collapse, barely able to reach the latch and swing the door open.

I entered the darkened room and dropped my purse on the floor. I took a deep breath--the sweet smell of jasmine in the air, unlike the stench of alcohol and drugs at the clinic. I sniffed again, and I stopped. And listened.

God, I thought. *I'm hearing things.*

I was so tired, I heard imaginary voices from somewhere off in the distance. I looked at my watch--near midnight. Bob was sound asleep, I was sure. I couldn't wait to be reunited with a real bed.

Suddenly I heard another sound. I stopped, listened

again, waited. *Nothing.* "Bob?" I called softly, thinking he'd heard me come in and gotten up. More silence. Then, suddenly, a thick, sweet smell tickled my nostrils. "Bob?"

I took several steps toward the living-room lamp but stopped short when I saw a soft, flickering light coming from the bedroom. "Bob?"

I heard more voices, unmistakable this time--a man's, a woman's. My heart sank. I walked slowly to the bedroom doorway and peeked in. There, rolling over in bed, was Bob, wearing only his shorts. The sweat on his brow danced and glowed in the candlelight. His eyes were closed, his lips parted as if in pain. From time to time he mumbled something unintelligible.

As my eyes washed over the bed, they fell on the naked body lying next to him. It, too, was covered with sweat, dancing and twinkling in the light. The glasslike beads stood out even more against the dark skin, made darker by the dim light. Her eyes, deep and sensuous, were open wide, fixed on a spot on the ceiling. Her hair was black, wrinkled, matted, falling in wet globules around her head, down her shoulders, above her two fat, spongy mounds. Several layers of dark-brown flesh rolled off a large Buddha-esque belly. One hand rested on her thigh, turned inward, pointing obscenely toward a thick, wet, matted mound of black. Her legs were large and bruised, her feet black from the Afghan earth.

She rolled her head toward the doorway, giving me a glimpse of cheeks that appeared grotesquely swollen, like the hind end of an ass. Her lips parted as if to speak, and her hand grabbed a large black tube and put it to her mouth. She sucked in deeply. I could hear her lungs expand, gobbling up all the thick white smoke they could hold as it rose from a bottle at the side of the bed. She held it inside for what seemed an eternity, and then it began seeping snakelike from the corners of her lips, curling its way gently toward the ceiling. Her eyes closed, and tiny bubbles of saliva formed on her chin.

Suddenly something inside me snapped. As if someone had reached deep down my throat, grabbed my stomach, and yanked it out through my mouth. Adrenaline surged through my body, charged down to my feet and up again to the top of my head until I felt I would explode. I leaped wildly through the doorway, my muscles tensed and straining, my head pounding. Mine was the body of a maniac, a demon-possessed beast ready to explode.

"What are you doing!" I grabbed a sham and threw it to the floor. "What the hell are you doing! What's going on here?"

Bob's eyes flew open, rolling wildly as he tried to focus. "Paula?"

"What are you doing!" I shouted once more, my fists involuntarily clenching, striking out at his body again and again. "What are you doing here with this goddam whore!"

"What ..."

I slapped his face as hard as I could, rolling his head across the pillow. I grabbed an ashtray and threw it in his direction, the butts and grey soot scattering over his chest, the glass shattering harmlessly against the hard clay wall behind him. "I'm gone for five days, working my ass off like a Goddam demon at the clinic, and I come home to *this!*" I grabbed a small wooden doll we'd bought at the bazaar and sent it hurtling toward him. "I come home and find my husband in bed with some fat, greasy *whore*!"

"Paula," he said, struggling to sit up, "it's not like that. It's not what you think!"

"Don't lie to me!" I screamed, pounding his head and shoulders, bouncing his six-foot frame around as though it were a toy. "I'm sick and tired of your lies!" I struck him again, and more, more. The harder I struck him, the more enraged I grew. I was completely out of control, running on some internal power. It swelled within my body, a nuclear reactor unleashed, growing as though it would never, *could* never, stop. I was racing. I was flying high without a chute. "You goddamn cheating son-of-a-bitch! You goddamn whoring, lying, cheating son-of-a-bitch!"

Tears streamed down my face. I looked over at the woman. Her eyes were still staring out the door, oblivious to my presence. "Who is she?" I pointed. "Where the hell did she come from?"

"That's what I'm…I'm…trying to tell you." He grabbed his jeans and struggled to get into them. He'd stuck both feet into one leg and fell over trying to stand up.

"Don't lie to me!" I leaped up onto the bed and, planting one foot against her side, pushed her with all my strength. She tumbled off the bed and onto the floor like a giant tree toppled in a great storm. The *hookah* went skittering across the room.

I jumped down and grabbed the blanket as she rolled around like a beached whale. I fought with her, pushed her arms down to her sides and finally managed to throw the blanket across her, then pulled it tight so that it covered her before rolling her over onto her back. I folded the ends of the blanket across her chest.

"Take it!" I ordered. "*Take* it, I said!" She struggled to a sitting position, her eyes glazed and searching. I reached out and slapped her across the face. "Take it, goddamn it!" I tucked the ends of the blanket inside her two trembling hands and grabbed her by the arms around the torso. With a mighty yank, I lifted her to her feet and, as she reeled unsteadily before me, pushed her stumbling out the bedroom door. I caught up with her and grabbed her by the arm. "Let's go!" I pulled her through the darkened living room. "*Faster!*"

When we reached the front door, she tripped and fell, the blanket opening like a parachute around her. With one final tug, I pulled her up again, faced her forward, and, planting my foot firmly against her ass, sent her flying out into the night. I grabbed the blanket, threw it after her, and slammed the door tight.

I fell back against the wall and took a deep breath. For an instant the turmoil inside me subsided; and then, just as quickly, it returned. I felt my legs moving toward the bedroom.

"All right, Bob, let's hear it!" I stood, arms folded, fuming.

"Hear what?" He was scurrying around the room, picking up the clothes, the dope, the litter, as though once out of sight, he couldn't possibly be held accountable.

"Everything! I want to hear what kind of excuse you've got before I leave you and go back to the states."

"What ... what do you mean?" he asked, panic in his voice. "You can't. You can't go back."

"I can and I will. Now, are you going to give me the satisfaction of knowing what the hell that fat, ugly whore was doing in my bed while I was gone?"

"Paula," he said, a young child about to plead with his mother not to punish him for doing something wrong. "Paula, you don't understand. It's not like what it seems. You don't understand."

"No? Then, what *was* it, Bob? Straighten me out, will you? Otherwise, I just might be forced to rely on what I saw with my own two eyes!"

"I know it looked ... *bad.*" He was weaving from side to side in the middle of the floor. "But she's no whore. Believe me, Paula. It wasn't like that at all. There was a reason. She's no whore."

"If you're going to tell me she's a respectable woman with whom you've fallen in love and want to marry ..."

"She's Raoul's wife."

"Terrific. Great news." I pulled my suitcase out from under the bed and threw the cover open. "That makes me feel better. That makes everything okay. If only I'd known sooner ..."

"You don't understand," he said weakly.

"Stop *saying* that! Stop acting like a whimpering, sniveling child! When are you going to grow up? You're a big boy now. When big boys do naughty things, they're supposed to be man enough to accept the consequences!"

"All right," he said, holding his head with one hand. "All right. I was wrong. I admit it."

"Bravo." I pulled some tops from the dresser and stuffed them into the case.

"But it wasn't like you think. Raoul loaned her to us as a maid. That's all she was ... a maid."

I stopped packing and turned to face him. "Oh," I said softly, "she's a maid." I clenched my fists again and felt my jaw tighten. "And I suppose one of her duties was to fuck my husband while I was away!"

"We weren't ..." He grabbed the edge of the bed as his legs buckled beneath him. "We didn't do anything like that. I swear to God. We were smoking, that's all. Raoul gave me some stash for her, some hashish, and we started smoking, that's all there was. He was ... he was supposed to stop by tomorrow and find her here ... early in the morning, with no clothes on."

"Well, he certainly wouldn't have been disappointed."

"And then ... and then he was going to accuse her of being unfaithful. Don't you see? It was all a setup. He was ... he was going to accuse her of being unfaithful so he could ... get her out of his house. But ... but we didn't *do* anything. We were just smoking. Don't you see?" he said, starting to weave again. "It was hot, and we had too much, that's all. We had too much and took off our clothes." He cradled his head in his hands and rolled it around in tight circles. "He was supposed to find her. I guess we just had ... too much."

"You were supposed to stay clean, remember, Bob? You *promised* you'd stay clean. How many times? How many times did you swear no more drugs?"

"I know. But it was a gift from Raoul, part of the plan. You can't turn down a gift, Paula. You can't tell an Afghan *no*. You know that, Paula. It's the custom. You just can't. It's the custom."

"Yeah, well, I know of an old American custom, Bob," I said, grabbing another stack of clothes and stuffing them into the case. "It's called divorce!"

"You know that, Paula," he mumbled, his speech suddenly slurred. "You know ..."

All at once he began to quiver and shake violently. His eyes opened wider than I'd ever seen them before and seemed to roll in two different directions at once.

"Bob?" I dropped the clothes on the bed. "*Bob!*"

"*P-P-Paula,*" he wheezed, looking up at me before

spinning around and crashing in a heap to the floor.

SEVEN

"How are you doing?" I watched as Bob's eyes opened into a narrow squint. They moved slowly across the cracks in the ceiling.

Jamal, a young Afghan boy in the bed next to him, giggled. "Howja doeen?" he mimicked.

"Who wants to know, you or him?" Bob replied.

"Both of us, don't we, Jamal?"

"Dunjwe, Jamal," he said.

"My mouth's a little dry, and my head feels like it's screwed on upside down and backwards." He let out a small groan. "Outside of that..." He worked his jaw up and down several times. "I feel fine."

I put my hand on his forehead. "The dry mouth is from the medication, and the upside-down head is normal."

Bob grabbed my hand.

"What's the matter? Does that hurt?"

He shook his head. "It feels good, actually."

I rubbed his forehead. "You look a lot better today," I lied. "Your temperature's gone down, too. Eyes bright. Mind sharp."

He struggled to swallow, but nothing went down. "Probably all the personal attention I've been getting from the nurses around here."

I lifted my brow and feigned surprise. "Oh?"

"Okay, okay, *one* nurse. Is that better?"

"Wan nurz. Eezat bay-tar?"

"Say," I said in a loud voice, "do you hear an echo?"

"An echo?" Bob repeated in Persian.

Jamal laughed.

"Yes, an echo." I turned slowly toward the next bed. "And if that little echo doesn't stop echoing soon..." I leaped up suddenly and pounced on Jamal's bed, digging my fingers into his sides. "I'm going to have to do something about it, aren't I? *Aren't I?*"

Jamal laughed and rolled from side to side, trying to break free.

"Aren't I?"

"No more!" he called in Persian. "No more! No more!" I gave him a playful pat and thought back years to a similar child, a similar time.

I'd been working in the hemodialysis ward at Children's Hospital in Milwaukee. Day after day, seven days a week, we admitted kids with failing kidneys, hooked them up to a dialysis machine, and set about removing the impurities from their blood that, in time, would kill them. The kids ranged in age from three or four all the way up into their teens. Some were worse than others; some had already experienced a complete kidney shutdown and were simply buying time until a compatible kidney became available for transplant. Or worse.

And then one year, somebody on the staff suggested that we take two weeks away from the hospital in the middle of July and spend them treating the kids off somewhere in the woods. One of the doctors owned a cabin on a large private lake and volunteered to host our dialysis sessions there. It was a way to lend hope to our kids, a way to show them that, no matter how bad things seemed, they could still lead normal healthy active lives-- up to a point.

So we packed up all the machines and the other equipment we needed and shipped everything north, and we made sure all of our patients and their parents knew how to get there. We spent the best two weeks of our lives boating, canoeing, swimming, horseback riding, golfing, playing volleyball, cooking over an open fire, and singing camp songs in the evenings. One of the kids who seemed to enjoy the experience most of all was a little Pakistani boy named Rajij. He was only five years old, with one failed kidney and the other failing fast. But he had a heart of gold and a winning smile along with a can-do attitude that just wouldn't quit. We all looked forward to his treatment days, usually three times a week. He brightened everybody's life from the moment he showed up.

Bob was there with me for the two weeks--most of them. He'd driven back home to take a test or something at the U after the first week and returned a couple days later. I was surprised at how he and Rajij bonded. He lifted the boy up onto his shoulders and carried him chest-deep into the chilly water, and Rajij dared Bob to throw him off. They parried back and forth for a while, and Bob cupped the boy's small feet in his palms and, growling like a wounded bear, tossed him high into the air where he seemed suspended in time before plunging into the water with a huge splash.

Of course, Rajij popped to the surface, laughing and coughing and begging for more.

"I'll bet you can't do that again!"

"Oh, you do, do you?"

And off they'd go, for hours on end.

It was the first time I'd seen Bob relate so well to a child. It actually started me thinking. *Why not?* Once Bob finished with school and got a job, why shouldn't we start a family of our own?

Those two weeks passed far too quickly, punctuated periodically by a visit from Dr. Jacobson, head of the Hemo Unit, and his wife Jean. When they weren't available, some other young doctors who wanted to donate their time and get away from the sterile walls of the hospital and the inner city dropped by.

When it was time to head back to town, we all saw the kids and their parents off, packed up our gear, and headed back to Milwaukee.

Two days later, we'd gotten the news. Rajij's second kidney had shut down in his sleep. He had passed quietly.

I shook my head and ran my finger across one eye. "Has Dr. Rashad been by today?"

Bob nodded, gulped down a mouthful of air, and said, "Yeah. He told me I'm coming along fine. He thinks ... maybe another week and I'll be good as new."

"He's a pretty nice guy."

"Yeah." A frown suddenly scored his face. "Did he say anything about keeping my records ... you know, *private*?"

I nodded. "He said to tell you not to worry. As far as anyone outside the clinic knows, you're being treated for an intestinal-tract problem. Dr. Rashad says that's a pretty common ailment to strike Westerners in their first few months here."

"Because if word ever got back to the embassy that I'm in here drying out ... Jesus, we'd end up *thumbing* our way back to the states."

"You let me worry about the embassy. All you have to worry about is getting well, do you hear?"

"Have you told Naim why I'm here? I mean, I know he's your friend and all, but he *does* work for the embassy. One slip of the tongue and ..."

"I told Naim you had a little medical problem, that's all. He didn't question it. He's a pretty sharp kid. He knows when to speak and when to keep quiet."

Bob slid over and patted the bed next to him. "Come on. Sit down here a minute, will you?"

"I don't have much time. What do you want?"

He motioned me closer. As I bent over him, he pulled me into his arms. "I've missed you," he said softly, squeezing me around the neck.

I hugged him back and kissed him on the cheek. "It's been a long time since you told me that."

"I know." He looked down. "Too long. I mean it, too. I really do miss you. I haven't exactly been the model husband the past few months. I realize that."

"You've been a real shit," I said, pushing him away.

"That bad?"

"Well ... *some* of the time."

"I know it. It's true. And I've been thinking about it lately. A lot, you know?"

"Well, that's a good sign." I smiled.

"And I think part of the reason, most of the reason, has been, well, you know--my problem."

"What problem is that?"

"*You* know what problem."

"I *know* I know what problem, but I want to hear *you* say it."

"Okay," he said, turning away. "My drug problem."

I squeezed his hand.

"It's not easy thinking about anyone but yourself when you're always trying to score a hit. It's like ... it's kinda like your whole life revolves around making those contacts, coming up with the bread, doing favors for friends ..."

"Trading your wife for a few joints?"

Bob's eyes dropped. "I'm sorry about that. I'm so sorry."

"No. I shouldn't have brought it up. I shouldn't have said that."

"Why not? It's the truth. I was wrong. I realize that now. It's just that, at the time, I was so involved in getting the stuff ... well, you know. Nothing else mattered. Just the shit. Just the stash. Keep the monkey fed."

I nodded. "I wasn't exactly guiltless."

He furled his brow. "What do you mean?"

"Well, I didn't do much to fight him off."

"You were out of your skull. You never could handle your dope."

I chuckled.

"It's a disease," he added. "A bad one. I guess I've always known I've had it. It's just that when it hits you, you don't want to admit it. You *can't* admit it. You're on a goddamn merry-go-round, reaching for the ring. You can't get off until you catch it. But each time around, someone moves it farther and farther away, and you end up getting more frustrated with each pass." He looked down again, a large tear slipping free from beneath a heavy lid and rolling slowly down the side of his face. "I just want you to know that ... I'm sorry. I was wrong. I was thoughtless. And I'm sorry."

"Look," I paused, wiping the tear away and touching my lips to his forehead, "I'm on break. I've got to get back before Dinara starts to wonder what we're up to. You just take it easy and follow Dr. Rashad's advice. I'll stop by again later, okay?" I got up, threw a smile to Jamal, who still seemed amused, and left.

I ran into Dr. Rashad coming out of the lab. "Doctor," I called, hurrying after him.

"Yes? Oh, Paula. Been looking in on your patient?"

"He seems to be coming along fine. He's in good spirits, better than he's been in days, and his temperature is down ..."

"That's good." We walked together down the hall. "He's making good progress. If he continues like this, I don't know why he can't go home by the weekend."

"That would be great. Really terrific." We paused outside the classroom where Dinara was covering for me.

"Anything else?"

"Well, just that ... I want you to know how much Bob and I appreciate your keeping this quiet. I mean, if the American Embassy ever found out he'd been messing with drugs ..."

He waved me off. "I understand. I only wish that everyone with a drug problem dared to admit it and come in for treatment the way Bob did. Here in Afghanistan, drugs have become an all-too-frequent way of life."

"But ... well, I guess I didn't realize that. Afghanistan is the *last* place I expected to find such widespread abuse. Islam forbids the use of drugs--or any type of stimulant, for that matter. Right? I never thought ..."

"Yes," he said, shrugging, "Islam forbids it. But ever since the days of the great China Opium Wars, the production of drugs has played an important role in our economy. Many an Afghan feudal lord has come to power over the centuries by cultivating his fields of poppies for distilling into heroin or opium and selling it to the West.

Sadly, the practice still exists today. It's all our local governments can do to control the flow of drugs inside our largest cities like Kabul. Bob is lucky that his dealings here didn't land him in the hands of the police. Our prisons overflow with *farangis* who were not so lucky, those who hold little hope of ever seeing their friends and relatives again."

I shuddered. "That's another reason we're grateful to you."

"It is I, Paula, who am grateful. For everything you have done for us. Now, before you make me sound like too great a humanitarian, remember that my motives here aren't totally unselfish. I appreciate your skilled handling of that measles outbreak. If you hadn't been here to take charge, many locals would have died. I am anxious to do whatever I can to encourage you to remain here in Kabul for as long as possible. We at the clinic need your help, your expertise, and so do the people of our country. And we need people like your husband, as well, people willing to teach our undereducated a better way of life."

I smiled and took Dr. Rashad's hand before heading down the hall to class. By the weekend, I was sure, Bob would be released from the hospital and return home, free of the monkey he'd been fighting for the past six months. Free forever.

I walked in on Dinara just as she was finishing a quiz on the possible complications involved in home birthing.

"What do you think about that?" she said softly, amazed, amused, turning toward me. She motioned to the eight young girls who would soon be released into the countryside to begin their jobs. "Everyone, an *A*. One received an *A*+ even!"

I smiled. Before long, they would attend the first commencement ceremonies for midwives in Afghanistan's long and labored history. All eyes would be on Kabul that day, and the city was using the event as an excuse to host a giant celebration.

On my way home from the clinic, I met Naim, and we went to the market together to shop for our dinners. His family was due to arrive in Kabul that evening from a small town half a day's journey to the south, and he was anxious to find a choice cut of lamb to prepare with rice and curry for their late-evening meal.

"Your mother won't want to do the cooking during their visit?"

He laughed. "That is *all* my mother wants to do! But this is a holiday for her so I will insist."

We walked from one vendor to the next, stopping half a dozen times to examine the various cuts of meats and to dicker over prices. At each stop, the scene was the same. Naim asked to see a pound of the vendor's best lamb, which the Afghan lifted from a slab, sending disappointed hordes of flies scattering. The bugs hatch out in late March and don't disappear until late November. Big flies, small flies, all kinds of flies. They flit freely from one open drainage ditch to another--ditches that serve as the city's drinking-water distribution system, washing machine, and toilet. Then, invariably, the insects end up at the marketplace to dine.

The Afghan women long ago made it a point to serve all meat well cooked, and the country, in general, has learned over the centuries to adapt quite well to the occasional bouts of dysentery that the *farangis* fight to control on a daily basis--the scourge that the British have come to call Ali Khan's Revenge.

When Naim had finally picked out a slab of pink-grey lamb tinged with goldenrod edges, I chose a plump young plucked chicken, and we said our goodbyes. On the way back to the hut, I stopped at a weathered, crumbling building that must have been old even in the days of the British-Afghan wars at the turn of the century. It, like Naim's lamb, was also pink and tinged with brown. The fact that it was still standing, still functioning as the city's only post office, was a testimony to both the construction techniques employed by the Afghans and the country's general unwillingness to waste even an ounce of material that someone, somewhere, might still consider of value.

The postmaster greeted me in Pashtun, smiling past

yellowing teeth and iron bars. Both looked as if they'd outlived their usefulness. He held out a white envelope stamped in half a dozen different places with blue and red words in English and Persian. "For you," he said with some flair, and I grabbed the letter and stuffed it deep inside my bag, as a miser might hoard a small cache of gold, and hurried off toward home.

At the hut, I threw my bags onto the kitchen table and stared at the envelope for several seconds, savoring what I imagined was written inside. It was from my mother, from Wisconsin--a home I'd known, it seemed, so very long ago. Even before I opened it, I felt the tears building inside of me. "Stupid," I cursed softly, trying to swallow back my emotions.

I slipped down into a chair, removed the letter from its pouch, and began reading. My mother's handwriting had a calming effect on me. Her words were so precisely drawn, each letter perfectly formed, as you would expect a schoolteacher's hand to be. By the time I'd finished, I was overwhelmed with homesickness. All the frustrations I'd experienced since arriving in Afghanistan, all the problems with Bob welled up inside of me, and the tears came spilling out.

It was a lovely, long, rambling letter in which I learned that father was doing well, had just gotten a promotion and a raise at the office where he worked as an insurance underwriter. And my Uncle Ned--all burley, barrel-chested, gruff and rough around the edges, the soft smell of alcohol on his breath whenever he came to call, alcohol or something bittersweet but never overwhelming--he had recently gotten a divorce, which I thought was terrible. But mom said it was best for all concerned. His wife didn't want any children and was becoming more of a financial burden every day. I could see her in my mind, all fat, lazy, disagreeable. I never did understand what had brought Uncle Ned and Lenora together at all, but I never stopped to think that, with his good nature, he would someday actually divorce her.

So as I set about blotting the tears from my eyes--not

tears for Uncle Ned or Lenora or anyone in particular, but for everyone. I slowly pulled myself up out of the chair and placed the chicken in the refrigerator. I removed a plate of cooked rice and carrots and set it on the stove. That would be all I'd need that night. The chicken would hold until the next day when I would make it for Bob. I wasn't in the mood for it, anyway. With Bob still away and my mother's words dancing through my mind, I would eat a few leftovers and be satisfied and go to bed early. There was no reason for staying up. None that I could think of.

That night, barely past nine, I rolled over onto my pillow, paused, and took a deep breath. The air was thick and sweet, the flowers outside the barred window working their magic even as the world around them slept.

Suddenly, I woke. My eyes bulged; my heart pounded. I took in the surroundings, squinted at the clock. *One-fifteen. Must have dozed off.* I'd been sleeping for more than four hours. I felt the sweat on my forehead, the damp nightgown clinging to my body. *Just a dream*, I told myself, only a dream. It was late at night, and I'd been alone in my parents' home, a young girl again, and it had been raining, thundering, lightning. I walked down the back porch stairs to the basement. Suddenly I stopped on the landing and looked out the back door. A tremendous lightning bolt flashed, and the wind caught the door and threw it open. There, standing just two feet before me was a hideous face covered with hair. Two deep-set, dark eyes stared at me--wolves' eyes, devils' eyes. A menacing growl escaped from blood-stained lips.

I shuddered again and reached over to turn on the lamp. Quickly I looked around. The room was silent. My hands were trembling. "Just a dream," I whispered. *Nothing real.* I took a deep breath and turned out the light, settling back against my pillow. I wished it were the weekend, wished Bob were there with me. I felt so alone, so vulnerable. *Foolish!*

Gradually my eyes closed and I lay still for several

moments. And then I heard a soft click from the other room. My muscles froze. Another dream? The machinations of an overworked mind? I strained my ears against the silence. Two minutes. Four. Maybe ten. It felt like hours. Finally, I reached out and turned on the light. Again I listened. Again I heard nothing.

Cautiously I climbed out of bed and slipped into my mules. Wrapping my robe around me, I rose and walked to the bedroom door.

"Hello?" I waited for a response, hoping to God I didn't get one. "Who's there? I know someone's there. Who's there?"

Silence greeted me as I looked for something to grab, something to hold, some kind of weapon.

"Hello?" I repeated, and I edged the bedroom door open and peered out into the dark living room.

My eyes adjusted quickly to the blackness as they scanned the room. I walked over to the lamp. With a sudden lunge, I leaped for the switch, nearly knocking the base over, and sent a shower of light spilling across the floor. I sighed, my heart pounding, my muscles still tense. Nothing stirred. Everything was as I'd left it: the dinner dishes on the table, the pot on the stove, my bag on the floor by the front door.

"Oh, my God," I said as my eyes fell on the door. It was open. Cracked little more than an inch, but it was open. It had been closed, I was certain.

Trembling, I reached over to a small table and picked up a long-handled flashlight that we sometimes used when the electricity failed. I hefted it like a club, getting the feel of it, balancing it just right, and then I quietly inched my way forward until I was within reach of the entrance. I was prepared for the worst, ready in case the door should fly open at any second and some creature burst in. I breathed in deeply before lunging against it, shrieking at the sound it made as it slammed shut. I quickly slapped at the bolt and gasped for breath, waiting to feel the sudden surge of strength against me. But the surge never came.

I hurried over to the stove in the center of the room and

grabbed a book of matches. I lit one end of a rolled newspaper and threw it into the beast's belly. I picked up a can of compressed sawdust, Afghanistan's answer to firewood. Holding it near the flame, I set it smoldering before lowering it into the pot, where it would continue to burn for hours. All the while I kept looking around, straining to be sure I was alone. I decided that if anyone, *anything,* was outside waiting to get in, I would make it as difficult for him as possible.

I pulled a heavy chair across the room and positioned it snugly against the door. I went around and checked all the shutters to be sure they were closed and latched tight. By the time I returned to the stove, the fire was crackling gingerly, a comforting warmth rising from the heavy black iron pot, taking some of the chill from my body.

I slipped the flashlight into my robe pocket and, looking once more around the room, began clearing the dishes from the table. Finally, I settled onto the sofa, facing the door, and waited, too frightened to sleep, for sunrise.

*   *   *

By mid-October, the pleasant fall weather had taken a turn for the worse. The north winds swept down out of Russia's Kirghiz Steppes, picking up speed and moisture over the Kush. Temperatures in Kabul dropped 50 degrees overnight. I knew winter had come, but still I was caught off guard. It's easy enough to throw on a sweater one day when the day before you could barely stand a light blouse; but to go from blouse to parka--it seemed impossible.

I hurried to the clinic that Thursday morning, walking as fast as I could to fight off the biting chill of the winds. I ended up running the last several hundred feet, but still I was shivering from inside-out by the time I slipped through the door.

"The Iceman Cometh," Dinara laughed when she saw my blue skin and shaking hands.

"Cute. Why didn't you tell me winter starts in Kabul at precisely 7 A.M. on October 19th?" I pulled off my sweater and slipped into a lab coat, and I wrapped the sweater around me again. I must have looked like an old *babushka*, but I didn't care. "How cold is it, anyway?"

"Someone told me it dipped into the low thirties last night."

"It feels colder than that."

"It's the wind. You'll get used to it."

"*Brrrr.*" I shook my hands to get the circulation going. "In a couple of months, maybe."

"Is not your native Wisconsin cold in winter?"

"Cold, yes; an icebox, no--at least not overnight."

"That's part of the charm of our country--the suddenness of the changing seasons."

"Right now I could use less charm and more heat. Is the kettle on?"

Dinara motioned for me to follow, and we entered the small office where she spent much of her day charting patients' progress, overseeing the staff, and ordering supplies. She did the work of half a dozen people. I wondered where she got all her energy. She was one of those people you admire from a distance, and even more so up close.

"Here." She handed me a cup of emerald-colored liquid and squinted at me through smiling eyes. "This will help."

"Thanks," I said, taking the cup and warming my hands against its sides.

"You didn't sleep well last night?"

I smiled. "Does it show?"

"No." She hesitated. "Well, maybe a little ... around your eyes."

"I hardly slept at all." I drank from the cup, paused, and sighed. "I was awakened by some noises and couldn't get back to sleep. Just silly stuff."

"You were worrying about Bob?"

"No, no." I slipped into a small chair before her desk. "Well, maybe just a bit. But Dr. Rashad says he can come home this weekend."

"That's good news, isn't it?"

"Yes, of course, but ..."

"But what? What is it? Something is bothering you

still?"

"I don't know. I guess I'm a little worried, that's all."

"About his ... cure?"

I nodded. "He says he's going clean, but that's hard to do. I *know* it is. I just don't want him falling back into the same trap again. But I don't know what I can do to prevent it. I mean, it's got to be his decision, doesn't it? I can give him support, and I can give him encouragement, but in the end, it's going to have to come from him."

"You are absolutely right. *You?* You can do nothing. It's in his hands now."

I lowered my head. "That's what I thought. I mean, I've always known that. That's what makes it so difficult, not being able to control my own destiny, my own marriage. I guess, when it comes right down to it, *he's* the only one he can rely on for help."

She looked at me, furrowed brow, squinting eyes. "Maybe yes. Maybe no."

"What do you mean?"

She wandered over to the window overlooking the courtyard. "I have the day off tomorrow. I'm going to visit my uncle in Pul-i-Khumri. It is a small village in the heart of the Kush where I grew up. I would like very much if you would come along to keep me company."

"Me? I mean, I'd love to. But why me?"

"It would be an excellent chance for you to see a part of my land that is very different from Kabul and for you to meet my uncle, Shah Khan Muhammad Nur Daod." She laughed, her dark eyes reflecting the overhead lights. "It is an impressive title, no? He is one of the last few remaining feudal lords within driving distance of Kabul. Most were long ago replaced by provisional heads of state. Or killed."

"But ..." I hesitated. I wasn't sure why. "I ... I have work tomorrow."

"I'll speak to Dr. Rashad. I'm sure he will agree that the clinic can spare you for one day. Besides, the trip will do you good."

"You sound as if I'd be going for my health."

"No, not for *your* health."

"I don't understand."

"So, if it is agreeable, I will have a driver pick you up this evening, about six. We can have dinner together, and you can spend the night at my home. In that way, no mysterious noises will keep you awake again. We will leave by Land Rover early in the morning and be back by sunset."

"Stay with you?" I thought for a few moments. It was a tempting offer. "But what about Bob?"

"Bob will be fine. Tell him you have a chance to visit a real, honest-to-goodness Shah and that you'll be back the first thing Saturday morning to pick him up. I'm certain he'll understand."

The thought of not having to spend another night home alone sounded too good to be true. And so did the prospect of seeing what I'd heard was one of the most beautiful parts of Afghanistan--the little mountain villages of the Kush.

I paused, set the empty cup on her desk, and rose. "In that case ... you're on."

"Good. This evening, then."

True to Dinara's word, we loaded our belongings into her four-wheel Rover and were out across the plateau toward the Kush at sunrise. It was the first time I'd driven anywhere with her, and I was stunned by her aggressiveness. She jammed the shifter into first, pushed the pedal to the floor, and then shifted into second or sometimes even third without bothering to clutch.

"Where did you learn that?"

"Where did I learn what?"

"It's called speed-shifting, isn't it?"

"Oh, that." She chuckled. "It's just a little habit I picked up driving a formula one while living in Italy."

"Formula One? You were a race-car driver?"

"Not personally. But I had friends."

"And in Italy. I didn't know you'd lived in Italy."

"Yes, after Paris. I met an Italian race-car driver, and

we fell in love. I lived with him in his villa on the Tevere River outside Rome. It was beautiful--lush gardens, gothic architecture, great museums, and the kind of weather we in Afghanistan enjoy for only a few weeks each spring."

"So what happened?"

"To us? He was driving his monster Ferrari at Monte Carlo one year and was forging ahead going into the chicane." She paused.

"And?"

"And he lost it. Somehow, he just ... lost it."

"Was he ... *killed*?" The words passed through unwilling lips. I didn't even know why I had said them.

She nodded. "Unfortunately, he was. Although not immediately. The car skidded off the road and hit some barriers. It was smoking badly as the ambulance and people from everywhere rushed out to help. They had trouble getting him out of his harness when a small fire broke out in the cockpit. Several of the men took off their shirts and were beating at it. They had just about extinguished it when a helicopter from a local news station flew up and hovered over the car to get some photographs."

"Oh, no."

"The wash from the blades fanned the fire alive again, and the car burst into flames before they could free him. By the time the pilot realized what had happened and cleared from the site, it was over. They finally extinguished the fire and got him out and to the hospital, but he was dead on arrival."

"Oh, my Lord. I'm so sorry. That must have been horrible."

She smiled half-heartedly, as though pretending the pain had gone. "That was a long time ago ..."

"I had no idea, Dinara ..."

She shrugged. "It was difficult to accept at first, but the long, lonely nights soon convinced me he would not return. It was then that I decided to come home to Afghanistan. I loved the villa and could have remained there forever. But, for what? A memory? No, I thought not." She shook her black hair from side to side. "That is not for me. I need more from life than memories."

We started up a long, gently sloping hill at the foot of the Kush. As if to prove a point, she dropped the shifter into second, and the Rover roared like a demon; then she slipped it into third, and it purred like a cat.

It was nearly 10 A.M. when the sun peeked over the top of the mountains to the east, and we rumbled out of the last of the tiny passes leading to Pul-i-Khumri. It is a scenic village, with many aging stone-and-clay structures standing shoulder to shoulder, like soldiers at dress parade. The huts looked to be hundreds, possibly even thousands, of years old. As we passed a small reflecting pool in the center of town, three very old, grizzled-looking tribesmen peered up at us before bowing as if to royalty.

"They have been expecting us. I cabled my uncle that we would be arriving this morning. Word travels fast."

"Since when does an Afghan elder bow to a woman?"

"When she is the descendant of royalty."

"*Ohhh.*" I nodded and smiled at the old men. "I am honored, Your Highness."

We laughed out loud as she jammed the accelerator to the floor and we took a sharp curve to the left before racing forward, down a steep slope, past a bazaar lined with tables sagging beneath the weight of dozens of Oriental carpets. We turned through a large open gate, driving for several minutes more along a tree-lined cobbled road until it veered sharply to the right. It looped back around to the left and up to a great stone building-- her uncle's home. She slammed on the brakes, and the Rover jerked to a halt in front of two giant men garbed in fine robes and sashes. A large curved scimitar hung at each man's side. One of the men had a carbine slung over his shoulder. I guessed that a small pouch fastened to his sash contained the cartridges.

"Good morning, Princess Dinara," the first man said in *Urdu* as he opened her door and took her right hand in his, kissing it gently. "We have been expecting you."

"Good morning, Chazhan," she replied. "You are looking well this morning. Is Shah Khan arisen yet?"

"Arisen, Princess Dinara, and anxiously awaiting your arrival."

"Good." She motioned with her hand. "And this is the friend I wired Shah Khan about. Her name is Paula Favage."

"Good morning, Miss Paula," the Afghan beamed as if genuinely pleased to meet me. He held out his hand and leaned forward to kiss me once on each cheek. "I hope your trip has been guided by Allah."

"It was a beautiful trip," I said in halting *Urdu.*

"And the driver was not too reckless?" A twinkle rose in his eyes.

"Reckless!" Dinara cried, feigning anger. "You think I'm reckless? You cursed jackal."

"I think only, Princess Dinara, that if you had owned a camel instead of an automobile, the poor beast would have been dead years ago."

"For your information, Chazhan, I once *did* own a camel ... and the poor beast lived for nearly three weeks."

We laughed as the Afghan ushered us through the great doorway into the Shah's home as if Dinara had never crossed the threshold before. We walked past beautiful objects of art--statues, weavings, paintings, pottery, all typically primitive in conventional Afghan style--all very old. It seemed to me that the Shah was financially well off. At the least.

"Has the Shah been well?" Dinara asked Chazhan.

"The Shah is ... the Shah," he replied with a smile. "Would anyone expect anything else?" He motioned for us to wait as he disappeared past a curtained doorway on the far side of the room. I looked around, speechless. I felt as if I'd been dropped into the pages of *The Arabian Nights.*

"He seems so ..." I paused, searching for the right word.

"Yes, you are right. He is that and more."

I laughed. "Not at all like the typical Afghan male."

"Chazhan is not typical by any means. He was educated at the Sorbonne in Paris. He studied English at Oxford. Shah Khan believes in the best possible for his family and staff. Chazhan is an Afghan through and through, though. Do not be mistaken about that. But he is hardly typical."

"And the other one?" I asked nodding toward the man with the carbine, standing behind us.

"He, too, is well educated. But in different ways."

"What do you mean? In what ways?"

"You have noticed the rifle he carries?"

I nodded.

"I have seen him split an acorn in two from a thousand yards."

"That's incredible."

"With his eyes closed," she added.

I started to grin, and then I noticed she wasn't smiling.

I walked slowly around the great room, stopping before each art treasure to admire its beauty and wonder about its origin. From what far-away lands had they come? India, China, Iraq, Iran? The spoils of war, or the tribute of loyal subjects? I could feel the Afghan's eyes on me and couldn't shake the thought of that shell hurtling through the air to shatter a tiny hull no larger than a thumbnail. If there were others like him around the estate, it was little wonder the Shah and his family had remained in power, despite all attempts by the government at democratization over the years.

"God, this is fantastic," I confessed when I had circled back around to her. "Does your uncle have any children?"

"None," she said. "I am his closest living family."

Chazhan reappeared and motioned us to follow. He wore a serious, pained expression, to which Dinara addressed herself instinctively:

"I hope you're not going to ask what you always ask."

Chazhan pulled at his sash. "I must do what Shah Khan requests."

"And he requests the *chaderi*," she said.

"Please, Princess Dinara. Shah Khan is growing old.

For his sake, if you would just wear this." He held out a fold of cloth beautifully woven with golden threads.

"I, too, am growing old, Chazhan, and I will not revert to pagan ritual. We are a civilized society now. Women are no longer required to hide their faces from Shah Khan or any man. Neither Miss Paula nor I will wear the *chaderi*. But I will tell Shah Khan that you offered it to us."

He bowed.

Dinara pushed past him into the next room. As I followed, I looked up into his eyes and almost felt sorry enough to wish Dinara had acceded to his request. Chazhan let the curtain fall behind us.

I was overwhelmed by the immense size of the room-- like a dozen rooms back home. The ceiling towered thirty feet above us, free of pillars, a clear-span marvel of architectural splendor with glorious ancient paintings etched across the dome, like the Sistine Chapel. Except for the ceiling's distinct greyish-brown cast, it could have been the uppermost reaches of the universe. I half expected to look up and see the twinkling of the constellations.

The outer walls of the room were pocked with porticos, nooks, and crannies, some filled with freshly cut flowers, others with various ornate vessels and sculptures similar in appearance to those in the anterior room. Brass-and-gold samovars glistened at us like the dew on the morning grass. The furnishings themselves were sparse: a large, ornately carved chair upholstered in red velvet and decorated with gold-and-black threads, a few small tables carved from wood and ivory, a long, credenza-type affair atop which reclined the figure of a Buddhist monk surrounded by serpents and dragons. The sculpture was carved of the purest white stone I had ever seen. On the floor lay assorted woven rugs of the Afghan style, as well as the huge Persian rug on which a solitary velvet chair stood sentinel.

I was about to ask Dinara how one greets a genuine Shah when suddenly a curtain to one side drew back and a small man with a long grey beard and white skullcap entered. He was dressed rather plainly in traditional cotton pants and shirt, with a long, flowing vest that reached nearly to his knees. Disappointed, I looked beyond the small man for some sign of the Shah, but none appeared.

"Dinara," the old man said in Persian, "may Allah always welcome you to my humble home and protect you against the night."

"Shah Khan," Dinara replied, reaching down to extend the traditional kisses and handshake, "you are looking very well these days. Obviously in good health."

"And you," he replied, "are looking more radiant than ever. Such clear skin, like the distant sands of the desert. You realize, however, that even the sands of the desert are occasionally cloaked from men's view by darkness."

I heard a soft groan from behind the curtain where we'd entered and imagined Chazhan cradling his head in his hands.

"In these enlightened times, a man can surely distinguish the sands even at night if only his eyes are not blinded by foolish superstitions."

He turned toward me and shrugged. "I have reared a rebel." He paused, shaking his head. "May Allah forgive me."

Dinara turned suddenly. "Uncle, I would like you to meet my friend."

"*Ahh*, yes--Paula Favage." He kissed my cheeks and grabbed my hand firmly, holding it for several moments while he looked deeply into my eyes. "Dinara cabled that you would accompany her to Pul-i-Khumri. I am pronouncing your surname correctly?"

"Yes," I said, amazed at how easily the Shah had slipped from Persian into English, which he enunciated as though he'd spoken the language all his life. "It rhymes with *savage*. That's the easiest way to remember." I laughed somewhat nervously, hoping he wouldn't take offense.

"Tell me," he said, still clutching my hand, "what nationality is Favage? I don't believe I have ever heard that name before."

"Probably not. It's mostly French, but there's also some German and Swedish mixed in."

"But no Afghan?" he asked, a slight twinkle in his eyes.

"No," I said, laughing. "At least none that I know of."

"The Swedish--that is no doubt where you get your beautiful blonde hair."

"Mostly it comes from a bottle." I smiled.

"*Ahh* ... the wonders of modern science," he mused, finally releasing my hand and turning toward the chair. He clapped suddenly, and Chazhan appeared in the doorway.

"Yes, Sahib?"

"Chazhan, pillows for my guests, if you please."

"Yes, Shah Khan," he replied, and within an instant, a woman dressed in full *chaderi* appeared with two large satin pillows, which she placed on either side of the chair. As he sat, Shah Khan motioned for us to join him.

"Now, tell me, Dinara, how are things in Kabul? What have you heard?"

"Things are calm, as is usual this time of year," she replied. "Winter is sweeping down from the plains, just as it is here in Pul-i-Khumri. It seems as though it will be a long one. The birds have already fled for warmer climates, and the leaves are off the trees."

"It will come three weeks early," the Shah said, looking out over the room, "and it will stay three weeks late."

"I wish not," Dinara replied. "Winter in Kabul seems so much harsher than here in the mountains, I think because here one expects winter and prepares for it accordingly. In Kabul, city life makes the cold so much more difficult to bear. The people tend to deny its coming and are caught unprepared. Even I."

"It is so." The old man leaned forward. "But, where are my manners? You must be hungry after your journey." He clapped again, and immediately Chazhan and two female servants appeared with a large teapot and a tray filled with halva, sweetmeats, fresh fruit, and cheese curds. This

Chazhan ordered set at our side as he poured tea into small gilded porcelain cups, which he distributed first to the Shah and then to Dinara and me.

"Now," Shah Khan said after some moments of silence, "tell me what besides an old man's love brings you such a distance from your home."

Dinara looked suddenly ill at ease. "It is not enough for a young girl to want to see her favorite uncle?"

The Shah laughed, reaching up to stroke his beard. "I know you better than that, Dinara."

"I'm afraid," she said hesitatingly, "that you know me too well. Actually, I wanted to show Paula the land where I was born and raised. But also, I have come because Paula is worried about the condition of her husband."

At the mention of my name, I started, but I remained silent.

"He is in the hospital in Kabul," she continued, "fallen prey to some ... I don't quite know how to say ..."

"The poppies grow wild in the hills," Shah Khan interrupted, and he turned to me. "Is your husband a *farangi* as well?"

"Yes. American."

Shah Khan nodded. "It is not easy for a *farangi* to accept the ways of life in Afghanistan without succumbing to the various temptations of our own little corner of the world. This is his first time in Central Asia?"

"No. He was here once before several years ago with the Peace Corps. We're working with the Corps again now."

"Paula is a nurse at the clinic--and a very good one. And her husband, Bob, *Robert*, teaches English at the university in Kabul."

"*Ahh*, yes," Shah Khan replied, emptying his cup and handing it to Chazhan for a refill. I watched as the servant carefully placed six cubes of sugar in the bottom before covering them with the green liqueur. "It is surprising how many *farangis* who visit our country return after several years' absence. There is a mystic allure to the land that calls them back. It is like the taste of sweetmeats." He offered a piece of cake to each of us. "At first, one finds them a bit too sweet, too thick, too intense for one's palate, but, before long, one returns for a second helping. And a third."

Without warning, tears suddenly came to my eyes, and I struggled to contain them.

"We were wondering…"

The Shah looked down. "Yes?"

"We wondered if it might not be possible for the great Shah Khan to exert some of his influence to help Paula's husband return to health … and to remain healthy."

The Shah looked deeply into my eyes, a thin smile on his lips. "Not even Shah Khan can change the flow of the mighty Kabul in the springtime. Nor can anyone but Allah himself melt the snows from the savage Hindu Kush in winter."

I dropped my head and began to sob uncontrollably.

"Bob is making excellent progress," Dinara continued. I felt her hand on my arm, felt its warmth, its sincerity. I breathed in deeply. "He's due to be released from the clinic tomorrow."

The Shah reached forward and lightly touched my head. His hand was warm, as well, his touch even gentler than that of his niece. It was hard to believe that this was the same man who had carved an empire for himself from the rough, barren countryside that has been the scene of fierce tribal battles and foreign warfare for centuries.

"If that is the case," he said softly, "perhaps there will be no rain falling on the poppy fields, and the crops around Kabul shall dry up, wither, and die before the delicate flower heads can be harvested."

I looked up into his warm, smiling eyes. "Then … then, you *can* help?"

"I can do only what little I am capable of doing," he replied. "The rest will be up to your husband … and to Allah."

"Thank you," I said, dabbing at my eyes with my napkin. "Thank you so much." I took his hand and squeezed it, and he placed his free hand over mine.

"Thank you."

"And now," he said, turning to Dinara, "you and your friend will take a short rest from your journey; then we shall tour the gardens together, as we used to do when you were small. Do you remember?"

Dinara smiled. "I remember."

"And you will stay the night before starting your trip back to Kabul."

"No, uncle, I'm afraid not. We would love to stay, but we must get back this evening. Paula must prepare for Bob's return home tomorrow morning. It has been over a week, and she is anxious to have him back."

"*Ahh*, yes," he said, thinking for several moments. "Yes, to be young, again."

"You will always be young at heart, my uncle."

He smiled. "It is best, then, that you return home to Kabul today. You will stay for the noon meal. We will walk the gardens, and you will catch me up on the family news."

"And you, me."

"And then you will depart in time to return to Kabul before dark. It is not safe for two such lovely young ladies to be out alone in the wilderness once the sun sets behind the Kush. It is said that even Allah hesitates penetrating the Afghan darkness."

We thanked the Shah again and followed a woman servant to a small chamber off the main room where we freshened up and rested for an hour before being brought once again to the Shah and given a tour of the sprawling gardens. By 2 P.M., we had loaded some gifts of bakery and fresh fruit in the Rover and were headed back to Kabul.

"One moment," Shah Khan said as we lingered in the palace, offering our farewells. He reached into his pants pocket and pulled forth a small trinket, a carving, something made of ivory. He took my hand and closed it around the figurine.

"What is it?" I said, opening my fingers to look at it.

"No," he said, clamping them closed again, his aging

fist completely encircling mine. "You must take this treasure and hold it in your hand for your journey back home. Thus secreted there, it will see you safely along to your destination. Once you have arrived, you will know that it is indeed your guardian ... what do you call it, a guardian angel? No matter its shape or size, it will see you safely through all adversity, if only you believe."

I looked into his eyes, deep and filled with passion, yet at the same time strangely devoid of the joys of life that surrounded him. He appeared tired, as though all of life, now, were nothing more than a game to him, a game he had learned to play well as a young man, a game that no longer held the spirit of competition, the sweet scent of victory.

"Thank you. I'm sure I will cherish it always."

He nodded, and after Dinara kissed her uncle goodbye, we left for the Rover and home.

Somehow, the trip to the Kush had been for me a cleansing experience. I felt as though I'd just finished a mountain retreat, a period of inner reflection and prayer that left my soul refreshed and my body rejuvenated. It was a feeling I would never forget.

"I ... I really appreciate what you did for Bob and me," I said after some minutes of driving. "I had no idea that's what you meant yesterday when you said ..."

"I have done nothing more than to visit a dear loved one."

"And I suppose it was just a coincidence that Bob's name came up in conversation?"

She shrugged. "It's so hard to think of things to say to an old person."

"And sometimes hard to think of excuses to give to a young one."

Dinara looked at me and smiled before returning her eyes to the road.

"Tell me something," I said.

"Yes?"

"Your uncle obviously loves you very much. Why hasn't he any children of his own? I would have expected a man like him to have many wives, children, and grandchildren."

"Shah Khan has led a rich life. He married first about 50 years ago. I think he has had either nine or ten wives since then."

"Not all at once, I hope."

"Usually no more than three or four at a time."

"But no children. I find that strange."

"He had, by his various wives, five. None survived."

"Oh. That's sad. It must have been difficult. And your father--was he the Shah's brother?"

"Yes. He fought alongside the Shah many times. The two of them ruled the Plains for many years. Until his death."

"How, if you don't mind my asking, did he die?"

"He was killed when I was only three. He died while defending Pul-i-Khumri from a band of Pakistani jackals who descended on the village and tried to steal some horses ... and make off with the village children. I was in his arms when a bullet from a Pakistani rifle pierced his heart."

"Oh, my God, that must have been horrible!"

"I don't remember much of the incident. I was so young. But, whether memory or fantasy, I sometimes lie in bed nights and feel the sensation of falling, falling far to the ground, and of lying there next to my father ... and crying."

"I'm so sorry. I can't imagine what they must have been like."

"Life is filled with tragedy. It is what makes it so ... *challenging.*"

"And you were raised by your uncle?"

"Yes, until I was old enough to go away to school, at which time he sent me to study in Paris. I have seen him, oh, maybe six or eight times since returning to Afghanistan nearly a decade ago. It is not often enough. I realized that today when we were seated before him, and I saw how old he has grown in the year since I last visited Pul-i-Khumri. It dawned on me, perhaps for the very first time, that Shah Khan will not be with us forever."

"You seem to have a rather stoic attitude toward death."

Her eyebrows rose and fell. "It is simply something one must accept. Stoicism. From the Stoic school of philosophy and the ancient Greek philosopher, Zeno. Roman Emperor Marcus Aurelius was one of the first great stoics. Strange. I had never before thought of the word in relationship to myself. But I suppose it is so. That one should bear pain in silence. But death and pain? I do not understand the relationship between the two. From his very first breath, man starts the long, arduous journey toward death. It is the one common element all men share. To fight it would be foolish. It should be everyone's goal in life to die with dignity, with grace, and with honor."

"Tell me more about your uncle," I said after some moments of silence. "He's such an intriguing man. A man of so many contradictions."

She chuckled. "There is not much I can tell. He was away during much of the time I was growing up in his household--that is before he became Shah, of course. Back then, he was a soldier in the old Shah's army. Gradually he worked his way up to become commander of the forces assigned to protect Pul-i-Khumri from the invaders to the east. It was his intimate knowledge of warfare, as well as his great acumen with a gun and a knife, that endeared him to the townspeople as well as to the former Shah so that when the old Shah died, my uncle was elected to take his place."

"I thought a Shah passed on his throne from one generation to the next."

"The old Shah had only one living son, the rest having been killed in battle. There was a brief reign by the son, during which he proved himself to be totally unworthy of the title of Shah, and he was overthrown. That is when my uncle was elected.'"

"And the old Shah's son--whatever became of him, do you know?"

She paused. "He died."

"In battle?"

"At the hands of my uncle."

I must have looked surprised.

"It was far better than he deserved."

Dinara turned the Rover south through the Baba-Khur Pass leading toward Kabul. As the long ribbon of road opened up before us, the Rover steadily accelerated until the few sparse trees and shrubs whizzed by us as though shot from a rifle.

"Has your uncle been to war lately?" I asked.

She shook her head. "There have been no attempts to subjugate Pul-i-Khumri since the last British invasion more than three decades ago. Now he mostly tends to the day-to-day affairs of overseeing the workings of the local government. And, of course, he has his crops."

"What kind of crops? I saw only the flower gardens."

"Oh, wheat, mostly. And..." She paused. "Poppies."

"Poppies! Your uncle raises *poppies*? For *heroin*?"

"It is a situation you undoubtedly find hard to understand. But do not think too harshly of him. It has been a way of life, a way of survival, for centuries. Without the wealth he and the entire region reap from cultivating poppies, Pul-i-Khumri would have long ago succumbed to the wandering Mongol hordes--or, worse, the shifting winds of time."

"I don't want to sound ungrateful, believe me. But ... I mean, doesn't that bother him? Doesn't that bother you, knowing that what he's doing is destroying lives each and every day that he does it?"

She shrugged. "As I have told you, death and destruction are inevitable facts of life. Only the way one dies may be open to conjecture, not *if* one dies."

I sat back in my seat and stared out the window, thinking about the day's events, about Dinara's words, peering out and thinking.

Perhaps she was right. Perhaps death was not what one should fear in life--the two are so inexplicably entwined, after all--but rather *living*. Perhaps it's not giving up life that counts, but failing to live life to the fullest while we have the chance.

We passed a small village made up of ten or twelve earthen huts, with a solitary woman bundled up against the cold walking along the roadway, a baby strapped papoose-style to her back. She glanced up only momentarily as we passed, and her eyes held the fallen look of defeat in them. As she dropped her shoulders, I caught a glimpse of the young infant's eyes, smiling and filled with life, hope, and the innate knowledge that his entire world still lay before him.

EIGHT

I had mixed feelings about the callousness of Dinara's attitude toward her uncle's business. It seemed so unlike her. It was difficult for me to conceive of her condoning her uncle's activities, especially after seeing firsthand what drugs could do to people ... what they had done to Bob. She was a nurse; she had been trained to minister to people, to help them through sickness and disease-- through afflictions of all types. Wasn't her casual attitude toward the poppy fields her uncle plowed for a living just a bit hypocritical?

Still, I realized that what her uncle did and what she did weren't one and the same. And I *was* grateful for her interceding with Shah Khan on Bob's behalf, although I didn't quite know what an aging poppy grower in the very bowels of the Hindu Kush some 200 miles from Kabul could do to see to it that Bob didn't fall back into his addiction. Could the man be so powerful that one word from him would dry up distribution in Kabul? And why had he promised to help us, anyway? Was it simply to salve an aching conscience? Or to endear himself to his niece? There were so many questions bouncing around my head for that first week Bob was home, questions to which only time might provide an answer--if *that*.

I worked that following week, although I came home each day to check on Bob at lunchtime, and I asked Naim to stop in whenever he had a chance. I knew how rough it would be on Bob the first few days back home, especially if he were alone for any length of time and had an opportunity to feel sorry for himself. Naim brought over a chess set from the British Embassy, and he and Bob proved to be worthy adversaries, sometimes playing through dinner and late into the night. They had actually begun a friendship of sorts. Of course, Bob invariably won their games, whether by chance or design I couldn't quite tell. Regardless, it bolstered his spirits and gave him something to think about besides himself--and what he was going through.

On Friday, a week after Bob's release from the clinic, I got off work early and came home to find him napping while Naim sat in the living room, reading a book I'd brought with me to Afghanistan. It was a novel by Henry Miller.

As I entered, Naim hurriedly rose. "Hello," he said, grinning sheepishly. "I hope you don't mind, but I found this on the table. Since Sahib Bob was sleeping, I thought I might read a little from it."

"Of course I don't mind, Naim. In fact, you can take it with you, if you like. I'm finished reading it."

Naim blushed. "Oh, no. I was only seeing how good my English is ... if I could read an American book."

"And?"

He shook his head. "I think it is surprisingly good. Although there are words in it I have not seen before."

"I'm sure." I laughed. "Just don't ask me to translate them."

Naim set the book down and motioned toward the bedroom. "Sahib Bob is doing well after his stay in the hospital, yes?"

"Yes. Very well. Maybe *too* well."

"How is that?"

"He seems a little edgy. You know, like he's anxious to get back to work."

"That is a good sign, I think, for a man to wish to return to his labors. It means he no longer suffers from what had ailed him."

"Yes, but I wish he'd learn to relax more here at home. His pacing and fidgeting are making *me* nervous." I reached around and pulled my hair together, and then I slipped a band around it to keep it in place.

"He will be returning to the university on Monday, then?"

"Yes. Dr. Rashad says it will be all right."

"I am sure he will be fine then. He seems to be much stronger now than when he first came home."

"Must be all that home cooking he's been getting-- three meals a day."

Naim smiled and clutched his stomach. "And Naim, too, is getting stronger, in places where he should not be, thanks to your cooking."

"Oh, right. As if you have something to worry about. You could gain 20 pounds, and you wouldn't show an ounce. Oh, that reminds me. Would you mind staying for just a little while longer while I run down to the market and pick up some meat for dinner? I won't be long."

"That is fine. I am in no hurry. There is no work for me at the embassy. In fact, Sahib Ingersoll is leaving next week for a vacation, so things will be slow for a while."

"Oh? Where is he going?"

"He is returning to the United States to visit some family there. He shall be gone for eight days."

"I suppose it'll be like a vacation for *you* while he's gone, as well."

Naim smiled. "I think there won't be quite so much running around as there is normally."

"Can you stay for dinner? We'll have plenty."

"Oh, no. No, thank you. Some of my friends and I are meeting tonight at a small restaurant in town. Then, afterwards, we will go to see the dance. There is a troupe passing through Kabul that is supposed to be excellent."

"That sounds exciting."

"Yes. It has been years since the last time I saw the dance. My father took two of my brothers and me to the market in Jalalabad, where we had lunch and enjoyed a fine performance. I am looking forward to seeing it again."

"And are any of your friends ... *girl* friends?"

Naim blushed. "Me? Girl friends? What would I want with a bunch of giggling girls around? This is a man's night out."

"Okay, okay." I paused. "If you don't want to tell me her name, just forget it."

"But I am telling you," he said, a large grin painting his face. "Three of my old classmates and I are getting together for dinner and the dance, that's all."

"Well, I hope you enjoy yourself." I reached for the door. "I'll be back as quickly as I can."

As I headed out the garden gate and into the street, the bitter winds rolled down from the north, picking up their intensity with each step. I threw my collar up around my face. The skies were cloudy and threatening, although it was unlikely they would release any snow. That normally didn't hit Kabul until mid-November or later. I stuck my hands in my pocket and walked as quickly as possible toward the square.

On the way, I thought about Bob, about the progress he'd made in two weeks. It seemed he had kicked his habit--as much as could be expected in so short a time-- and even though he'd been somewhat fidgety the past few nights, he was more like the old Bob, the person I had married, than he'd been for years. He seemed, too, more helpless, more dependent on me. While he was perfectly capable of making lunch for himself, he enjoyed my coming home to do it for him. He also seemed to enjoy all the pampering I was giving him.

It was as if we were courting all over again, and it was nice. I felt I could very easily get used to the idea of playing the traditional feminine role, the way Afghan women did, and not miss the liberated-woman model I'd embraced for years. Being a liberated woman has its advantages, but it also presents some challenges. Sharing the responsibilities of providing for the household was a task I could easily have lived without. It's only right that women should receive equal pay for equal work--and equal respect, for that matter. But who's to say that a woman's work *couldn't* be at home, split between the kitchen and the family?

Someday, I mused, when our Afghan adventure was over and we returned to the states, Bob would get a good job, we'd have some children, buy a small home in the country, and live a good life, the kind of life I used to dream about when I was a child. If he just continued making progress, if he could just stay clean ..."

I turned the corner and came upon the stall of Jalal, the butcher, a Pakistani who had moved his family to Kabul to avoid the conflict in his native land. I waited around for several minutes until he had helped a local Pashtun choose just the right turkey. Its feathers and head were still attached, its neck clamped tight with a leather cord so that the bird retained the blood to be used in soup. Finally, when he'd finished with his customer, he turned to me.

"Yes, Mrs. Paula. And what is your pleasure today?"

"What have you that is wonderful and fresh?" My *Urdu* was still weak, but at least I could make myself understood. When I had first tried speaking the Pakistani dialect, I had the local merchants howling in laughter.

"Today we have excellent goat's meat, very clean, very fresh, only 550 *afghanis*. Truly a delight for the young schoolteacher's wife."

I wrinkled my nose and turned my head. "Why would *anyone* pay that much for this smelly old goat?"

Jalal's eyes grew bright, and a smile came to his lips. "Old goat? This is freshly cut and butchered just this day by my own two hands! I helped in the slaughter myself. The skin is hanging on the side of the shop. See for yourself if it isn't still wet with life." He was thoroughly enjoying the game.

"This meat hasn't been wet with life for two days," I said flatly. "Besides, I had more of a taste for something ... like this." I pointed to a pink chunk of meat that I thought might be mutton.

"Karakul. The finest in the marketplace. I should have known this is what you would hunger for on so fine a day as this."

"Karakul? That's for making sweaters, isn't it? I wish

mutton for a meal."

"Karakul *is* mutton for a meal," he growled. "You *farangis* spend three months in a land, and you think you know all there is to know about it. This is the absolute finest Karakul mutton you will find in all of Afghanistan. It was slaughtered and brought to me just this noon. I have sold nearly forty pounds of it in three hours. This is the last I have. You will have to hurry if you want it before someone who knows a fresh piece of meat sees it and snatches it from your very hands."

"How much?" I asked.

Jalal rubbed his stubbled chin and peered at me for several seconds. "For you … six thousand *afghanis*."

"That's outrageous! Why, I wouldn't pay six thousand *afghanis* for a *dozen* pieces of meat like this!"

"Five thousand!" he shouted.

"Three thousand and not a cent more!"

"Four thousand five hundred," he replied, "and not a cent less!"

"Four thousand two hundred-fifty, and you can throw in the skin!"

This brought laughter from the small crowd that had gathered to see the young blue-eyed *farangi* dicker with the age-wizened old butcher. Jalal's eyes were aglow with delight. He smelled profit in that crowd. Like a carnie sideshow operator.

"By Allah, if I can withhold my temper!" He gnashed his teeth menacingly. "Four thousand three hundred *afghanis* for this prime cut of Karakul mutton and not one cent less!"

"Excellent!" I shouted triumphantly, digging through my purse. "Here are two thousand. Cut the piece in half. It's more than I need for one meal."

Jalal muttered under his breath and moved a razor-sharp knife across the flesh, severing it in two, and gave me the smaller piece, which I slipped into my bag.

"*I'll* take that other half for two thousand *afghanis*," a woman standing next to me called out.

"Two thousand one hundred!" Jalal cried. He cursed

through it all, but his eyes continued to dance with delight.

"That was quite some dickering you did in there."

I turned to find a tall Afghan smiling past a glowing, sun-warmed face and brown-grey eyes. Slowly he raised his hand and pushed a shock of hair off his forehead. He was ruggedly handsome, well-built and muscular, with small wrinkle lines below deeply set piercing eyes, taut skin across his cheeks, and the kind of chiseled jaw and full, thick lips a male model might sport.

"You speak English well."

"And you, *Urdu. Very* well."

"No, not very. I'm more comfortable with Pashto."

"May I carry that for you?"

I pulled my bag back. "*No*! I mean, no, thank you. I'm all through shopping. I'm on my way home."

"Then, I will accompany you." He smiled. Dressed in tan cotton pants and a bright-blue linen shirt beneath a long black vest, he looked the modern Afghan. On his feet were moccasins, the sort many Afghans wear even in winter. At his side hung a straight, short dagger, the type the military often carry.

"That won't be necessary."

"It cannot be too much to ask to allow a humble servant to carry your bag home from the marketplace."

"No, really. Thank you, but I don't live that far. And my husband is waiting for me. I really should ..."

The man reached out suddenly and grasped my arm. I instinctively tugged back, but he held it so firmly that struggling was futile. "It is not safe in this part of the city with darkness closing in."

"Please. I must go."

He released my arm as suddenly as he'd taken it, and I stepped back.

"Do you come to the market often?" His gaze swept my body, burning through to my very soul. Silhouetted in the setting sun against the towering Kush, he seemed stark, threatening, someone to avoid at all costs; yet, his eyes told me otherwise.

"I ... come every day. With friends."

"Then I will see you again. Soon."

He made a short bowing motion with his head, turned, and, like the wind on the sand-swept plains, disappeared. I stared after him for several minutes before I realized my heart was pounding. Why? Was it that he had surprised me so? Or frightened me? Or had he entranced and captivated me? I had never had that happen to me before--someone come up to me out of the clear blue sky and leave such an impression, certainly not in Afghanistan. He was an Afghan, no doubt about it. But he seemed different from any others I had met.

I took several steps toward home, and then I stopped and looked around to see if by chance he was still there, watching, following. I saw nothing but a wall of people huddled around Jalal, who was still slicing meat and cursing.

By the time I returned to our hut, I was furious with myself for having been taken so by the stranger. I had stood there, gawking like a small schoolgirl, without having the courtesy even to ask him his name or where he was from or any of the dozen other questions I was dying to have answered. Was he a soldier? A politician? Or, perhaps, a dreaded Pashtun rebel?

I chuckled before throwing the thoughts out of my head, but they kept creeping back. That evening, I told no one about the Afghan at the marketplace. But I was dying of curiosity to know more.

We spent most of Sunday, the day before Bob's scheduled return to the university, cleaning up the few fruits that remained in the garden and mounding up soil around the perennials. It's a job the embassy's gardeners normally do, but I thought it would be good therapy for Bob. He had been cooped up in the hospital and at home for far too long. Though not much of a gardener, he seemed to enjoy working under the cloudy grey skies, stopping from time to time to stare out over the Kush looming over us always. He said he could see the mountains changing as winter drew near--just as the people in Kabul change. Both, he said, shifted gradually into their winter coats, the Afghans to warmer clothes and the Kush to a darker, more somber cover of wild grasses and shrubs. Any day now, it seemed, would bring the first snowfall of the season to the mountains, and we wondered if it would be a light dusting or a thick slate of white.

That evening, Bob grilled his specialty, curried lamb, and he ate as if he hadn't seen food for a month. Working outside had given him an appetite. It was good to see him hungry, nice to see him smile, walk around with the same spry steps he had before the drugs and booze had taken their toll. It was good to see him healthy again. I only hoped that someday soon all the problems that his dependence had created would be gone forever. Then we could pick up with our marriage where we had left off.

We crawled into bed early that night, and Bob was sound asleep in minutes. I was tired, too, but for some reason I lay awake, tossing, turning, looking at him in the dark, thinking. It felt so nice to have him home, the real Bob, the one I knew and loved. Several times I reached over and stroked his bare chest. He didn't stir. After a while I, too, began to drift off, images of Bob in the garden and Afghans at the market and Naim and the river and the mountains all melding into one.

I shook my head and muttered something half out loud. Bob was making his way awkwardly through the darkness of the room.

"What? What's the matter?" I asked, still dazed from my drug-like trance.

"I thought I heard something in the next room. I'm going to check on it."

"What was it?" I asked.

"Probably just the wind. Go on back to sleep."

"Maybe the door. The front door blows open sometimes if it's not bolted."

"Go back to sleep," he repeated. "I'll check."

As Bob's slippers shuffled out of the room, my eyes closed of their own accord, too heavy to resist. I had almost dropped off again when I heard voices. Puzzled, I sprang up and listened. From the next room came excited, high-pitched voices speaking in *Urdu*. There was Bob's and at least one other, all talking so fast I couldn't make out a word. I began to tremble.

"Bob?" I called. "Bob? What is it? Who's there?"

Suddenly all sounds stopped. Then, just as suddenly, Bob screamed out in pain, and there was a crash and a quick series of loud bangs, as though someone was pounding on the wall with a hammer.

"Bob?" I leaped out of bed and flew to the door. My heart froze in my chest as I stared out into the dimly lit room. Bob was lying face up on the floor, a steady stream of blood seeping from a gash opened along his temple. In the doorway stood a towering man. He clutched a great wooden club in one hand and a small, pointed dagger in the other. He caught sight of me, his eyes stripping me down to my soul. I tried to scream, but nothing came out. He took one step forward, as if intending to silence me, and then he stopped. *"Farangi* traitors must die!" he spat in thick *Urdu*.

The Afghan whirled around--his long, cotton coat flailing out behind him like a great swirling cape--and disappeared into the night.

"Bob!" I cried, rushing to his side. I raised his head and placed my hand over the gash. He moaned softly as the warm blood trickled through my fingers and settled in a pool at my knees. "My God, Bob! You're bleeding. Bad."

I looked around, kicked the door closed, and I laid his head back down before running into the bedroom where I rummaged through our belongings until I found a small first-aid kit. Throwing open the top, I scattered the contents across the bed and picked out a small bottle of Mercurochrome and a roll of gauze. Racing back, I tore off a piece of the flimsy fabric and pressed it against his temple. The blood had already started to clot, the pressure slowing down the flow enough so that, working quickly, I was able to wind the remaining gauze around his head several times, enveloping the wound. I folded the end of the roll several thicknesses deep and tucked it up under the wrap.

Releasing the pressure on his temple, I waited for several moments until I saw a tiny red splotch show through the bandage.

Struggling to move him away from the door, I pulled him over to one wall and propped him up --anything to get his head elevated.

"Bob." I stroked his face. "Bob, can you hear me?"

His head moved slowly to one side, and his eyelids opened partially.

"Bob, it's me. Paula. Can you hear me?"

He groaned and looked up at me.

"Bob, listen to me. You're going to be all right. We're going to go to the clinic."

His hand reached out and grabbed my arm.

"It'll be all right. Everything will be all right. I'm going to go for help. I'll have the embassy contact Naim and tell him to bring the Jeep. You'll be okay."

"No," he said, suddenly clutching at me, his eyes opening wide. "No clinic."

"Bob, it'll be all right," I assured him. "We'll get you to a doctor."

"No, no doctor. I'm okay. I don't need anyone."

"But you're *bleeding*. You've got a bad gash on the side of your head. You may need stitches."

"No," he said again. "I just fell, that's all. Just a scratch. I don't need a doctor."

"Bob ..."

"You take care of me, fix me up."

Slowly he loosened his grip and rolled toward me. I took his head in my hands and worked my way behind him, cradling him in my lap.

"I'll be all right," he repeated. "You take care of me. I'll be all right."

NINE

I sat in a small meeting room the size of a postage stamp, green painted walls and concrete floor, a few windows overlooking the harsh countryside. The room doubled as the employee's lounge. A small row of metal cabinets lined one wall, next to a blackboard. Across from that, a wooden table held a small microwave oven.

I sipped absently from a cup of chai and stared out the window. What two days ago had been a starkly beautiful land had grown suddenly ugly--or perhaps it was my attitude that had changed. Where once trees sprouted with life, now there hung skeletons in brown and black, misshapen aberrations dotting the landscape, scarring it, making an ugly scene seem even more grotesque.

They don't belong in Afghanistan, those trees staring back at me. Nothing belonged in Afghanistan but the sand and the rats. Certainly not me. And not Bob.

Dinara had come in and slipped down into a chair across from me. She startled me when she spoke.

"I'm sorry," I said, clutching my chest. "I didn't see you come in."

"Apparently not. You seem preoccupied with something out there. What is it--the wolves?"

"What wolves?"

"Those vicious, man-eating creatures that descend upon Kabul each winter to devour all that stands in their way?" A wry smile crossed her lips.

"What *are* you talking about?"

She laughed. "Those are Michener's creatures. Haven't

you read *Caravans?*"

"James Michener? No. Why?"

"Well, in one passage of his book, a howling, hungry pack of wolves moves down from the sparsely timbered mountainside in search of food. They kill several people, some just for sport. The incident upsets the entire city, of course, especially the American and British Embassy personnel, who set off after them--to do what, I am not quite sure."

"There are no wolves in Kabul?"

"Not the four-legged kind."

I smiled. "It's all fiction, then?"

"Well"--she hesitated--"not all. There have been wolves spotted by shepherds in the outlying areas, where the wilderness still reigns and few men dare to travel. But it's not likely one would stray so close to civilization, *or* attack a human."

"Unless it was hungry?"

"It would die of starvation first. Wolves are notorious cowards. In that respect, they vary little from most people. So far as I know, there has never been a case of a wolf attacking a man without provocation. I'm sure it could happen if a man strays too close to a mother's den or tries to kidnap its babies for a zoo exhibit somewhere or to capture one to train as a dancing seal. But, even then, it's more likely that the mother would simply pick up as many cubs as she could carry and spirit them away, abandoning to the intruder those whose lives she could not save."

"I didn't know that. They have such a vicious reputation, at least in America."

"In much of the world, I believe ... perhaps due to the story, *Peter and the Wolf.*"

I smiled.

"Well, well," Dinara said, her shimmering black hair cascading over one shoulder as she cocked her head. I was amazed at the clarity of her skin, from her face down her neck, along her arms--the purity of it, the whiteness, the healthy look to it, so elastic and alive. "Do you realize that's the closest thing I've seen to a happy face from you all day?"

"I'm sorry. I guess I just haven't felt very ... smiley today."

"Do you wish to talk about it?"

I shook my head.

"You are sure?"

"I just don't know what to say."

"My uncle, Shah Khan, has a saying: When words fail you, speak from your heart."

"Your uncle is a liar!" I snapped. The words had just leaped out.

Dinara's brow lifted for an instant. "I have heard Shah Khan called many things by many people over the years, but never a liar. I wonder what pain is inside of you that makes you say such."

I lowered my head onto my folded arms and stared into my lap. "Your uncle said he would see to it that Bob didn't get into any more trouble with drugs."

"Shah Khan said that he would do what he could. On that, he gave his word."

I lifted my head and stared into her large brown eyes. "Last night we had a visitor. Someone broke into our hut. When Bob went to see what it was, he was jumped and beaten nearly senseless--by an Afghan."

"Oh, no. How badly is he hurt?"

"He has a deep gash on the side of his face. The blow missed one of his arteries by half an inch."

"Where is he now? Why didn't you bring him to the clinic?"

"He wouldn't come. He was afraid that if he didn't show up for work this morning, he would lose his job and be sent back to the states. I bandaged him up. I applied some pressure and got the bleeding to stop."

"And he is better?"

I shrugged. "He went to work."

"But what did the intruder wish? Did he say? Could you tell? Was he a thief? Kabul is filled with thieves who would rather take from others than work for their rightful share."

"He was no thief. He was a ... drug dealer. Bob said he thinks it was someone who sold him some drugs several months ago, back when he was still using."

Dinara shook her head. "I find it hard to believe that a dealer would do such a thing."

"Bob owed him money--nearly ten million *afghanis*--for some cocaine. He said he'd forgotten all about it, and I believe him. With the way he was using that stuff, with the shape he was in ..."

"But a dealer would not risk his own personal safety by attacking a man in Kabul--not for ten million *afghanis*, not for fifty million! There's not a dealer this side of Khumri who is not known to the police. He would be apprehended and imprisoned for life the moment he stepped within fifty kilometers of the city."

"But he *must* have been a dealer. Bob said ..."

"Did Bob recognize this man, or was he someone acting on behalf of a dealer?"

"I don't know." I thought for a moment, and I added, "No, I don't think he recognized him. I think Bob said he got the drugs through someone he knows--a friend. The friend gets them from a dealer Bob has never met."

"Did Bob say what his attacker looked like?"

"He didn't have to. I saw him."

"*No.*" The word had a flat ring to it. Dinara's eyes widened, and her face grew pale.

"Don't worry, he didn't harm me. For an instant, when I first saw him standing in the doorway, I thought he was going to ..." I breathed deeply, thinking back to the horror of the night. "But he muttered something in Persian and then he left."

"In Persian? Are you sure it was in Persian and not in *Pashto* ... or *Urdu*?"

"Yes--no. No, on second thought, it *was Urdu*, I think. Why? What difference does it make?"

"It makes a great deal of difference. Try to recall."

"Yes, yes it *was Urdu*, because I had trouble understanding him. He had such a thick accent, like someone from ..." I stopped as my brain sent a sudden charge of electricity racing through my body.

"From the hills," Dinara finished. "Yes. And what did he look like? How was he attired?"

"He had on a white cloth coat, very long, so that it swirled when he moved, and a wide red sash ... or brown-- it was hard to see in the dim light--and a turban ... I think. Oh, God, now I'm not sure! I just can't remember. It all happened so fast."

"And did he speak to you, or only to Bob?"

"He said something to me about *farangi* thieves. *Farangi* thieves must die ... something like that. No, it wasn't thieves. It was *traitors*. *Farangi traitors* must die. That's it. That's what he said."

Dinara stared intently out the window as though searching the landscape for something--something important, something hideous, as though looking at the brown and barren countryside would surrender something to her that it would never give up to me, a mere foreigner. "It was no dealer who visited your home and attacked your husband last night." She sighed. "And I doubt that there was anything even the great Shah Khan could have done to prevent it. I don't know how your husband escaped with his life."

These last few words were uttered softly, as though they had slipped out of her lips as an afterthought, without her knowing. I watched the expression on her face harden and her eyelids narrow to tiny slits. I hardened myself to ask.

"Well, who was it, then--a thief?"

"Not a thief. Not exactly."

I was puzzled. "Who, then?"

Dinara suddenly turned back to me. "Did this Afghan take anything from your home--money, jewelry, valuables of any sort?"

I shook my head. "It all happened so fast, he wouldn't have had time."

"And you say he was alone?"

I nodded.

"You saw no one else? You *heard* no one else?"

I shook my head. "Wait a minute." I suddenly remembered. "I *did* hear something."

"What?"

"Another voice. I think. Yes ... someone outside the door saying something--in Persian or *Urdu*, I'm not sure. I couldn't hear clearly. But someone said *something*."

"You're sure you didn't hear what?"

I shook my head. "Does it matter?"

"It could matter very much. It could be the reason you and your husband are alive today."

"Why?" I asked. "What are you talking about? Who were they? Who was the man who attacked Bob?"

"He was a drug dealer ..."

"But you said ..."

"*And* a thief."

I stared at her. She wasn't making any sense.

"*And*," she continued, "a Pashtun soldier."

My eyes involuntarily widened, and I leaned forward over the table. "A rebel?" I paused. "Here in Kabul? What would he be doing here?"

"The Pashtuns often earn money for their fight by selling drugs to Kabulis, who then sell them to the *farangis*. With the money they make from the sales, the rebels buy high-powered carbines from other governments, and shells for the guns, and even more powerful weapons, like mortars and machine guns and rocket-propelled grenades, when they can find them."

"But what did they want from Bob?"

"They must be preparing for an offensive somewhere, most likely against the Pakistanis. They are seeking funds for munitions. That is what they wanted from Bob. When a *farangi* promises a dealer money for the drugs he has received and fails to keep that promise ... well, more than one person has lost his life in that manner. Oh, the rebels may let the debt slide for a while, but sooner or later, the piper becomes due, as you say. They will take cash ... or take out payment in other ways. That is why I was surprised Bob did not meet a sterner fate."

Her last few words cut into my brain like a scalpel,

echoing over and over again, a loud voice crying out from deep inside a cave: *a sterner fate ... a sterner fate...*

"What can we do?" I felt my muscles tug involuntarily, my tendons tighten of their own will. "They didn't get any money. They didn't get anything. They ... they'll come back, won't they? They'll keep coming back until they get what it is they want."

"The simplest thing to do would be to pay them the money that is owed them. They are savage people, fierce warriors who would just as soon slit a man's throat as talk to him. They're a proud people, too. I remember my uncle talking about them, about how bravely they fought with him against the British, how fiercely they fought *against* him for control of the great poppy fields to the north of Pul-i-Khumri. When they feel that something is rightfully theirs, they will fight to the last man to get it. That is why the Pakistanis are having such great difficulty subduing them in the Northwest Frontier, even though the Pakistani soldiers outnumber the Pashtuns a thousand to one."

"But we don't have that kind of money--nowhere near that much. If you're talking about paying for the drugs that Bob ..."

"Then, you must borrow it."

"From whom? We know no one in Kabul who would loan us that much."

"I will speak to Shah Khan. Ten million *afghanis* to him is early morning dew on the flowers. He would surely loan that small an amount to his only niece. And I, in turn, will loan it to you for your husband."

"That's not possible. How would we pay you back? On what the Peace Corp gives us, it would take years."

"There will be no hurry." She rose and placed her hand on my arm.

"But ..."

"I will have the money for you tomorrow morning. Meanwhile, you should go to your husband at the university and tell him to meet us after work at my home. You will be my guests tonight. It will be safer if you don't return to your own home until you have the money in your hand."

I watched as Dinara walked toward the door, paused a moment, and looked back over her shoulder.

"Don't worry. It will be all right."

But I couldn't help worrying. The sight of the wild-eyed Pashtun kept dancing through my head. His words kept ringing in my ears. Not the words so much as the spiteful, hate-filled tone that carried them, a torrential rain on a blinding wind. I knew that Dinara hadn't exaggerated in describing the Pashtuns' fury when aroused. And I kept wondering how many other Pashtuns there would be, how many other terror-filled nights. If Bob couldn't recall owing money to one, how could he remember the others he might still owe? How many purchases had he made that he hadn't yet paid for? I couldn't take it anymore. First Bob's addiction, now this. Where would it all end? And when?

I reached for my cup, but I was shaking so hard I couldn't lift it from the table. I pushed it away and stared out the window. "If only I could push our troubles away as easily," I said softly. But I knew deep down inside that simply wasn't possible.

After Dinara gave me the rest of the day off, I stopped by the university to see Bob. He agreed to meet me at Dinara's after work. He also agreed that we had to get our lives in Kabul back on track--along with our marriage. Best of all, for the first time in a long time, he seemed serious.

After that, I went down to the Kabul marketplace to find a new winter coat. I'd brought my ski jacket with me to Afghanistan, but if November was any indication of what lay ahead, I'd need something a lot warmer to see me through the harsh winter that loomed ahead.

I entered the small main-street shop of Daod-Faisel around noon--not the best time of day to go shopping in Kabul. It was a typical Kabuli storefront showcasing a large open-air window with numerous pieces of pottery and some Afghani carpets on the hard brick floor. From the ceiling, bulbs hanging from their cords cast light onto two racks of clothing along the walls and one running down the center aisle, while two large fans whirred thanklessly overhead.

The proprietor--a funny-looking man, too short atop his long legs and too long for such a short, thick torso--wore a brushed cotton sports jacket of taupe-and-rose atop dark green trousers and blood-red oxfords. On his head sat a fez that gave his bulbous face far too much emphasis for its own good. Except that, when he smiled, his cheeks widened into a small ocean of warmth, and you felt that everything about him, from top to bottom, was perhaps not so out-of-sorts after all.

He came up to me, bubbling with enthusiasm, and shook my hand. He kissed it while bending deeply forward from the waist. It was obvious that he was anxious to wait on a rich American *farangi,* although he seemed equally anxious to close shop for lunch. I hoped his mounting hunger might work in my favor.

"How much is this one?" I asked about a mid-length coat with full sheepskin collar and cuffs.

"This one, for you ..." He thought momentarily, rubbing his chin stubble and peering up at me over small, wire-rimmed glasses. The glasses made him look more like an accountant than a furrier. "This I can let you *steal* from me for nine million *afghanis.*"

"Nine million? That's absurd."

"You are right," he said, practically pulling the coat from my shoulders. "I should have known better than to show you this coat. It is obviously more than an American can afford."

"I'll give you one million for it." I turned away from the small man and pulled the coat back around me. I pirouetted in front of a full-length mirror--one of two in the shop.

"I'm sorry, but that is out of the question. It cost me twice that much just to buy the fine Karakul lambskins from which I myself tailored this fine garment only last week."

"Really? There is a herdsman who grazes his sheep not three kilometers from my home who would sell me the same skins for five hundred thousand. Perhaps I should buy them from him and have you work them up into a coat."

"Yes, yes," he said, peering anxiously at his watch, "perhaps you should."

"Or, better still," I said, taking a short stroll around a table on which lay some fine-crafted leather boots, "I could give you his name, and you could buy your furs directly from him at quite a savings, which you could then pass along to me."

"Yes, yes, that would be fine, too."

"In that way, you could make fine-quality Karakul coats at a fraction of the price."

"I'm sure I could." He reached for the coat just as I turned and strolled back to the mirror.

"Of course, in the meantime, I would have nothing to protect me from the cold, harsh winds. And I do need protection. I can't afford to be sick this winter."

"None of us likes to be sick. That is why so many people would gladly pay four million *afghanis* for such a fine coat as this. And that is what I will sell it to you for. But I warn you, it is below my cost and my absolute final offer."

"You see, I'm a nurse at the clinic, and I must stay healthy in order to take care of our sickly patients."

"What's that you say? A nurse?" He rubbed his small, stubbled chin once more and looked the coat over closely as though for the first time. "In that case, I should let you *steal* the coat from me for, say, three million *afghanis* ... my absolute lowest price."

"It's such a shame." I paused, deep in thought. "I could pay, perhaps, one million-five. No more. You see..." I lowered my voice as though about to divulge some great government secret, "they pay American nurses very little at the clinic. Not that I complain, you understand. My reward comes not from money but from the satisfaction I get in caring for the sick and wounded, especially the little children. I do so love little children. Little Afghan children."

"You work with children, too?" He frowned.

"Yes."

He looked once more at his watch and seemed to be growing increasingly agitated. "Children are indeed a joy."

"Do you have any of your own?"

"Yes, yes, I have seven," he replied. "Now, if I could show the American nurse a shorter Karakul coat more in her price range ..."

"Then, perhaps I shall one day care for them, as well." I ran my hand up and down the sheepskin and admired the coat in the mirror.

"For whom?"

"For your children. You know, if they ever get sick and need care at the clinic ... Allah forbid."

"You speak Pashto very well." The man was beginning to sweat. "Perhaps *too* well."

I smiled, and I looked at my own watch. "My goodness, but it's getting late. Luckily, I have already eaten lunch, so I'm in no hurry."

"Lunch?" A sudden look of panic swept over him. "Yes. Yes, well, perhaps I could make the American nurse a very special offer."

"Oh?"

"Say, two-and-a-half million *afghanis*. That is below my own cost, as Allah is my witness."

"My husband would explode. He is a teacher at the great university right here in Kabul. He would never allow me to spend more than two million. And he would probably beat me for that!"

The door to the shop swung open, and a very attractive young woman strolled in. I watched as the man's eyes caught hers, and I was sure I saw her smile. She wore a plush coat of sheepskin, and her face, though veiled, still revealed two beautifully dark, expressive eyes. I watched those eyes smile at the shopkeeper before they quickly turned away as she pretended to examine several Karakul hats displayed on a table near the door.

"For the wife of a teacher at the university, perhaps two-million-three. But not a cent less!"

"I don't *know.*" I turned the coat collar up and rubbed my cheek against the soft, warm fur. "I'm sure we couldn't afford that. Yet, I do so want the coat. It would mean so much to know that I would be warm and protected from the cruel winter winds. Did I tell you we're with the Peace Corps? We came to Afghanistan this July from America. I was surprised at how hot your summers can be. We have a small hut just outside of town, down the main road. It's not very large. We couldn't afford what many people ..."

"All right, all right," he said in exasperation. "Two-million-two. And my brother will *die* when I tell him."

"Two-million-one," I countered.

The old man glanced nervously at the young woman, who herself had taken on a very anxious expression and seemed to be edging toward the door. "Very well. Two-million-one, and it is yours. Will you wear it?"

Before I could answer, he hastily scribbled out a receipt. I carefully counted out the money into the man's palm.

"Wear it in good health," he said, again looking toward the young woman. "And may Allah be with you."

As I strolled out of the store, I smiled at the young Afghan woman, who had lowered her *chaderi* long enough to reveal thick, lush lips beneath her dark hair and a clear complexion. She wore beauty as lightly as a whippoorwill's call on a starry night. I thought of stopping to thank her as I passed through the door. Obviously, but for her, I would still be wearing my ski jacket.

I hadn't gone more than ten steps under the clear, cold sky when I stopped to rub the collar of my new coat against my face. Suddenly a familiar voice behind me spoke so softly I wasn't sure I had heard it at all.

"It looks good on you."

I turned and saw him. The man I'd met at the market.

He had caught me by surprise, but this time it was a pleasant surprise. I had wondered when I might see him again, wondered when I would get to know more about him, get to ask him ... so very much. Now, more than ever.

"What?" I fed him my coolest, least interested look.

"That coat is you. Is it new?"

Despite my determination to remain aloof, I cracked a small smile.

"Did I say something amusing?"

"I'm sorry, but you sound like a bad poet: 'It is you. Is it new?'"

He grinned and shook his head. "Only an American *farangi* would take a compliment and turn such a compliment into a joke. In the future," he said through thin, tight, smiling ups, "I shall have to choose my words more carefully. I can see that."

"Oh?" I raised my brows and half-turned from him so that I looked past the vendors lining both sides of the street. "And what makes you think there will *be* a future?"

He took hold of my arm as he had done the first day we met, but more gently. "What is there to life ... without a future?"

"A quote from the classics?"

He shook his head. "A quote from Shadar."

I turned around to face him. "Shadar? Is *that* your name?"

He bowed low, emulating an English nobleman, and craned his neck upward. "At your service."

"That's a good way to throw out your back," I said flatly, turning out into the street. I strolled across the thoroughfare to the shop of a small vendor on the other side. I stopped and stared in amazement. "That ... that's my coat," I said to no one in particular, pointing to a small rack of Karakul wraps hanging behind a table. "That's my coat *exactly*."

Shadar came up behind me just as a short, balding Afghan emerged from behind the rack. "*Ahh*, the young lady and her gentleman friend wish to purchase a Karakul coat for the coming winter? It is an excellent idea. One cannot have too much of a good thing."

"No, no. I just bought this in there. Just this very minute." I pointed to the small shop across the street.

The old man slammed his palm against the side of his head. "Why did you do that?"

"Because I needed a coat, and because he gave me a good price."

"A good price?" The man spat into the dust at the edge of the street. "Daod-Faisel? He is a thief and a jackal. He would charge his own mother a hundred times more than the coat cost him and still not be satisfied."

"No. Really. He gave me a very good price." I paused, glancing from the man to Shadar and back. "*Really*."

"Oh?" the man replied, raising his brows in disbelief. "So he gave you a good price? And what, may I ask, did the pretty young *farangi* pay for so magnificent a coat as this?"

"One-and-a-half million *afghanis*," I lied.

"One-and-a-half million!" His eyes rolled upward, and, for a moment, I thought he was going to fall to his knees right in the street. "One-and-a-half million, and I sold him that very coat only this morning for three hundred thousand and still made fifty thousand on the deal!"

"You didn't! I don't believe it."

"I *told* you he was a thief."

I felt the blood pulsing through my veins, my temperature rising by the second. "He *did* cheat me!" I turned to Shadar. "He said he bought the skins from some herdsman and sewed the coat himself!"

"Liar!" the man cried as a small crowd of spectators gathered. "May Allah damn him to eternity for his sins!"

Shadar stepped forward. "The young and beautiful American *farangi* wishes to know what you would have charged her for the very same coat."

I turned to see Shadar rummaging through his pockets before finally extracting a brown goatskin wallet.

"*Ahh*," the merchant smiled, his voice growing suddenly softer. "I didn't realize the lady was with you."

His eyebrows lifted and fell, and a large, toothy grin crossed his face. "In that case, I should be a thief if I charged anything more than eight hundred thousand *afghanis.*"

"You should be a thief if you charged any more than *three* hundred fifty thousand," Shadar said.

"*Three-fifty?* That is an insult! Why, this coat cost me …"

"Two hundred and fifty thousand *afghanis,*" Shadar said. "At least, that's what you told us you paid for it only a moment ago. And I'm sure *you* are not the same lying, cheating jackal that Daod-Faisel is, preying on the misfortunes and innocence of others. Allah would not smile on such as that."

A loud buzz of agreement rose up from the Afghans who had heard the harangue with the shopkeeper, like the singular notes of a cantata from a string quartet, the crowd gradually pressing in on all sides the better to see the confrontation firsthand.

"So here," Shadar continued, "are three hundred fifty thousand *afghanis,* for which we will gladly accept this fine Karakul coat." He reached over the table and pulled the coat from the rack. "I trust that is agreeable, that it is an honest man's profit."

The crowd again murmured its consent, and the merchant smiled sheepishly and pocketed the money, all the while muttering softly under his breath.

Shadar, clutching the coat, took my arm as we worked our way out of the assembly.

"That was pretty slick. I can see I'm in the presence of bargaining royalty."

"It was only right. The old man and Daod-Faisel often prey upon *farangis* so. It is a game they play. When one sells a Karakul coat or sweater or hat, the other tells the purchaser he was robbed and offers to make up for it by selling a second item at a lower price. If you had gone to the street merchant first, he would have charged you ten million *afghanis,* if he thought he could have gotten it."

"Why, those two crooks!"

"Most Kabulis know of their little game and enjoy the rare occasions when it backfires. At least now you have two coats for your money." He held out the second Karakul coat. "For you."

"But I don't *need* two coats."

"Don't be foolish. Take it; otherwise you'll be out the two-million-one you paid to Daod-Faisal, and I'll be stuck with a woman's coat I don't need."

"How did you know I paid that?"

"How did I know you paid what?"

"How did you know I paid Daod-Faisel that much for the coat? I told the street merchant I paid a million-and-a-half."

He thought for several seconds, his brow contorted, and he finally shrugged. "That is easy enough to answer. I followed you to the store and eavesdropped while you were dickering with the owner."

"You followed me? Why?"

"Well, I ... wanted to be sure you were not taken advantage of by my own people. And, I must say, you learn our ways fast. Unfortunately, you're not quite in a league to compete with our craftiest vendors ... *yet*."

"Well, thank you for your concern and kind compliments, but I couldn't take your coat. You bought it; it belongs to you."

"Well, then, I'll tell you what we'll do. You sell me *your* coat for what you paid Daod-Faisel." He opened his wallet and counted out some money from a large fold of bills.

"Why would I do that? Then I would end up back where I started, without a coat."

"But you won't. I'll sell you *my* coat for three-hundred-fifty thousand *afghanis*. That way, neither of us will lose."

"Except you. You'll be out ..." I added it up in my head. "You'll be out nearly two million *afghanis*."

"Look at it this way: These are my countrymen; I feel responsible. Let me salve my aching conscience by allowing me, at least, to refund the overage you paid to

Daod-Faisel."

I shook my head. "Absolutely not. I'm afraid your conscience will just have to ache. Besides, I'm not at all convinced your conscience is the real reason you want to reimburse me."

"What other reason could I possibly have?"

"I'm not sure, but I suspect you have an ulterior motive."

"I never have ulterior anythings. Well, perhaps I should not say *never*."

"*Um-hmm*. I thought so. But I told you before. I'm married!"

"Yes." He sighed, shaking his head. "But that is not the motive of which I speak."

"It's not? What, then?"

"I will tell you over lunch if you have not eaten yet. I know a very fine café just around the corner."

"*Uh-huh*. Well, if that's not your motive, you're wasting a really good line."

"Honestly," he said, suppressing a smile. "Look into these eyes and tell me what you see. Is this the face of a liar?"

I leaned forward and searched for several seconds as he bent toward me. They were dark, strong, honest eyes. His skin wore the weathered look of a farmer or a herdsman; yet his hands were smooth and free from the roughness farmers' hands develop from their daily chores.

"Well, go on. Tell me. What do you see?"

"I see a very strange Afghan man who speaks perfect English, and I'm puzzled by it and by him. But I still don't trust you."

He shook his head and took me by the arm. "*Farangis!*"

We turned the corner to a small outdoor café, a shop called *Yeh Thora Parind*--The Little Bird--where the owner met us at the front door and smiled broadly. We exchanged handshakes and a few poor attempts at humor in English. The proprietor, a short, stocky man in his mid-to-late forties, wearing a turban and a brightly colored print shirt over beige pants, took our orders. Chicken with curry sauce and almonds for me, and fish with rice and peppers for Shadar. In the back of the café, I could see the large, open grill over which the chef toiled happily, as though cooking were the only thing in his life that mattered. I could hear him humming and singing, that high-pitched nasal wail so common to the countryside. Nearly half a dozen tables were filled, some by university students, a few by *farangis* in suits, some by Afghan businessmen. I looked at Shadar and broke into a smile.

"What?"

"I'm sorry. But the chef ... his voice ..."

"Yes? What about it?"

"It's terrible! I hope he is not the 'little bird' after which this café is named!"

Shadar laughed. "Shall I call him over, then, so that you may ask him to his face?"

I panicked. "No! No, my God. I would never ..."

I looked at the sly smile working its way up from his lips into his eyes before he spoke. "It wouldn't matter to Ahmad. I tell him he has a terrible voice all the time. He just laughs and says he would rather have a terrible voice than no voice at all."

"It must be nice to be that happy." The smell from the grill, from the roasting bird, the lamb, and the goat dishes waved gently across the room, stopping passers-by who squinted into the darkened café before shrugging and moving along, perhaps promising to return another day. A few could not resist and were quickly met at the door and escorted in.

After some small talk, a little verbal sparring, some sharing of my background with him, I found myself wondering certain things. Would I have the courage to ask? Or maybe he would voluntarily share something of his inner self. He had hinted that he was self-employed, which I took to mean that he either owned his own business or drifted aimlessly across the shifting sands of the desert. Yet, he didn't look like any entrepreneur I'd ever known.

After several minutes, the owner brought our lunches and set the plates before the two hungriest customers in the room. Shadar thanked him and ordered our tea.

"So? What do you think?" He bit into his second mouthful of fish, grilled golden brown, rich in its own bastings, while I pursued my own entree, seared to perfection and carrying the scars of the grill, which had been maintained at the perfect temperature for its task.

"*Mmmm!*" I pointed to my mouth. "*Mmmm.* Just a minute ..." I swallowed, breathed out, and took a sip of water.

"Yes? No?"

"Oh, God, yes! It's magnificent. I can't believe how juicy it is, how tender. And your fish?"

He pulled a bit of it over to one side of his plate, spearing it at the end of his fork before handing it to me.

"*Ummm. Ummm*, this is great, too." I handed the fork back to him. As he took it, his hand brushed mine. He turned toward the kitchen and sent a thumbs-up sign across the room, and as I looked back over my shoulder, I saw Ahmad smile and throw a kiss toward our table.

I glanced at Shadar, stuffing himself as though he hadn't eaten in weeks, or perhaps expected not to do so again. He motioned with his fork.

"What? Me? More about me?"

He nodded, swallowed, and drew a breath from the steaming tea. "*Ahh*, yes. All I know of you so far is that you are a nurse at the clinic, you are here with your husband, a teacher at the university. And you are not very happy."

I paused. "I never said I wasn't happy."

He nodded. "Yes. You did."

"When?"

"When Ahmad was singing. You said it must be nice to be so happy."

"I didn't mean ..."

He held up his hand. "It does not matter. Are you happy now?"

"But ..."

He reached suddenly across the table, pressed a finger against my lips, pursing his own as you would talk to an infant. "*Shhh*. It does not matter. What matters is ... are you happy *now*?"

I smiled as he withdrew his hand. "How could I not be? This is the best meal I've had since we left the states."

"And?"

I looked at him. "Oh, and, of course ... the best company."

He broke into a toothy grin, his rugged good looks standing out all the more against the dark brown of the clay wall behind him.

"Except ..."

He paused, the smile fading suddenly from his face. "What? I have done something to displease you? I know. I eat like a pig. That's it, isn't it? I eat like a swine."

I chuckled. "No, your manners are impeccable. But you haven't told me anything about *you*. Do you always make it a habit of picking up young, married *farangi* women and taking them to lunch? Do you work for a living? Are you married, divorced, separated? Are you independently wealthy? A mass murderer? A student?"

He swallowed. "Yes."

"Yes? Yes to what?"

He placed his knife on the edge of the plate and finished filling my cup with tea and set the pot off to one side. "Yes, I am a mass murderer."

"Oh, great. Thanks."

He laughed. "Actually, there is not all that much to tell. I'm afraid my life is not so filled with drama and intrigue and adventure as yours, traveling to a foreign land, working with exotic new people. I, on the other hand, was born very near here, in a small village just north and west of Kabul. I went to school here, attended some colleges in America, came home, got a job, got married, and settled down to a life of eternal bliss."

"*Ohhhh*," I said, absently. "I was right. You *are* married." I tried not to sound disappointed and couldn't understand why I felt so. What should it matter to me, anyway? Deep down inside, I had pictured him as a lone wolf, a solo rider, someone who lived, worked, played, and traveled only for himself. Perhaps it was that he didn't seem the marrying type. Perhaps he seemed the type who was filled with the need for adventure, a lust for life, a larger-than-real action hero. Someone who could enthrall me with tall tales of high adventure. I wasn't at all expecting to hear tall tales of high tea.

"I said I *got* married, not that I *am* married. My wife died three years ago in a plane crash."

"Oh. I'm so sorry."

He shrugged. "Who can understand the will of Allah?"

"But that still doesn't explain how you came to speak such perfect English. You went to college in the states. Still, a few years are hardly enough time to learn to speak English as well as you do."

"A few years, no. But also seven years in Berlitz, the language school?"

"Berlitz? You must have wanted to learn to speak perfect English pretty badly."

"My ... *position* at the time required it of me."

"What position was that?"

"I worked for a large international organization that specializes in inter-global trading."

"So, you were a salesman?"

He chuckled. "Something like that, I guess you could say. But enough. Let's talk more about you."

I seemed to detect a sudden nervousness in his tone, and I wondered if it had something to do with his former job. "What did you sell?"

"What?"

"You said you were a salesman. I asked what it was that you sold."

"It's really not important," he said again, pushing his plate aside and dabbing his lips with a silk cloth.

"But, I'm curious. I'd like to know."

He looked straight at me, squinted slightly, and replied, "Guns."

"*Guns?*"

He motioned me to lower my voice. "It's not something everyone in this room should know."

"I'm sorry," I whispered. "I just wasn't sure I'd heard you right."

He nodded. "Yes, you heard me right."

"Was it some secret-type thing--you know, selling guns to the military or the rebels?" I could feel my eyes light up, my pulse racing at the thought. This was more like what I had expected. Here sat the most intriguing, the most mysterious man I had met in ages telling me he had worked as a salesman when actually he was a gun runner! It was a staggering thought, almost frightening. It made Shadar seem all that much more exciting ... and dangerous.

"No, no. Nothing like that. I bought guns from the U.S. and sold them, with the full knowledge and consent of both of our governments, to developing third-world nations."

"For revolutions?"

He hesitated, cocking his head, and laughed. "You do have the strangest sense of curiosity."

"Well?"

"Well, hardly for revolutions. At least not that I know of. These were hunting guns--shotguns, .22-caliber rifles, things such as that."

"Hunting guns!" Once again my excitement level plunged to the basement. "I don't believe it. Then, why so hush-hush? Why so secretive?"

"In this part of the world, when you mention the sale of guns, many people would ... get the wrong impression." He must have seen the disappointment in my eyes, for he reached out and touched my hand. "Have I let you down?"

"No, no," I lied. "It's just ... I mean, I thought ..."

"Yes." He nodded. "I know. That is exactly what everyone thinks. But tell me ..." He motioned to my plate. "After your meal, what? Are you filled, or have you saved room for dessert?"

"Oh, no. I am *stuffed*. Really. I've never had this dish

before. It really is magnificent. So simple, yet so elegant, if that makes any sense."

"I'm glad to hear that. This has always been one of my favorite restaurants. The owner loves to see me come in. He knows I always bring a hearty appetite--and, of course, a thick wallet."

"About that ..." I paused.

"About what?"

"I mean, you said you used to sell guns. But you haven't told me what you do for a living now."

"Oh, I guess you Americans would call me a gadabout. Sort of a jack-of-all-trades. I do a little of this, a little of that, whatever is needed." He pulled out his wallet and began fishing through it for some bills.

"You make good money for a gadabout."

He smiled. "There is good money all around if one knows where to search for it."

"Tell me where."

"Well, the Russians and Germans and French, for example, are always seeking good, reliable workers with strong backs for many of the construction projects going on in Afghanistan."

"You work on a construction crew?"

"At times, yes."

"Building what?"

"Sometimes roads, sometimes bridges, sometimes buildings. It all depends on what my government feels is of the most pressing nature at the time. That may change from day to day."

He noticed me looking at his hands. "Don't let them fool you," he said as if reading my mind. "They're small, but they're strong."

"My father was in construction. His hands were always rough, callused, cut. Yours seem so smooth, like the hands of an artist."

"I take care of them." He pulled his hands back as though I'd suddenly embarrassed him. "Are you sure you would not like some dessert? I'm afraid my country's desserts aren't nearly as glamorous as what you're used to, but ..."

"No, thank you. I've already had more than I usually eat for lunch. I'm *stuffed*."

"Well, then, I take that as a compliment, for the prophets say, 'When one eats to capacity, one knows the fullness of life.'"

I stared at him for several moments. Though we had only met, I felt comfortable with him, secure, as though we'd been friends for ages. Partly, I suppose, because of the lack of any detectable accent in his voice, but also because he seemed to care about me. That's something I'd been missing and was relieved to have found again. In *anyone*.

"What are you looking at?"

"Oh, I'm sorry. I was just thinking."

"About?"

"About why it was we came to lunch. About that motive of yours, remember? You said you'd tell me over lunch, and you haven't said a word about it."

A sudden pained expression came over his face. His eyes grew sad, as though he'd lost a loved one or a good friend. "It is hard to discuss."

"Shadar ... I was only kidding. But you ... you are serious. You *did* have an ulterior motive."

"It's about last night."

I sat up straight. A sharp chill raced through my body. I was afraid to ask; yet I heard the words come tumbling out. "What about last night?"

"About what you ... and your husband ... went through."

My mouth fell in astonishment. "How do you know about that? I told no one except my closest friend only this morning, and she would never ..."

"There are times when one should not ask questions but merely listen carefully." He leaned forward and pulled his chair closer to the table. "I know what happened last night, and I know how you must feel. I just wanted to tell you that it was all a mistake, that neither you nor your husband will ever be bothered by them again. Ever."

My heart leaped inside of me. Had this been the other Afghan I heard outside the door to our hut? Was he a Pashtun rebel after all? Did he have something to do with the attack on Bob?

"How do you know about last night?"

"I cannot tell you that. I can say no more except that I am sorry for whatever anxieties you may have experienced because of the incident, and I assure you it will not happen again."

"I don't know if I should thank you or throw this cup of tea in your face. You know all about last night, and yet you ..."

"Some things are better off left unspoken. And as for the tea ..." He paused. "I would just as soon a simple thank you."

I stared into his eyes. They were stern, confident, caring. Mine were still too shaken to move. My hand clutched the corner of the table. But as I looked at him, looked through his eyes down into his heart, I believed him. For some reason, I believed him. His words were slow and sure. He had not the slightest quiver in his voice as he spoke, the way people do when making up a lie. Those eyes, more than anything, that told me he was telling the truth, that he sincerely cared about what had happened to Bob and me. Suddenly I looked beyond him and spotted a familiar face.

"What is it?"

"It's Naim, a friend, a young boy I know from the American Embassy."

Shadar grasped my hand and leaned far over the table, coming so close that I feared for a moment he was going to kiss me. "I must go," he said softly. "But I will see you again. Soon."

"What? Where are you going? When will I see you?"

"I don't know." He placed several *afghanis* on the corner of the table. "But if you ever need me, if you ever need anything in Kabul, don't hesitate to call on me. I live in a large home three doors down from the corner behind the post office. Remember, three doors down."

Before I could respond, he got up and disappeared as if by magic through a curtained doorway opposite the entranceway to the street. I sat thinking for a while, wondering what had happened. It seemed like a dream-- the suddenness of our meeting, Shadar's abrupt departure.

"Hello," Naim said, bringing me back to reality. "I did not expect to find you here."

"Naim, what are you ..."

"I am picking up lunch for Sahib Ingersoll. The proprietor here makes an excellent chicken-and-rice dish that Sahib enjoys to eat." Naim looked after Shadar before motioning toward the curtains.

"Is that a friend of yours?"

"Yes. Well, no. Not really a friend. Actually, we met at the market several days ago. He's a salesman or ..."

"I think, then, maybe he was not the person I believed him to be. In the darkness of the café, it is sometimes difficult to distinguish faces."

"Who did you think it was?"

"For a moment, I thought it was a freedom fighter who sometimes comes to Kabul for supplies."

"A freedom fighter?"

"Yes," he said. "A Pashtun rebel."

TEN

The night came and passed quickly. The next day, Dinara gave me ten million *afghanis*, as promised. I told neither Bob nor her about Shadar and the incident at the café. I didn't want to alarm either of them. Besides, I wasn't sure that he actually *was* a rebel--or anyone, for that matter, who might affect our stay in Afghanistan.

Yet, as Shadar had said, no one else had come calling, despite the ominous warning that fateful night. It was as if someone, somewhere, had put the word out that we were taboo, off-limits to the special brand of violence and aggression, the peculiar form of punishment and justice so widespread in Afghanistan and alien to us in the Western world. Still, I was anything but relaxed during the week that followed-- tottering at the brink of a steep cliff, ready to leap back to safety. Or tumble over the precipice into only God knew what.

I hadn't seen Shadar at the market since the day of our lunch, which made me wonder if Naim had been right. Maybe he really *was* a freedom fighter. Perhaps he had suddenly been called back to the Frontier where the Pashtuns had been battling for independence from Pakistan. I began to wonder if I would ever see him again. Was he alive and well ... or lying in a ditch somewhere with a gaping hole in his heart from a Pakistani carbine?

Bob, too, was edgy. But that had been a way of life with him since we'd left the states. He feared another attack, as well he might since he'd been getting his drugs from three different sources and couldn't recall whether or not he had squared accounts with any of them.

It was Sunday, one week after the attack, when I approached him about something that had been playing on my mind. It was time, I had finally concluded. I'd had enough.

"Bob," I said as we sat on the sofa, "I want to go home."

He looked up from the paper he'd been reading. "What?"

"I said I want to leave the Peace Corps, leave Afghanistan, and go back home."

"What are you talking about? We've got a job to do. We signed a contract. We can't go home, not until our stint is up."

"This isn't the French Foreign Legion. We can quit anytime we want to."

"Sure, and lose all our back pay."

"I'd rather lose that than my sanity, and I'm going crazy over here. I just can't take it anymore. Nothing seems worthwhile. Nothing seems to matter, not when our safety, our happiness, is at stake. I want us out of here, and soon."

"Look. Let's not get crazy here." He slid over and wrapped his arm around my shoulders. "We'll be done and on our way home before you know it. We've only got a year-and-a-half to go. What happened here the other night *happened*. Nothing is going to change that. But it's over with. You've seen that. We haven't had a speck of trouble since. It was just an isolated incident. I'm not even sure anymore if I owed *anyone* any money. That guy who attacked me was probably just some drug-crazed Afghan who thought he'd found an easy mark. But it's over, so just try to forget about it."

"It's *not* over. The memories aren't over. The nightmares keep coming, night after night." I began to sob, pressing my head against his shoulder. "I'm sorry, but I can't take anymore, Bob, I just can't."

"Hey, hey, hey, come on, now. That's not the girl I married. Where's my little scrapper, where's the little trooper who wanted to come to Afghanistan with me to help change the world? Where's the gal who wanted to see Asia, who wanted to savor life, to enjoy new experiences?"

"She's dead," I said softly, "and so is the dream. Now all I want to do is get out."

He pulled his arm away and squirmed to reach his wallet. Opening it up, he pulled out a small sheet of paper. "Here. Look at this."

I took the paper from him. It was a clipping from the local English newspaper. "Wanted: full-time employee to act as translator for large multinational corporation. Excellent salary; good benefits. Applicants should speak fluent English, Persian, and *Pashto*. To be stationed in Kabul. Generous relocation expenses paid. Write Box 4073."

"What's this about?" I grabbed a tissue and dabbed at the tears in my eyes.

"It's a job. I applied for it last Tuesday. I wasn't going to tell you about it until I heard back from them. I didn't want you to get your hopes up."

"Here in Kabul?"

"Here in Kabul. But with the kind of money they pay, we could live anywhere we wanted. We could rent a villa outside of town ... a palace, if we want. We could even buy a place of our own. Have our own maid, our own gardener. Whatever you want."

"But, it's still here in Kabul, and I don't feel safe here anymore."

"Well, you're going to have to *learn* to feel safe. I'm telling you, if I get this job, we can *buy* our safety. We can buy anything we've ever wanted."

"But what about what we're doing now? What about the Peace Corps? If we quit, wouldn't they send us back to the states? They wouldn't just let us stay here ..."

"Fuck the Peace Corps! We can quit any time we want, like you said. Once we have enough money. So, if that's what's bothering you, the Corps, well, hell, we'll just leave them. You could take a vacation, go back to the states to visit your folks for a while if you want. Then come back and join me here. We'll be able to afford to travel if I get this job, as often as we want, anywhere we want to go."

"And ... and, for how long? I mean, do you have any idea what ..."

"I'd work for them just long enough to get a little seniority so I could request a transfer back to the states. They could just as easily use my skills as a translator in New York or Chicago or L.A. as they can here. They must need people all over the world."

"And I'd get to quit the Corps?"

"Sure, if you want. Or you could stay on at the clinic. Quit the Corps but keep working with Dinara. Hell, the Corps wouldn't care. Ingersoll would see to that. And the clinic would be delighted. But the important thing is, it would be up to you. It would *all* be up to you. You wouldn't *have* to stay on. You wouldn't *have* to do anything. Not unless you wanted to. And I'll have my first real job--a good-paying job, the kind I've always told you I was going to get."

"What's the company's name, do you know?"

He shook his head. "*Uh-uh*. I asked around, and there are several multinational corporations with branch offices here in Kabul. It could be any one of them."

"How long would you have to work for them before you had enough seniority to get transferred back to the states?"

He shrugged. "Who knows--maybe six months, maybe two years. It's hard to say. But if we find out after a while that things aren't going the way we want, I could quit and, with the experience I get here in Afghanistan, get a translator's job with the U.S. government or with another large company back home. Maybe even at the United Nations."

"Do you think so? Oh, Bob, don't string me along here. Could you really do that? I mean, if it was best for us both?"

"Of course I could. Don't you see? This is perfect. It's a golden opportunity. It's what we've been waiting for. A chance to get a great job and lots of experience. A chance to write our own tickets back to the states, to live and work anywhere we want."

It was a nice thought--going home again. And Bob seemed excited about the job, more excited than I'd seen him in months. Still, I wasn't sure. I had to admit it sounded ideal. I mean, they were looking to hire someone to move to Kabul, and we were already here!

On the other hand, it almost sounded too good to be true, and Bob sounded too much like all the other times with all the other half-baked schemes he'd concocted over the years. I couldn't let myself be sucked in yet one more time. Not again. So I told him we would see. We would see what happened with his application, see what happened with the Peace Corps, with Afghanistan, with Kabul, with us. We would play it by ear, make the best of whatever happened. We would see.

But as Christmas approached, I found myself growing more depressed. Bob had gotten the job with Monrovia, and it seemed to be everything he said it would. They were a German-based corporation with strong corporate ties in the Middle East. He even had a title: Assistant Vice-President of International Communications. But whatever hope I had for our lives getting better never materialized. If anything, Bob's work kept him away from home longer than his job at the university had. And the fact that few people in Kabul considered Christmas anything but another workday didn't do much to bolster my spirits.

It helped some that we received a package from my parents. It was stuffed with Wisconsin baked ham, cheese, and salami, as well as some imported chocolates. In turn, we sent them goat-cheese curds, halva, and wild rice imported from Bombay, plus two pairs of Karakul mittens. It wasn't much, but it was enough to show them we were thinking about them.

Christmas Eve fell on a Thursday, and both Bob and I worked as usual. Bob, in fact, had to work late to finish up some loose ends before the holiday.

The snows, as if on cue, had arrived several days earlier. I bundled up in my Karakul coat against the cold northwest winds and walked home from the clinic the afternoon of the 24th. The flurries danced and swirled through the air, each flake a tiny ballerina putting on a show. Bob was making enough money now so that I could have quit the Corps, but that would have meant enduring the long, lonely days at home. I wasn't ready for that. And, with jobs as hard to come by as they were, there was little hope of my finding work outside the Corps. Besides, Dinara wasn't sure if they could have hired me if I quit, since their original contract was with the embassy, who had contracted with the Corps. I probably could have gotten a job at the embassy doing secretarial work or something, but I couldn't *stand* the thought of being in the same building with Ingersoll. So, I decided to stay on at the clinic until my stint with the Corps was up. By that time, I hoped Bob would be ready to transfer back home.

On my walk home, I turned the corner and headed past the post office when I stopped. At first, I thought I might go in to check for mail. But I'd already received all the holiday correspondence I was expecting, and I had nothing more to send out. Then, gradually, I became aware of my eyes searching up the alleyway beyond the post office, searching out a house--the third house from the corner, Shadar's house. I'd all but forgotten about him in the weeks leading up to Christmas. With Bob's changing jobs and Christmas shopping and all, I hadn't time to think about phantoms and rebels and gun-runners.

I forced the image of the handsome young Afghan once more from my mind. And when I came to the American Embassy, I instinctively turned in. I was desperate for some holiday spirit. Surely *they* would have a Christmas tree with all the trimmings, the lights, and maybe even a plastic angel or a lighted star on top. And hopefully, George Ingersoll would be nowhere in sight.

I entered the waiting room and stopped. *Oh, yes! Look at that. Oh, my goodness.* There it was. It was puny--a store-bought plastic tree--but it was a *tree*. With its spindly trunk and sparsely placed branches, it looked more like a mop stick with green spray-painted coat hangers springing out in all directions. But it had lights and icicles and ornaments, and there were garlands and strings of popcorn running round and round like a spiral staircase from the base to the very tip, where the garland surrendered to a gaudy, gold plastic star.

I stood there looking at the tree for what seemed like an hour until the marine on duty walked into the room.

"Oh," he said, startled to find me there. He snapped to attention. "May I be of service, *ma'am*?" The words were crisp and loud and somehow didn't seem to fit the occasion.

I looked down at a small plastic manger beneath the boughs, at the figures huddled around the crib. Slowly I bent down for a closer look. "There's no Mary," I said softly.

"Beg your pardon, ma'am!" the marine said.

I looked up at him through blurry eyes. "I said there's no figure of Mary here."

"No, ma'am."

"Why not? What happened to her?"

"I'm not sure, ma'am!"

I felt suddenly foolish, childish, like a little girl playing tea party with her dolls and discovering one of the saucers missing.

"May I help you, ma'am?" the marine repeated.

I rose slowly and looked one more time at the tree. "No," I said finally. "I was just leaving."

I had never realized how difficult getting into the holiday spirit in a non-Christian country could be until we moved to Afghanistan. Bob and I had planned to have a small Christmas dinner of baked ham and yams with bulgur wheat and unleavened bread. It was as close to traditional turkey and stuffing as we could come.

As I sat beneath the lamp, reading from a book of poetry I'd purchased at the university bookstore, I was surprised by a knock at the door. At first, I thought it was Bob, and then I thought Naim. But, when I went to the door and called out, a strange voice answered in Persian. It was a messenger.

"Delivery for Paula Favage."

"Can you slip it under the door?" I asked, afraid to un-latch the lock.

"It's too large," the messenger said.

"Then, just leave it outside. My husband and I are busy right now. We'll get it later."

"My instructions are to present it personally to Mrs. Paula Favage," the voice replied.

I glanced over at the loose board beneath which I'd hidden the ten million *afghanis* Dinara had loaned me. I'd placed it there for safekeeping--from thieves and from Bob, who might be tempted to use it for ... I wasn't quite sure what. He'd been furious when I refused to tell him where I'd hidden it. He said I didn't trust him, that I was just as much as accusing him of still being a junkie. But I wouldn't relent. I felt a special obligation to give the money back to Dinara as soon as I was convinced we wouldn't need it. I wanted to be sure it would be there--*all* of it--when the time came.

Slowly, cautiously, I unlatched the door. With the toe of my foot wedged firmly against the heavy wooden planks, I cracked it open. There stood a young boy, innocent-looking enough. In his hand he held a small package, neatly wrapped in red paper and topped with a blue bow. I opened the door wider and took the package from him, thanked him, and quickly closed and latched the door.

I listened for several moments to the crunch of the boy's footsteps on the snow-encrusted path. Only when I'd heard the metallic clang of the front gate did I let out a long, deep sigh and dare to look down at the package in my hands. It was not much larger than a small teacup and quite carefully wrapped. It reminded me of the packages I used to have wrapped at Gimbel's back in Wisconsin. For a moment, I thought about placing it under the tree, a small potted fig Bob and I had dug up and brought in before the snows blew down off the steppes. I had decorated it with several yarn bows and spotlighted it from behind with a small reading lamp.

Finally, my curiosity got the better of me, and I slipped my fingers beneath the edge of the paper. Removing the top, I found more tissue, and inside that, a ring--a magnificent gold ring adorned with three small diamonds.

"Oh, Bob!" I cried out loud, taking the ring out and slipping it onto my finger. It was too large, but it fit my middle finger perfectly. As I held it up, admiring its beauty, the jewels caught the light from the lamp and sent it shimmering across the room in a dozen tiny sprays of green, yellow, and blue.

It was the most beautiful ring I had ever seen, the most thoughtful gift I'd ever received. I suddenly realized that my spirits were sky high. I was flying on a cloud of joy, and it was absolutely wonderful. How insignificant the gifts I'd gotten Bob seemed in comparison. I thought about rushing to town to try to buy him something more, but it was late ... and dark.

I quickly rummaged through the tissue for a card or note and finally found a small slip of white paper folded once, lying in the bottom of the box. Taking it out, I opened it and held it up to the light:

"For the joy you have brought to me, from your land to mine."

I thought for a moment. "That's odd," I mused aloud. "From your land to ..." And then it struck me. "*Shadar*!"

I searched the paper for some clue, a signature, an initial. Nothing. "It *must* be from him." A flush of excitement swept my face. He was alive. And well!

Outside, I heard a car door slam, followed by several loud voices. I slipped the ring from my finger and tucked it safely into my pocket. I gathered up the box, note, and paper and threw them into the stove, where they burst into flame.

"Paula, open up! It's me!" Bob banged his fist against the door. "Come on. It's cold!"

"I'm coming!" I slid the latch to one side as he burst in.

"Brrrrr," he shuddered, shaking the snow from his head. "Jesus, it's fucking freezing out!"

"Yes." I gave him a quick peck on the cheek and felt suddenly guilty. "They said on the radio this morning it's supposed to dip down into the teens. I think it might get even colder than that."

"Goddamn." He hurried over to the stove.

My eyes widened suddenly as I saw the open stove door and the blue bow peeking out from inside.

"Why's the door open?"

"What? Oh, because I was going to throw in another can of sawdust when you knocked."

"You don't need another can. The fire's large enough." He slammed the iron grate and stood facing the stove, rubbing his hands together furiously, a Boy Scout trying to coax a flame from two sticks.

"So," I said, strolling casually up to him, "how was work?"

"Same as usual. Maybe a little slower. We mostly sat around and chewed the fat. Nobody really felt like starting any projects today, you know? I guess with the holidays here and everything, everyone was a little lazy."

"Not you, though." I poked him in the ribs.

"Well, hey, you've gotta go along with the program, you know what I mean? I didn't want to make everyone else look bad."

"Uh-huh. I know. I wish I had that luxury. We were swamped at the clinic today. Some kind of flu going around. People were lined up out into the hallway."

"Oh, say. I almost forgot. I have some news."

"What?"

"We're going out tomorrow."

"Out? On Christmas Day? Where?"

"The big brass is throwing a shindig to celebrate the occasion. Dinner, cocktails, the works."

"But I planned on having dinner here. I've got the ham all ..."

"Screw the ham; we can have the ham Saturday. I told

them we'd be there. You know, this is the first big bash we've been invited to. It's a chance to get to know Mr. Kronhausen and some of the other bigwigs. A chance for you to meet some people, too. Never hurts to brush up to the brass. You know what they say."

"Sounds like you're really into corporate life--a big-time executive." I went over to Bob and lightly rubbed his neck. "Next thing you know, you'll be telling me about your promotion."

"Don't do that!" He pulled sharply away.

"What? What's the matter?"

"Nothing. It's just that I'm ... cold. Give me a chance to get the chill out, okay?"

"Okay. Sure." I put my hand into my pocket and felt the hard lines of the ring. I wondered where Shadar was now ... if he was home in Kabul or out somewhere far, far away. And I wondered why I'd wondered. "What time is this dinner?"

"They said to be at the office around four. We're supposed to meet for cocktails and get-acquainted chatter, bullshit like that. Then we're going to a private club the vice-president has reserved for the evening."

"I didn't know there were private clubs in Kabul."

"There are a lot of things you don't know about Kabul."

I looked up at Bob. "What do you mean?"

"Say," he said, turning away, "speaking of food, what's for dinner? I'm starved."

I caught what I thought was the smell of alcohol on his breath, but it passed quickly. "I thought we'd have roast mutton. We haven't had that for a while."

"Great. Let me go get cleaned up, and I'll be right out."

Bob disappeared through the bedroom door, and I pulled open the oven door and took out the leg of mutton I'd bought earlier that day. It was done to perfection--golden brown on the outside, and tender and juicy when I sliced into it. I put the meat and bread on a large platter and set it on the table before bringing out the green beans.

"Hey, what's this?"

I turned to see Bob standing in the doorway, holding two packages wrapped in brown paper and decorated with yellow yarn. I sighed. "Bob! You weren't supposed to find those until tomorrow!"

"What are they?"

"What do you think they are, silly!"

He shook one. "For me?" A sheepish look came over him as his eyes swept mine.

"What's the matter?"

He shook his head. "I'm afraid I got so carried away with the new job and everything, I didn't have time to buy you a gift."

My heart dropped, and I looked away for a moment. I forced a slight smile. "Hey, that's all right. I understand. After all, Christmas in Afghanistan isn't exactly like Christmas back home. We'll have plenty more years to celebrate."

"I meant to stop by the marketplace this afternoon. Really. But I didn't have a chance. Then it sort of ... slipped my mind."

"It's no big deal. Really it's not. Not like back home."

"Yeah, but you got *me* something."

"Not much. Just a couple little ... somethings. Come on, now. Let's eat. You can open them later."

Monrovia opened the corporate doors to its executive conference room and stocked the bar so well that, by six that evening, most of the employees were already staggering from room to room. That included A. J. Kronhausen, himself--vice-president and manager of the Kabul branch. He was a likable enough cherub of a man, with his broad smile and round, puffy, potato-dumpling cheeks. When he spoke, his thick German accent made him sound like my own grandfather might have sounded in the Old Country. He had a gold wedding band on his finger; but if there was a *Mrs.* Kronhausen anywhere around, I hadn't met her.

By seven o'clock, Bob was showing signs of too much liquor on an empty stomach. He wandered around, bouncing from one group of employees to the next, trading risqué stories with the men and flirting with the women. I'd had three Old Fashioneds, but I felt as sober as when I'd gotten up that morning, which was my plan.

I was wondering if we were ever going to eat when Kronhausen, himself, climbed up onto a chair overlooking the conference table in the center of the room and, banging an empty beer stein against a crystal chandelier overhead, asked for quiet. A hush fell over the crowd, and A. J., in his most somber tone, invoked the blessing:

"Chentlemen und ladies ... At least I tink dere is still some ladies present. Vee vill achurn now to das Club Mecca for food und drink. Oh, yah," he added as an afterthought, "und to make Mary!" Some people helped him down from the table before he stopped short. "Whoever she iss!"

Bob and I followed the group out of the office and played caboose to a couple dozen people rolling down the center of Kabul's main street. We turned into a long, dark gangway that led to a brownstone building on which was inscribed "Club Mecca--Private." Inside, a giant of a man wearing a tall, comical-looking fez and sporting an anything-*but*-comical-looking scimitar in his sash greeted us. He led our group, stumbling and laughing, to the main dining room, the sash trailing after him as one of Bob's coworkers tried to ignite it with his lighter.

Kronhausen had selected the main room for some pre-dinner entertainment. It was situated at the end of a long corridor dimly lit by half a dozen oil lamps, goose-necked high up on the walls so that they cast eerie shadows on the occupants. Inside the room sat three tables, each filled to capacity with various trays of relishes and appetizers. A number of chairs made of wood and upholstered in red leather stood guard around the room's perimeter. Dozens of pillows had been scattered in front of a small, temporary stage hastily erected at the far end of the room.

As I sipped from a glass, I noticed Bob had disappeared. I finally spotted him as he worked his way through a throng of people back to my side.

"Hey, you," I said poking him in the ribs. "What are you doing? Where have you been?"

"Hey, honey. Having a good time? This is a great party, huh?"

"Yes, everybody's having fun. But when are we going to eat? I'm beginning to get a little tipsy."

As if on cue, a waiter passed by, carrying a tray filled with cheese cubes and crackers, and I grabbed a couple, tossing one in my mouth and feeding another to Bob. I caught sight of a small, balding man across the room. "Say, isn't that Ingersoll over there?"

"George? Where?"

I pointed across the room to a small group of men and a stunningly attractive blonde wearing a black-satin dress and making small talk.

"By God if it's not. It's old George. Now, what the hell would *he* be doing here!"

"Hey!" a voice behind us bellowed out. I turned to see a tall, lanky Swede with a great yellow beard and deep-set blue eyes. He had come up behind us and slapped Bob between the shoulder blades, scattering the remains of his drink across the tile floor. "Favage, you sly fox. Why are you hoarding the most beautiful woman here?"

"Hey, Eric. No, no hoarding. This is my wife. Paula." I wiped some of Bob's drink from the front of his coat.

"Oh, your wife? Well, I'm Eric Nordheim, and I'm pleased to meet you, Mrs. Favage."

I smiled at him. "Yes, I know. We met over cocktails at the office earlier."

"We did? By jingo, now how could I forget a thing like that!"

"Hey, Eric." Bob said, grabbing his arm. "Speaking of women. You know old George Ingersoll from the American Embassy, don't you? Paula and I were just trying to figure out who that is with him."

Eric strained his eyes, peering across the room. "Where?"

"There." Bob pointed. "The guy standing next to that deformed creature in the low-cut gown."

"I see the creature, but I don't recognize old Ingersoll."

"That's not him? The short guy with the bald spot on his head?"

"I don't know." He began to snicker. "I never met the man!"

Bob laughed for several moments before the Swede wandered off, and I followed my husband across the floor, losing sight of him when I stopped to grab another piece of cheese. I looked around. The room had swollen with people. Suddenly I smelled the thick, acrid scent of pot. I instinctively peered around for Bob and took a deep breath when I spotted a group of three women and two men huddled in the corner. They were passing a joint and laughing. One of the men held it out so that a full-bosomed redhead, wearing a V-neck clingy orange dress, had to stretch to reach it. As her fingers grew near, the man pulled the joint away, causing her to stretch even farther; all the while her giant melons threatening to burst out of their flimsy confinement. Before long, several others had gathered around to admire the redhead's assets. The men found it all quite amusing, and the redhead didn't seem to mind.

I looked around again for Bob, concerned that he, too, might try to get in on the action. He was nowhere in sight. I watched as Eric gravitated toward two others--a tall, dark-haired, pockmarked man and an exquisitely attractive brunette in a tight, short skirt and white blouse. The three of them moved slowly in the direction of the group huddled in the corner. I kept searching the crowd, trying to pick out Bob's face, with no luck.

"Well, well. Mrs. Favage, I see."

I shuddered. Even before turning around, I knew who it was. I could feel his beady little eyes roving over me. "Hello, Mr. Ingersoll."

"George, remember?" He laughed foolishly. "Yes, indeed. Fine party. Just excellent. I'm glad you and your Mister could come. It's been so long. Too, too long, don't you see. And that's not right, now, is it?" He let an empty little chuckle escape from his lips, and I smiled when I saw the deep crimson spot on his cheek.

"Why, Mr. Ingersoll, whatever happened to your face? Not coming down with something, are you? Maybe you should go to the clinic."

He grabbed my arm and leaned close, his eyes flitting to my bosom. "If I were sure *you'd* be my nurse, I'd check in tomorrow."

"Don't count on it," I said flatly, pulling my arm free and turning my attention back to the crowd.

"If you're looking for Mr. Favage, my dear, I'm afraid he's not here. I saw him leave just a few minutes ago."

"Leave? Leave where?"

"I don't know. But I'm sure they'll be back."

"They will? Who's they?"

"I'm so, so sorry." He grinned maliciously. "But I didn't catch the lady's name." Ingersoll leered at me, allowing his eyes to roam freely over my body before turning and sauntering back into the crowd.

For a moment, I was tempted to fling my glass after him, to see it shatter off his greasy, thick skull. But I thought better of it. After all, he was still technically my boss.

I turned away from temptation and bumped into Eric, again. "Whoa, whoa, there."

"Sorry," I said, juggling my drink.

"That's all right. No harm done." He grinned as he raised his hand to his lips to lick off some of the spilled liquor. "It's getting kind of crowded."

"Yes. I was just looking for ..."

"Bob?"

"Yes."

Eric furled his brows and scanned the room for several seconds. "Nope. Don't see him anywhere."

"Well, he probably just stepped out for some air ... or something." I pretended to scan the room for some sign of him.

"*Uh-huh.* Say, look who's here," he said, grabbing the arm of a young woman and pulling her toward us. "Have you two met?"

"No, I don't think so."

"Hi," the redhead said. "Mary Forrester. Glad to meet you."

"Paula Favage. Nice to meet you." I shook her hand, warm and white, the skin blotchy, as I looked up at her face, past the liner applied too heavily to her eyes. She wore an orange-red rouge that was applied too heavily and clashed with her fire-engine lipstick and mauve dress, making her look as if she'd just thrown herself together.

"Mary works at the company, too. Executive secretary." He winked at me as if the words held a secret meaning. Mary shook her head and poked him in the side.

"Oh, stop, already!"

"Mary's husband's name is Bob, too," Eric said. "Just like yours."

"Not Bob," the woman corrected. "Robert. It must be Robert or else he gets terribly upset."

I smiled, trying to appear interested.

"He told me on the eve of our wedding that his mother had named him Robert after his father, who had been named Robert after *his* father, and so on down the line for ten thousand years or something ridiculous like that, and that if I knew what was best for our marriage, I would call him Robert. He always thought the name Bob sounded like something you do for apples." She chuckled to herself. "Oh, not that I'm making fun, mind you."

"Of course not. I completely understand."

"As for Robert, he'd just as soon call me Megs as Mary," she continued, not missing a beat. "And do you think I'd mind when my own mother named me Mary after my grandmother on my father's side? After we were married, he asked me if I minded him calling me Meg, and said he could call me anything he wanted just as long as he don't call me late for dinner!"

She laughed, and Eric laughed along with her, eyeing her cleavage all the while.

"That is … something," I said.

"Mary's one of our most popular employees," Eric added. Mary feigned a blush.

"Quit, now. I'm nothing special. Just another hard-working girl."

Eric's eyes narrowed. "*Very* hard working."

She pursed her lips and poked him in the ribs again. "Get out of here, you big Norske," she said. "Leave us girls alone."

"That's a first!" He took a sip from his drink, leaned over and kissed her on the lips before backing away, pausing to crane his head toward my ear. "She likes women almost as much as men, so watch your step."

I looked up at him, my eyes opening involuntarily. He nodded and ran his hand quickly across my ass before melding into the crowd.

"Don't pay any attention to him, whatever he said." She took a sip from her drink. "Say, where is your husband? That good-looking hunk who has the entire office buzzing?"

"I … I think he stepped out. For some air."

"And leave all this?" She motioned with her head before she spotted a waiter carrying a try of fresh drinks. Her eyes lit up as she motioned him over. She put her empty glass on the tray and grabbed a refill with each hand. She held one out to me, and I shook my head.

"I'm still good," I said, holding up my glass.

She shrugged. "Well … down the hatch." She lifted one glass to her lips, swallowed several times in quick succession, and set the empty on the tray before smiling at the waiter. "Thanks," she said, taking a sip from the second glass. He smiled and bowed before moving on.

"I'm gonna get a piece of that before the night is through, I guarantee you," she said, looking after him.

I struggled to keep my face from betraying my shock as I stood there, speechless.

"I'll bet you never would have guessed that a fine, young Irish girl like myself could end up in a heathenistic hellhole like *Afghanistan.*" She said the words with considerable contempt, as though spitting out a bitter pill. "Sometimes I have to wonder how it happened, myself." She paused, reflecting, before her eyes darted back to me.

"Have you been here long?"

"Here? Oh, you mean in Afghanistan. No. Five or six months."

"Oh, my God. You've got a ways to go, dearie, to catch up."

I smiled and looked out over the crowd. "Say, will you excuse me?" I edged slowly away from her. "I'm enjoying our conversation, but I think I'd better go find my husband."

She grabbed hold of my arm, her eyes narrowing to tiny slits. "Now, why would you want to do a thing like that?" She cocked her head to one side. For a moment, I thought it was because she was drunk.

"Because," I replied, "I don't see him, and I'd like to know where he is."

"You know, these parties that Mr. Kronhausen throws for his employees at Christmas, they really are extraordinary. He takes such good care of his people. Always puts them first."

"Yes, they really are something. But I have to ..."

"They take a bit of gettin' used to, if you know what I mean." She paused to take another long swallow from her drink.

"No," I said. "I'm afraid I don't."

"Well ..."

"Hello, Mary!" A large-boned Englishman who'd been introduced to me simply as Toby came by and grabbed her around the waist. "And how's my favorite compatriot and fellow Brit? Keepin' busy, are you? Boring the company, here?"

Before she could reply, he bent forward and covered her lips with his own. While they juggled their drinks, he reached down to her skirt, pulled up the hem, and slid his palm across the soft white flesh of her thigh, kneading it for what seemed an eternity. I stood there stunned. I felt I ought to look away, pretend not to have noticed, but my eyes had a mind of their own. When he began making long, guttural sounds deep within his throat, she responded by slowly grinding her pelvis against him, and then she suddenly broke from his kiss and half-heartedly pushed him away.

"Now, see here, you bloody Englishman, what are you doin' in front of me company this way? You dirty little bugger."

"What do you think I'm doing?" he replied, nuzzling his lips against her neck. "And I'm not all that little, if you know what I mean."

She laughed, he laughed, and she turned back to me without missing a beat. "The first time I came to one of Mr. Kronhausen's parties, I was a bit surprised, me bein' a sheltered girl from the shores of Ireland ... *and* a strict Roman Catholic, no less. But it's soon enough when you spend years in this hellhole that you realize you deserve all the fun you can get from life. So why not take whatever anyone gives you?"

Toby pressed his mouth against her ear and whispered something that caused her to giggle.

"I'm sorry, darlin', but I've got to move along. It was nice talkin' with you. Drop by the house sometime when you and the mister are free." Her hand brushed the man's crotch, and she reached up and kissed him lightly on the lips before they turned and disappeared into the crowd.

I stared after them for what seemed forever before putting my drink to my lips and emptying the glass just as Eric returned.

"Here--let me get you a refill."

"No. No, thanks. I've had enough."

Before he had time to respond, a bright light fell across the stage, and a short, funny-looking man wearing a fez-- similar to the one on the doorman--appeared from out of nowhere. He pulled a sheet of paper from a tailored jacket.

"Ladies and gentlemen," he cried out, "welcome to Club Mecca. I am Faroud, your host for the evening. And I hope you are having a wonderful time." A cheer went up from the crowd, and Faroud executed a deep, exaggerated bow. "Thank you so much. And now, for your evening's pleasure, all the way from the foothills of the mighty

Hindu Kush, from the villages of Zandahar, by way of Bombay, Tehran, and Minsk, Soviet Russia, it is my sincere pleasure to give to you a dancing troupe of unparalleled excellence. Ladies and gentlemen--The Xabalii Community Dancers!"

The little man stepped back out of the light, and a spot opened up on the stage as a sudden clash of cymbals and the strumming of a balalaika split the smoky night air. I turned to Eric, who was squatting on the floor, clearing a spot for me to join him.

"Come' on. This is something you won't want to miss."

I stooped down next to him. "What is it?"

"You've never seen the Xabalii?"

"No."

He smiled. "You're in for a treat."

With the flutter of a finger cymbal and the rustle of the bells, three dancers burst into the room. Their flowing costumes of red and gold shone with thousands of glistening sequins that sent the light shimmering across the crowd. With filmy veils that barely concealed their rouged faces, they swirled their black hair through the air as they twirled and leaped to the music. One dancer--the star of the troupe, I guessed--had a small dagger at her side, which she periodically withdrew from a scabbard and brandished around her body as she bent to the most amazing contortions, her feet gyrating to the pounding rhythm of the instruments.

"They're fantastic," I said over the catcalls of the crowd.

"I *knew* you'd like them. The leader has been studying dance from the time he was two."

"*He?*"

He laughed. "Queer as a three-dollar bill."

I looked back at the dancers. "And the others?"

"Probably his faggy concubines. Damned good dancers, though. I wouldn't mind taking *him*--I mean *her*--for a spin around the floor." His eyes pranced across the stage, glued to the lead dancer. "*Damned* good."

As I watched, I saw the performer making suggestive moves toward the men in the crowd. The other two dancers watched him carefully, like mother hens guarding their young.

"Why men?" I shouted over the din.

"I don't know. I guess it's tradition. It's no big thing to be gay in this god-forsaken country. Most men out with their flocks would just as soon relieve themselves with another man as with a sheep or goat!"

I cringed at the thought. Eric must have seen me shudder; he drew close and shouted, "What's the matter? Don't the little buggers turn you on?"

"No!" I shouted back. "Not particularly!"

"They do me … sort of. In a way."

I felt Eric's hand reach beneath my skirt as he quickly worked it up to my thigh.

"Don't!" I cried, pushing him away.

He looked at me long and hard for several moments. "All right," he said finally as if granting me a great favor. "For now."

I turned back to the dancers who had just lured the buxom redhead out onto the floor. They were teaching her how to move to the music; she was a fast learner. One of the two backup dancers wrapped a red shawl around her neck, and she pulled it down to her waist, running it back and forth as though drying herself with a towel. Slowly, she lowered the shawl and bent forward, swaying her torso to the beat of the cymbals. The lower she bent, the louder the hooting from the men--and women--closest to her, until I could see right down her dress--see her mammoth breasts swinging freely, bound only by the lightly woven knit material trying to restrain them.

Suddenly one of the men in front reached up, grabbed her garb, and, with a swift tug, ripped it off her shoulders so that it dangled at her waist. Her giant breasts swung free, dancing as if they had a life all their own as she wiggled and gyrated to the music. The other dancers ran their hands along her body, making suggestive motions with their hips and thighs. Several of the men in the crowd reached for the hem of her dress and tried pulling it off, too, but she managed to slip away at the last moment, which only served to heighten their frenzy.

I looked away, feeling suddenly dizzy from the liquor and weak from lack of food and the stuffiness of the room. A loud cheer went out from the crowd, and when I looked up again, the redhead was completely naked except for a skimpy pair of see-through black panties. Behind her, the dancers groaned and moved to the music, rubbing their pelvises together as the leader reached down into his own pants and, still swaying to the music, began pulling on himself.

Eric leaned closer and whispered in my ear: "I think now is a good time, yes?" He threw the full weight of his body against me as I tumbled backward into a group of people, my crossed legs pinned beneath against the floor. I struggled to get up, but he had pulled my blouse free from my slacks and worked his hands up beneath it, grabbing for my breasts, squeezing until they hurt.

"No!" I screamed. "Stop it! *Stop it*!"

In a moment he had straddled me, and then I felt the rhythmic pressure of his pelvis grinding, grinding, as his hips sought to cover mine.

"*No!*" I shouted one more time, and, with all my might, I worked my right leg free and jerked up suddenly on one knee as hard as I could. It struck deep into his groin.

"*Aeeooow!*" He rolled over, doubled up in pain, as I clamored to my feet. My heart pounded; my blood raced. The crowd was crying out--whether for me or for the dancers, I couldn't tell. I wasn't about to stick around to find out.

Eric grimaced, still clutching his groin, as I kicked out a second time, catching him on his thick, squared chin, sending saliva flying through the spotlighted room. He tumbled backward as I quickly turned and picked my way through the crowd, stepping on bodies sprawled across the floor, knocking over several drinks.

When I finally burst out into the corridor, I stopped and stooped forward, taking several deep breaths. For a moment I thought I was going to vomit. Smoke clung to the dull black walls like a thick coat of stucco. I stumbled down the corridor toward the entranceway and was about to reach for the latch when I stopped.

What will I do outside? A woman alone, a farangi *after dark in downtown Kabul?* I searched up and down the hall for another option. *Bob!* I had to find Bob. He *had* to be there. *He wouldn't just leave me. He wouldn't!*

I grabbed the knob on one of six doors standing sentinel along the hall, turned it until it clicked, and pulled it open. Inside a small, darkened room, I heard moaning and someone muttering something unintelligible as I squinted at the glare of images on a screen.

"Hey! Shut the door!"

I scanned the room quickly. Against the far wall, a man and a woman larger than life were wrapped in a tangled web of arms and legs. She was groaning, he was puffing. The tinny music from the video's audio track filled the room, adding to the eroticism.

"C'mon! Close that door!" another man's voice cried.

"Yeah, or come on in," another said. "You can sit on *my* lap anytime!"

Somebody laughed, and somebody else echoed him. Someone said something about tits, and I backed out and slammed the door.

Goddamn it. Goddamn it, what has he done now? What has he gotten us into? I could feel the anger welling within me, racing through my body, unstoppable, a raging fire, a roaring engine running flat out. *What has Bob gotten me into this time?* I wanted to stop, to leave the labyrinth far behind, but I knew I couldn't. Not alone. Not at night.

I grabbed the knob on another door, turned it slowly, and paused. I started to pull on the doorknob but couldn't. I was frozen in time, ceasing all function. What if there were more of the same inside, what if there were more people? What if Bob was in there? I had to find out. I had to find him. I just had to find him so that we could get the hell out of there and back safely to our home.

I jerked the door open and looked inside. The light was dim, slightly brighter than in the previous room. *Thank God, no video, no porn flicks.* As my eyes struggled to see through the haze hanging in the air, they fell upon a rattan sofa set against the far wall. It was stacked with silk pillows, ornately festooned with fringe and brocade. Upon them, two couples entwined themselves in a wild embrace. The thick smell of joss sticks mingled with a thicker, sweeter smell--something stronger than pot. I squinted, straining my eyes to see.

"Bob?" I stepped into the room.

I saw my husband's glassy eyes peer up over his shoulder and toward me before looking back down at the woman he was straddling. I watched the two of them roll onto the floor, still joined at the hips, and heard her cry out.

"God, oh, God, don't stop, baby, I'm so close! Don't stop. Harder. Now!"

The couple next to them began grunting, deep and hard and savagely, the rhythm of the woman's guttural sounds spurring her partner on. In a split second, I thought about yelling, about crying, about screaming, charging in, slapping him, hitting him, *killing* him. I thought about every option that was possibly available to me. And then, for one reason or another, I settled on the one that made the least amount of sense.

I stepped back outside, looked one more time into the room--to be certain, I suppose, that I hadn't made a mistake--and then I slowly, calmly closed the door. Of the room. Of the night. Of my life.

I stood there, staring at the knob blankly for several moments. Any minute the anger would strike. Any moment the wave of disgust would sweep over me, and I would fling the door open, burst in, and pull him off of her. I would order him to get dressed and take me home, after which I would break into tears. And then I would tell him once and for all that I was leaving him. Leaving for America. Leaving for good.

But no anger rose up. No tears formed. I had simply

gone numb. The din from the main room down the hall had swelled into a roar. I could only imagine what was going on inside. I felt for my top, straightened it out, tried to push out of my mind what had just happened, what had happened with Eric, what had happened with Bob.

Or maybe I had been wrong. Maybe it hadn't been Bob I had seen behind the door. Maybe, in my state of mind, I had merely imagined it had been Bob; it was dark, after all. Maybe that was it. I was losing my mind, hallucinating, imagining all sorts of things. Maybe the Swede *hadn't* attacked me. Maybe I had simply tripped and fallen over backward, and he merely tumbled to the floor with me, struggling to get up, to help me up. When I felt his weight, I panicked, kicked at him, and raced out of the room.

But he grabbed me. He fondled me. Didn't he? Or maybe it hadn't been him. Maybe it had been someone else, someone crazed with alcohol and drugs, someone spurred on by the redhead dancing naked on the stage.

Was I going crazy? Was I going mad? Was the entire world crumbling around me? Or was it my mind playing tricks on me, over and over again. Because I was frustrated, unhappy, frightened. Maybe it was the depression, the confusion, the fear of living beneath the terror of the unknown each and every day of my life. That was it. That *had* to be it!

"So, are you getting the hang of it yet, darling?"

I snapped my head around at the sound of the voice and saw Mary. Good old Irish Catholic Mary. Her hair was rumpled, and her skirt was on backward--the zipper to the front. Her makeup had been badly smudged. Whiskey or some other dark stain ran in a line from above her breast down her blouse to her navel. I stared at her blankly. What was she doing here? Had she, too, been hallucinating? Was *she*, too, losing her mind?

"I say, are you getting the hang of it?"

"I ... I think that's my husband in there." I pointed to the door. "I think ... he's having sex with another woman."

"Well, doll baby, what did you expect?" She reached up and stroked my hair casually, as a young girl might do to her favorite doll.

"But it's dark, and I'm not sure ..."

She smiled and took my hand. "Now, then, it's not that dark, is it? You saw with your own eyes. And what else would you expect? After all, he paid a lot of money for the privilege."

"What?" I jerked my hand back and gazed at her as through a chintz curtain. She was larger than life, she was less than real. She waved her hand, and a thin trail of smoke followed it down to one side.

"I said he paid a lot of money."

The words sounded hollow, as though spoken through a tube. I shook my head. "I don't understand."

"Five million *afghanis* isn't exactly the going rate for a slice of cheese and a cup of green tea, now, is it, love?"

"Five million ..." I stared into her glassy eyes for several minutes, my brain struggling to function. "No," I said, backing toward the exit. "No, it's not. No."

"Where you going, honey? The party's just begun. Come on in. Come on in with me. I'll take care of you. I'll protect you." She held out her hand, again, the ruby-haired Wraith of God, the angel of death, palm up, arm extended, beseeching me to take hold. Beseeching me to enter into her world of depravity and dysfunction. She was weaving slowly from side to side. I couldn't tell if she was swaying in one spot or perhaps walking slowly toward me. Yes, that was it. She was walking toward me, stalking me, waiting for just the right moment to pounce. A crazed, lust-filled animal blood thirsty and hungry for the kill.

I took one step back, two, three, and before I knew it, I had pressed my back up against the entranceway through which we had originally entered the club, pushed up against it and felt instinctively for the latch. I looked past her, at the long labyrinthine hall that seemed to stretch on forever into eternity, the lights on the sconces grown dim with the night or with the numbing of my senses.

"Come on, honey, I'll take good care of you. You've just had a li'l too much to drink. I know just what you need, my love. Come on with me."

I moved my head back and forth, up and down. I knew better. I knew better than to touch her; I knew what lay just beyond those outstretched palms. I knew only too well.

"Oh, God, *nooooooo*!"

* * *

It was pitch black and bitter cold when I stumbled into the courtyard of Naim's small apartment. I felt my way along the stone-walled portico, tripped up two steps, and stopped when I reached the first doorway on the right. I knocked several times. In the stillness of the morning, the sounds reverberated like cannon shot. I waited before knocking again. Behind the door, I heard shuffling followed by the sound of voices.

The lock clicked and the doorknob turned; a young Afghan boy peeked out at me with startled eyes. Behind him, I could see the soft flickering of candlelight.

"*Naim*!" I breathed in deeply and, composing myself, repeated, "Naim ... is Naim here? Is this where Naim lives? I need to speak to him. *Please*."

At first, I thought the young boy hadn't understood. He stood staring at me for several moments. Finally, he turned and spoke in Persian to someone behind him. "A woman--a *farangi*. I think it is your friend. She asks for you."

The young Afghan disappeared, and two familiar eyes peered out.

"Oh, Naim," I sobbed, falling against the threshold. "Thank God you're here!"

We walked together to the embassy, closed and shuttered because of the holiday, and found the Jeep behind the building. Naim reached beneath the front left fender and, after fishing for several moments, finally pulled out a small metal case, from which he withdrew a key.

"I do not know this is here. It is in case one of us empty-headed locals loses the key we are given, and someone from the embassy has to come out to pick us up."

I climbed into the passenger seat and sat stiff-backed in a vacuous stupor as Naim started the engine and goaded the Jeep out of the compound. Before I realized it, the vehicle ground to a halt outside my cottage. Naim reached over and touched my arm and asked if he could help, and I yanked it suddenly away from him.

"I'm sorry," I said, my breath coming in pants. I felt myself trembling. "I'm sorry. Please. Just wait here."

I climbed out of the Jeep and hurried up the path. Struggling with the lock under a moonless sky, I finally got the door to open and pushed past it. I clicked on the lamp and, with the light spilling across the floor, gazed down at the boards beneath the stove. I slid over toward the spot and ran my hands across the wooden slats until my nail caught on the one that was loose. I pried it free. The small cardboard box was there, where I had left it. *Thank God!* I grabbed the box, replaced the board, and set it back in place. I slipped off the rubber bands holding the lid closed. The top sprang free, and I reached inside. The stack of ten million *afghani* notes seemed light. I thumbed through them, counting out loud as I went.

"Five million," I said, slamming the money down into the box. "That goddamn thieving son-of-a-bitch!"

I slipped the lid back on and secured it again with the rubber bands, and I took what remained of Dinara's money into the bedroom and stuffed it into my suitcase. I rifled through the drawers and jammed in as many of my personal belongings as I could carry.

All the while I worked, I thought of Dinara. I was off until Monday, two more days. By then I had planned to return the loan--*all* of it. How could I do that now? I'd managed to save eight or nine hundred thousand *afghanis* from my pay--less than two hundred dollars. Perhaps there were a few more lying around the house that Bob hadn't found. But five million! Where would I come up with five million *afghanis* in two days?

I hurried into the living room and picked up a pad and a pencil. Hastily I scrawled a note:

"Bob, I've left you. I am sick of the drugs, the whores, the lies, the stealing. I'm gone for good. You will hear from a lawyer about the divorce. I want the money--Dinara's money--within two weeks, or I will press charges with the embassy and the Afghan Police. And I MEAN IT!!!"

I threw the pad face-up on the table and flung the pencil toward the kitchen. That part about getting the money back, I knew, was wishful thinking. Bob didn't have it. He'd spent it on membership in his "club." I was just thankful he hadn't taken it all.

As far as suing him went, I knew that, too, was a pipe dream. In Afghanistan, the man controls the household funds. He has all legal rights to it. The wife can say nothing, do nothing. We were American citizens, and that might work in my favor. But no court in *this* land would ever convict him of stealing. Unless he was foolish enough to return voluntarily to America where he could be prosecuted, the money was gone. I would simply have to face up to it, face up to Dinara. I would even have to face up to myself--to the fool I'd been for believing him, for staying with him, for thinking I could change things.

I grabbed my case and hurried out the door and down the path to the Jeep. Naim came around and helped me pack the bag into the back seat, then took me by the arm as I climbed up into my seat.

"Are you all right?"

My hands were shaking. My muscles were tense, my neck strained, my eyes blurry. I nodded, and he hurried around to the driver's side.

"Where to?" he asked, throwing the Jeep into gear.

I looked at him blankly. "What?"

"Where would you wish me to take you?"

"I ... I don't know." The thought suddenly struck me. I had nowhere to go. I might once have gone to Dinara's, but not now, not now that Bob had stolen the money. I couldn't possibly face her now. And I couldn't go to the embassy for help; it was locked tight. Nor could I stay with Naim. He had a tiny one-room flat, which he already shared with a roommate. "I ... I have a friend," I said finally, "who lives here in town. Do you know the alley-way behind the old post office?"

Naim nodded.

"There's a house there, the third one from the street. My friend lives there. I can stay with ..." I caught myself, paused, and added, "I'm sure I can stay with my friend tonight." *If he's home. Oh, God, please let him be home!*

As we raced through Kabul, the shock of the evening finally caught up with me. The realization of what I was doing. Of not knowing what came next. Me, Paula Favage, the very married wife and someday-hoped-to-be mother, had just left her husband. For good. *Forever.* I felt as though I had suddenly died, as though my life had just passed before me. I saw the letter to my parents:

Dear Mom and Dad. A funny thing happened to me the other day. Bob took me to a sex club, got stoned, and stole some money, so I left him. Will wire when I find work. Love, Your Idiot Daughter Paula.

I began to cry, softly at first, turning away from Naim so that he wouldn't see; but it quickly built up; and soon I was weeping bitterly, uncontrollably. I could feel the tension in the Jeep, feel the confusion in Naim, sense his eyes alternating between me and the road. I knew he wanted to speak; but he couldn't find the words. What words were there? What could he say to ease my pain? What could *anyone* say?

Naim cut the wheel sharply, and we sped past the embassy before we turned down the alleyway behind the post office. Suddenly I looked up. There it stood--the third house from the corner.

Could I do it? Could I find the strength to knock on the door and enter the house of a Pashtun rebel? The lights were out. What if he wasn't home? What if he was miles away--hundreds or even thousands of miles? What would I do then?

I looked at Naim, the panic clearly visible in my eyes. He looked frightened, too. He started to speak and stopped.

"This is it," I said.

Naim craned his neck and peered up at the house. "It is dark."

"Probably sleeping. It's late. It'll be all right."

Naim nodded. "I will help you with your bag."

"*No!* No, that's not necessary. I can manage."

He looked at me, and the pain I felt was reflected in his own young face. "Are you sure?"

I hesitated before nodding and reached for my bag. "Thank you, Naim." I leaned over and kissed him lightly on the cheek.

There were tears in his eyes to match those that had been falling from mine. "I will wait until you are safely inside, Paula Favage."

I climbed out of the Jeep and struggled up the walk to the front stoop, each step an agonizing exercise in hopelessness. With a backward glance at Naim, I set the case down and grabbed the metal door knocker. Once, twice, three times I lifted it and banged it back down against the heavy wooden slab. I felt like a convict who had just walked the last mile and now waited to be strapped into the electric chair. Just a few more moments and it would all be over. Like a convict, I wondered how it would feel.

"Please, God," I said softly. "Please, oh, please let him be home." I waited for what seemed forever. With each passing second, a new tear formed in my eye, sending the one that had preceded it trickling down my cheek. "Oh, please," I said again. *Please!*

He wasn't home. I knew he wasn't home. Because I needed him, because I had been a bad girl, an idiot, a weak woman, he wasn't home. It was my penance, my sentence for not having lived a better life. I looked back at Naim one more time, and then I raised the knocker again. Suddenly I saw a light through the shuttered windows, and in a moment the door opened, and Shadar stood before me.

"My God," he said. "What's happened to you? Are you all right? Come in. *Hurry!*"

He reached down and took hold of my case, and I turned and looked at Naim one last time. I stood there for several moments and watched the Jeep start slowly down the road back toward the embassy. Soon, the taillights were swallowed up by the dark Afghani sky.

ELEVEN

I lay still against Shadar. Our bodies pressed so closely to one another that I could feel the heat of the blood coursing through his veins. I could feel the beat of his heart. Or perhaps it was mine.

The flames in the stove danced and crackled. How different they seemed from the flames that burned within me, ready to consume me, impossible to extinguish. In a way, I found being with him comforting. In another, it was agonizing. I had dreamed, as a schoolgirl might dream, of meeting my very own Prince Charming somewhere, sometime, when we would walk through the fields under a sky of brilliant blue until we came to a small orchard. There, in a sun-drenched grove, we would stop. It would be quiet, still, and our eyes would find one another and hold each other tight. He would reach out, stretch his arms around to encircle my back, and stroke my hair. And his lips would press against mine. And mine would explode against his, seeking, searching, demanding, hungrily devouring that which they had so willingly sought out. My hands would reach up to his head, caressing his hair, pulling him closer, forcing him against me until our teeth brushed and our souls cried out.

"What are we doing?" I would ask.

"Everything."

"Where are you taking me?"

"Everywhere."

But that was fantasy; *this* was reality. I was shaking, trembling from deep within, unsure of what lay ahead.

Unsure of whether or not I should have come. But I'd made my decision, and now I had to live with it.

Shadar leaned his head against mine and kissed me on the cheek, far more gently than I would have imagined possible. Far more gently than in my fantasy. Taking my chin in his hand, he looked deeply into my eyes. "Would you like to go to bed with me?"

Those words, too, I had once dreamt of hearing. But not now, not under these circumstances. I looked up at him, studying his face for a long time. He was ruggedly handsome, not in a boyish way like Bob. Shadar's eyes were grayish brown--like a cat's--encircled by deeply etched lines that made him look far more mature up close than he did from a distance. More mature and wiser ... and more compassionate.

"I can't. I ... just can't."

He pulled me tighter still against him, warming me and soothing me at the same time. "I understand," he whispered.

"You can go to bed. I'll be all right, now."

"I will sleep here with you. Or I will lie awake the rest of the night. It does not matter to me. All that matters is that you are here, and you are safe."

I had told him I'd left Bob and had nowhere else to go. He hadn't asked for an explanation. He simply took me in. When the time was right, he must have realized, I would tell him everything. Until then, it simply didn't matter.

The following morning, I opened my eyes to the sound of clanging metal. I looked around the room. It took some time before I realized where I was. I was drugged, hungover, tired; but I was safe, too, and relieved. I inhaled deeply and actually felt the air funneling through my lungs. I was free.

As my eyes traveled the room, I was surprised at its size. In the dim light of the evening fire, I had seen little. Now, with daylight falling through the slats in the shutters, I could make out a huge open space with many antique furnishings--chairs, tables, a settee, and a deep-pile Oriental carpet. The walls supported several paintings, including two that appeared to be French. Shadar had done well for himself, for a jack-of-all-trades.

"I *did* wake you." He peeked in from a doorway. He crossed the room and knelt down beside the sofa. "I'm a good cook, but a noisy one." He reached out and stroked my forehead. "How do you feel?"

I yawned and threw the quilt off me. "Tired. As if I could sleep for another three days."

"Breakfast would be cold by then."

"Breakfast? What time is it? It seems as if I just dozed off."

He held out his arm and squinted in the dim light. "*Ummm.* I would say it looks as if you just dozed off four hours ago. It's seven forty-five."

"In the morning?" I yawned again and put my hand to my head, surprised to find it in the same place I had left it the night before.

"You slept soundly," he said, rising and going to the windows. He reached out and unhooked the shutters. The white light emptied across the room, as a spotlight changes a theater from night into day. "Does that hurt your eyes?"

"No, no. It's fine," I lied.

"Good. I hope you're hungry because breakfast will be ready in a few minutes."

"And what did I do to deserve all this attention? Besides barging in on you in the middle of the night."

"Don't forget about forcing me to stay awake all night." A smile crossed his lips. "But, mostly, you came here, and now you are safe. Now, enough talk about last night. The bathroom is through there, in case you wish to freshen up."

"I must look a mess."

"You look radiant." He touched his lips to my forehead before heading back to the kitchen. I got up from the sofa and looked around for my suitcase.

"Oh," he called, "I put your bag in there. It was heavy. I hope that is all right."

I shuffled around the living room, taking in the surroundings. Everything seemed so clean, so neat. I had expected chaos in the house of a bachelor.

I made my way down the hall to the bathroom, peeled back the shutters, and peered outside. Beyond several snow-covered trees stretched a large expanse of ground that in the summer could have been a garden or a patio. Two looming statues and a marble birdbath reached up from their blanket of white.

"It's snowing," I called.

"We've gotten six inches! Radio Kabul is predicting up to a foot by this evening."

"A foot!" It was hard to believe. Even deep in the Snow Belt back home we rarely received more than a few inches at a time. And the Afghan winter had only begun. It looked as if Dinara's uncle had been right. It *was* going to be a long, cold winter.

When I had finished washing and dressing and brushing out my hair so that I looked like a human being, again, I joined Shadar in the kitchen. It, too, was neat and orderly. At one end stood an aging white-porcelain stove. Butting up to it: an ancient wooden icebox. Shadar stood over a long counter to one side of the sink, where he worked at arranging an exotic-smelling meal on two large plates.

"I hope you like duck eggs. I fixed them to my own recipe."

"I don't know. I've never had them."

"And you're from the great farming state of Wisconsin?"

I picked up a small slice of cheese lying on the counter and pushed it against my tongue. "How did you know that?"

"What?"

"That I'm from Wisconsin? I don't think I ever mentioned it."

"I know many things about you that you never mentioned."

"Oh? Such as?"

"Such as, you were born in Milwaukee in 1954, which would make you ... let's see, now ... twenty-five."

"*Uh-uh*. Twenty-four. I haven't had my birthday yet."

"*Ahh*, yes. You're right, of course. December 30th, isn't it?"

"Yes," I said, surprised.

"I'm afraid math is not one of my strong points."

"That must be the only thing."

"All right, now. Where were we? Oh, yes. You were an 'A' student in college, your mother's name is Dolores with an 'o', and your father's name is Fred, short for Frederick, with a 'k'. Everyone at the firm where he worked until he recently retired called him Freddie."

My mouth fell open. "How do you know all that?"

"Actually," he replied, adding a green onion and parsley garnish to the plates, "I guessed. Most people named Fred are called Freddie sooner or later in life, and since your father is now sixty-six years of age, I assumed he had recently retired."

"But ... all those other things. How did you ..."

"Magic," he said softly.

"*Hmm*." I thought for several seconds. "Unfortunately, I don't believe in magic."

"No? More's the pity."

"But I do believe I know how you found all that out."

He raised his brows.

"I'll bet you got that information from my Peace Corps application at the American Embassy. You *stole* that information. You're nothing but a common thief!"

He shrugged. "I have never been called *that* before ... *common*."

"Well, you are. And I knew I couldn't trust you from the day we met." I leaned in close. "Something about your eyes."

"What about my eyes?"

"They're *verrrrry* shifty, *very* suspicious-looking. Never trust a man with shifty eyes."

"I guess the ... what is the expression? Oh, yes. The jig is up." He grabbed the plates and walked toward the back door.

"I was always interested in journalism, you know," I said. "Thought for a while I might become an investigative reporter. *That's* how I figured out where you got my bio. My deductive reasoning."

"You're right. You would have made a very fine investigative reporter."

"Damned straight."

"Oh, bring that container of yogurt on the counter, will you? You like yogurt with your eggs."

I turned to get the container, then stopped short and looked around. "How did you ..."

He smiled, and he disappeared through the door. I grabbed the container and followed him into a glass-walled atrium lined with exotic flowering plants--dwarf citrus trees in full bloom, some with oranges and lemons and limes and kumquats hanging from their branches, plus gardenias, azaleas, orchids, violets, and several plants I'd never seen before. Just the other side of the glass wall, snow settled in stark contrast into sloping white mounds against the panes.

"My God, this is gorgeous. It's just like the Garden of Eden."

"Well, I don't know about *that*. But thank you. I'm glad you like it. It's a bit like eating outdoors without some of the, uh, inconveniences."

I laughed.

"What's so funny?"

"*You*," I said, as he pulled a red-cushioned chair out for me and I settled into it. "You're remarkable."

"Yes. I've been told that before. So often, in fact, that I'm beginning to believe it myself."

I laughed again.

"You're remarkable, too."

"Me? Why is that?"

"To be able to laugh the way you do ... after what you've been through."

The laughter suddenly died on my lips as thoughts of the night before sped through my mind. "Yes," I said finally. "Well, what's over is ... over."

"Very true. And what hasn't yet begun, hasn't yet begun. Such as ..." He paused, leaning toward me as though about to share an intimate secret.

"Yes?" I met his eyes across the table.

"Such as ... *breakfast* ... which is going to be terribly cold and terribly bad if we don't eat terribly soon."

I grinned and sat back.

"Now," he continued, "some bread?"

"That looks wonderful. And it's hot!"

"Naturally."

I took a piece from the covered dish he held out to me. "Now, don't tell me you've been baking all morning while I was asleep."

"I was *going* to tell you that but, since you and your deductive reasoning obviously wouldn't buy it, I'll tell you instead that I got it from the finest baker in all of Kabul only an hour ago. And, yes, while you were asleep."

I noted the skill with which he handled himself at the table, the way he poured the tea, passed the bread, held his silverware. Even his conversation. He was clearly a man of breeding and no mere laborer. In fact, I wasn't quite sure *what* he was, but I was going to find out.

"You've grown suddenly quiet. I hope not for lack of stimulating conversation."

I looked at him for some time. "You're an excellent cook. The eggs are wonderful."

He nodded at the compliment.

"I don't suppose you would tell me what else you are."

"Meaning?"

"Meaning ... you know. What you *really* do for a living."

"I told you."

"*Uh-uh.*" I stuffed another forkful of egg into my mouth and took a sip of juice. "I don't buy that gadabout stuff. Not you. You're not the type."

"I see. Then, what *do* you think I do for a living?"

"I'm not sure, but I have a friend with the American

Embassy who thinks ..."

"Yes? Go on."

"He thinks you are a Pashtun freedom fighter."

I expected some surprise, some small display of emotion as the words fell from my lips. Shadar sat calmly considering them for several moments.

"And you? Do you think so, too?"

I shook my head. "I really don't know *what* to think."

"Is it important? Would it make a difference to you *what* I did for a living?"

He was setting me up. I could tell. If I answered one way, I would be crass and materialistic; if the other, I would be a Hollywood romantic.

"Yes," I said finally, "I think it would, but only because of what I've been through with ... I've been hurt once in a relationship. I thought I had married one man, and it turned out I had married someone completely different--a stranger, someone I had never even known. Not really. Until it was too late."

"It is never too late."

I paused. "I suppose that's true."

"Besides, you can't mean that you're thinking of marrying *me!*"

"That's not the point. It's just that I don't want to get attached to anyone again so soon. I don't want to feel something for someone, the way I might feel something for you, until ..."

"Until you know more about him."

I nodded.

"Well, then, let me assure you that I am not engaged in anything illegal or otherwise subversive, dangerous, or disgusting--at least, not at the moment."

"You're crazy," I said, smiling. "Here I am, trying to hold a serious conversation, and you're making jokes."

"Let me ask *you,* then. If I *were* a Pashtun freedom fighter, would it be so wrong? Do you know why the Pashtuns are fighting for freedom?"

"A little."

"Well, then, you probably *don't* know that the Pashtun

people developed their own form of government, their own society, and their own laws centuries ago. They also developed their own fields and worked hard to turn barren, rocky soil into fertile, productive land. They are a fine, God-fearing people with a long and proud heritage. They fought against the Axis powers in World War II because they felt that the indiscriminate extermination of any race of people--or the domination of one people by another through force--was not only illegal but also immoral. They would rather lay down their lives than say a bad word about anyone. But they have been exploited, pushed from one country to another, stolen from. Their children have been abducted into slavery; their women, raped; their livestock, slaughtered and left to rot in the broiling summer sun."

"I had no idea."

"A while back, not so very many years ago, the Pashtuns reached a crossroads. They'd had enough. They had become, for all practical purposes, an independent nation of people. This they announced to the world. All they wanted, they said, was the land they had occupied for so many centuries. That, and peace. But the Pakistanis, their neighbors to the east, couldn't accept that. They couldn't stand the thought of losing some of the lands they desired for their own, even though they hadn't occupied it since before the days of Muhammad. So, when the Pashtuns announced they were a free and independent nation, the Pakistanis moved several heavily armored divisions against them. They rooted the Pashtuns from their homes and chased them over the fields and through the mountain passes, scattering them all over northern Afghanistan, the Northwest Frontier, into Russia, and as far as Iran. They banned those whom they could not catch and kill or place on trial as traitors to the government of Pakistan. They placed bounties on their heads so that any dog of a man interested in making a few dollars could do so easily enough by placing a high-powered shell through the back of a Pashtun rebel's head at a thousand yards."

Shadar paused as if suddenly realizing how emotional he'd grown in telling the story ... realizing, too, that *I'd* noticed it.

"So," I said softly, "you *are* a freedom fighter."

"Actually," he said, picking up the kettle and pouring tea into his cup, "I'm an electrician. Now, eat your eggs."

I had never met a man like him before. He dove into life with the same zest and vigor my own father showed when I was a young girl, and he was still a young, vital man. In many ways, Shadar reminded me of my dad, though worlds apart and of a different race. Shadar, too, was rarely at a loss for answers to my questions, whether about the great mosques of Kabul or the people of the barren plains, whom we met on a Jeep trip to the foot of the Kush that Sunday afternoon.

A couple miles outside of town, we found ourselves plowing through snow drifts three feet deep with no sign of things letting up.

"*Brrrr!* It's colder than it looks."

He turned the heater to high and goaded the vehicle slowly through the snow. "Nervous?" he asked.

I smiled. "A little. Are you sure the Jeep can handle all this snow?"

He laughed, suddenly reaching out and pulling me up against the console. He held me tightly against him while he steered with his left hand.

"Sure? Let me show you." He threw his lips hard against mine. I felt my body melt and fire race through my veins. When he finally broke free, I let out a long low moan.

"Is that supposed to relax me?"

"No good? Perhaps we need to try again."

I poked at him. "Just keep both hands on the wheel and drive more carefully, mister. I'd like to be sure we actually get where we're going."

"Doctor's orders?"

I looked at him and shook my head. "Worse than that. *Nurse's* orders."

"*Hmm.*" He nodded, freeing his right hand and planting it firmly against the wheel.

We rolled on like that through the countryside, our view broken only periodically by a row of huts or an occasional solitary figure on horseback. By mid-afternoon, we had reached the village of Charikar, set upon the plains at the foot of the Kush. The mountains towered over us as a parent over a young child. Narrow sluices carved thin ribbons of grey through the pure white of the slopes surrounding them. Up and out the couloirs radiated like the spokes on a bike, up into the sky, into the clouds, into heaven itself until you couldn't see where they stopped and where the mountaintops peaked.

The shrouded summit climbed thousands of feet above the snowstorms and bitter squalls that swirled around us-- an everyday occurrence in winter, where accumulations of ten to twenty feet of snow or more at once were common. Occasionally, I noted a small window open up, and we caught sight of the wild sheep and goats that made the craggy cliffs their home. During summer, these sure-footed beasts traveled high up the sides of the mountains in search of the tender green shoots that grew near the summit; during the savage winters, they instinctively sought the protection and shelter of the lower elevations.

"Well? What do you think?" Shadar peered up through the frosted glass of the Jeep.

"I think that anyone who doubts the existence of God has never seen this."

Shadar nodded toward the west, and I peeked out the window opposite me. "A hunting party from Charikar."

"What are they hunting?"

"Karakul, probably. And wild goat."

"You mean them?" I pointed to the animals on the mountainside.

He nodded.

"Honk your horn."

He looked at me. "Why?"

"To scare them away!"

Shadar smiled. "You do not understand the ways of the

hills."

"You mean kill or be killed?"

"Something like that."

"We can't just sit here and watch them be slaughtered!"

"But for the animals that travel the snowy mountain passes of the Kush, these people and others like them would perish. There aren't many supermarkets in Charikar."

Shadar watched patiently as the villagers approached the Jeep. Straight from the pages of a Tolstoy novel, six large, hulking beasts, themselves picking their way awkwardly through waist-deep drifts, encircled the car. Each man huddled beneath an enormous fur coat, each head and face obscured by an oversized hat fastened under the chin with leather bands. Even as they gathered around, I had trouble distinguishing the dark skins of their hats from their shaggy black beards. Except for the carbines they carried in their hands or slung over their shoulders, they could have been mistaken for wild animals themselves--mysterious creatures that walked upright and peered out through tiny slits of eyes to survey the harsh winter surroundings engulfing them.

"Wait here. Keep the engine running to stay warm."

"Where are you going?"

Shadar opened the door and stepped out into the blowing snow. "Hello!" he called in Pashto. The wind whipping down from the mountainside picked up his words and scattered them across the tundra.

"*Hello!*" the lead beast called as the men met beside the Jeep.

Shadar motioned toward the Karakul clinging to the side of the Kush. "You have an elusive quarry today," he shouted. "The howling winds and snow make the sheep leery. They are a difficult target."

"The Karakul are always leery. They are always a difficult target. It is this way whenever the winter is so harsh so early in the season."

Two of the men peered curiously into the Jeep through

the driver's side window. I wondered if Shadar had left it cracked open on purpose. Obviously, they had never seen a blonde, blue-eyed *farangi* before.

"That is a fine-looking rifle," Shadar said.

"The leader held his hand up to his ear, and Shadar repeated the words more loudly.

"It will do its job." The Afghan slipped the carbine off his shoulder to give Shadar a closer look.

"Italian?"

"Yes. From a good friend. It's a .308."

Shadar nodded and hoisted it to his shoulder. "It is a good gun for summer hunting, but difficult to use at long range."

The man scowled and pulled the rifle back. "It will do the job," he spat again. "Besides, it is not the gun that kills the beasts but the man." He turned to the others and pointed toward three large sheep clinging to the mountain.

Two men in the back of the pack struggled forward, fighting upwind against the biting sting of the icy snow. They advanced twenty or thirty yards before bogging down in a drift. Buried nearly to their chests, they raised their rifles to their shoulders and pointed them up the slope.

I watched in fascination, more intrigued than horrified, as I waited for the sound. I had never seen hunters up close before. I had never seen a firsthand fight for survival. Shadar was right: if these people did not produce some food, they would starve ... or freeze to death. Perhaps in days, hours, possibly even minutes.

Shadar stood motionless as the two lead hunters, their rifle stocks glued to their shoulders, let loose, and two resounding cracks split the still afternoon air. As the sound from the rifles bounced off the mountainside, the sheep leaped off to one side and started their slow, arduous climb farther up the slopes toward safety.

The old man with the Italian carbine muttered something unintelligible and raised his own rifle to his shoulder. Standing well back behind his two clansmen, he fired once, twice, three times, but his shots landed far short of their target. The sheep continued their slow, contemptuous climb upward until within minutes it was difficult to see them at all.

"This wind! It is the devil's wind!" The old man shook his head while working his way back toward the Jeep. He stopped and turned to the hunters behind him, equally upset about their squandered opportunity.

"No one in his right mind should be hunting in this god-forsaken weather," one of them shouted. "For this, we should beg Allah's forgiveness!"

The man with the Italian carbine put his hands over his eyes and peered up the mountain as if hoping the sheep had tired of their game and decided to make themselves an easier target. I looked to Shadar, but he had disappeared. I thought at first he might have bent down for some reason and pressed my nose up against the driver's window to see.

A sound from the back of the Jeep startled me. I whirled around.

"I won't be long." Shadar had lowered the rear gate and was tugging on a large wooden crate.

"What are you doing?"

"I'm just ..." He grunted as he pulled the crate out onto the tailgate. "I'm just helping out a friend."

"I didn't know you knew these men."

He swung the box around and lifted open the top, reaching inside to withdraw a long, thin wrap. Untying one end, he slipped a rifle from its sheath. He pulled the bolt back, peered at me over the crate, and--satisfied--set it closed again. He looked into my eyes, a look of calm determination. "I don't. I meant *you*."

I stared at him blankly as he shoved the crate forward and lifted the tailgate up, again. I waited for him to reappear around the side of the Jeep. The leader of the hunting party had made his way through the drifts to help retrieve one of the other hunters who had fallen into the snow and was nearly buried. Together, the two Pashtuns pulled their friend free and brushed one another off.

From the corner of one eye, I caught a glimpse of a

fourth figure, half-covered with snow.

Shadar! He had come around the passenger side of the Jeep and trudged up onto a small ledge overlooking a deep ravine that fell thirty feet before slowly starting its long, gradual rise up the base of the mountain. Waist-deep in snow, he raised the rifle to his shoulder and wrapped the sling snuggly around his left forearm. He turned the rear ring of the scope until he was comfortable with the range, and then he pressed the butt of the rifle against his right shoulder, nestling his face against the stock. Standing perfectly still against the vortex whipping down against him, he paused. Ten seconds passed. Twenty. He stood like that for what seemed an eternity until I began to worry that something might be wrong. And then it happened.

"Kerrack!" the rifle called out. I jumped as the sudden burst rattled the windows. The hunters, too, leapt back, startled. Before the echo of the retort had returned from the hillside, one of the sheep had fallen in its tracks.

"Kerrack!" A second burst split the air, and a second sheep fell, this one tumbling into a snow-lined couloir and sliding halfway down the mountain, sending a small avalanche of snow tumbling down before it.

Shadar looked over at the old man, who gazed at him in shock. Struggling down off his perch, he paused before the leader of the group, who motioned to the others in the party to begin the trek up the mountain to fetch the sheep. He shouted something to the old man, who had reached out his hand to grasp Shadar's, but his words were lost to the bitter howl of the wind. The windows in the Jeep rattled again, more fiercely this time, and I felt my feet begin to numb as each second the storm picked up in intensity.

The old man took the rifle from Shadar, who pointed to the solitary animal still clinging to the cliffs. The man hefted the gun to his shoulder and, taking some moments to adjust the scope, followed the movement of the sheep as it disappeared behind a small squall that blew down from a ledge hanging over it. When the sheep reappeared from the ice and swirling snow, a third shot rang out. The animal paused, raised its head for a split second, and then fell in a heap.

The man turned toward Shadar and broke into a toothy smile as the two trudged back toward the vehicle. I scooted behind the wheel and rolled down the drivers-side window as they drew near.

"That will feed your families until the weather eases and the snows let up."

The two clenched hands and hugged, and then the old man motioned the others to retrieve the last kill.

"Our homes are always open to you and your woman," the man shouted back to Shadar. "Both today and every day."

"Allah would be pleased! But we must return to Kabul where we have work to finish. Someday, though, we will come again to share your food and hospitality. When the weather is more hospitable."

The two laughed as the old man slipped the sling off his shoulder and held the rifle out to Shadar. He held up his hand and shook his head. Reaching inside his coat pocket, he pulled out a box of shells and handed them to the man. "To go with your new rifle," he shouted above the wind. "Seven-millimeter mag." He hesitated. "You can find more shells in Kabul."

The old man stared in disbelief, looking first at Shadar, and then down at the gun in his hand, and finally back to his young countryman. The man's cheek quivered below one eye, from the wind or from something else, I couldn't tell. He went to remove his Italian carbine from his shoulder as a goodwill gesture, but Shadar waved it off.

"Where you call home," he yelled, "you cannot have enough weapons."

The old man nodded, started to say something, and stopped. His eyes had said enough. Finally, he turned and began the long, solitary trek up the mountain to join his companions.

It was nearly dark by the time we saw the lights from

the city stretched out along the horizon. I had grown sleepy and had snuggled up to Shadar on the way back. As I stirred, I looked out at Kabul rushing across the plains to greet us and felt a sudden wash of relief.

"There is something sinister about the vast reaches of the endless Kush." It was as if an aura of death had hung over us at the base of the mighty mountains, like a large white curtain ready to fall. On one side lay warmth and happiness and life; on the other, an endless, cold abyss from which one's return was never imminent.

"How long have you been awake?" Shadar said softly.

"*Umm.*" I yawned. "Just now. I had a dream about the mountains … and the hunters."

"I had a dream, too."

I raised my brows and peered up at him.

"A daydream. Driving back from Chitral."

"A daydream about what?"

"You remember what you told me earlier--about the five million *afghanis* your husband stole from you and your friend."

"Yes?"

"Well, I think I have a solution."

"To what?"

"To where you can get the money to repay your friend."

"What? Where?"

"I will lend it to you. That way, you would be able to pay your friend back, and your conscience would be clear."

"Oh, right. Except that then I'd owe *you* five million *afghanis*. I'd still be no closer to paying off my debt."

"Yes, but I can afford to loan you the money until you get the money back from your husband."

"Which may be never."

"Which may be never, you are right. Regardless, at least you would be able to hold your head up at the clinic. And you would be revered and recalled as an honorable and trusted employee."

"You make it sound as if I'm about to die."

"I hope not," he laughed. "But it is difficult to say just how long you will remain at the clinic. What if you were to decide to leave?"

"What if I did?"

"You would not feel comfortable doing so, knowing you still owed your friend so much money. Would you?"

"And what if I take you up on your offer and we have a big fight or something? How would I feel about leaving *you* if I owed you money?"

"That's ridiculous. Anyway, it's totally ... *different*."

"Oh? How?"

"Quite simple. First of all, you *are* going to leave the clinic. Second, you *aren't* going to leave me."

"Ever?"

"Ever."

"You're quite sure of yourself, aren't you?"

He smiled. "In this case? Quite."

"Don't forget. I've already left one man who thought I was going to stay with him forever."

"That's where you are wrong." He paused. "He was no man."

I stretched over and looked at the small electric clock on the nightstand. Three-fifteen.

Shadar started. "What? What is it? What's the matter?"

"Do you know what time it is?" I asked.

"I have no idea. Why?"

"I have to get up in less than three hours to go to work."

"*Mmm.*" He pulled me closer to him, cuddling up against my back and kissing the nape of my neck.

"Hey," I said, turning to meet his lips with my own, "If I'm going to get up for work, I've got ... to ..." I kissed him several more times--short, light kisses followed by deep, longer ones. "I've got to get ... some ... sleep."

He kissed me once again, his warm, wet, willing lips melting against mine, his hands sliding down my hips, thighs, then slowly working their way up, lingering gently, lovingly working their magic until I thought I would explode.

"Shadar, I really should ..."

With a deep sigh, he released me. "Rejected again."

"We went to sleep only four hours ago!"

"See what I mean?"

I laughed. "You wouldn't worry about feeling spurned if *you* had to get up in three hours to take care of a clinic full of sick people."

"I thought you taught midwives ..."

"That's finished. They'll be graduating next weekend."

"Then, your work at the clinic is through?"

"My work at the clinic is never through."

"But, with your students it is finished."

"Yes. With them."

"So, you can leave."

"Sure, assuming I don't ever want to eat again."

"No. That is nonsense. I am talking serious, and you are spurning me again."

I looked closely at his eyes. I thought about Bob, about our first date in Chicago, his promises, his optimism, the certainty of it all. And how that turned out.

"Now *you're* talking nonsense."

"No. I'm serious. If you are finished teaching your classes, you could leave, quit the Peace Corps."

"Why would I do that?"

"So that you could be with me."

"Every hour of the day? Wouldn't that grow a little monotonous?"

"I mean leave with me for Dailut-Ya. It's a small town on the Afghan-Soviet border, just north of Chitral."

"Why?"

"I have some work to do there. For a couple of days."

"You'll be back?" I heard the fear in my voice as the words slipped out.

"Yes, of course, as soon as possible, but not to Kabul."

Panic seized me. "What do you mean?"

"My services are not needed here."

"What services? And where else would you go?"

"I told you. Come with me to Dailut-Ya. Wherever we

go after that, we'll be together."

I reached over and turned on the light. His eyes were aglow.

"You're serious, aren't you?"

"Yes, of course. We will leave the day after tomorrow, Wednesday. We will stay for two days, maybe three. It depends."

I thought for a moment. I had wanted to leave Kabul for weeks. The only reason I hadn't left already was Bob. And now, with him no longer an excuse …

"But I can't just up and leave. I can't just quit."

"Why not?"

"Well, for one thing, I still owe Dinara ten million *afghanis*."

"I told you. Not a problem."

"And for another, I have a contract with the Peace Corps."

"Consider it canceled."

I shook my head. "This is crazy. You're talking like a madman."

"Why? What is so mad about wanting to be with you?"

"I don't know. I mean, what would I do? Where would we go after you're finished in Dailut-Ya?"

"You told me that you miss your parents."

I paused. "Yes."

"Well, we will go to America to see them."

I shook my head. "I don't believe this."

"What? Why not?"

"It's too much, too soon. I don't know what …"

"I am giving you the money to repay your friend at the clinic. You can tell her about your breakup with your husband. Tell her you're going home to America. She will understand."

"And what will I do while we're in Dailut-Ya?"

"What every woman does in Dailut-Ya. Cook and bake and weave."

I laughed. "I don't know how to weave."

"It will be a good opportunity to learn."

I shrugged.

"Fine," he said. "Then, it is all settled."

"Wait a minute. It is *not* all settled. I can't just pack up and quit my job, quit the Corps, and go chasing around the countryside with you."

"Why not?"

"Well, for one thing, it ... it just wouldn't be *right*."

"Since when is it not right for one person to be with another when both are in love?"

I looked at him closely, studying the light shining in his eyes, the shape of his brow, the hard, firm edge to his chin. It was the first time he'd used that word, the first time I'd heard it in months. I knew he was right. I *did* love him. Perhaps more than I should have. He gave me something I hadn't had in so very, very long. He cared about me. He needed me. And I needed him, just as I had once needed Bob. The difference was that Shadar fulfilled my needs. He watched over me, pampered me, made love to me, *cherished* me. Somewhere along the line, Bob had grown away from all that--if he'd ever known it at all. Just as I had come to love Bob, he had grown to love only himself.

"Do you mean that?"

"Of course." He paused, furrowing his brows. "Do I mean what?"

"That you love me?"

He smiled. "That's an easy one." He reached over and switched off the lamp, and for a while, we were both silent. And at last he whispered, "More than you will ever know."

"And you will return with me to America?" I asked just as softly.

"By this time next week, we will be in Milwaukee."

"Oh, my God. I don't know. It's such a big step, so sudden. I have to think about it. I mean, everything is happening so fast. I'd have to make arrangements, talk to Dinara, have my passport updated. That all takes time."

"Time is one thing we do not have."

"Why not? You could go to Dailut-Ya, and I'll stay here to make arrangements. Then, when your work is finished and you return to Kabul, we can make whatever last-minutes arrangements are necessary and then fly back to the states."

"No. Once I am finished in Dailut-Ya, I cannot return to Kabul. Not ever."

"Why not?"

"I ... cannot tell you."

"But if it involves you, it should be something we can talk about. If you love me, if you really do, you should be willing to confide in me. I don't want to get hurt again. I don't want to make the wrong decision. If I was to leave with you and something happened to us, something happened to ... I just don't know if I could cope with it."

"What I must do in Dailut-Ya I cannot tell even my own brother."

"You don't have a brother."

He hesitated. "That is another reason."

I thought for several seconds. "Is it dangerous?" I felt the sweat forming on my brow.

"Yes," he replied softly. "Very."

I felt tears spring to my eyes. "Would I be in danger?"

"I don't know. Possibly. But I think not," he replied, adding, "if all goes right."

I rolled over and buried my face in my pillow, trying to hide my tears. I felt his hand on my back, his warm breath against my neck.

"Why?" I asked, sobbing. "Why does life have to be so complicated? Why can't it just go on the way it's been these past few days?"

"I don't have the answer to that," he said, stroking my temple lightly. "I wish I did."

TWELVE

I knew it would be difficult telling Dinara I was leaving. But when I arrived at the clinic the following morning, she had a surprise for me

"What is it?" I asked.

She looked me squarely in the eyes. "You're fired."

I stared in disbelief. "*What?*"

She smiled and pulled me close. "I already know."

"Know what?"

"That you're leaving the Peace Corps and leaving the clinic."

"But how … when …"

"Shadar sent a message earlier this morning. He said that Bob had abandoned you at the Christmas Party at the club. And that he's back doing drugs."

I nodded. Grabbed her. Held her close.

"It's okay. It's all right. I'm so happy for you. You'll be returning to your home in Wisconsin soon, and you'll get to see your parents again."

"Oh, God, Dinara. I'm looking forward to it. Although …" I struggled to fight back the tears. "I'll miss you so much."

"And I, you. But who can say what the future holds? Maybe one day soon, under different circumstances, you will return to Afghanistan, and we can go to meet my uncle again and next time enjoy more of his hospitality. And Shadar, too."

I smiled. "I would love that."

"You will always be in our hearts. For all the

wonderful things you have done for us here at the clinic … and for our people."

I told her I had wanted to stay until I figured out a way to pay her back the remainder of the ten million *afghanis,* but I insisted I would get the money once I returned to the states. I said I would wire it to her first thing.

"He didn't tell you?"

I paused. "Who? Tell me what?"

"Shadar. He sent ten one-million-dollar notes along with the messenger. Your debt is repaid in full."

"Oh, my God."

"You didn't know?"

"He left a note on the bed for me this morning. He said he'd be busy all day making plans for our departure for Dailut-Ya. But he never mentioned …"

"He purchased some new luggage for you and had it delivered here as well."

"I can't believe it. Everything is moving so fast."

"It may seem that way to you now. But perhaps everything only *seems* to be moving fast because of your new friend and newly emerging life. And how mired in lethargy your life had been before."

"I guess that could be true. I never thought of it that way."

She paused as we walked to her office. "Is he good for you?"

"I … I think so."

"And do you love him?"

I hesitated for only a moment. "Yes."

"Then everything is moving exactly as fast as it should."

Before I could respond, someone knocked on the door. Dr. Rashad peeked in.

"Is this a private party?" Three of the nurses followed after him.

"What's this?"

He smiled. "Only what you deserve."

One of the nurses presented me with a cake with the words, "Happy Birthday and Good Luck," scribbled in

English. "I wrote the message myself," she beamed. I smiled, fighting back the tears, and reached out to her, hugged her, and kissed her on the cheek. Salay held out a package--a combination "Birthday and going-away present." I opened it through swollen eyes. Inside was a plump Karakul hat, with a fur brim that turned down to cover the ears, and a note.

Thank you, Paula Favage, for all you have done for us. You will never be forgotten. - Dr. Rashad and Staff

"We will miss you," Dinara said, squeezing me so hard, I felt the muscles inside my chest ache. As she clutched me, I could feel the tremors in her body. I would miss her, too. Most of all, I would miss her.

When we had finally finished, Dinara called a cab and helped load my belongings into the trunk. She kissed me on the cheek. As I got in, tears formed in my eyes. I rolled down the window, squeezed her hand one last time, and told her I would remember her always. And then the car lurched into gear and began our lumbering journey over the ice-and-snow-packed roads back to town.

At home, I set the luggage in the bedroom and opened the largest bag first. Inside I found another note, this one written in Persian:

Will be home around 7. Bad weather coming to the plains necessitates our leaving tonight. Be packed. Love, S.

As I labored that afternoon over the stove, I couldn't help but think about him--where he was, what he was doing. And I thought about us--where we might be three weeks from then, three months, three years.

I tried to take things one day at a time, not to plan too far ahead, not to fall into that trap. Still, I couldn't help but wonder what life with him would be like. In a few days, we would be free of the yoke of Afghanistan, of the drugs and the rebels, of the midnight calls by thieves and murderers, and we would be back in the states. Certainly, we would live together once we got to Milwaukee. Or maybe it wouldn't be Milwaukee. Maybe we would visit my family there, and then we would find another place to live. Chicago, St. Louis, Kansas City, Minneapolis. I just wanted to stay in the Midwest, somewhere not too far from home, to be near my parents as they grew older.

Then, one day, perhaps, Shadar would ask me to marry him. Or maybe *I* would propose, and *he* would say yes. And we would have children--a boy who looked just like his father, and a girl with dark eyes and fair skin. And after a trying day of tending to skinned knees and sprained fingers, I would welcome Shadar home from the university, where he would be teaching.

At night, he would light the fire, and we would settle in on the sofa, the children fast asleep. We would hold hands and talk--about little things, about our days together, about our pasts, and make plans for our future: a large home in the country; perhaps more children; a pay raise, tenure, and a full professorship for him teaching Central Asian history.

"You idiot," I mumbled to myself, upset for stringing out the fantasy so long. There would be plenty of time for daydreaming later. First I had to finish the quiche I was preparing for dinner. Shadar really *would* be home before long, and we would need to stuff as much of our luggage as we could possibly fit into the Jeep.

We would have to leave Shadar's furnishings behind, and that upset me. He had some beautiful antiques, some things I was sure had been passed down from one generation to the next. Still, parting with them didn't seem to bother him. He knew we could use the money from their sale, especially after he had paid my debt to Dinara. I didn't know how well off he was, but I knew he wasn't rich.

I had lost some of the salary I had accumulated from working at the clinic when I broke my contract with the Corps. All I had to my name was a little over a hundred thousand *afghanis*, and I really owed that to him.

I heard the sound from outdoors. "Hey, you." I said as I swung around. Shadar peeked through the doorway.

"Are you addressing *me*?"

He closed the door behind him and swept me into his

arms, kissed me on the lips, his hands working small, firm circles at the base of my neck as I moaned in delight.

"Oh, God, I've missed you."

"Me, too," he said softly, and he kissed me again. When we finally broke, I looked up into his eyes. There was no doubt in my mind. Not when I was with him. We would work things out. No matter what. Or where.

After dinner, we set about packing his things.

"How far is it to Dailut-Ya?"

"A full night's journey ... *if* the weather cooperates. If not, possibly two, three, four days. Maybe more."

"We'll have to take plenty of warm clothes and food. And water."

"I've already taken care of that. I've packed enough supplies to see us through a month."

"And in Dailut-Ya, we have a place to stay?"

"That has all been arranged."

"Were you able to sell your furnishings today?" I asked.

He looked down. "I'm afraid not. I could find no one interested in buying them." He sighed. "Money in Kabul is tight in winter. I asked three people who I thought would be interested in acquiring at least some of my furnishings, but no one wishes to pay even a fraction of what they are worth. We'll just have to leave them for now and hope we are able to send for them--or sell them--later."

"Maybe not. I grabbed a pen and paper and quickly scribbled a short note. "Tell me what you want me to pack, and I'll do it while you take this to Dinara. I've told her what is here and what it's worth and asked her to pay whatever she can if she's interested."

"What makes you think she'll be interested? Or that she has any money to buy?"

"I happen to know that she recently came into ten million *afghanis!* Besides, she is descended from royalty. Her uncle is Shah Khan of Pul-i-Khumri. He will have a place for these things if she doesn't."

His eyebrows rose. "In a shah's palace?"

I laughed. "No, silly. But he knows people. And he has servants. Surely he recognizes the value of fine furnishings."

"Paula ... how much do you know about Dinara?"

"You mean about her past? She explained all that to me."

"She did?"

I looked up. "Yes. Why? What more should I know?"

He looked at me and smiled. "Nothing. Nothing more."

By the time he had returned, I had stuffed the last of four suitcases full of clothes and personal belongings.

"What did she say?"

"She said that she would pay twenty million *afghanis* for the furnishings, and she wished us the best of fortunes. I told her we would leave a key to the house under the front mat when we depart, and she said she will have some friends move the furnishings out tomorrow."

He handed me the envelope she had given him. I opened it and placed the bills on the table. I unfolded a small piece of paper. "She wrote us a note," I said. "How thoughtful."

My gift to you. May it atone for some of the misfortunes you have endured in my country, and may you always think of your friends here kindly. Allah bless you both. – D

I was puzzled. "What does she mean, *gift*?"

Shadar shrugged. I picked up the bills and counted them out.

"My God," I cried.

"What?"

"You said she paid you twenty million *afghanis* for the furniture."

"Yes, why? How much is there?"

"It's ... more than *fifty* million!"

"What? Let me see."

I looked at the note again as Shadar counted out the money.

"We can't possibly keep this. There must be some mistake."

He sighed. "I am afraid we must. You can't return a gift--not without insulting the host."

"But, fifty *million*! That's nearly ... ten thousand dollars! Why would she do such a thing?"

Shadar set the money on the table and crossed the room to the sofa. He patted a spot next to him, and I sat down.

"Paula, I must tell you something that may make it easier for you to understand my people."

"Tell me something? About what?"

"Please. Listen to me. Dinara is a woman of great ... stature in my country. She is descended from royalty."

"Yes. I know. She is Shah Khan's niece."

He shook his head. "No."

I looked at him, half expecting to see him smile. His face was somber. I had never seen that look on him before.

"What do you mean?"

"Shah Khan ... is Dinara's father."

"What? He can't be. Her father is dead. He died holding her in his arms while defending the city. She told me so, herself."

He shook his head again. "Dinara's father died, yes. But only in the eyes of his daughter."

"I don't understand. I met Shah Khan. He called her his niece."

"When Dinara was born, Shah Khan was already a widower. His wife had died several years before."

"I don't understand. Then how could she ... and who is Dinara's mother?"

"One of Shah Khan's concubines. A woman with whom the Shah had an affair. A servant."

"But, why didn't she tell me this? I would have understood."

"It is not something she can ever tell anyone. By being born to a servant, even though her father is the great Shah Khan, she would be looked upon as nothing more than a jackal, an illegitimate child who could not ever be part of the royal line. She would have lost her heritage, her stature, her wealth, everything. She might even have lost her life."

I struggled to digest the information. "Why the elaborate story about her father being a hero and how he had fought alongside her uncle to save the city?"

"The Shah had to protect her from something else, something with which he is involved. Something illegal."

"You mean poppies. And heroin."

"Some, yes. But the real source of Shah Khan's wealth does not come from the sale of a few poppies. It is from the sale of arms."

"Arms?"

"To the rebels."

"I ... I don't understand."

"Shan Khan has been a major supplier of firearms to the rebels for more than two decades. Not everyone knows this, of course. It is not the kind of thing one is anxious to reveal about oneself. But our government knows. And so do the Pakistanis. That is why Shah Khan made up the story about Dinara's father--his brother--having been killed defending Pul-i-Khumri from the Pakistanis. If word had gotten out that Dinara was really the Shah's daughter, she would have been the target of assassins and kidnappers long ago. She would most likely have ended up imprisoned, assassinated ... or worse."

"My God. So she's been forced to live a lie her entire life!"

He nodded.

"But how do you know all this?"

"I deal in many things," he said somberly. "I am, in effect, an importer-exporter. Of sorts."

"An importer-exporter of what things?" I felt the hair on the back of my neck begin to tingle. I wasn't sure I wanted to hear the answer.

"Those things that are most valuable to people intent upon resting power from others."

"Like guns?"

He nodded.

"And drugs?"

"Occasionally."

I felt crushed. I felt as though I were sitting with the enemy. I was the victim of a husband who had succumbed to drugs who had thrown his wife to the wolves because of his addiction. Now I was in the home, in the very arms, of the man who might have been responsible for selling them to him.

"But only to be traded to the Kurdish rebels in their fight against the Pakistanis within their own land."

"But ... but ... how can you be sure they don't end up ..."

"Because," he continued. "I also deal in information. That is the main commodity that I offer for sale."

"What do you mean? Information about what?"

"Clandestine information."

"Are you ..." I hesitated. "Are you ... one of the rebels?"

He sat silently for several moments, pondering my words. Finally, he leaned back, dusted off his pants, and rose from the sofa. "That is all that you need to know for now." He strolled back toward the table. He picked up the bills, folded them once, and slipped them into his pocket. "That is all I can tell you ... for your own well-being."

I traced his steps across the room. "Are you in danger? Will *I* be in danger?"

"Did you pack everything?" he asked.

I nodded. "Everything I could fit."

Shadar went into the bedroom closet. "Don't close that yet." He reached up above the doorway and pulled something from a concealed shelf.

"Here." He held out a small semi-automatic pistol.

"What's this for?"

"For you," he replied. "For your safety."

It was nearly 10 P.M. by the time we'd finished loading the Jeep and set off for Dailut-Ya. The weather was fair, a light misting of snow in the air, but calm. By the time we had arrived at Charikar, Shadar's fears had come true. The winds had picked up, and the storm intensified. It was dark and cold, and though the Kush loomed a scant twenty miles before us, we could see nothing beyond the headlights of the Jeep, and that diminished steadily with each passing kilometer.

Another four hours on the road and we were deep among the mountains, approaching the tiny pass of Ilhalmid. It was a little-traveled route to Chitrat barely over the Pakistani border. As we crossed through the pass, I could feel the immensity of the mountains looming over us, as if attempting to squeeze us, to force us back, to crush the life out of us.

We drove on, and the pass grew narrower. The sides of the mountain rose steeper as we ventured farther from Kabul. The snow on the ground was so deep that the nose of the Jeep was kicking it up and spraying it over the windshield. The wipers had trouble handling the load, and we had to stop several times to get out and scrape the glass clean.

When we'd traveled two-thirds of the way through the pass, I began to breathe more easily. The snow seemed to have lightened, and Chitral lay just thirty kilometers ahead.

"Does anyone ever get stuck in these passes?"

Shadar glanced at me before returning his gaze to the road. "It is said that Alexander the Great lost nearly one-fourth of his army while trying to negotiate the Kush in December."

"Too bad he didn't have four-wheel drive."

Shadar laughed. "Yes, that would certainly have helped."

We drove for several more minutes in silence, the nose of the Jeep snaking its way up the pass, higher and higher until it seemed we were poised at the very threshold of heaven.

"I suppose no one gets stuck these days," I said casually. "I mean, with four-wheel drive and all."

Shadar glanced at me again. "Are you worried?"

"No," I lied. "Not with you driving."

"Good."

Suddenly, fifty feet in the distance, the lights fell on a large, dark object. At first, I thought it was some beast of the wilderness--a great sheep perhaps, or a bear--but as we drew nearer, I could see white numbers painted on its side.

"What is it?"

"I'm not sure," Shadar replied. "Some sort of truck … an abandoned vehicle or something."

We pulled alongside it, buried nearly completely in snow, and got out to take a closer look. In the light from our own vehicle, we saw that the soft top on the disabled truck had been ripped open, the canvas flapping in the stiff mountain wind. We tried to open the doors, but they were frozen shut. I rubbed the glass to take a look inside, but the ice was too thick and refused to yield its secrets.

"Who do you think it belongs to?"

"I don't know. But, from the looks of the serial number on the back, I would say it is German. Possibly from the embassy in Kabul."

"Why would anyone from the embassy have abandoned it here so far from the city?"

Shadar pulled out a pocket knife and began chipping away at the ice on the side window. When he'd finally cleared a small portal, we peeked in.

"Maybe there are supplies inside," I said.

As the ice slowly succumbed to Shadar's knife, he pulled out a small flashlight and shined it into the vehicle.

I screamed suddenly and jumped back. "Oh, my God!"

"What? What is it?"

I motioned toward the light falling on two large eyes staring out.

Shadar pulled me away and threw his arms around me.

"My God!" I cried again. "Did you see? There's a man in there. We have to help him."

"Yes. Yes." He took my hand and led me back to the Jeep. "We must go."

"But ... we can't just leave him. He needs our help. We

can't just ..."

"He cannot use our help. Not now."

"But he ..."

"He is dead."

Shadar opened the door to the Jeep and forced me in before hurrying around to the driver's side.

"What are you doing?" I asked as he turned the key in the ignition. The engine roared to life.

"We're getting out of here."

"We can't leave him here. We can't just *leave* him. He's hurt, freezing. He may still be alive. I'm a nurse. He needs our help. We have to ..."

"Paula, *he is dead!* He is frozen *to death*! There is nothing more we can do for him!" He paused, and he added softly, "Not now. Not anymore."

I sat horrified, glued to the door of the Jeep, frozen as surely as the driver we had just left.

We pressed deeper into the mountains, but I couldn't clear my mind of the image. I had never seen anything like it before in my life. Those eyes. The icicles hanging from his beard. The light from our Jeep dancing off the snow that had settled around him. Most of all, the look of pained agony on his face.

We followed the contours of the mountain pass, plowing a road where there was none only moments before until finally we started heading down, down toward the few sparse lights of Chitral. I stared blankly out the window as Shadar shifted into third, and then into second, the Jeep growling and bucking as though begging to race on.

"There is a roadblock up ahead."

"What?"

"Up ahead."

"Is it trouble?"

"It could be. I'm not sure."

I stared out ahead of us but saw nothing, felt nothing. Even Shadar's words sounded hollow, empty, like the sound of a tin can landing on a metal roof.

He nudged me lightly. "Are you all right?"

"I ..."

"Paula, are you all right?" he asked again.

"I ... think so."

"There will be Pakistani border guards at the roadblock. Just remain quiet and keep your composure. Don't panic, no matter what happens. I will take care of everything. Do you understand?"

I nodded. "Yes."

The Jeep's gears ground suddenly as Shadar downshifted and leaned steadily on the brakes. Finally, we pulled to a halt, and two bouncing white lights approached from a small wooden shack on the side of the road. The figures behind the lights were bundled up against the cold and the snow, which had begun falling harder again. Shadar pulled his own collar up around his neck, opened the door to the Jeep, and stepped out into the heavy night air.

I watched as he greeted the men, pointed back toward the Jeep, and then pulled his wallet from his inside coat pocket. Fishing for something, he finally selected a document, which he unfolded and handed to the guards. They looked at it in the light from their beams, looked back at the Jeep, and paused. One of the guards began walking toward me, and I could hear my heart beating wildly. Louder and louder the sound grew with each step the man took until finally he reached the vehicle and signaled for me to open the door. I was petrified, immobile. Should I do it? Or should I wait for some sign from Shadar? The guard motioned again, and I instinctively slid my hand over to the latch and pulled up on it.

When the door opened, the guard poked his head in and said something in Pakistani. I stared up at him blankly. I was sure he could hear the pounding of my heart, see the sweat on my brow, feel the tension between us. What if he decided to search me? What if he asked to see my passport? What if he asked what I was doing in Chitral, in Pakistan? Would I tell him that I was blindly following directions from my rebel lover?

At that moment, I heard Shadar say in Persian, "She is

sick." He repeated the words in Pakistani. I coughed once, then, turning toward the guard, coughed again as he put his hand up to his face. He glanced quickly around the Jeep, exchanged some words with Shadar, and looked at the second guard before finally waving us on.

Shadar climbed back into the driver's seat. The guard slammed the passenger door. Briefly, he stared in at me, and I out at him, before the Jeep slowly began to roll down the road toward town.

"That was close," Shadar said when we'd traveled a thousand yards.

I breathed deeply. "What are we doing in Pakistan?"

"It is a shortcut to Dailut-Ya. The main pass through Afghanistan is sure to be closed. We had no choice."

"Why did you say that was close? What was close?"

"The Pashtun rebels recently launched an attack against the Pakistanis. If the guards had mistaken us for Pashtun sympathizers ..."

"Where was the attack? Nearby?"

"Yes," he replied. "In Dailut-Ya."

Shortly after noon on Tuesday, we reached our destination. Like a small jewel set in a large ring, it was a quaint town with short, squatty buildings and a great, round-topped mosque in the center of the square. The snow in some areas had drifted as high as the windows on the homes. Nowhere was there sign of life except for the occasional light trail of smoke snaking its way from a rooftop chimney.

The Jeep rolled to a stop in front of a small, shuttered hut; silence washed over us. Nothing made a sound--not the chirping of a bird, not the cry of a baby, only the occasional whistle of the wind whipping down off the steppes and funneling through the narrow alleyways separating the buildings.

"It looks abandoned."

Shadar shook his head. "The people are here, but they have locked themselves in against the winter winds--and war."

We got out of the Jeep and trudged through knee-high snow, Shadar dragging two large suitcases that left long, narrow tracks on either side of our footprints. I stopped at the front door to the hut, and Shadar motioned me to open it.

Once inside, we quickly set about building a fire to protect us from the bitter cold that rattled down upon us. All of the windows of the hut were either shuttered or covered by snow. I searched for a lamp in the darkness.

"There--on the table." He pointed to one side of the large main room.

I looked at him curiously as he pulled a lighter from his pocket. "No electricity." I brought the kerosene lamp over to the stove. "But this will do." He lifted the glass chimney and touched the flame to the wick, and soon the room was bathed in a soft glow of gold.

I looked around the hut as Shadar went out to retrieve the rest of our belongings. It had been hours since we'd eaten. Except for one small table, two high-backed chairs, and the stove, there were no furnishings. "Too bad we couldn't have brought your things from Kabul. We could have used a bed."

He grunted.

I walked through a small doorway at the far end of the room and found the bath, which consisted of a second small table, a black kettle filled with frozen water, a cracked mirror, and a small commode. I shivered.

I came back out into the main room, where Shadar had set the rest of our belongings before slamming the door shut. He beat his gloved hands together and danced around the stove for a few seconds before pulling off his hat.

"Well," he said, glancing around, "what do you think?"

"What's there to think?"

He smiled and nodded slowly. "Pretty bad, huh?"

"If you think *this* is bad, you ought to see what's in there." I nodded toward the bathroom.

"*Uh-huh*. Let me guess. A Dailut-Ya special."

"And what's that?"

"One pot to wash in, and another to ..."

"You're clairvoyant." I snuggled up against him, reaching up for a kiss, and then I squeezed him as tightly as I could.

"What's that for?"

I told him I wasn't sure, and we laughed.

"Well, how about some food, then?"

"I get the honor?"

"Come on." He motioned toward his pack. "I'll help."

We finished a lunch of dried fruit, goat's cheese, and dehydrated lamb that reminded me of beef jerky except stronger in taste, and we unfolded two sleeping mats next to the stove. We spent the rest of the morning cleaning up and trying to make the place look livable. By mid-afternoon, we were exhausted. We curled up for a short nap and ended up sleeping through the night.

The following morning, as the sun peeked over the distant mountains, I lolled lazily under a blanket, listening to Shadar fumble with the stove.

"Come on, sleepy head. Nap time's over."

"What time *is* it?" I asked.

He held out his watch. "It is precisely ... Wednesday."

"*Wednesday*?" I shot up and looked around the room. "Wednesday? You're kidding."

"I never kid about Wednesdays. Mondays, Tuesdays, maybe even Thursdays. Never Wednesdays."

I pulled myself from bed and, shivering in the early morning cold, hurried into the bathroom. I grabbed the kettle of frozen water and brought it to the stove to thaw. While Shadar rummaged through his case, I set about fixing breakfast. We were hungry enough to finish off some salted mutton, halvah, and rice, along with a pot of tea. I had just put a second pot of water on the stove when a knock sounded at the door. Shadar opened it cautiously, peeked out, and then he threw it back wide.

"So, my friend. You have arrived safely in Dailut-Ya!" The largest of the three men standing in the doorway spoke in clipped *Pashto*. He was wrapped in a goatskin coat that hung nearly to the ground, and over his shoulder: the ubiquitous carbine.

"Come in, come in! We are just preparing tea. It will take some of the chill out of those old and crusted bones."

The men entered, and the one with the carbine pulled off his hat, sending a sudden flurry of snow to the floor.

Motioning to me, Dalal said something I couldn't make out.

"Well, if you'll give me a second. Dalal, this is a good friend of mine--Paula Favage. Paula, this is Dalal. And Jamal," Shadar said, pointing to the second man. "And this fellow here, the ugly one, is Jahad."

"Hello." I smiled. "It's nice to meet you. All of you."

"By Allah, Shadar," Dalal said, "a *farangi* as beautiful as a nightingale, yet who speaks the language of our forefathers! Why did you not tell us you would be traveling with a little sparrow so beautiful as this?"

"I can't tell you *everything* I do!" The three Pashtuns laughed.

"She is your wife?" Jamal asked. He was thin, with a full mustache and deeply set eyes.

"Not yet." Shadar beamed at me.

"Then, you must make plans soon so we shall dance at your wedding!" Dalal's black eyes glistened as a huge smile broke across his face. He had a twinkle in one eye, set deeply amidst a face scarred by the elements of war, similar to the glint I had seen so many times in my own grandfather's eyes. "A man would have to be a fool to let one so beautiful escape his grasp!" He stepped forward suddenly and, grabbing me in two huge, bear-like claws, lifted me off the floor like a rag doll, spun me around the room, and finally dropped me down next to Shadar.

"But, by Allah, she is a light, young thing, no bigger than a mynah bird! Are you sure she is sturdy enough to make you a good wife?"

"If not," Jahad said, "I'm sure Dalal would consent to step in and take your place, by Allah!"

"What are friends for? You need only ask, and your wish is my command!" Dalal leaned forward. "Just so you do not forget and tell my wife! She would have me skinned alive."

All of us laughed, deep and hard, and I found myself instinctively moving closer to Shadar's side. Suddenly serious, he motioned with his head toward the door. "The weather is bad, yes?"

"The weather is as usual," Jamal said.

"Then, there are likely to be few Pakistani patrols out today."

Dalal spat on the floor. "Let them come. We will be ready for them."

"You heard of the battle that took place outside Charikar yesterday?" Jamal asked.

Shadar nodded. "We ran into two border guards at Chitral, and they told us."

The three Pashtuns laughed deep and hard. "Good news travels fast."

"Good news?"

"What else would you call ten dead Pakistanis? We captured six Soviet machine guns and four Kalashnikov rifles. The Pakistanis are contributing nicely to the welfare of the new Pashtun state, no?"

Shadar glanced back at me, and then he motioned the three men outside.

I ran to the window and peeked through the slats. Against the stark-white snow, I could see Shadar talking to them as they listened intently. But then a cold, mean look came over Dalal, and I heard his voice boom out in the early morning air. Shadar listened calmly before continuing with what he was saying. Jamal and Jahad tried to soothe the huge man, which took some doing before he finally grunted, rubbing the ice still clinging to his thick, scraggly beard, and then nodding once to Shadar.

As the door to the hut opened, I quickly slid away from the shutters. "Where are your friends? Aren't they joining us for tea?"

"I'm afraid not. And, worse, I'm afraid I cannot stay, either." He came up to me and took me in his arms, squeezing me tightly and pursing a kiss against my lips.

"Don't tell me. Let me guess. You're going with them."

"That's what I like about you Americans. You never waste words saying what's on your mind."

"When will you be back?"

"I'm not sure."

"In time for dinner?"

"A late dinner. Perhaps, yes."

I looked into his eyes and met a pained expression. "What is it? Can you tell me?"

He shook his head. "Nothing. Nothing that I can discuss right now."

"You discussed it with them. Why can't you tell me?"

He pushed me suddenly back. "You were listening!"

"I was *not!*" I said indignantly. "I would *never!*"

"Then, how did you ..."

"I was *looking*. Through the shutters. There's a difference."

Shadar winced and reached for his coat.

"Can't you tell me? Please? I'm going to be worried sick not knowing what you're doing."

"If I could, I would. I promise you that. Besides, nothing bad will happen to me this day." He slipped his coat on and fastened it tightly against the bitter winds of the plains. I looked at him for several seconds before I threw my arms around his neck and squeezed as hard as I could.

"I wish you didn't have to go. I know you do, but I wish you didn't. There's danger out there that you're involved in. I don't know what I'd do if anything happened to you."

Shadar reached out and brushed a single tear from my cheek. Holding my chin, he moved closer still to me, cocked his head to one side, and placed a long, firm kiss on my lips. I closed my eyes and imagined that we were somewhere else--far, far away from Afghanistan, from Pakistan, from the dangers of rebel forces and government troops. When I opened them again, he was gone.

"Be careful!" I called, racing out into the cold morning air. "All of you!"

I stood waist-deep in the snow that had accumulated outside the stoop overnight. Shadar turned around and threw me a kiss, "I'll have some villagers call on you later, so you won't be lonely."

I watched him slide behind the wheel of the Jeep. As he coaxed the engine to life, an old, battered truck parked farther down the road also sputtered and growled, sending a huge black cloud of smoke belching from its exhaust; and the two vehicles pulled away, rolling off into the glistening white horizon.

THIRTEEN

I stood next to the stove, transfixed at the sight. It was like being in the bazaar in Kabul, only *it* had come to *me*.

"Would you like the chair placed here?" Sharmani spoke in thick mountain *Pashto*.

"Yes," I answered. "Yes, that would be fine."

The small, greying wife of Dalal arranged the chair next to three others that she and her friends had brought with them from their homes. They also brought a small table, several large baskets of food that they had carried on their heads, a number of pots and pans, a large incense burner complete with a handful of homemade joss sticks, and six children--including the most adorable young girl I'd ever seen. The children ranged in age from three or four to nearly adult. They had come at Shadar's request to keep the young *farangi* woman company, to help her get settled into the hut, and to protect her from the wilds of Dailut-Ya.

But who's going to protect me *from* them?

Once the new furnishings had been arranged to my satisfaction, the Pashtuns emptied out large sacks of Karakul yarn, from which they prepared to produce the *pièce de résistance*--a woven rug to place before the stove. It would complete the metamorphosis from caterpillar to brilliant moth. The yarn was hued like a rainbow, orange and red, brown and ochre, green and yellow. It was thicker than any I'd seen before.

"Where did you find such vibrant colors?"

"We make them from the dyes in the mountain plants

that grow high in the Kush during spring. We collect the plants and pound them on stones until they are shredded into thin, tough strands. These we place in kettles of water and the renderings from young lambs. The kettles must then be made to boil ever so slowly for three days."

"That's remarkable," I said, fingering the wool.

"It is something my mother taught me," Sharmani replied, "something she learned from her mother and she from hers. There is an old saying among the Pashtun mountain people: From a mother one learns how to bake, how to cook, and how to dye wool."

"And not," one of the other women interjected, "how to satisfy a husband?"

The women all laughed.

"That," Sharmani confided, "is easier said than done."

"When will *I* learn how to satisfy a husband?" Sharrnani's daughter, a girl of fifteen, asked.

"On your wedding night, no less. There is plenty of time for that. Do not be in such a hurry." The woman turned to me. "She is anxious. She is to be wed next year to Joban."

"He was one of the men who came here with your husband and Jamal this morning, wasn't he?"

She nodded. "Yes. That is the one."

"Well, congratulations," I told the girl. I held out my hand.

"There are better men," Sharmani said flatly. "*Much* better."

"He is a *fine* man," her daughter insisted. "He will make a wonderful provider. He is an excellent hunter. He never fails to bring back the largest ram when the men go on the hunt into the hills."

"True. But he is old enough to be your father. A man's eyesight fails him in time. Soon Joban will no longer be able to give you the largest of *anything.*"

The others laughed.

"You are too easy on him," said a woman with huge breasts and a chin marked with a single crescent-shaped dimple. "He is not only old, he has the memory of a yak."

They laughed again, and I was beginning to believe them.

"You sound as if you're not pleased with your daughter's marriage to Joban."

Sharmani shrugged. "Pleased, no. But Joban and Dalal reached an agreement. It is too late to change things now."

"Why too late? Didn't Dalal consult with you or your daughter?"

"Why would he? It is the place of a young girl's father to decide which of his daughters marries, and to whom."

"Don't be so hard on the old man," another woman said. "There are worse in the world. *Somewhere.*"

"Like Old Nadir," a third woman said, and they all laughed. Sharmani turned to me and, holding out a strand of yarn, asked, "Have you ever before woven a rug?"

I shook my head. "I've never woven *anything.*"

She looked at me as if to ask, *Why would a man choose for his companion a woman who cannot weave?* "Well, it is not hard to learn. You will know by the time Shadar returns from the plains."

"I thought it took years to learn."

"Six hours with Sharmani will *feel* like years," one of the women said. The older woman threw a skein of yarn at her.

I paused, watching as Sharmani prepared the yarn, and thought out loud. "Do you have any idea of when the men will be back? I was hoping Shadar would ..."

She shrugged. "One cannot say when freedom fighters will return ... or what skirmishes they will encounter."

Freedom fighters!

"Now," she said, pulling her stool nearer to me. "Pay attention to the needles. Always watch the needles, for they tell you when you have made a mistake so that you can go back and correct it before you go too far. That is very important."

As my lesson wore on, the others beat their yarn against the hard clay floor to soften it, after which they rolled it into skeins. Sharmani and Dari--the dark-haired, plain-faced woman who had defended Joban--showed me how to lace the yarn on a large wooden frame pierced with inch-long spikes. In no time, they had produced a platter-sized mat that would serve as the core of the rug.

By the time three o'clock rolled around, I was weaving. The rug had somehow managed to take shape, growing as if by magic from a single strand of wool into a circle nearly three feet across.

As the others packed up their belongings and bundled up their young, I laid the half-finished rug out before the stove.

"By this time tomorrow," Sharmani said, "it will be complete."

I had hoped there would not be a tomorrow filled with weaving. I had hoped that Shadar would return that night, his work finished, and that we could ready ourselves for the rest of our lives together.

"It's beautiful." I was proud at having been part of the process. "Thank you so much for teaching me."

"A woman should know how to weave if she is to make a man a good wife."

For a second I considered telling her that Shadar and I weren't betrothed, just dose friends, but I decided against it. I wasn't sure what customs the mountain people had, and the last thing I wanted was for them to think of me as some wanton *farangi* hussy with her eye out for any good-looking Afghan who happened to come along. "Yes. I'm sure she should."

"And a woman in the mountains of Dailut-Ya should know certain other things, as well. Especially so young and attractive a woman as the American *farangi.*"

I looked at her for several seconds. "What kinds of things?"

"Like how to protect herself."

I smiled. "Don't worry. I can take care of ..."

She cut me off with a wave of her arm. "You have a gun?"

"A *what?*"

She held out her hand and pulled on her thumb, as

though cocking the hammer of a pistol.

"No," I said. "I ..."

"Shadar said he gave you a gun before you departed Kabul for Dailut-Ya."

"Oh!" I suddenly remembered. "He *did* give me a pistol, yes." I went over to my case and pulled out the small weapon from beneath some clothing. "Here." I held it away from me as if it were a dead mouse. "I almost forgot."

Sharmani took the weapon from my hand, pulled back the bolt, and slid the small clip from the butt. Looking inside, she mumbled something under her breath and jammed the clip back in until it snapped. "Well, it is not much of a gun, but it will have to do. Come. I will show you."

The others had already scattered to the winds when Sharmani and I stepped outside the hut. The sun was low along the horizon, casting contorted shadows across the glistening snow. Scanning the horizon, the woman's eyes fell on a large, round, snow-covered bale a hundred feet away.

"This," she said, pointing to a small latch on the side of the pistol. "This is the safety. When it is in this position, so"--she pulled the latch back--"it will not fire. Moving it forward, like this, releases the lock on the trigger and frees the firing pin. Do you understand?"

I nodded, amazed at how efficiently she spoke, as though she had run through this very talk many times before. An icy wind blew down from the snow-covered valley engulfing the town, and I wrapped my arms around my body to protect myself.

"Here," she continued, pointing to another small latch. "This is the release for the clip, which holds the cartridges. Pull the bolt back so, press the release down like this, and the clip will slip out of the handle of the gun." She removed the clip and held it up. "Inside the clip are the .38-caliber shells. Ten of them."

"They look so small," I said, my teeth chattering.

"They are large enough to kill," she said calmly.

"Now, to replace the clip, slip it into this slot until it clicks, so. Push the bolt forward, and the top shell moves from the clip into the chamber, where it can be fired. Until the first shell is in the chamber, the gun will not fire. It is like a second safety." She raised the pistol high in the air and lowered it slowly to eye's height, her arm extended before her. I watched as she held her breath and pulled gently back on her finger.

"Kerrack!" It was a small, muffled sound that barely carried to the mountains and back--not at all like the boom of Shadar's rifle the previous day.

"Did you hit it?" I asked, not quite sure how she could expect to miss something as large as a bale of hay at a hundred feet.

Sharmani walked out onto the road and across to the hay as I followed. She pointed to the frayed edges of a length of hemp no thicker around than a shoelace. I hadn't even *seen* it from across the street.

"You did *that?*" I asked.

I followed her back to the hut, where she turned and handed the pistol to me. "Now you," she said firmly.

"Do I have to cock it or something?"

"It is an automatic. It will be ready to fire again when you are."

Struggling to keep my chattering teeth from throwing off my aim, I lifted the pistol in front of me and, still not seeing the hemp, fired in the general direction of the hay. The recoil kicked my hand back over my head, and I was sure I'd missed the target entirely.

Sharmani suppressed a smile.

"Here. Let me get behind you. And hold both your arms steady, so."

"I wasn't expecting the gun to kick back like that."

"It is called recoil. Now you are expecting it. When that happens, again, don't fight it. *Expect* it. You must first aim by closing one eye and aligning the sight on the gun with the target. Once you have done that, you hold your breath to prevent shaking. Then you squeeze the trigger as if you are milking a young ewe. Gently, slowly, until it goes off, so."

With her head nestled close to mine and her finger atop my own, she slowly increased the pressure until the gun exploded.

"I did it! I actually hit the target! Did you see? Did you see the snow fly?"

She smiled. "You will soon learn to shoot like that without any help. But you must practice, like weaving. Then you will succeed."

We went back into the hut, and I slammed the door solidly behind us. Huddling next to the stove, I watched Sharmani throw on her coat and pick up a few remaining pieces of yarn, which she stuffed into her pocket.

"Shadar will be returning soon, Allah willing. You will need some time to prepare his meal. You will find plenty of food in the baskets we brought."

"They'll be back yet tonight, do you think?"

She nodded and shrugged. "Allah be willing."

"Thank you," I said, still shivering. "I don't know how I can ever repay you."

"If there is anything else you need during your stay here in Dailut-Ya, Shadar knows where to find us."

"Sharmani," I said suddenly as she moved toward the door. She stopped and looked back at me. "Where is Shadar? Where did he go?"

She eyed me suspiciously for several moments. Finally, she said, "With the others, on the plains."

"I know that, but why? What is he doing there?"

"He is helping do what all Pashtuns must do: protect the Frontier from the Pakistani dogs." She said it easily as one might recite a poem. No animosity in the words, no look of fear or hate in her eyes.

"But why?" I asked again. "Why did he bring me here? Why did *he* have to come to Dailut-Ya?"

She pondered the question briefly, and then, turning the handle on the door, replied. "Because it is his home."

Shadar returned to the hut around six that night to a meal I'd thrown together of flatbread and mutton.

Throughout dinner, he sat quietly, barely picking at his food.

"What is it? What's the matter?" I paused. "Is my cooking that bad?"

He shook his head and gave me a weak smile. "It's just that I'm tired ... and a little depressed. It will pass."

"Depressed about what?"

"About the fighting, about the fate of the Pashtuns."

I looked at him, at his deep-set eyes made even deeper by the flickering glow of the kerosene lamp. He appeared exhausted, defeated, not at all the same person who had left me that morning.

"Why didn't you tell me you are a Pashtun?"

He paused. "Didn't I?"

I shook my head. "I wonder why."

"Now, now." He pulled his cup closer and poured some honey-and-herb tea from the pot. "Don't go thinking the worst. Just because I'm a Pashtun, because I was born in the village of the Kush, doesn't mean all sorts of exotic and mysterious things. Nearly half of Afghanistan is made up of Pashtuns. It is hard to travel anywhere from north to south without running into someone who speaks Pushtu."

"But the Pashtuns of Dailut-Ya--the rebels--they are in danger, aren't they?"

"If you consider extinction danger."

"From the Pakistani soldiers?"

"From the Pakistanis ... and the Russians."

"The *Russians*? What do *they* have to do with anything?"

He sipped from the cup and set it on the table, hesitating as if trying to decide where to begin. Or *if*!

"The Soviets have gained control over Tajikistan, Turkmenistan, and half a dozen other satellite nations between Soviet Russia and Afghanistan. They have never been able to subdue the Afghans, or the Pakistanis, for that matter. They fear that, with resistance fighters traveling north from Kabul into the Soviet satellites, there will be uprisings against the Russians, civil wars, new break-away republics. With their shared border with

Afghanistan, the Russians are anxious to see a pro-Soviet regime in Kabul. There's a strongly pro-American Iranian government to the west and a pro-Western Indian government to the east. It is crucial to Russia's best interests to maintain good relations with the Afghans and Pakistanis so that the Russians retain access to the Arabian Sea. They want a pro-Soviet buffer state in Afghanistan, one that will allow them access to key military posts from which they can monitor Iranian and Indian military and political activities. At the same time, they want a post from which they can keep a closer eye on the southeastern provinces of China."

"You mean spy posts?"

Shadar laughed. "You make them sound so ... *vile.*"

"Well, aren't they? I don't think it's funny. They spy on us, we spy on them. Why do countries have to maintain all these undercover operations, anyway? They just strain international relations and stress global peace."

"But if every country in the world stopped spying on every other country in the world, millions of people would suddenly find themselves without a job."

"Funny. Very funny."

"A bad joke. Forgive me."

"Well, *I'm* not joking. I think it's time *all* countries got together and banned the CIA and the KGB and SAVAK and INTERPOL and the KAA and ..."

His ears pricked. "What do you know about the KAA?"

"Only that it's Afghanistan's answer to the CIA, isn't it? Why?"

Shadar leaned back in the chair and rubbed his palm across his forehead as if to soothe a throbbing head.

"Nothing."

"What's the matter with you tonight? Why are you so tense?"

He peered at me intently. I think it would be best if you forgot about the KAA, especially while we're in Dailut-Ya. Do yourself and me a favor and don't ever mention them again, do you understand?"

"No, I don't understand. Why?" I stared back into his eyes. I had hit a nerve by mentioning the Afghan secret police. Shadar was keeping something from me that was right on the tip of his tongue, just at the edge of slipping out. I wanted to know what it was.

"Because it's ... just not *safe* to talk about them. That's why."

"*Why* isn't it safe? What's all the secrecy about? I'm Paula Favage, remember? Your friend, your lover, the woman you want to spend the rest of your life with. And I'm not exactly sitting back in a warm apartment in Kabul, waiting for a telephone call from my sister Bitsy."

"You don't have a sister Bitsy."

I frowned. "You know what I mean. I'm right here with you in Dailut-Ya. I'm right here where two days ago there was fighting, bloodshed, murder in the streets. I'm here where every man, woman, and child I meet handles a gun better than I use a fork, where the respected mother of eight and the wife of the village leader took me out in the fields to teach me how to shoot a pistol. I think I have a right to know if we're in danger here. Are you going to tell me what's going on or not?"

I could feel my blood surging, my face flushed with anger. All the frustrations of living through the danger without even realizing how great the danger was had finally overwhelmed me. My fists clenched tightly, and my veins bulged. I wanted to grab Shadar and shake him until he said it: *I'm a Pashtun rebel. I'm here to fight for the freedom of my countrymen. We're in grave danger!*

Instead, he reached calmly into his pocket and withdrew a short, half-smoked cigarette. Holding it between his lips, he set a match to the tip, inhaled deeply, and turned his head, blowing a long stream of smoke across the room. He pulled a pack from his pocket and held it out to me.

"When did you start smoking? I never saw you before."

"I started, oh ..." He thought back over time, "I guess it was around two this afternoon. Dalal gave me a pack to hold for him." He inhaled again, and, suppressing a cough, he dropped the butt into his half-drained teacup, where it hissed softly before expiring.

"*What* are you doing?"

"Putting it out," he said.

"But you just lit it."

"I only wanted a short smoke."

I looked down at the cup and then up at the smoke still lingering in the air, and then I looked down once again at the cup. "My God," I said softly.

"What's the matter?"

"I'm in love with a lunatic."

He patted his knee. "Come here. Sit with me."

"Why should I?"

"Because I would like to see if I might grow to enjoy it."

I set my tea down and glared at him before getting up. I stopped.

"Well?" he said, craning his head.

"Well, pull your chair back so I can fit in."

He made room for me, and I nestled into his lap and snuggled up against him.

"You know," he said as I threw my arms around his neck and stared into his eyes, "you remind me of something I used to watch as a young boy."

"Oh? What's that--a Laurel and Hardy cartoon?"

"A what?"

"Never mind."

"No. You remind me of a young mynah bird, like Dalal said."

"Oh, gee, *thanks!*"

"No, I mean it. Did you ever see one just out of the nest?"

"Afraid not. We don't have many mynahs in Wisconsin."

"Well, it's really an amazing thing. At first, the bird sits on the limb nearest the nest. The limb is stout enough to support the weight of the nest, all the young birds, and both parents. But soon the youngster grows bolder and ventures farther from the nest, hopping to ever thinner branches and ever smaller limbs until finally ..." He made a falling motion with his hand.

"He waves goodbye?"

"No! He crashes. And then he picks himself up, looks around, and lets out the most terrifying yell as if he were being strangled to death."

"And I suppose that's me. The part where he squawks just before being killed."

"He doesn't squawk before being killed; he squawks just until he realizes he's safe, and then he's quiet again."

"And that's what I remind you of?"

"How does that fine old Yankee saying go: 'If the shoe fits, put your foot in it?'"

I laughed, grabbed him by the neck, and shook him as hard as I could. "How about if *this* shoe fits, you put *your* foot in it!"

He let out a crisp laugh that turned into a soft smile. It was the same smile he'd worn the day I met him at the market in Kabul--self-confident, superior, *sexy*. I moved closer to him, my lips suddenly attracted like a magnet to a piece of steel. I felt the warmth of his breath, tasted the honey-sweetened tea on his lips as I nibbled first the top and then the bottom until the passion deep inside me, the anxiety and fears, the longing welled up, culminating in one long, deep, hard kiss.

"Well!" he said when I let him up for air. "I never saw a mynah bird do *that* before."

"Perhaps you never watched closely enough."

"Perhaps not," he said. He reached inside his jacket pocket.

"What are you doing now?"

"Getting another cigarette. Want one?"

"No," I cackled. "And neither do you."

I reached inside his jacket to grab the pack from him. Instead, my fingers folded around something small and hard. I pulled it out.

"What's this?" I held it up to the light.

He smiled again--filled with anticipation this time. "Go

ahead. Open it."

I slipped the small ribbon from around the case and opened it to reveal a ring. A sparkling ring with a Marquis-cut diamond in the center, surrounded by a whirling cluster of smaller stones. Set in a band of gold adorned by several smaller opals and rubies. It was turned into the shape of a tree. And on the back, where the converging branches met, sat a beautiful little bird.

A mynah bird.

"Happy birthday, Paula Favage."

I looked at him in amazement. "How did you ..." Tears welled in my eyes as he took the ring and slipped it onto my finger.

"Oh, Shadar!"

"Do you like it?"

I threw my arms around him and squeezed him tightly, tears streaming down my cheeks. "It's beautiful. It's the most beautiful thing I've ever seen."

"Then, why are you crying?"

"I don't know," I said. "Perhaps all mynah birds cry when they're happy."

The following day had begun as surely as the preceding night had ended. Shadar had gotten up before I did and left me a note:

My Little Mynah, pack our belongings for our trip to Islamabad. With luck, we will leave tonight--tomorrow morning at the latest. There we will catch a flight for Bombay and then New York. Love, S

I set the note aside and looked down at the ring. It glistened even more brightly in the natural light of day. Or maybe it was my eyes that sparkled. Could it really be that by this time Monday morning we'd be home? In New York? And then Milwaukee? After all, I'd been through, after so many grueling months in a hostile land, it was hard, *impossible*, to believe. I was sure I must have been dreaming.

I read the note once more, and I crinkled it in my palm and tossed it high into the air.

"Whooweeee!" I yelled at the top of my lungs. *"Whooooooo-weeeee!"*

I ran for the suitcases and started looking around for things to stuff inside even before washing up and fixing my hair. It was too good to be true. I kept telling myself over and over. *We're going home. At long last. We're going home!*

By midmorning, I was ready for the Jeep. Or ox cart. Or *anything.* I had calmed down and seated myself next to the stove, our four cases packed and ready to go, while I worked on the rug that I would take with me to Milwaukee. It was more than a rug; it was a symbol of survival, of all I'd endured. It was innocence sprung from worldliness. It was life from the loins of death. Someday, I would look at that rug stretched before a great stone fireplace and tell my children the tale of how their mother had gone to the faraway land of Afghanistan--a wondrous and frightening land of camels and goats and shepherds, of murderous thieves, of women who shot pistols in the streets, of ...

Suddenly there was a knock at the door. Before I could rise, Sharmani burst in. She was breathing heavily, her eyes swollen with terror.

"Sharmani! What is it?"

"We ... we have just gotten word from Radio Kabul. The city has fallen." She stopped and gasped for breath. "The government has toppled."

"What city has fallen? What are you talking about?"

"Kabul," she said, her voice still trembling. "There was an uprising, several thousand Soviet-armed troops. They killed the foreign minister, and the president has fled for his life."

"No! Not Kabul! We were just there. You must be mistaken. We ..."

"There is gunfire in the streets. Hundreds of people have been killed. The militia is in shambles."

"Are you sure?" I felt foolish at the question, not wanting to believe.

"We heard it on the shortwave. And then the broadcast stopped. The station went dead."

"Oh, my God! My friends! Dinara, Naim, the nurses at the clinic ..."

"That is not all," she said, her eyes dilating wildly. "There are Pakistani troops marching on Dailut-Ya at this very moment."

"Here? What should we do?"

"A group of fifty of our men was dispatched to meet them at the pass leading to town. There will be gunfire. There will be deaths."

"Shadar! Where is Shadar?"

"He and the others are out on the plains west of town. Two of our best riders have set off on horseback to find them. I do not know if they realize yet what is happening. They could find themselves stumbling into a trap."

I climbed to my feet as she turned toward the door. "Wait! Where are you going?"

"I am going back to my children. They are alone and frightened."

"I'm going with you."

"No. It is better that you stay here for Shadar. Lock the doors and bolt the shutters. Let the fire die out. The Pakistanis will pass the house if they think it is empty."

"Sharmani," I said, clutching her arm, "I'm frightened."

She looked me in the eyes, reached out and touched my cheek with her fingers. "We are all frightened." She slipped free from my grasp and was halfway out the door when she looked back and shuddered. "Allah be with you, Paula Favage."

I was trembling, as much for Shadar as for myself. What if he should run into a Pakistani patrol? What if he should be captured ... or *worse?*

I quickly bolted the door and checked all the windows to make sure they were closed and shuttered. If only there were something to shove up against the door, but there wasn't. The stove was the only object heavy enough in the entire house, and it was secured in the middle of the room.

Suddenly I remembered the gun. I ran to my case and flung it open, strewing clothes around the floor, until finally I felt it against my hand--the hard, cold steel of the barrel.

I pulled it out and stared at it. What good would a pistol do against an entire army of seasoned soldiers? I felt the sudden urge to cry but fought it off. I fumbled with the pistol, trying to remember how to work it. I found the latch to release the clip. Inside were ten cartridges, lined up obediently and ready to use, just as Sharmani had left it. No, not ten. We had spent two cartridges the day before.

"Oh, shit," I cursed--as if two fewer shells might make the difference between life and death.

I slammed the clip back into the slot and pushed the bolt forward, sliding a shell up into the chamber. Then I slipped the safety on and carried the gun back with me to the stove. I sat down and picked up my weaving, laying the gun in my lap. I would remain there and work on the rug. And wait.

There was nothing else to do.

An hour came and passed, and then another. At one point, I thought I heard the distant din of gunfire--three or four shots--but as I strained my ears against the howling mountain wind, I couldn't be sure. Several times I had left off my weaving and gone to the shutters to peek out into the street. Not a soul stirred. All the men and boys old enough to carry a gun had long since left for battle, leaving the women and the girls, the small children and infants behind locked doors. Like me, they waited anxiously for whatever news would come.

I stretched my arms out and yawned. I needed some tea--something to warm me and help keep me awake. I set the gun and the yarn down on the floor and got up to put the kettle on the stove.

I stopped short and strained my ears against the wind. I thought I'd heard a noise, a small rustling. Maybe it was Sharmani with some news. I crossed to the door, listened closely, and slipped back the latch to take a peek outside.

Suddenly the door burst open and a burly man with a long black mustache and blacker eyes pushed past me, followed by two others. The man with the black eyes swept the room with his carbine, settling the rifle muzzle finally on me. I dropped the kettle to the floor, and the soldiers jumped.

"Who is in there?" the man said in choppy *Pashto*, pointing toward the bath.

"N-n-n-no one." The words came from far away.

"Come out of there, or we shall kill you!" The man motioned two soldiers forward, and they snaked quickly along the walls, flanking the doorway, before bursting into the tiny room.

"It is empty," one of them said upon returning.

The man with the carbine trained between my shoulders stepped forward. "Where is he?" His voice was brusque, his eyes menacing.

"Where is ... who?" I asked in *Pashto*.

The man looked around the room, his eyes suddenly stopping at the foot of the stove. My heart leaped into my throat as I looked down. There, peeking out from beneath the rug, was the gun--just a shadow of the deep blue muzzle showing. I wasn't sure whether or not the soldier could see it from where he stood.

"I am Sergeant Mandat Foud of His Majesty's Royal Pakistani Patrol. I am seeking a Pashtun by the name of Shadar. This is his home?"

"No," I said. "I live here alone."

"You lie!" he shouted, taking two short, menacing steps forward.

"I ... I am Paula Favage. I am working here with the Peace Corps. I'm a nurse with the clinic in Kabul."

The sergeant eyed me suspiciously, weighing the weight of my words against the feeling he had deep inside his gut. He pulled a thick piece of dried meat or something black from beneath his coat, bit off a section, and returned the rest to his pocket. He paused, his eyes seeming to mellow momentarily as he swallowed. In seconds, the smell of dung and urine reached my nostrils.

"What are you doing here in Dailut-Ya, then? You are a long way from Kabul."

"I … I have a week off from the clinic. I came here because I was told that some of the finest yarns in the world are used by the Pashtun mountain women of Dailut-Ya. I wished to buy some yarn and to learn their secrets for turning it into fine weavings. You see?" I pointed to the rug on the floor.

The soldier stooped down and, lifting an edge of the rug, rolled the material between his fingers.

You idiot! I screamed at myself. *Why did you tell him that? If he tilts the rug up and finds the pistol, it's over.*

I watched anxiously as the sergeant released the rug and stood upright. He quickly scanned the room again. "You have papers?"

"Papers. Yes, I have a passport in my case. And orders from the Peace Corps. Yes."

He motioned for me to get them, and I scurried over to my suitcase--thank God Shadar's bags were in the bathroom. I fumbled around inside and finally pulled the papers out. The sergeant took them and, holding them up to the light, examined them carefully. Satisfied, he returned them to me, nodded, and motioned with his head toward the door. "You have come recently?"

"Y-yes, only yesterday."

"An American *farangi,* traveling alone?"

I nodded.

Suddenly, he turned and took two steps toward the entranceway, motioning the others to precede him out. As the soldiers exited, the sergeant stopped and looked back at me. "You will leave at once for Kabul. It is not safe here for *farangi* women." He spit on the floor and jammed another piece of meat into his mouth.

As the door closed behind him, I let out my breath. My heart beat furiously, straining to break free from its bonds. I felt weak. My legs threatened to collapse. I pulled out a chair and plopped down. I had never been so frightened in my life. If he was an example of the type of men the

Pashtuns were fighting, I could understand why Shadar had been so concerned. The sergeant's presence alone seemed enough to cow any army. I couldn't believe I was still alive to think about it.

Suddenly I heard a light tap at the door. *Sharmani,* I thought. The soldiers had left, and she was checking to see that I was all right.

Hurrying to the door, I threw it open, and there, shivering in the cold, was a young boy of no more than seven. He looked frightened and tired, his breath coming in short, quick gasps as if he'd come a long way. Perhaps one of Sharmani's sons.

"Yes? What is it?"

He removed a small bag of rice from his pocket and fished out of it a sealed white envelope, which he handed to me. Then he fastened the bag closed, again.

I pulled the youngster inside and closed the door. Looking at the envelope, I noticed some words hastily scrawled on the back:

P - <u>Extreme</u> danger. Get the enclosed message to the American consul in Kabul. Do not open it. Do not let it out of your possession. I will meet you tomorrow at slip number 3 at Chakai, 11:00 p.m. If I am detained, you are to board the Khani-G. Captain Ilhami will transport you to Bombay, where I will join you as quickly as possible.

- S

I turned to the boy to ask him where he'd gotten the note, but he had gone, slipped out while I was reading. It was in Shadar's hand, I was sure. I stared at the envelope for several seconds, and then, despite orders not to open it, I withdrew its contents--a small piece of paper with the neatly printed words "J-G. Action 2. Urgent. PUN."

I studied the cryptic message. It, too, was in Shadar's writing. But what did it mean? Was it a secret code? I shook my head. Too ridiculous, too bizarre. Still, I went over to the table and, my hands trembling, struck a match. I knew I was to convey the message to the consul, but Shadar wrote those instructions not knowing how close at hand the Pakistanis were. I set the match to the enveloped and set it in the incense holder to burn. Then I lit a joss stick to disguise the strong stench of expectorant the sergeant had left on the floor, still clinging heavily to the air. Suddenly I heard voices and a muffled, high-pitched yell from outside the door. Before I could react, the door burst open again.

"Search her!" the sergeant ordered, rushing in and followed by the same two soldiers. The men set their rifles against the wall and grabbed me, checking first my pockets, then frisking along my arms and legs. When they found nothing, they stepped back.

"What is this all about?" I asked.

The sergeant scowled and motioned toward the open door, through which a fourth soldier dragged the young messenger. "This Pashtun child. You have seen him before?" He glared at me while my mind frantically searched for a cover-up.

"Why?"

"*I* will ask the questions," he shouted, "and *you* will answer!"

"Yes," I said. "He was just here."

"Yes. I thought so." He glared at the boy. "Excellent. And tell me, what was he doing here? He gave you something, yes?"

"He tried to ... to sell me some rice," I lied. "He had a small bag that he said he wanted two thousand *afghanis* for. But I am leaving Dailut-Ya, as you told me. I sent him away. I have no need for rice."

The sergeant's face dropped. "*Rice!*" He snorted and looked around the room before adding softly, "Rice."

He paused in mid-sentence as I stared at him. He was short, stocky, probably well built. His face wore the look of determination that comes only after years of service to one's country.

He thought quietly for several seconds, took one last look around, and turned toward the soldier holding the boy in the doorway. He muttered something ominous-sounding in Pakistani. The soldier looked down, as if embarrassed, and removed the bag of rice from the boy's coat pocket.

"This?" the soldier asked, taking the bag of rice from the boy and holding it out for my inspection.

"Yes. That's it. That's what he wanted to sell me."

He turned back to the doorway and ordered his charge to leave.

"Where is he going?" I asked. "What are you going to do to him?"

"He will be freed," the sergeant replied. "Eventually. But it is a good thing for you that you have told us the truth."

"Why should I lie about rice?"

"We found the rice on the child just before we took him into custody. I thought him to be nothing more than a beggar, but, still ..."

I watched as the two soldiers who had frisked me picked up their weapons and followed the sergeant out of the hut. He turned back at the door and snarled at me. "You will be gone from Dailut-Ya in one hour, do you understand?"

"One hour? But I can't possibly ..."

"One hour!" He turned on his heels and stomped off through the snow.

FOURTEEN

Sharmani's son Muhammad forced the wheel to the right, and the truck veered sharply around a curve. We were heading down to the tiny Pakistani hamlet of Kodeez. Muhammad had returned from the pass only moments before we departed. I saw the look of disappointment in his eyes when Sharmani asked him to go back, this time carrying a passenger--a farangi *woman* passenger--but he had obediently complied.

"Is it safe?" I knew he had just returned from fighting off the Pakistanis.

"It will be safe ... for a while," he replied. "We sent the *farangi* dogs scurrying back to Gilgit for reinforcements. The pass will remain open yet the rest of the day. And possibly tomorrow. After that ..." He shrugged.

Muhammad, Sharmani's middle son, was barely fifteen and still wearing the baby smoothness of youth. He looked hardly old enough to carry a gun, let alone battle foreign invaders.

"Have you ... ever shot a man?" I asked blankly as the truck bounced and jostled its way through the pass.

"I have killed seventeen Pakistani soldiers since July." He said the words proudly as if he were announcing the results of a high school basketball game.

I lowered my head, thinking about a fifteen-year-old boy who might never know the meaning of peace. The thought sat heavily on my mind. I wondered if any Pashtun children--of *any* generation--would ever again know peace with honor and dignity. It somehow seemed unlikely.

"I know what you are thinking."

I raised my head and looked at him. "Oh?"

"You are thinking that I am too young to be involved

in the fighting, too young to carry a rifle, to aim it at another and to pull the trigger, to see him come to the end of his life ... sometimes in great agony."

"Something like that, yes."

"But you are wrong."

"I could be. But I don't think so. Not in this case."

He looked surprised at my response. He had seemed just a little cocky, just a little too confident of himself earlier, as though he thought himself better than an American *farangi*--particularly a female *farangi*. But once we'd gotten into the truck--after Sharmani had asked him to drive me to Kodeez, where I was to meet another Pashtun who would see me to Chakai--he seemed to have mellowed some, to have dropped that chip from his shoulder. It was clear he would still rather be chasing Pakistanis across the mountains than piloting women to safety. But it was also clear also that he was surprised at my interest in the Pashtuns.

"It is not easy, taking a stand," he said after a long pause. "Sometimes I wake up in the middle of the night and cry out loud. I see the faces of the dead and wounded--the Pakistani faces ... and the Pashtun. But, even worse than that, I see the faces of those who have yet to fall--my father, my brothers, my friends. The faces are twisted in agony. The tears stream down, and the mouths cry out for help, but no one comes to their aid. No one ever comes."

"It must be terrible."

"It is just as in real life. No one ever comes."

"How about the Afghan government? Don't their troops support the Pashtun cause?"

"Yes--for what that is worth. Lieutenant General Daud has said repeatedly that Afghanistan lays claim to the lands occupied by the Pashtuns in the Northwest Frontier. But, without the ability to move troops into the area to protect us from the Pakistanis, it is little more than lip service, fig leaves blowing in the wind."

"Why are we stopping?" I peered out into the darkness that had sneaked up on us and veiled the mountains from view.

"We are in Kodeez. This is where we must part."

I was puzzled. It was dark, but not that dark. I was supposed to meet the Pashtun at the bus depot, but I could see nothing--no buildings, no lights at all.

I got out of the truck, pulling my case behind me, as Muhammad exited the driver's side. He stopped, stretched, yawned, and looked first right and then left.

I looked after him. "But where is the depot?"

He looked off into the night. "There," he replied, pointing to one side toward an empty skeleton that had once passed as a building.

"That? That pile of rubbish is a bus depot?"

"It was once. The locals tore most of it down when the buses stopped running between Pakistan and Afghanistan. The wood makes excellent tinder for burning on a cold winter's night. It is rare to find a wooden building still standing in this part of the world. When one is left unguarded, it is sure to disappear quickly."

"I don't see anyone," I said, following him toward the building's skeleton. "Where is the man who is supposed to take me to Chakai?"

"He will come. This is a well-known meeting spot among the Pashtuns. It is out in the open, not easily defended. It would be difficult to set a military trap here. Also, the main road to Chakai runs right past the building to the south."

I brushed away some snow from what was left of the depot platform and set my case down. "I hope he comes soon. I have to get an urgent message to the embassy in Kabul."

"There is a public telephone in Chakai that you could use," he said, "but ..."

"But what?"

"I have heard today of an uprising in Kabul. I do not know in what state the city is."

"Did you hear anything about the American Embassy there?"

He shook his head. "Only that Soviet forces have invaded the city and taken over much of its communications and government buildings. The president has fled. It is hard to know how things go in Kabul."

"I hope ... the embassy is safe."

"You are worried about someone?"

"I have a friend, a young man named Naim. He reminds me very much of you, except that he's a few years older. He works for the embassy. I only hope that ..."

"He will be safe," Muhammad said resolutely. "Allah watches over the good and the just and keeps them out of harm's way."

I wished I could believe him. "Thanks." I smiled, and I stared again out over the plains, trying to pierce the darkness, but saw nothing, heard nothing.

"I would suggest that we move your case to the front of the depot," Muhammad said, pointing. "It is from there that your ride will come."

"I'll hear him coming, don't worry," I replied.

"That is not the point. If he does not see you, or if he cannot get a good close look at you, he may decide it is too dangerous to stop. He may be frightened away even before he arrives.

I did as Muhammad advised, placing my satchel between the building and us, and stood there peering into the emptiness. Suddenly Muhammad placed his hand on my arm and said softly, "Go in peace. May you and Shadar have a safe journey, *Insha'Allah*."

"Wait," I said, confused. "Where are you going?"

"I am going back to Dailut-Ya. There will be wounded coming in from the pass tonight. They will need caring for. And there will be rifles to clean and cartridges to load before morning."

"But...but what about me?" I felt the ice surging through my veins and shivered involuntarily at the thought of being left alone.

"I can wait no longer," Muhammad said firmly. "If you hear a convoy of several vehicles, throw your case to one side and hide in the snow, beyond the glow of their headlights. A convoy means that the Pakistanis are coming."

I stood watching his silhouette as he walked toward the truck, opened the door, and climbed in. For a moment, I wanted to run after him, jump in beside him, go back to Dailut-Ya. At least there I knew what I was up against.

I wanted to, but I didn't.

I watched as the engine roared to life and the truck lurched forward down the road to the Tirich Mir Pass, from where we had come.

Don't go! Please come back! Don't leave me here! a voice within me cried. But my lips were pursed tightly together even as my eyes followed the faint glow of the taillights until they were mere specks in the back of my mind.

A sudden veil of fear blew across me. I thought of moving, but I couldn't. I thought about Muhammad's words, about what it was I should do if a convoy came through. I wondered if I would be able to move even then.

Get hold of yourself. This is no time to panic!

And yet I could not fight back the urge to cry. I did not give in, did not sob, did not weep openly, but the tears came anyway, slowly, one at a time, first from one eye, and then the next. And all I could do was let them come, snaking their way down my face, settling on my upturned collar, where they turned to crystalline rivulets of fear.

I had been waiting for more than an hour. Another fear suddenly struck me. What if my ride *never* came? What if I were forced to spend the night in the open, and then face the day anew, alone and afraid, in the middle of nowhere? I looked down at my watch, trying to make out the figures in the dark. I guessed it was sometime after six. The wind had picked up, blowing down out of the north--just the direction I was facing. I kneeled back against a small corner of the depot still standing and pulled my case before me to act as a shield from the wintry blasts.

I thought about my other belongings--my brand-new shoes and my partially completed rug. I had to leave them with Sharmani in Dailut-Ya. She said she would send them to us--to Shadar and me, although I didn't think it likely. How would she find us? Where would we be? In Kabul? Islamabad? Milwaukee? A Pakistani prison? *Dead?*

"Think of it," I said aloud. "This may be it--the end. Paula Favage, born in Milwaukee, died in some God-forsaken snowdrift, with a dream in her heart and a block of ice for a head."

I was cold--beyond cold, *numb*. I tried moving my fingers beneath my gloves. If I hadn't known from blind faith that they were there, I would have sworn they didn't exist at all.

So this is how it ends: I slowly freeze to death. They say you lose all feeling just before you die. The cold isn't cold. The pain isn't pain. Everything is fine. Just don't go to sleep. Whatever you do, don't go to sleep.

But as the minutes dragged on and the temperature dropped, I grew sluggish. I half-stifled a yawn against my shoulder and let my head dip down. My eyes closed, and I jerked my head up, slapped my cheeks, and felt for the sting. It did not come. Nothing came. No feeling, no pain, no anything.

There was no use in fighting it, no use at all. I closed my eyes, again--unable any longer to keep them open, to fight the feeling of numbness that had swept over me--and shifted my weight back onto my haunches. I could feel the warm glow, see the images of sunshine and water, crystal blue and sparkling, on a warm summer's day. It felt pleasant, invigorating, stimulating, alive. I wondered how long it would take. And whether or not I would know when it came.

My head jerked up suddenly, and my eyes popped open. Nothing but darkness greeted me. And then I heard it. Somewhere from far, far away, I heard the faint sound of an engine. A motorcycle. A hundred motorcycles. It was a race. *Thousands* of motorcycles, all lined up on the edge of a huge dirt track that stretched across miles and miles of desert. Suddenly the green flag fell, and the engines roared and hissed, screamed and clanged, as a huge bellow of smoke rose up from the pack.

"Motorcycles," I whispered, my head snapping back as I put my hand to my ear to close out the sound of the wind. I looked around and saw nothing. Had I imagined it? Was I hallucinating? Suddenly I heard it again. Yes, this time I was sure. It was growing louder, clearer. It *was* the sound of a motorcycle!

Peering into the dark, I saw a tiny white light dancing in the distance. Up and down it flitted, bobbing and weaving from side to side like some magnificent prizefighter, increasing in brightness and dying out again like a shooting star on a clear summer's night.

"A motorcycle!" I paused to make sure. "Yes!"

My bones creaked as I struggled to my feet, and the pain shot up my spine as I stretched out. All the while, my eyes were riveted to that dancing white spot as it grew larger, bolder, the buzz of the engine increasing until it was unmistakable. A lone vehicle. Down the road from nowhere to nowhere. It had to be my ride. It just *had* to be!

I thought about waving, about shouting out madly, but I held back, as Muhammad had told me, and stood where I could be seen. The light was growing stronger by the moment. It fell on the side of the depot, illuminating the strange maze of pipes clattering in the wind and the snow that had begun to fall. Illuminating *me*.

"Oh, thank God!" I said aloud. "Thank God he came. Thank God I'm alive!"

The motorcycle roared up, the oversized knobby tires biting and spitting up the hard, crunchy snow on the road. The helmeted driver cocked the front wheel to one side and killed the engine. He glanced nervously around, turning the handlebars first one way, and then the other, so that the light illuminated the entire area like a searchlight. "Are you the American, Paula Favage?"

I thought for a moment that I recognized that voice, and a shiver went through my body; but I quickly dismissed the thought to an overactive imagination. "Yes, yes. Yes, I am. Oh, thank God you're here!"

"You'll have to leave that case," the figure said, motioning toward the depot. "We have no room for it on the bike."

I thought quickly about what was inside--a few personal belongings, a change of clean clothes. A toothbrush. Surely I could take my toothbrush! "I ... understand."

"Throw it down in the ditch there. We don't want anyone to find it and come after us."

I hauled the case to the ditch and flung it as far into the night as I could, and then I hurried back to the cycle. The driver had gotten off to stretch and had slipped off his helmet.

"You must be tired. Have you driven far?"

"Yes. Now we'd better be going."

He took two steps toward me, into the wash of his own headlight.

"Oh, no," I said. "Oh, God, no!" *It couldn't be!*

The Pashtun's eyes grew large as they fell on me. Thoughts of that night with Bob flushed over me, that night in Kabul when the Pashtun rebel had beaten him, sliced open his head, and left him for dead. But not before warning me, not before scaring me to death.

"Please," I said, my voice quivering. "Please, just leave me. Leave me alone. Go away."

The Pashtun looked back up the road from where he'd come, straining his ears to the night. Then he mounted the cycle. "Hurry," he said firmly. "We must depart for Chakai."

"Please," I said again, "just leave me alone! I haven't done anything to you. I can't go with you. I *can't*."

The Pashtun lunged out and caught my arm, squeezing it so tightly that I cried out in pain. "Shadar sent me," he said, shaking me. "Don't you understand? Shadar sent me to get you."

"No, you're lying!" I shouted. I flailed out at him, striking out with my free hand, striking at his face--at the face I had seen so many nights in my dreams, that terrifying face with its scowling lips that had delivered their heart-stopping threat.

Suddenly he reached out with his free hand and slapped me, sending a small spurt of blood and spittle flying from my mouth. I screamed out again, and I started to sob.

"Listen to me!" Slowly I looked up at him. "The Pakistanis may be following me. Now, I don't care what you think, and I don't care what you want. I don't care if you wish to come or even if you live or die. All I know is that Shadar sent me to meet you and to take you to Chakai, where you are to call the American Embassy in Kabul and deliver the message sent to you. However, if you will not come, I cannot force you. I will send word to him that I could not find you, that the Pakistani soldiers caught and arrested you. Or that you were frozen to death when I arrived. Whichever you choose."

"Is ... is he all right?"

"Shadar? He is alive and well."

"Then, why didn't he come for me?"

The Pashtun's eyes dropped for a second. "Come. He pulled me toward the cycle. "Get on, now. There is no time left for games."

I stared at him, trying to feel something inside, some instinct, but it was no use. I was tired, cold, numb from the inside out. Slowly I approached the cycle and swung my leg over the saddle, climbing on behind him. He lifted up on the starter and threw his weight down against it. The engine roared to life.

"Take off your hat," he shouted back at me, "and put this on. It will keep you warmer, and safe." He held out a helmet. "We are an hour's drive from Chakai ... *if* we can stay clear of the Pakistani patrols."

The Pashtun revved the engine, and the tires churned and crackled as we began cutting our way through the cold night air, on toward the Pakistani river town of Chakai, where I was to call the embassy and then board the boat that would eventually take Shadar and me to Bombay--and to safety.

Eleven o'clock, I thought. *He'll be there by eleven. But what if he isn't there?* I shook my head, shook that thought free, and lowered my helmet against the Pashtun's shoulder, clinging to him tightly and wishing he were Shadar.

It was nearly nine o'clock when we pulled into Chakai. The Pashtun had suspected trouble on the main road, so he decided to take instead a snow-covered secondary road through the city's back alleys.

We stopped before a large government building.

"Where are we?"

"At a German diplomatic station. There is someone on duty here twenty-four hours a day, and--more importantly--there is a public phone. Do you speak German?" He motioned for me to dismount.

"A little. Not very well."

"Pakistani, then?"

I shook my head.

The Pashtun frowned. "I will have to go in with you and ask them to put through a call to the embassy in Kabul."

"Thank you."

"I do not tell you for you to give me thanks," he snapped. "It is dangerous for me to show my face in this city. Many Pakistani soldiers could recognize me. If we run into one of them inside the building, we will be in serious trouble."

He turned to watch two Pakistani men walking down the street. He returned his attention to me. "Have you a gun?" he whispered.

I reached into my coat pocket and fingered the pistol. "Yes," I said softly.

"Good. Be prepared to use it."

"But I ..."

"Just ... be prepared."

He pulled himself off the bike and swung around on his heels before walking briskly up the stairs leading to the doorway. I followed behind him, glancing from side to side. Every face in the street, every window in every building harbored hostile eyes--eyes bent on destroying us, eyes that could send us to prison ... or the grave.

The Pashtun rebel glanced once quickly from side to side, and then he reached for the door.

"Just a minute."

He stopped and turned to face me. "What?"

"Back on the road, where you picked me up."

His eyes stared at me, through me, carving their way into my soul. I knew first-hand what danger those eyes possessed. "Yes?"

"You recognized me ... from that night in Kabul."

He thought for several seconds. "Yes," he said finally. "I recognized you."

"Why?"

"Why what?"

"Why did you do that to my husband?"

I felt inside my coat, wondered if he knew I had wrapped my palm around the butt of the pistol, wondered what he would do if he found out.

"Your husband was a danger to us. He was buying drugs from a friend of his, a man named Raoul." I stared at him, my fingers tightening around the pistol. "It was a dangerous situation."

"Why? Why should you or anyone care what my husband was doing? What's so dangerous to you about his doing drugs?"

"Raoul has connections to the Pakistani underground. That is how he obtains his drugs, by supplying the Pakistanis with information. It was only a matter of time before a slip of your husband's tongue endangered us all. Either that, or he would have enlisted with Raoul as an operative. That would have been even worse."

I felt my hand move inside my pocket, felt the muzzle of the gun shift involuntarily upward. I sensed that he felt it, too.

"Do you understand what I am telling you?"

I struggled to put that night into perspective, that night that I had so long ago put out of my mind. Bob had been with Raoul, he'd admitted that. He'd gotten his drugs from Raoul. What had the Pashtun said to me that night as he left? What had he told me? Farangi *traitors must die*. Yes, that was it. He called Bob a traitor.

"I say, do you understand?" he repeated.

I looked at him, ran my eyes across his face. It was the same face I had seen that night, but it was no longer filled with anger. It no longer held the threat of violence, thinly veiled behind those cold, grey eyes.

"Yes," I said finally. "I understand."

His eyes narrowed, and I thought I saw his hand move toward his coat. Then he motioned with his head as he turned and slowly entered the building. I let out a deep sigh and followed him through the doorway and into the bowels of hell.

The Pashtun stopped before a large oak desk littered with papers. *"Guten abend,"* he said to the clerk, seated behind a typewriter.

"Guten abend," she replied. *"Wie gehts?"*

The Pashtun explained that we wanted to use the telephone to place an emergency call to the American Embassy in Kabul. All the while, I had the uneasy feeling that the man seated at the desk behind the clerk--a Pakistani--was eyeing us suspiciously. Did he recognize the Pashtun? My hand was still wrapped around the butt of the gun, my fingers pressing up against the back of the trigger guard, running around the loop, brushing the trigger, as though wanting to know exactly where everything lay, how everything fit together, in case I needed to act. I felt like a commando about to launch a terrorist raid on a hostile government.

In an instant, a dozen guns would be trained on us, blazing away, the deadly spray falling to either side before hitting us, dropping us finally in a pool of blood.

"Paula!" The Pashtun's voice snapped me back to reality. He was standing beside a door at one side of the room. I smiled at the young German and hurried to join him.

"Through here." He motioned past the open doorway. Once inside the small cubicle, I let out a sigh. "That was close."

The Pashtun lifted the receiver and asked in Pakistani for the American Embassy in Kabul. Then he turned to me. "What do you mean?"

"That man, the one behind the clerk--didn't you see him looking at us?"

He shook his head.

"I think he might suspect something."

"Could be," he said. He handed me the receiver. "I'll stand guard while you talk to the ambassador."

A voice over the receiver answered in English.

"Yes," I said. "Hello. Is this the American Embassy? I'd like to speak to the ambassador, please. It's *urgent*."

Several seconds passed, and then another voice came on the line: "This is assistant ambassador Ingersoll speaking. May I help you?"

I muffled the mouthpiece and turned to the Pashtun. "It's Ingersoll! He's the ambassador's assistant. What do I do now? I can't let him know it's me."

The Pashtun hesitated before grabbing the phone. "Mr. Ingersoll, this is the consulate general of the Afghan Internal Affairs division. I have an urgent message to give to the ambassador regarding the status of the takeover by the Revolutionary Army of the Republic of Afghanistan and the safety of the American Embassy personnel in Kabul. I must speak with the ambassador at once."

I watched the expression on the Pashtun's face as he listened to the voice on the other end of the line.

"No," he said. "I'm sorry, but this message is for the ambassador's ears only."

Again the Pashtun listened.

"I'm sorry," he said again, "but I am afraid I will not be able to relay the message to you in place of the ambassador. I must go now. Please be sure to arm yourself heavily and relay to the ambassador my greatest sympathies at ..."

He paused, a thin smile creasing his lips as he listened to Ingersoll on the other end of the line.

"Good," he said finally. "I will wait."

The Pashtun smiled.

"Oh? He did? Just this minute? How fortunate for us all. Please put him on. Yes. And thank you."

The Pashtun gave me the receiver. "Just takes a little *chutzpah*," he whispered, handing the receiver back to me.

"Hello, is this the American ambassador?" I asked. "Yes. Yes. My name is Paula Favage, and I have an urgent message for you." I looked up blankly for several seconds, pushing my brain to come up with the cryptic message I had burned earlier that day. *Oh, no!* I'd had no doubt I would remember it always. I'd not had the slightest doubt.

"What's the matter?" the Pashtun said. "Give him the message!"

"I ... I ..."

The voice on the other end of the line sounded anxious. "Well?"

"The message," I said finally, "is this: *J-G. Action 2. Urgent. PIN.*" I paused. "No, *PUN.* Yes, that's it, *PUN.* Did you get that?"

There was silence on the other end.

"Hello?" I said. "Did you hear what I just told you?"

"Who is this?" the ambassador asked.

"Did you hear the message?"

"Yes, yes. Who are you? Are you safe?"

"I ... I think so." I looked up at the Pashtun, who had pulled his revolver from beneath his coat and was leaning against the door. He looked anxious.

"Then, tell the sender that the message was received and that an appropriate response is underway. And thank him--and thank *you*--very much."

"I ... think I should ..." The phone clicked suddenly. "Hello? Hello?" I listened to the emptiness at the other end, listened to the hollowness of death. The Pashtun stared at me as I set the receiver in the cradle.

"Is that it?" he asked.

"Yes."

"Good. Let's get out of here." He slipped his pistol into a shoulder holster and buttoned his coat. I took a deep breath and, still clutching the handle of my own gun in my pocket, followed him back out into the receiving area. We tried to appear casual as we passed the clerk and walked out the front entranceway to the top of the steps. Once there, we scurried down to the cycle.

As we were climbing aboard, I noticed two Pakistanis huddled outside an office door. They looked vaguely familiar.

"Now let's get you down to the pier," the Pashtun said softly. He kicked the starter once, did so a second time, and the engine growled to life.

"*Look out!*" I shouted as the two men on the street began running toward us. I pulled the pistol out of my pocket and slipped the safety off, aiming it quickly at one of the Pakistanis.

Kerrack! Kerrack! Kerrack, it screamed, and the man in the lead stumbled and fell, a large automatic pistol tumbling from his hand.

"Hang on!" the Pashtun yelled. He fed the machine a sudden spurt of gas, and it leaped forward, slipping from side to side before the oversized tires finally grabbed the snow and ice and we raced away down the street.

Burump, a shot from the second Pakistani's gun cried out. I ducked down behind the Pashtun, who cut the wheels sharply around a corner, the engine whining as we picked up speed. I clung to him savagely as we hit a bump. The bike bucked wildly, nearly knocking me off, as we turned into a fenced area and sped off toward a long, narrow road.

It seemed like hours, with me looking back over my shoulder every minute or two, but it was far less than that. I clutched the Pashtun as tightly as I could, and after several more minutes, I heard the roar of the engine dim and bike begin to slow. I looked up and out over my driver's shoulder, my gaze following the sweep of the headlights along the oceanfront, onto a pier and beyond that to the waters of the Indus River straight ahead. Several boats were tied to the dock. One of them was sure to be the *Khani-G.*

The Pashtun came to a stop and threw his legs out

wide. "Okay," he said as the engine idled softly, "this is it."

Trembling, I got off the bike and looked back one last time to make sure we hadn't been followed. I peered down at the pistol in my hand. I saw again the Pakistani soldier fall against the snow and heard the retort of his companion's gun. I shivered and took a deep breath before slipping the pistol back into my pocket.

The Pashtun eyed his watch. "It's quarter past ten. What time are you to meet Shadar?"

"His note said at eleven."

"And you know the name of the boat?"

I nodded.

"And the captain?"

"Yes."

He looked at me for several moments before peering back over his shoulder. "I don't think we were followed; but I must take no chances."

"I understand."

He slowly backed the bike up and pushed it forward with his legs until he was turned around. He revved the engine once and looked back at me. "You lead a charmed life, Paula Favage. Take care of yourself, *Insha'Allah*."

I nodded, and the Pashtun took off down the road into the inky stillness of the night. I looked around and cursed myself for not having picked out the *Khani-G* in the glare of the headlight. Now, with no moon or stars to guide me, it would be next to impossible to tell one boat from another.

I took a few steps toward the water and stubbed my toe.

"Damn!" I cursed under my breath as I picked my way forward. I could hear the lapping waves beating softly against the icy shore, slapping the boats' wooden hulls up against the dock. The wind rolling across the bay was harsher, stronger than at Kodeez. I stopped and pulled my hat from my pocket. I slipped it onto my head and down over my ears.

"You are?" a voice in the night said suddenly.

I leaped back, my heart pounding, and scanned the darkness, but I saw nothing. Was I imagining things? Was it the sound of the waves? An overactive imagination?

Suddenly a hand grasped my arm.

"Owww!" I cried as it squeezed tightly.

"You are?" the voice demanded, more sternly this time.

"I'm ... I'm looking for Captain Ilhami. I'm looking for the *Khani-G*." The hand released its grip, and I peered at the silhouette in the darkness. Just then a bright light split the night air.

"I am Captain Ilhami," the figure said, turning the light from my face down so that it illuminated the ground at my feet.

"Shadar!" I said excitedly. "Is he here?"

"You are the first," he growled in *Pashto*. "Follow me."

The man turned and walked along the dock. I quickly scurried after him and the bobbing light. At the water's edge, he placed the light on a large piling and stepped aboard an old fishing boat. Holding out his hand, he helped me aboard, and then he grabbed the light and extinguished it.

"What time is it?"

The captain pulled a match from his pocket, struck it on the bulwark, and touched the flame to the end of a floppy cigarette. He inhaled deeply, holding his breath for several seconds before blowing out a long stream of smoke, dancing like waves in the cold, damp air off the river. "Ten-thirty," he said, adding, "We sail at eleven."

The captain drew again on the butt and finally stooped to tinker with the engine housed in the hold. I looked around for a place to sit and found a folded canvas tarp. I pulled it open and nestled myself down in the center of it, pulling the ends up over me for protection.

"The water looks cold," I said, leaning back against the rail and peering out to sea.

The old man drew again on the butt, the small orange glow illuminating his nose and eyes against the blackness of the hold. Finally, he stood up and lifted his foot onto the rail. I suddenly felt very alone, and afraid. I squirmed against the hard, cold bulwark and looked up at the man.

"What if ... Shadar doesn't ... *get* here by eleven?" I paused, anticipating the answer, dreading what I knew I was going to hear. "What ... what do we do then?"

He drew again on the cigarette and exhaled softly. "We sail at eleven."

I was nodding--nearly asleep--when the sound of footsteps awakened me. "Shadar?" I called out. "Shadar? Is Shadar here?"

The captain was slipping the ties off the pilings. In the background, I heard the soft purr of the slowly idling engine.

"We can wait no longer. It is eleven. We will sail."

Panic raced through me as I watched him prepare to shove off.

"But ... we can't! We can't leave without him! He'll be here any second. I know he will."

"It is time."

"*Please!*" I begged. "Let's wait just a little while longer. He's coming. *I know* he is." I got up and hurried to the rail where the captain was standing. "He'll be here any minute. He *must* be here. He told me he would. We can't leave now. Just a little while longer. *Please!*"

"You are in my way!" He pushed past me. And as he slipped the last of the lines free, I felt the ship begin to drift from the pier. I felt, too, the panic of being suddenly alone, alone at sea, with a captain I had met not an hour earlier. And where was I going? What would I do when I got there? I was supposed to meet Shadar here, in Chakai, and we were to sail to Bombay together. How could I sail without him? How would he find me? *If only he would come,* I thought, my eyes piercing the dark for some sign, some indication he was on his way.

I slipped my hand into my pocket and suddenly remembered the gun. Could I do it? *Should* I do it? Force Captain Ilhami to delay sailing until Shadar arrived?

And what if he refused? Would I have the strength to ...

I watched the captain go around to the stern, grab a large lever, and push it forward. The engine began to sputter and throb, lightly at first, and then more loudly as it slipped into gear, sending the boat lurching forward and chugging through the choppy water. I reached deeper into my pocket and closed my hand around the pistol grip.

Captain Ilhami spun the wheel round and round, and the boat began snaking its way through the icy film, the bow turning southward toward Bombay. I slipped my hand, empty, back out of my pocket and, tears forming in my eyes, settled down beneath the tarp to await whatever fate had in store for me.

I had drifted off to sleep, the sway of the boat like a hit of heroin. I dozed off and woke, dozed off and woke again. Each time my eyes popped open, and I looked around for Shadar, as if somehow magically he would appear. But each time I knew what I'd find, and it was the same. And then, finally, I saw him ... in my dreams. We were together and safe, just the two of us, his arms wrapped around me, his voice, soft and comforting, telling me he'd never let me go, his eyes sparkling like the stars over the Kush ...

"Miss," a hushed voice called out just as I was nodding, preparing once again to join Shadar. My eyes flew open, and I threw back my head, banging it sharply against the rail.

"*Miss!*" the voice cried again with more urgency.

I looked around the deck, slowly focusing on Captain Ilhami hovering near the rail across from me.

"Yes? What is it?"

"There is trouble. A ship--the Pakistani border patrol. They are heading right for our bow."

I stared out to sea but could see nothing. From the distance, though, came the faint sound of a motor above the waves slapping at the *Khani-G's* hull. And then I saw the light. At first, it was green and small, a tiny speck on the horizon, but it grew larger by the moment.

"What are they doing out here in the open sea?" I asked.

"They are looking for stowaways. For illegal aliens. For smugglers. For Pashtun rebels and sympathizers."

"What should we do?" I shivered suddenly, as much from fear as from the cold.

"There is only one thing to do." He looked over the side. "You must go overboard. If they find you here, they will confiscate the *Khani-G* and throw us both in prison ... or worse."

"Overboard!" I looked over the rail at the choppy blackness of the water. It held the look of emptiness, of death. Panic seized me.

"When the Pakistani ship draws near, you must leap into the water and stay there until they have boarded and searched the *Khani-G.*"

"And ... and then what?"

"Then," he said softly, "I will turn around and come back for you."

"How?" I asked, my voice cracking sharply. "How will you find me? How will you know where I am in the dark? How will I survive? I won't last five minutes."

"We have no choice," he said, gripping my arm. "It is either that or face the patrol. See how their course cuts ours in two? They know we are here, and they have a much more powerful boat than the *Khani-G.* We cannot outrun them. And they are heavily armed. Here." He held out a life vest, which I quickly struggled to strap around me, working mechanically, a machine suddenly devoid of all feeling and thought. From off our bow, the roar of the powerboat grew steadily louder.

"Quickly, now," Captain Ilhami said. "Climb up onto the rail and wait until I signal you to jump. Try to keep within sight of the *Khani-G.* Keep your arms and legs moving; it will help keep you warm in the icy waters. When you see the patrol boat leave, call out to me ... as loudly as you can. But only after the patrol boat has left, do you understand?"

I understood everything. I understood nothing. All of life was a blur, a fleeting, timeless image in a bad dream. So this was how I was to end. My life flashed before me. All the good, too much of the bad.

I lifted my leg over the rail, and I slowly brought the other alongside it. The waves, churned up by the wind, lapped hungrily at my feet. I stared at the large, choppy whitecaps and felt a rush of frigid air sweep up off the water's surface and across my face. I couldn't do this. I *wouldn't* do this. It was all a horrible dream. A nightmare. It was insane, utterly useless. The moment I hit the water, I would be dead. I would be pulled into the icy abyss, sucked under by the current and the waves, and never again break the surface.

The engine from the powerboat quickly grew into a raging demon, screaming in the night, intent upon my destruction. Suddenly a strong beam of light poured across the bow of the *Khani-G*, spilling onto the deck and running steadily sternward until nearly upon us.

Squatting precariously on the bulwark above the sea, I prepared to push up and out with my legs, out through the frigid night air and down into the inky-black water. In a fraction of a second, it would all be over. Forever.

The *Khani-G* lurched sharply in the wake of the other boat, and I felt one of my hands slip free from the rail. Suddenly the light grazed my arm, and I heard the captain shout, "Now! Jump *now!*"

I tensed my entire body and shoved my feet against the bulwark as hard as I could. I could feel myself sliding down, scraping the hull of the boat as I fell, when suddenly my body snapped violently. A sharp pain raced up my arm to my fingertips. Someone had caught me, or *something*! I dangled helplessly against the hull just inches above the water.

"Captain Ilhami!" a familiar voice rang out from the sea.

Dazed, I looked up into the eyes of the captain, who was bent over the rail, his two strong hands clutching my arm.

"Captain Ilhami of the *Khani-G,*" the voice called again.

"Pull up on my hands!" the captain yelled down to me. "Pull tightly against my hands and use your feet against the hull!"

Slowly I felt myself inching upward. I worked my right leg up and over the side of the boat and onto the rail, where Captain Ilhami got a good grasp on it and, with a sudden yank, jerked me back onboard. I tumbled in a heap to the deck, breathing frantically, barely believing I was still alive. I had never again expected to feel anything solid beneath me.

"Ahoy!" a voice called out. "Anybody here?"

Shadar! I looked up at the rail, and there he was, his eyes peeking over the top.

"It *is* you!" I cried, struggling to my feet and stumbling forward. It's really you! Oh, my God!" I reached out for him as he hauled himself up over the rail and jumped down onto the deck. I felt his arms reach me, grab me, squeeze me, just as in my dreams. "I don't believe it!" I sobbed. "I just don't believe it!"

He held me close and gently lifted my face up to his, placing a large, long kiss on my lips, a burning, hurting kiss that I would remember for the rest of my life.

"We had a little misunderstanding," Captain Ilhami said finally.

"Oh?" Shadar smiled down at me. "And what was that?"

"We mistook you for the Pakistani Border Patrol. And your lady, here, very nearly went for a swim."

Shadar looked down at me. "Did you really do that?"

I nodded, the tears streaming from my eyes. I wanted to be strong. I wanted to show him how brave I had been. But it was hopeless. "Yes," I said, sobbing at the thought, and I buried my face against his chest.

"She is a very brave young woman." The captain grinned. "If I were twenty years younger ..."

Shadar smiled, and my heart sang. "If you were twenty years younger, she would *still* belong to me."

The captain swept him slowly with his eyes and shrugged. "Yes, perhaps you are right."

Still clinging to one another, we leaned back against the bulwark and slowly slipped down to the deck. I grabbed him by his hair, pulled his face to mine, his cheek to mine, and held him there as he grabbed for the tarp beneath us. Gradually, awkwardly, he pulled it up and around us, and we huddled there for several minutes in the warmth of our own two bodies, wrapped in silence.

"Oh, Shadar. I didn't want to tell you, but I was so afraid."

He wiped my eyes with his gloved hand and turned my chin up. "There's nothing wrong with being afraid. But it is over, now. You don't have to be afraid anymore."

"But ... but how will we ever get out of the country? We have no money, we have no passports. Everything we owned I had to leave behind."

"We have more than you think, my little mynah," he said softly as the *Khani-G* corrected her course and veered south toward the Indus Sea and Bombay. "We have each other."

EPILOGUE

In the months that followed our return to the states, I heard nothing of Bob except for what I learned second-hand from friends and his parents. One year later, I was granted a divorce by the courts in Chicago, where Shadar and I had decided to live.

Three months after the divorce, I received my first correspondence from Bob--a short letter asking for five hundred dollars. The return address was in care of the Australian Embassy, Kabul. The note said nothing else-- not whether he was well or ill, whether he wanted the money as a loan or a gift ... nothing. Before I had a chance to respond, I learned from his parents that they had received word from the American consulate that several Americans had been killed in a clash between Soviet forces and Afghan rebels, implying that Bob was among them. Shadar doubted that it was true since he'd heard nothing about such an incident from either the Afghanistan Relief Corps or official sources.

Several months later, however, Bob's parents received a small parcel of personal belongings in an unmarked package stamped, "Postes Afghanes: Kaboul." Since then, all of their attempts to acquire information about Bob proved futile. The U.S. Embassy claimed they had no record of Bob's death. And the British and Australian embassies in Kabul similarly claimed no knowledge of his status.

Whether or not Bob actually wrote the note requesting the money is unclear. Whether or not he is alive or dead is also a mystery. The only possible lead is a small piece of blue paper, found folded up and tucked securely into the change section of the wallet forwarded to Bob's parents, and then on to me. On it, hastily scribbled in what looks to be Bob's handwriting, are the words, "Islamabad. Twenty kilos. One hundred fifty thousand *francs*. Thursday."